Wh
Die

The Roses Trilogy
Book 3

Susan Agatha Davis

ERCILDOUNE PUBLISHING

Newport, Vermont 05855

This book is a work of fiction. Nothing in this book is intended in any way to present, represent, or resemble any real person or incident. References to real and/or existing locations, businesses or sites are used strictly to establish a fictional background or atmosphere and do not intentionally present, represent or resemble those locations as they exist in reality.

WHEN ROSES DIE
Copyright © 2016 by Susan Agatha Davis. All Rights Reserved. No part of this book may be reproduced or transmitted in any form or by any means, electronic, mechanical or by any other means, without written permission of the publisher or author, except where permitted by law.

Cover Art by **BetiBup33 Studio Design**
Cover Design by **Anthony Smits**
NEK Editing, Newport, VT, Tracie Ashman

Published by:
Ercildoune Publishing, 25 Northern Ave., Newport, VT 05855

ISBN-13: 978-1539051176
ISBN-10: 153905117X

Published in the United States

Disclaimer:
Rated M for Mature: This book contains adult content including sex, violence, and obscene language. It also includes references to childhood trauma.

ERCILDOUNE PUBLISHING

Newport, Vermont 05855

Acknowledgments

Special thanks for the hard work, inspiration, and support of the following people:

Joseph Fletcher, Tracie Ashman, Karen Karlovich, Paula Holland, Anthony Smits, and Virtual Writers Inc.

Other Books:

When Roses Weep

When Roses Break

Saynte and Sinners:
A Rick Brandt Novel

Rick Brandt: Resurrection

Rick Brandt: Hawk's Curse

WHEN ROSES DIE
Chapter 1
Very Early Monday Morning

Candace Knight brushed her jet-black hair from her eyes and shivered in the cool air of the medical examiner's lab. She had left her purse on a table by the door and now pulled her heavy cardigan tightly around her arms. She moved slowly to the table. A bright light shone down on the shrouded body. Candy's mouth went dry, and her hands balled into fists. She looked up at the medical examiner and nodded her head. "I'm ready."

She wasn't, of course. No one is ever ready for death, especially the death of someone they care about.

As the sheet was pulled back, Candy closed her eyes for a second then opened them to see the still, ivory features of a twenty-something woman with streaming blonde hair. The woman's make-up had been removed and she was naked under the sheet, but she was still beautiful, with the kind of quiet, statuesque beauty one would expect of a fairytale princess – a princess who had been strangled by the very thorns that protected her castle.

Candy's eyes fell to the torn and punctured flesh of the woman's delicate throat. She bit her lip as tears welled into her eyes. Her hand moved forward a bit. She wanted to touch the young woman. She wanted to whisper into her ear, "It's going to be all right. I'll get you a warmer blanket.

I'll take you home. I'll fix this." Candy half expected the woman to open her eyes and look up at her and smile.

None of that happened, of course. Candy pulled her hand back and spoke to the medical examiner. "What did this?" She indicated the torn flesh.

"She was strangled with a spiked dog collar turned inside out. Nasty piece of work. Some asshole really enjoyed doing this one."

"When was she killed?"

"We're estimating sometime before midnight."

Candy shuddered. "Yes, that's her. Pamela Mayhew, 27, married, two small kids. I'll give Detective Saddler the contact info as soon as I check my records."

"You knew her well?" the doctor asked as he replaced the sheet.

"I know all my girls well." Candy's voice was soft and trembling, but the lab seemed to echo her words back at her. She did know all her girls well, just not well enough to save their lives.

Candy picked up her purse and walked from the chilled lab out to the warmer hallway. She sank onto a wooden bench and leaned against the cool, tiled wall. She gripped her heavy purse tight to her chest and fought back the rage that tried to consume her.

"Dr. Knight?" someone asked.

Candy looked up at a young lab tech. She forced a smile. "Yes, that's me."

"I'm Edgar Mitchell. I'm the new forensics guy here. Well, not 'new' new. I started just before you left." He smiled back.

He was wearing a lab coat that was spotless and freshly pressed and his black shoes shone with new polish. Dressed to kill, or at least to study those who were killed, Candy thought.

"I heard you're teaching now, forensics, at UNLV?" he asked.

"Yes, it's a small class. One evening a week. But don't you already have your degree?" Her mind slipped into professor mode like a rabbit seeking a friendly burrow in a storm.

"Yes, but I heard about your lectures, and I know you used to work here. I was wondering about auditing a class." Mitchell shifted his stance in front of her, and for a moment she imagined him offering her an apple.

"Of course, just check with the registrar's office. There are a few seats left."

"Thanks, Dr. Knight." He smiled. "Have a good day!"

He turned and walked briskly away. He never asked why the former director of the forensics lab would be sitting outside the medical examiner's office and hugging herself while on the edge of tears. Maybe he didn't want to know. Maybe he didn't want to invade her privacy, she thought. Maybe he already knew.

She closed her eyes and leaned back again.

"Candy?" said a quiet male voice.

"Tom?" Candy opened her dark eyes, looked up, and smiled for the first time that morning.

Detective Tom Saddler offered his hand, and she stood up and wrapped her arms around him, holding him as he comforted her. He didn't speak. He just held her and rocked her gently. He was a muscular man, a former college athlete turned cop, and his arms were strong under his nylon jacket. As he held her, she could feel the gun and holster strapped to his chest.

"I'm glad you came. The girl—" Candy pulled herself away and looked into his hazel eyes.

"Was one of yours. I heard. The sheriff called me and said you were here. Let's get some breakfast and talk about it."

Something about just having him there made her more relaxed. If anyone could solve Pamela's murder, Tom could, Candy reasoned, with a little help from her, of course. She slipped her arm into his and let him support her as they walked.

It was almost four a.m. The diner was quiet. A tall, dark man in an expensive gray suit flipped through the Wall Street Journal as he drank his coffee. A couple of young women, surrounded by stacks of books, were taking a break from a night of studying. An older couple sat by the window and waved at the little white poodle still in their car.

Candy and Tom found a booth with a coin-operated music box and a view of the parking lot. The smell of coffee, bacon, and fresh rolls wafted through the warm air.

Candy flipped through the song selections. "I haven't seen one of these in years. You sure know how to show a girl a good time." She nodded to the petit blonde waitress who poured Tom some coffee without asking.

"Only the best for you," Tom joked. He smiled at the waitress. "Morning, Kelly. Steak and eggs, medium, over easy, two slices of raisin toast, and a large orange juice."

Candy chuckled. "You must exercise like hell to keep the weight off." She shrugged off the sweater.

"Care to join me sometime?"

"In my line of work, a fit body is a professional necessity." Her eyes lowered. She was looking at the menu, but she was seeing Pamela.

"Teaching?" Tom asked.

Candy looked up at him, her eyelids half closed, her lips pursed. She felt something she seldom felt around men – embarrassment. Tom knew her too well, and he knew what she was talking about, and yet there he was, forcing her to explain herself.

"I'm not actually talking about a job, and you know it."

"And for you, ma'am?" the waitress asked, pen and pad at the ready.

"Something with a lot less grease and meat in it." Candy scowled at Tom. "How about some oatmeal, a side of whatever fresh fruit you have, some yogurt, and hot tea with lemon."

The waitress smiled and left, and Candy turned her attention back to Tom. "Do you always eat like that first thing in the morning?"

"Trying to change the subject?"

Candy looked down at her hands. "I thought you didn't want to know about that part of my life. I thought it made you uncomfortable."

"That was before it became relevant to a homicide investigation," Tom admitted.

"Ah. Now I get it. It's the case that has your attention, not me."

It was Tom's turn to feel uncomfortable. "It's not that – exactly."

"Then exactly what is it?"

He was having trouble meeting her eyes. "You always have my attention, Candy. You have since the first day you propositioned me."

"I never –"

"I believe we were standing inside a large kink store, and you said something about how good I'd look in a pair of chaps, and then you tried to get me to put them on." He blushed.

"I wasn't – Well, okay, maybe I was propositioning you, a little, in a friendly, harmless sort of way. You can't arrest me for hitting on you."

"No, but I could have if you'd asked for cash later." Tom finally met her eyes.

Candy felt a deep heat rise up her back and burn her neck and cheeks. "I am NOT a prostitute," she snapped.

Tom tensed, leaned forward so only she could hear, and whispered. "I'm not saying you are, but you engage in BDSM with high-end clients, and I'm sure they don't just pat you on the ass and say thank you."

He knew he was in trouble the second the words left his mouth. He tried to never let his opinion about her lifestyle taint their friendship, but there it was. His unease about Candy practicing BDSM affected his entire view of the case.

Candy leaned forward, her face a few inches from his, her voice low. "I'm a dominatrix, you asshole. I whip them, I humiliate them, I make them crawl around on the ground and lick my boots. I do NOT have sex with them." She straightened. "Now, I know, and you know, that many D/s couples have sex. But for me, that requires a committed relationship, and I'm not in one. I provide a service and that's all. If I was having sex, you can bet it wouldn't be for money."

He met her stare for stare and they both held their breath for a few seconds. Candy wondered if Tom had any idea how badly she wanted to sleep with him and how much he had just sliced her to ribbons.

He finally looked down in a gesture of surrender. "I'm sorry. I really don't know what you do, and I don't want to know. I just want to solve this murder, and you're the only one who can help me do that."

"That's all you care about? Solving the murder? Not about me?" Hurt flashed in her eyes.

Tom felt like he shrank to two inches tall. "That's not what I meant." He tried again. "Of course, I care about you. Solving this murder IS caring about you."

"If you want to know what I do with my clients, all you have to do is ask." Candy leaned back herself as the anger ebbed out of her. "Apology accepted, for now. In the meantime, you need to eat better."

"Hey, my day is just beginning, and I need all the energy I can get." He tasted the black coffee and grimaced. "I'm trying to do with less sugar." He looked up, saw the sadness in Candy's eyes, reached across the table, and took her hand. His eyes went from accusatory to soft and kind. "Tell me about your girls."

When he touched her, Candy took a deep breath. "Well, there's five of them, usually. They come and go, but I never have more than five at a time. They range in various ages. Pamela was the youngest at 27. Lois is the oldest at 65. They all have one thing in common, they want to learn the lifestyle. They want to know what it means to be a submissive. Some want to be a dominatrix. In general, though, they're curious, bright, sexually active, and good people." She smiled slightly. "Sometimes I'm their teacher and sometimes their mentor and sometimes their counselor, but mostly we have fun with it."

"How often do you meet?" Tom asked.

"Every Thursday, late afternoon, before the husbands get home."

"Do you know if anyone has threatened any of them before?"

Candy shook her head. "No, not that I know of." She looked at the way he was holding her hand and stroking it gently as she spoke. "That's quite an interrogation technique you have there."

Tom released her hand.

"I didn't say you had to let go."

"What about Pamela? Any personal issues you're aware of? Anyone want to hurt her? How about a husband or boyfriend?" Tom ignored Candy's comment.

"Most of the women don't tell their partners what they're up to." Candy nodded politely as the waitress set the tea down. "Pamela was different. She was young and her husband was supportive. In fact, he talked to me one day after a session. He wanted to know more. They appeared affectionate with each other. I never heard her say anything bad about him."

Candy's cell phone rang. She checked it, screwed up her nose, and let it go to voicemail.

"You need to get that?" Tom asked.

"Nope. You were saying?"

"Well, I believe Pamela's death has something to do with your little group. She was found dressed in a dominatrix-styled outfit, leather corset, black hose, black stilettos, the collar –"

"Inverted and used to strangle her." Candy rubbed her arms and wondered if food was a good idea. "I talked to the M.E., remember?"

"What do you make of the flowers?" Tom asked.

Candy frowned. "What flowers? The M.E. didn't mention any flowers."

"They were tucked into the top of her corset – six sweetbriars."

Candy's eyes widened. "Sweetbriars? Those are beautiful, but their thorns are nasty."

"There were six of them, all tucked in nice and neat. Any ideas?"

"Not a clue."

"Did Pamela's husband usually pick her up after a class?"

Candy shook her head no as the waitress delivered their meal. "I only saw him that one time, but he seemed nice. Usually, she took the bus home." Candy picked up a spoon and poked at her oatmeal, then scooped some yogurt into it and started stirring it around. "I don't understand what she was doing out in the middle of the night. She usually stays home in the evenings, makes supper, and spends time with him and the kids. Did he report her missing? How did that happen?"

"According to her husband," Tom stopped, dug a notepad out of his jacket pocket, glanced at it, and put it back, "Howard, or Howie – anyway, according to Howie, they had just finished supper when she received a call from a friend of hers. He said it was a woman, but he couldn't remember the name. Pamela told him her friend was having a hard time and wanted to get some coffee and talk. When Pamela wasn't home by nine, he started making calls but couldn't locate her. Someone found her body around two this morning." Tom dug into his breakfast.

"She was lured away, then."

"Apparently by a woman, possibly even by one of your girls," Tom said as he ate.

"Or somebody posing as a woman. I find it hard to believe that any of my girls did this. I've been working with this group for almost a year now. Anyone with an issue usually doesn't last more than one or two days. It's a supportive and mature group of people. You have to be both of those things to survive in the lifestyle."

"How do you like the new apartment? Did you sell your house yet?"

"It's still on the market." Candy picked at her food. "I took my toys out of the attic and turned it into a spare bedroom. I think it will sell faster that way, but who knows? The apartment is okay – small but useable for now. There's no place for me to play, but, at the moment, I don't have anyone to play with." She grinned and gave him a wink. "Once I sell the house, I can shop around for something better."

"Miss the lab?" he asked.

Candy sighed. "Yes, definitely. Teaching has its perks, mind you. I'm enjoying it. But there's nothing like sinking my teeth into a murder case."

"Then I expect full cooperation from you, young lady," Tom grinned.

Candy frowned, put down her spoon, and leaned forward. "I want this son-of-a-bitch caught. I texted my girls and warned them. We're having a brief meeting tonight to talk about it. No one should be victimized because some asshole doesn't understand our lifestyle."

Tom stopped eating and looked into her intense eyes. "Whatever you need from me, just ask."

"I know you'll do your best. You always do."

"In the meantime, there's something I need from you."

"What?"

"I need to interview your girls." He could feel her tense without looking at her.

"Their privacy –"

"Takes a back seat to a murder investigation." Tom offered Candy an apologetic smile. "Look, this has to be done, if not by me, then by someone else in the department. You know I will do my best to be discreet.

Nothing I learn will find its way into ink unless it's relevant to the case. I promise."

Candy wasn't happy. She crossed her arms. "I can't make them talk to you. I'm not even sure you can force me to tell you who they are."

"True. I can subpoena their names and addresses from you, of course, then show up at their homes and start asking questions."

Candy glared at him.

Tom put his fork down. "Or…"

"Or?"

"I could meet with them at your place tonight. One at a time. Privately." For the first time, he realized how right Sheriff Hodge had been to force Candy to retire from the lab. She was given a choice – her job or her lifestyle, and she had chosen the lifestyle, something Tom never understood.

Candy finally nodded. "Come early. I'm going to have to warn the girls."

"It would be better if you didn't."

"For you, maybe, but not for them. If someone refuses to show up, you can always subpoena the information on that person."

"I'm trying to meet you halfway, Candy."

"I know." She picked up her tea. For a moment, she considered throwing it at Tom. Instead, she took a long, slow drink.

"Come on, I'll give you a ride home," Tom said as he wiped his mouth with a napkin, slid out of the diner booth, and stood up.

She shook her head. "My car is back at the lab."

"Then I'll take you back to the lab, but I'm going to follow you home and make sure you get there safely."

Candy's eyes widened a bit. "You think I'm in danger, too? Or are you just being overly protective, detective?"

"You think you're not?" Tom countered. He wasn't smiling.

Candy was quiet for a few minutes as she thought about it. "I suppose you're right." She sighed and finished her oatmeal while Tom paid the check.

They drove in tandem to Candy's apartment, Tom's unmarked cruiser behind her silver Mini Cooper. He pulled into the parking lot of the apartment building, parked behind her, got out and surveilled the street before he opened her door.

"Thanks, Tom" Candy kissed him on the cheek.

"I'm going in with you. I want to make sure the place is secure."

She was used to attention but not this much attention. "It's all locked up. You know how cautious I've been since the attack." Her fingers went involuntarily to her throat, which still bore the scars of a recent surgery. It was four months since Toni de la Rosa, a former police detective and, it turned out, deranged serial killer, tried to strangle

Candy to death with an electrical cord. Candy shuddered at the memory.

"I'm not taking any chances. I'm just doing my job."

"Is that really all you're doing?"

Tom ignored the question.

Candy let Tom lead her into the small apartment building. The place had recently been remodeled, and fresh vinyl siding shone in the early morning light. She unlocked the outside door, they took the stairs to the third floor, and she slipped the key into the lock of her heavy door. Tom entered ahead of her.

Inside, the apartment was cool and dark. He flipped on the lights and began a careful search, going from room to room and checking in closets and behind or under furniture. Finally satisfied, he joined her in the tiny kitchen area.

Candy had thrown open the curtains and stood by the sink as she watched the sun rise over the buildings. "I'm always amazed at this view."

Tom stood behind her and looked out the window. Ribbons of pink and orange held up the sky. "It is beautiful."

"I sometimes think how nice it would be to find a cute little house in the country, something with horses and a garden and a big front porch where I can sip tea and watch the sun come up," Candy said.

"And what would you use the barn for?" Tom teased.

"Oh, the usual." She turned toward him, winked, and added, "Hay bales." She stroked her thumb across his lips.

"Okay, I think I'd better get going before I don't get out of here." He turned to go, stopped, and looked back. "You're missed at the lab."

"By you?"

He grinned and headed out the door.

Candy sighed and sat down at her kitchen table. She checked her phone. None of her girls had messaged her back yet. It was still early. She doubted they were awake. But soon they'd learn what happened to Pamela, and then the fear would set in, the fear that was already crawling into her bones. She needed protection, she realized, the sooner the better.

Her phone rang again. Candy glanced at it, scowled and let it go to voicemail. Then she made a call that woke Rick Brandt from a sound sleep. His voice sounded muddled on the phone.

"Yeah? What's up?" he asked.

She could just picture him – stretched out in bed, his deep scars and Marine Corps tattoos accenting his muscles, his buzz cut, and next to him his lover and Candy's closest friend, Fran Simone. Candy wondered if she'd interrupted them.

"One of my girls is dead – murdered," Candy explained. "Tom seems to think I may be in danger. He's working on the case, but I was thinking –"

"That you could use some help?" Rick asked.

Need help? Call Rick. It was a mantra with Candy as it was with others in her circle.

"Yes. At least have someone check in on me now and then. Something. You think I'm being paranoid?" Her hand went to her throat. That memory was dying hard and slow.

"Yup, but that don't mean someone ain't out to get you. Be home later?"

"I'm home for the day. The house is locked up. I have some people coming over but not for a while." Candy heard a woman's voice mumbling in the background and knew it was Fran.

"I'll be there in about an hour. Don't let anyone in and don't go anywhere." He hung up.

She placed another call. "Charlie? It's Candy Knight. Are you awake yet?"

"Nope. I'm talking in my sleep," said a man's gruff voice.

"I need a gun. Something light."

"You haven't got a gun?" He sounded surprised.

"I had one once. Never used it. So, when I quit the crime lab, I got rid of it. I was nervous about having it in the house. Now I'm thinking I need it again."

"Got a permit?"

"Yes. Totally legit. I just want something at home – just in case."

"I'll be at the store in about thirty minutes," he said.

"Thanks." Candy hung up and took a deep breath. She walked into the quiet living room and looked around. Her peace was unexpectedly destroyed once before. She didn't want that to happen again.

She double-checked the locks on the doors and windows, then slipped into the shower and tried to wash the smell of death from her skin.

***

Alex de la Rosa, his brown eyes and square jaw reflected in the car's window, ducked behind a map as he sat in his black Corvette across the street from Candy's apartment. He watched as Tom and Candy went in, and then watched again as Tom came out. Alex frowned. He ran his fingers through his thick, dark brown hair and picked up the manila envelope from the passenger seat. He opened it and pulled out the photo of Pamela Mayhew, her body prone on the concrete, her eyes open, a pool of blood around her throat and staining the flowers at her breasts. Her wig was dark and looked like Candy's hair. She was dressed in a pink and black corset.

Alex slipped the photo back into the envelope and looked at Candy's apartment. He had to go in. He had to see her. There were things he needed to tell her. He folded the map and started to open the door when he saw a small blue Ford pull up. Alex waited and watched as the driver of the other car pulled out some binoculars. Apparently, Alex wasn't the only one interested in Candy's actions that day. He shut the car door.

As the man with the binoculars began to scan the area, Alex ducked down and stayed hidden. He waited a few minutes and then peeked through the window. As he watched, the man in the Ford answered his cell phone. He appeared irritated, but he finally hung up and drove away.

Alex never got out of his car.

***

Rick Brandt turned over in the warm bed and slipped his hand under the sheets and around the naked body of his lover. He leaned forward, brushed back her hair, and kissed her neck.

"Who was that?" Fran Simone rolled over and smiled at him, her long red hair splayed across the pillows. Her fingers traced the Marine tattoos on his chest. She kissed him.

"Candy. One of her girls is dead," he said.

"Her girls?" Fran looked confused.

"One of the girls she mentors, some housewife dreaming about being a slave or dominatrix or some such shit." He kissed her again.

"Oh, THOSE girls. She must be scared to death."

"Yeah. She wants some protection."

Fran wrapped her hands around his neck and looked up at him. "I'm not sure I like the idea of you working for a dominatrix." Her blue eyes twinkled with humor. "What if she appeals to your baser nature?"

Rick laughed. "Baby, you're the only one who does that, and you do it so well." He kissed her again.

***

Candy waited for Rick to show up before going to pick up the gun. Maybe she was being paranoid, she thought, but could it really hurt to be careful? She tried to nap but couldn't fall asleep. Even coffee seemed unappetizing. She considered something stronger, but it was too early in the day. By the time Rick got there, she had been pacing the apartment for an hour.

She peeked through the security hole and instantly recognized the hard-lined face, the keen gray eyes, and the scar at his hairline. She opened the door with relief.

"Rick. Thanks for coming."

Rick stepped into the small apartment and gave it a cursory look. "You living with anyone?"

"No."

"Anyone you know drive a black Corvette?"

Candy shook her head no. "Why?"

"One just took off from in front of your building. I called Saddler. He filled me in. What's your plan?" Rick was all business.

"First, I'd like to find out how much you charge and what I can get for that," Candy said.

Rick chuckled and tilted his head, eying her carefully. "You're right. A man is only worth the price he sets on himself. On the other hand, we ain't strangers. We can work something out."

Her shoulders relaxed. She shut the door. "Look, I know we haven't always been on the best of terms, but—"

He raised a hand to quiet her. "Past is past."

She took a deep breath. "I have a friend who owns a gun and ammo shop in Paradise. I thought maybe we could start with a trip out there. You can show me what I can get, maybe even how to use it." She shook her head. "I don't like guns, but under the circumstances, better safe than sorry."

"I agree. You shouldn't own a gun if you don't respect it." He licked his dry lips, remembering the taste of a steel barrel that was once shoved into his mouth. He was much more familiar with guns than he ever wanted to be. "Ready to go?"

"Yes. Let me get my purse."

***

L&L Cook's Sporting Goods was a cramped, dusty cross between a militia hideout and a hay barn. Its rough, wooden floors hoisted a maze of wooden and metal shelves loaded with survivalist supplies, hunting and fishing gear, and outdoor clothing. Candy walked in first and waved to the owner from across the room. Rick followed her.

Charlie Cook looked like he was about to swallow his cigar. "Shit! Rick Brandt! What the fuck? I thought you'd died and gone to hell, man!" He laughed.

Charlie was a big man with large, rough hands, a long dark beard, and thick, curly, dark red hair. He was wearing camouflage pants and a green t-shirt that sported an American eagle across his broad chest.

"Close. I went to Mexico for a while." Rick grinned. "I thought I smelled the stench of your cigar when we drove up. You finally give up chew?"

"Workin' on it."

"You guys know each other?" Candy asked. "Figures."

The men shook hands and Charlie turned to Candy. "So, what can I do you for, sugar?" he asked with a wink.

"She needs something light, easy to use, and deadly," Rick answered. His eyes scanned the wall-mounted firearms with appreciation. "She's got a stalker, someone who's already tasted blood."

"Shit. A pretty lady like you don't need that," Charlie told Candy. "Let's see what we can find."

"You still got the range out back?" Rick asked. "She should try it first and make sure it works for her."

"Sure thing."

Charlie led them to the counter, stepped behind it, and looked over some pieces locked in various cases. He then pulled out three of them, spread a cloth over the countertop, and set them in front of Candy. Charlie leaned on the counter and studied her quietly, waiting.

"She's not your type, Charlie," Rick joked.

"You'd be surprised," Charlie said with a grin. "Why? She your gal now?"

Candy nearly choked. "I'm not his type either." She nodded toward Rick. "What do you think?" she asked the men, indicating the guns.

"Well, for starters, you need at least a .380 ACP." Rick picked up the first pistol and hefted it in his hand. "Nice weight to it." He put it down, picked up the next one, and glanced at her hands. "Here, hold this, tell me how it feels."

Candy's hands were shaking as she held the piece.

Rick took the gun and placed it properly in her hands, then turned her hands upright. "There. I want you to feel the weight of it. Does it fit? Is it too big?"

"I can handle it, but it feels like I'm stretching a bit." Candy put the gun down and flexed her fingers.

Rick nodded and picked up the third one. He hefted it in his hands and smiled. "The M&P has a laser with it, right?"

Charlie nodded. "That's called the Bodyguard. It's a .38 special. Light, easy to use, easy to conceal. The laser makes it easier to aim and shoot. Great for self-defense and built for a woman."

"The recoil has a bit more bite to it than some others," Rick added. "Why don't we try it out?" He slipped the gun into Candy's hand and watched as she tested the weight of it. She nodded.

Charlie locked the guns back up and signaled for a guy in the back room to watch the store while he grabbed some ammo and led Rick and Candy to the range.

Rick loaded the gun, lined Candy up with the target, got behind her, and propped up her arms. "Here, higher. Now, watch the light. See it?"

"It's easier to see at night," Charlie said.

Candy nodded. "I see it, but barely."

"There, give it an aim and expect recoil." Rick stood behind her.

Candy was sweating, and not just from the hot sun. She swallowed, aimed, closed her eyes, and fired. The gun kicked back. She yelped and nearly fell backward.

Rick caught her. "Good girl."

"Of course, you might hit the target if you keep your eyes open," Charlie laughed.

Candy, now flushed with embarrassment, gripped the gun tighter. "Again," she said.

"Again," Rick told Charlie.

About the fourth time around, Candy was able to keep her eyes open and hit the target. Her arms ached. Her hands shook. Her heart was pounding in her ears. She was scared and excited and proud of herself at the same time. She lowered the gun and handed it to Charlie. "I'll take it."

"With ammo?"

"With ammo." Candy turned to look at Rick and saw the gleam in his eyes. "You enjoyed that, didn't you?

"Fran told me once that you knew how to shoot."

Candy blushed a little. "Yeah, well, she didn't want you worrying about her."

"I gotta have a talk with her about that," he said. "She's not allowed to lie to me."

"Who's Fran?" Charlie asked.

"Not allowed?" Candy asked in surprise.

Rick reached behind his back and under his jacket with his left hand, pulled out a Smith & Wesson M&P45, checked to make sure it was loaded, spread his feet a bit, turned, and fired with both hands. Candy jumped. Her eyes went from the intense look on his face to the way he held the firearm to the target in front of him. He shot carefully and deliberately.

"Ya gotta take your time." He shifted his weight and fired with his left hand alone. "Ya can't afford to miss." He smiled as he finished off the rounds.

"You still got it," Charlie told Rick as he walked up behind them. "I got paperwork for you to fill out, sweetie. She's wrapped up and ready to go."

Candy was beginning to understand the allure of the gun – the adrenalin rush, the sex appeal. She took a deep breath and looked up at Rick. "Now, with any luck, I'll never have to use it."

"You need to practice though, just in case."

"Like using a whip." She turned and walked back into the store, leaving the men to stare after her.

"I always liked that woman," Charlie said.

"Someday you'll have to tell me how you two know each other," Rick responded.

"You know I sell whips too, right?" Charlie smiled and followed Candy into the store. "So, who's Fran?" Rick just grinned.

Chapter 2

Late Monday Morning

Tom Saddler dragged himself back to the squad room. He was up most of the night and needed sleep, but something about the Pamela Mayhew case bothered him. It seemed so random and yet so deliberate. The clothing, the flowers, the collar all sent a message, but Pamela Mayhew wasn't anybody that anyone wanted dead. He spoke to the husband and got nowhere. The man was so distraught that he had to be hospitalized. The victim's children had been ferried to her mother's house – a house also in mourning. Tom sat down at his desk and pulled out a notebook and pen. The air conditioner was whirring as he started writing down all the ideas that raced through his head.

"You wanted these?" Edgar Mitchell asked as he approached Tom's desk.

"What's that?" Tom took the documents from the young man in the starched white coat.

"Trace analysis. Nothing we didn't expect, but we'll keep looking." Mitchell walked away just as Sheriff Joe Hodge, a somber look on his thin face, appeared.

"You need sleep," Hodge said as he flipped a chair around and straddled it in front of his detective. The sheriff looked gaunt and tired. His gray hair was military short. A string bolo hung around his neck.

"Yeah, well, I'll sleep plenty when I'm dead," Tom repeated an adage. "What's up?"

"We got another one."

Tom stopped breathing for a moment. He leaned back in his chair and stared at the sheriff. "Same MO?"

"Identical."

"Shit." Tom threw down the pen. "Got a name?"

"Andrea Ortiz. A housewife from the valley. Think she's another one of Candy's girls?"

"Only one way to find out." Tom started to call Candy and then stopped. She'd been through enough that morning. Calling her now or an hour or two from now wouldn't make any difference.

"Problem?" Hodge asked.

"I should tell her in person. I'll go over there in a bit. Let me finish up a few things here, first."

"I thought you'd want to come out to the scene with me," Hodge said.

"The body is still there?"

"Yup. Coming?"

"Hell, yeah."

Hodge nodded and stood up. "I expect you to treat Candace Knight like any other suspect."

"Suspect?" Tom slipped on his jacket. "Why would she be a suspect?"

"We got two dead women, dressed in that BDSM gear, and both are associated with Candace Knight. You don't think she's a suspect?"

"We don't know that the second one –" Tom started to say.

"Wanna put money on it?"

Tom sighed.

Tom and Joe Hodge arrived at the small diner to find the area cordoned off and several patrol officers keeping the public at bay. About a dozen people rubbernecked from outside the yellow police tape. Inside the tape, Detective Angela Simmons spoke with four people – a waitress, an older couple, and a man in a nondescript, long black coat who turned out to be a minister.

"Sheriff," Simmons said as she nodded at Tom. "This is Reverend Lawrence Blackwell. He was having breakfast with his secretary…" Simmons indicated the older woman, "…and her husband when the waitress came in all upset and said there was a body by the dumpsters. He followed her outside and called 911."

Blackwell, dressed in khaki pants and a button-down blue shirt under his long, lightweight coat, leaned against a large, intricately carved cane with a rubberized grip. "Call me Larry," he said. He indicated the couple with him. "This is Melissa Pearson and her husband Jim. I'm not sure what we can tell you, really. Our waitress went out back, for a smoke I think, and came running in and told me what she saw. I came out with her and called the police."

"So, you didn't see anything suspicious?" Tom asked.

"This is Detective Tom Saddler," Hodge explained. "He's working on a related case."

"No. Whatever happened, well, I guess it happened long before we arrived," said Blackwell.

"Why would the waitress run inside and tell you about the body and not her boss or someone else in the kitchen?" Tom asked.

The minister shrugged. "I suppose because she knows us. We eat here pretty often, and she was waiting on us. She attends my church."

"I may need to talk to you some more." Tom offered Blackwell his card. "This afternoon, maybe?"

"Sure. Just stop by my office anytime."

Tom excused himself as he approached the body. "We have an ID so soon?" he asked Detective Simmons.

She tucked a strand of blonde hair behind her ear and started to answer but was interrupted.

"I recognized her," the waitress said. She was hugging herself, puffing on a cigarette, and leaning weakly against the building.

"How do you know her?" Tom asked.

"She's a regular. She comes in for lunch once or twice a week."

And you are?" Tom asked.

"Missy. Missy Barber." She stamped out the butt of her cigarette, dug another one out of her pocket, and lit it.

Tom waved the smoke away but didn't complain. "Did you get her contact information?" Tom asked Simmons as he indicated Missy.

"Yes, sir. I have all of 'em."

"Great." Tom turned to the waitress. "Missy, do you know who Candy Knight is?"

The woman looked surprised. "Sure. Everybody knows Candy. That ain't Candy."

"I know it's not. But you know her? You know Candy?"

"Of course."

"Have you ever seen Candy and this woman," he checked his notes, "Andrea – together before?"

"Yeah, they have coffee here a lot, you know, like once a week anyway. Nice people. Always smiling."

"You never saw them argue or disagree about anything?" Tom was aware that Hodge was nearby and listening.

"No, not at all. They were friends."

"Thanks, Missy. If you think of anything, anything at all, call me, okay?" Tom handed her a business card.

She nodded, took the card, and slipped it into her apron pocket. "Can I go back to work now?"

"Yes."

For the first time since getting there, Tom approached the body. His eyes went immediately to the victim's torn and bloody throat. His jaw tightened. The woman's hair was the same style and color as Candy's and her face was half-hidden behind a lace mask. For a moment, Tom felt a surge of panic, but he'd just left Candy and he knew she was safe, at least for now. Tom bent down, slipped on some evidence gloves and brushed the bangs aside only to discover the victim was wearing a wig over auburn, curly hair. He glanced up at Detective Simmons. "Forensics guys here yet?"

"Mitchell just pulled up," Simmons said.

Tom stood up and looked at Hodge. "Was the Mayhew woman wearing a wig?"

"I'll have to check the report. I don't remember."

Tom let out a long, slow sigh and turned back to the dead woman. "Damn waste." That was when he spotted the roses. He waited impatiently for forensics and the medical examiner to do their jobs before asking about the flowers.

"Five of them," Mitchell told him. "Sweetbriar roses."

Tom looked up at Hodge. "There are five women in Candy's group. Candy would make six. The first victim had six flowers pinned to her breast. This one has five."

"Serial killer," Hodge said with a grunt. "Damn, and I thought – Hell, never mind what I thought."

Tom thought about Candy. She was going to take this one hard.

Hodge seemed to be reading Tom's mind. "You headed over to her place now?" He didn't have to say Candy's name.

"Yeah."

***

Alex looked like a slick businessman in a suit and tie at the coffee shop table, impressive but nothing more, until he slammed down his cell phone. A number of people turned to stare. He slunk into his seat and picked up the phone again. He was afraid to look at it, afraid to see the photo of the second victim. Just a woman – just a friend of Candy's. A nobody in the grand scheme of things, and yet certainly a somebody to someone.

Alex shut off the phone, straightened out his suit jacket, and walked out of the shop, leaving his coffee sitting on the table. He looked around. He didn't know if he was being followed or not. He sprinted across the street and got into his Corvette. His hands gripped the steering wheel. He swore. He wondered if there was any place where he could hide and still keep Candy safe.

The phone rang and he answered it.

"Second thoughts?" a man asked.

"I told you I'll do it, and I'll do it!" Alex shouted. He hung up and drove off.

***

Fran Simone stood in the busy corridor of the Eighth Judicial District Court of Clark County, Nevada, and faced off with Assistant District Attorney Allyson Stone. Stone had stepped into her space. He was a head taller than her, and his finger was a few inches from her nose. She wanted to bite it.

"This was murder, plain and simple. You're damn lucky the D.A. went for vehicular homicide and you should be grateful we don't want more time," Stone said.

His tone rankled her. Fran stood her ground, her beige suit jacket tossed over one arm, her briefcase at her feet. Her red hair was pulled back, and her blue eyes were cold. Her jaw locked as she listened to his rant, then she stuck her finger into the belly of his snug-fitting white shirt and stepped forward.

"Get the hell out of my space and don't you dare shake that finger at me. My client's been in jail eight months on this charge, and we're already hitting speedy trial issues," she argued, lowering her voice a bit as people passed by. "You don't have a strong enough case for a jury. Let it go. We'll take a misdemeanor plea and time served."

"I can't do that," Stone countered. "A man is dead. Your client killed him. I'm willing to accept a felony conviction, three years inside followed by probation. You know that's a sweet deal."

"Your victim was drunk, angry, and looking for a fight. He stepped in front of a moving vehicle. What did he think was going to happen?" she fired back.

"A sweet deal!" he countered.

"It's only a sweet deal if he's guilty!" She found Stone irritating, the way one finds a bee irritating when it's buzzing around inside your car while you're driving. She kept verbally swatting at him, but he wouldn't go away. She was going to have to stop the car, get out, and kill the damn thing, metaphorically, that is. "Okay, I see we're obviously not making any headway. Set the damn case for trial and let's get it over with."

She picked up the briefcase, opened it, slipped the file inside, and snapped the case shut. She regretted taking this case. She turned and marched away, her high heels clicking on the tiled floor. As the main door opened, the hot, late morning sun struck her hard. Fran stopped a moment on the top step of the courthouse as she adjusted to the heat. Her heart was still racing.

"Miss Simone?"

Startled, Fran jumped and turned. She half-expected to see Stone following her outside but instead found herself facing an older man in a dark navy suit. A rim of white hair framed his shiny head, and his thin body leaned precariously on the handle of a black umbrella.

"Miss Simone?" he asked again.

"Yes, I'm Fran Simone. If you're looking for representation, you'll have to contact my office." She reached into her skirt pocket, pulled out a business card, and handed it to him.

He took it with a smile but shook his head. "No, Miss Simone, we have other business we need to talk about, the business of business, if you get my drift."

"I'm afraid I don't, mister?"

"Hawksworth. Rupert Hawksworth." He pocketed her business card and offered his hand.

She shook it reluctantly.

"I'm here on behalf of the board of Max-Mil Enterprises." He waited, expecting a response.

Fran frowned and shook her head. "Is that supposed to mean something to me?"

"It should." He pursed his lips together and looked at her over the top of his glasses. "You own fifty-one percent of it."

"I do? When? How? What does a Maxy-Mil Enterprise do?"

"Max-Mil and it doesn't do anything. It's a real estate investment firm. We own property all over Clark County, predominantly small hotels, some bars, a few office buildings, a handful of apartment houses, and a very large parking garage."

Fran's eyebrows went up in surprise, then realization hit. "It was one of my father's–one of Max Simone's holdings, wasn't it? I have a lawyer and an accountant sorting through the inheritance. I still don't know everything he left me." She had this odd feeling that she needed to apologize to Mr. Hawksworth for her obvious ignorance, but she resisted the urge.

"Some members of the board thought as much. There's a board meeting Friday to discuss the future of the company. You should have gotten a notice to be there."

Fran shook her head. "Not that I've seen. I don't know who sends out those notices, but it's possible they don't have my new address. I moved to Henderson about six months ago."

He nodded. "Yes, it's quite possible." He pulled a brass business card holder from his trouser pocket, removed a card, and slid a silver pen from the breast pocket of his jacket. Balancing carefully, he wrote some information on the card and handed it to Fran. "That's the meeting time and location. I strongly suggest you be there. You currently have controlling interest in the company, but that is about to change – swiftly."

"Someone is stealing my company from me?"

"You don't understand." Hawksworth lowered his voice and looked around to be sure they weren't being overheard. "Your father was involved in some very shady dealings."

Fran wasn't surprised.

"About a year ago, the company, with Max Simone at the head, hired Jax Saynte to be CEO." Hawksworth checked around again, which made Fran nervous. "I believe Max and Saynte were using the company for various criminal activities. Can I prove it? No. But I have some evidence, and I have my suspicions. When Max died, his interests fell to you. Since you weren't close to your father, I'm assuming you're in the dark about these things. Am I wrong?"

"You're not wrong. I barely talked to the man."

"You need to be at this meeting. You need to get to the bottom of this for your own sake. You could wind up in jail or worse." Hawksworth hobbled away, leaving Fran standing on the step, the sun pounding into her back and the card in her hand.

"What the hell?" she mumbled to herself.

Fran hurried to her silver Mercedes and climbed in. She quickly lowered the window and turned on the air conditioning as she dug her cell phone out of her briefcase. She had Rick Brandt's number on speed dial. When she got call waiting the first time, she tried again. She got call waiting again and swore. The third time, he picked up.

"Where the hell have you been?" she asked.

Rick laughed. "One of those days, huh?"

"Do you know anything about Max-Mil Enterprises?"

"No. Should I?"

"Apparently I own a majority share in the company that Max was using to front illegal activities, and I have no idea what the company does, where its offices are located, or anything about the guy who runs it." Her voice was tight, high-pitched, and panicked.

"Settle down, boss," Rick said gently. "I'll see what I can find out and meet you at the office."

"I'll be there in ten."

"I'll be there in thirty," he responded.

"Where are you?"

"Taking care of business, boss." He hung up.

Fran sighed, exasperated. She loved that man, but he was forever a puzzle she couldn't quite solve. Maybe that was a good thing, she thought. Maybe that's what kept her interested. That, and he was the best damn private investigator her law firm ever had.

Fran put the phone away and drove to her office.

***

Monday At Noon

Rick had Paris on his mind. Maybe it was the travel ad he saw in the newspaper that morning. Or maybe it was driving by the Vegas version of the Eiffel Tower later that day. At any rate, it was an odd thing to be thinking about as he drank his coffee at Grizzly's Bar while canned country blues played over the speaker system.

He had left Candy at her apartment and had arrived at Grizzly's to question witnesses in the case Fran was handling. He glanced at the young woman sitting on the stool next to him and smiled. "Ever been to Europe?" he asked.

"No." Blonde hair fell loosely on tanned shoulders. She wore a faded pink tank top over denim shorts. Her long and shapely legs ended in gym socks and flower-print sneakers. "Is that an invitation?" she asked with a smile.

Rick chuckled. The idea played in his head for a few moments before he was able to swat it away. "As much fun as that would be, sweetheart, it ain't gonna happen."

The young woman reached out and ran a finger over the scar at Rick's hairline. "Where'd you get that one?"

"That's a long story for another time," he said with a wink.

"So, what is it you want today, Ricky?" She leaned toward him and rested one smooth, pretty hand on his thigh.

Her other hand reached into an oversized quilted bag and pulled out a package of cigarettes. The bartender scowled at her, and she put it back.

Rick signaled for another coffee. "You remember a fight in the parking lot about two months ago?"

She laughed playfully. "Honey, folks are always fighting around here. Sometimes over me."

"Your shift started ten minutes ago," the bartender said as he warmed up Rick's coffee.

She gave the bartender the finger and then smiled at Rick.

"Yeah, but this time one of the guys got into a car and hit the other guy with it. Killed him." Rick took a long drink of his coffee and waited while she thought.

"Oh, that fight." She nodded. "Phil, I think. Some guy from outta town. He was being a real ass, drunk as hell, and carrying on. Got into it with a regular, Bennie Gray. Why?"

"Gray got arrested for it."

She straightened up. "I heard about it on the news. That's too bad. He's a nice guy."

"Did you see what happened?"

"Not really." She shrugged.

Rick's phone rang. He glanced at it and ignored it. "Was Gray drunk?"

"Not really. I mean, he had a few but he could hold it, you know? He's a big guy. Friendly like. Always tipped well. "

"No red eyes? No slurred speech? No problem walking? None of that?"

She shook her head no. "Now that you got that outta the way, what do you say we find someplace nice and private to get reacquainted. You've been gone too long." She draped an arm around his neck and grinned.

Rick leaned back a little, staying out of her orbit. His eyes appreciated what he saw. "Sorry, babe. I'm off the market."

Her eyes widened in surprise, and she dropped her arm. "You gotta be kidding me! You? I didn't think that was possible!"

Rick laughed. "Yeah, well, things happen." He finished his coffee. "Anyone else see what happened that night?"

Rick's phone rang again. Again, he glanced at it but didn't answer it.

"That your squeeze?" the woman asked, looking at the phone.

"Just answer the question, sweetie."

"You mean the fight? Yeah, Steve. Actually, I think his name is Stavros but he goes by Steve. He was trying to break it up."

"How do I find Steve?"

"I don't know his last name, but he comes in every Tuesday after work. It's his thing." She stood up and stretched her legs. "You know, if you ever find yourself with some free time, you can still call me." The young woman winked at him. "I'm not the jealous type."

"I'll remember that." Rick stood up, paid his tab, and turned toward the door. Stopping a moment, he looked back and added, "You really should see Paris while you're young." Rick climbed into his battered, second-hand Jeep and started the engine when he answered the phone call. "Yeah, babe?" He smiled as Fran shouted at him. "One of those days, huh?" He laughed. He got used to her small panic attacks years ago, and he found them a bit amusing, although he wouldn't tell her that.

"I'll be there in thirty," he finally said as he hung up.

Rick put the Jeep in gear and cranked up the radio. It was nearly noon. The traffic seemed heavier than usual.

Fran called again. Rick sighed, glanced down at the phone, and decided against answering it. Instead, he shut it off and tossed it into the glove compartment. That cost him the few seconds he needed to make the next light. He sat in traffic and stared ahead, thinking about that morning and how warm Fran felt in his arms.

A car honked its horn. Rick looked up, realized the light had turned green, and pulled ahead. He didn't see the moving van run the red light until the last second, and he didn't have time to react. The front end of the van struck hard against Rick's driver's side door. His arm went up instinctively to shield his face. His vehicle was pushed about twenty feet, leaving burned rubber on the pavement. When the screeching ended and the world stopped spinning, Rick leaned back in his seat. It took a minute for him to realize the left side of his body was in pain from his head down to his foot.

"Shit!" He cradled his injured left arm against his chest. He could feel the bones move and he knew it was broken. He wanted to get out of the vehicle, but he could barely see, and his crumpled door was pinned shut by the front of the van. He reached down, unhooked the seatbelt, and considered climbing over the shift box to the passenger side to get out, but when he tried to move, he found his left leg was pinned. "Fucking shit!" He looked at the van and saw the driver slumped over the steering wheel.

Traffic stopped. Horns blared. One of those horns was his, Rick realized. He reached for the steering column and turned off the ignition as people ran up to both vehicles. Pain ripped through him, and he screamed, "Fuck!"

"Hey! You okay?" a man asked. He was dressed in a business suit. His glasses reflected the sunlight as he stared into the Jeep from the passenger side window.

"Fuck, no." Rick tried to focus through his right eye. "Get me outta here."

"We got help coming." The stranger glanced at Rick's arm. "Shit. That's not good."

"It's my leg. It's stuck!" The leg didn't hurt anymore, but Rick knew that was a bad thing. Something was cutting off the circulation and, with it, any feeling he had there. He leaned over a bit, opened the glove compartment, and grabbed his phone. He speed-dialed Fran and got her voice mail.

"I'm going to be late," was all he had time to say. He suddenly felt very cold and dizzy. The phone dropped into the empty seat as Rick fell into a dark void.

***

Fran got the message. She expected him to be ten minutes late, or twenty, or maybe even thirty, but when an hour had gone by and he still wasn't there and wasn't answering his phone, she started to worry.

Fran pushed herself up from her office chair and looked out the vintage arched window behind her desk. Her lunch, which consisted of a small bag of nuts and some coffee, sat on her desk. She heard the phone ring and go quiet as her secretary, Margo, answered it. There was a brief conversation, but the only thing Fran heard was Rick's name. Heart pounding, she turned and hurried to the outer office. "What's going on?" Fran asked Margo.

Margo, a young woman with purple-streaked black hair, looked worried but tried to smile reassuringly as she hung up her phone. "He's okay, sort of."

"Sort of?" Fran was nearly shouting.

"There was an accident. That was someone from the ER. He told them to call you. She said he's going to be okay," Margo explained.

"Who was that? Who just called? What kind of accident?" Fran demanded to know.

Margo shrugged. "I didn't ask."

"Did they say – anything? Is he hurt? Idiot, of course, he's hurt, or he wouldn't be there! How bad was the accident? What did the doctor say?" Fran was pacing the floor. She stopped and looked at Margo. "What's on my schedule?"

"You have a client meeting at two and another at four."

"Cancel. Reschedule. I need to go to the hospital and check on him," Fran instructed.

"Why don't you go to the hospital first and then let me know what you want rescheduled," Margo suggested.

"Yes, yes. Good idea." Fran rushed to her office for her purse and ran out the door.

"Drive carefully!" Margo yelled after her.

Fran's heart raced as she pulled into traffic. Ever since she had given up booze, she found herself increasingly agitated. She wanted to reach into her purse and pull out the flask, but it wasn't there. Rick had given her an ultimatum: him or the scotch. She chose him. She sighed and grabbed the breath mints, popping a couple into her mouth out of habit.

"I'll be damn lucky if I don't start gaining weight," she muttered to herself, although she had lost five pounds since giving up liquor.

As she turned the corner toward the hospital, a tow truck went by her with the wreckage of Rick's Jeep on a flatbed. Fran gasped. She turned her head to look at it and nearly ran into the car in front of her. Slamming on the brakes, she checked the rearview mirror, but the tow truck was gone.

The emergency room was crammed with people. Fran grabbed a passing nurse and asked, "Rick Brandt, accident?" The woman nodded to one of the small, curtained-off areas and kept walking. Fran hurried past staff and patients, yanked back a curtain, and caught her breath when she saw him on the examining table.

Rick's shirt had been cut off and tossed onto a nearby trash can. Someone with magnification goggles and tweezers was bending over Rick's battered and bleeding face while they pulled glass from around his eye. Rick's pant leg was sliced open to the knee. Blood ran down his chest, and his left arm was strapped to a board. His right arm was hooked to an IV bag. A wide band held his head tight to another board.

"We have a major hematoma but no broken bones on the leg," a doctor said as he checked the x-rays and then turned his attention back to his patient. "I need this leg wrapped up tight. Now, let's take a look at that arm."

"You have to leave." A nurse tried to push Fran out of the way.

"No!" She circumvented the medical staff and grabbed Rick's right hand. "Rick, I'm here, I'm here."

The band across his forehead kept his head immobile. His left eye was bloody and swollen shut. A tear crouched in the corner of his right eye as if afraid to fall. His jaw was locked.

"Please, miss, you need to step aside!" Someone tugged at her arm.

"I'm not leaving him," Fran said.

Rick squeezed her hand. "I'm okay, babe. Now shut the fuck up and get the hell outta everyone's way, will you?"

Fran choked down her fear and backed up as the doctor and nurses continued to work. Someone took her arm and escorted her to the waiting area. Fran collapsed into one of the cushioned chairs and reached for her cell phone. In a minute she had Margo on the line.

"How is he?" Margo asked.

"I don't know. Not good. I saw his Jeep. It's totaled. He was struck at the driver's side door. I don't know anything about the accident."

"But how is he?" Margo asked again.

"I know he has one eye in bad shape, and his left arm is broken, possibly shattered. He's got a problem with his leg, too, but the doctor said it wasn't broken. He's awake. He talked to me, but he's in a lot of pain." She paused. "Cancel the appointments. I'm not going anywhere."

"Will do. Should I call Tom Sadler and let him know?"

"Good idea. Do that. Thanks." Fran hung up, slipped her phone into her pocket, and leaned back into the chair to wait.

Chapter 3

Monday Afternoon

Detective Tom Saddler was standing at Candy Knight's door when his phone rang. He ignored it. It was just after lunch, and he was worried. It appeared two of Candy's "girls" had been murdered. His gut tightened as he wrapped on the door and tried to come up with the words to tell her.

Candy didn't want to wake up. After Rick left, she took some sleeping pills, threw on a large, terry robe, and passed out on the sofa. When Tom's knocking woke her, it took her a few minutes to remember all that had happened that morning. Then the grief hit.

"Who is it?" she yelled from across the room.

"Tom Saddler."

Candy dragged herself over to the door and answered it. She tried to smile when she saw him, but the attempt didn't last long. He looked tense and exhausted.

"You found out something about Pam's death?" she asked as she let him in.

"I wish that was the case." Tom stepped into the cozy apartment and motioned toward the sofa still covered in pillows and a blanket. "Sit down, Candy."

"Oh, shit." She shut the door, moved to the sofa, and settled into it. Pulling her robe tight around her, she leaned forward and watched as Tom slid a chair closer to her and sat down.

"What happened?" she asked.

Tom looked down, composed his thoughts, and looked back up at her. "Andrea Ortiz."

"No." Candy trembled. "No! No! No!" She grabbed the pillow next to her and hugged it. "When? Where? How?"

"She disappeared during her morning walk. A waitress found her a few hours later by the dumpsters near a diner that you and she frequented, the Yellow Hen."

"How was she killed?"

"I'm still investigating, but the MO is the same, right down to the collar and the flowers, only this time there were five of them, flowers that is. Not six."

Candy stood up and paced the small living room. She chewed on a thumbnail as she continued to hug her pillow. "This can't be happening. I texted all the girls early this morning. She must not have read her texts. I need to call and warn them. This can't be happening."

Tom walked into her path and stopped her. He took the pillow from her, tossed it to the sofa, and pulled her into his arms. "I need to talk to those girls, now, not tonight. I'm sorry to do this to you, Candy, but I have to have their names and contact information. Don't make me get a warrant."

She buried her head in his chest and nodded. "Okay. I just can't believe – They wouldn't do this. I know they wouldn't."

Tom cupped her face in his hands and tilted her head to look at him. Tears streamed down her cheeks, and he wiped them away with his thumbs. "I'm going to find out what's going on. I promise, but I can't do it without you."

"I went online this morning and checked on the flowers. The sweetbriar is a type of rose. I'm not sure if you know this, but all roses have meanings according to their color or type," Candy explained. "The meaning for the sweetbriar is 'the wound that heals,' perhaps because of the thorns. I'm not sure."

"Tell me about Andrea," Tom said.

"Andrea was 45 or 46. I can't remember. She just had a birthday."

Tom nodded and listened.

"She got divorced last year. She has a son, fifteen. He's in a special school. Some kind of disability, severely autistic, I think." Candy slipped out of Tom's arms. "What am I going to do? What am I going to tell them?"

Tom's phone rang and he pulled it out of his pocket and scowled.

"About the case?" Candy asked.

"I doubt it. It's Fran's office. I can get it later." He let the call go to voicemail and put the phone back in his pocket. "So, if you can get me that information –" he prompted her.

"Yes, of course." Candy went to an old roll-top desk. She pushed back the cover, opened a small drawer, and retrieved a leather-bound notebook. She sat down, pulled out some floral stationery, and began transcribing names, phone numbers, and addresses.

Tom stood quietly for a while as she worked. Then he approached her and gently rested his hands on her shoulders.

She looked up at him curiously.

"I want to apologize for this morning," Tom said. "You're right. I should have just asked. I shouldn't have presumed."

She nodded but didn't say anything. She went back to her writing.

He left Candy and went to the kitchen to call Margo at Fran's office.

"There you are!" Margo said, clearly relieved when she heard his voice.

"It's not like I left town. What's Fran want now?" He was tired and dealing with two dead bodies. He wasn't in the mood for Fran's demands.

"It's Rick. He was in a two-car accident. Pretty serious. He's at Valley Hospital now. Can you call Fran? She's panicked."

"How serious?"

"Well, she said he was alive and conscious but in bad shape."

Tom glanced back into the living room where Candy was still writing. "Okay, I'll call her in a bit. I've got my hands full right now. Tell Fran I'll get in touch with her a little later."

"She'll have a fit," Margo said.

"I'm not her boyfriend anymore, and she's not the center of the universe," he snapped.

"Okay. I'll tell her." Margo hung up.

Tom groaned. He walked back into the living room.

Candy put down her pen and handed the paper to Tom. "Everything okay?"

"That was Margo. Rick Brandt was in a car accident. He's at Valley Hospital now. She just wanted to let me know."

"Oh my god! Is he okay? I just spent the morning with him."

"You, too?" Tom muttered under his breath.

"How is he?" she asked.

"Margo said he was conscious but pretty banged up. Fran's there. I'd go down but…" He waved the paper Candy had given him. "…priorities."

"Of course. Get to work. I'll check on Rick." Candy stood up, let the robe slip from her shoulders, and made a mad dash to the bedroom in her thin slip.

Tom watched her go and had to smile. "I'll let myself out," he called to her. "Be careful. Hear me?"

"Yes, sexy. I'll be fine," she yelled back.

Tom stopped. He didn't want to leave her yet, and he didn't want her to be alone after all that happened. "On second thought, I'll give you a ride over just to be safe."

"Does the hospital have a rule against guns?" Candy asked.

"I'm a police officer."

"I meant for me!"

***

Tom and Candy found Fran in the operating room waiting lounge.

"What's going on?" Candy asked as she walked through the door.

Fran stood up and the two women hugged. "Rick's in surgery, but he's going to be alright. That's what the doctor said. He's going to be alright." Fran hugged Tom as well. "Thanks for coming. I know you're busy."

"More than you realize." Tom gave her a cautious hug and tried to keep the bite out of his voice.

Fran heard it. "Something big?" She sank back into the chair.

"Candy can tell you about it. I need to get back to work. Call me with any news." He nodded at the two women and left.

"He's still pissed at you for falling in love with Rick," Candy said as she sat down next to Fran.

"He's going to have to get over it. I didn't plan on this, Candy. I didn't. All I knew for sure was I wasn't ready to marry Tom and probably never would be. We would have broken up even if Rick hadn't come back into my life."

"I know. Still –"

"Yes, I know." Fran rested her elbows on her knees and held her head up, feeling exhausted. "I don't know what's taking so long. Rick was in the ER earlier. They were removing broken glass from his face and chest. His arm was –" She paused a moment, fighting back her panic. "It's his eye I'm worried about. It looked bad."

"How's your daughter doing?" Candy changed the topic to give Fran something else to think about.

"Lauren? Ah, well, she's thirteen. It's a tough age for a girl. I wish I was there to help her through it."

"You don't have custody back?" Candy asked, surprised. "I figured, with your ex-husband dead, she'd just come back home."

"You would think, wouldn't you?" Fran said sarcastically. "Because he beat her, child services got involved, and she ended up in state custody, but placed with his widow. Lauren hasn't lived with me for almost a year, and it's driving me nuts."

"You must have visitation, though, right?"

"Every weekend, but you know how it is with teenage girls. She has places to go, friends she wants to be with, and sports. She does track and field and she's very good." Fran smiled proudly. "She's got my legs, thank god!"

"So, what happens next?"

"We go back to court. Hopefully, they'll send her home. I miss her terribly, but she doesn't want to be around Rick, which is a problem. That's why he has his own place, somewhere to go when she's with me."

"That has to be tough." Candy squeezed Fran's hand. "Rick came to the house this morning. He took me gun shopping."

"Gun shopping? What the hell is going on?"

Candy stammered a bit before saying, "Two people were murdered, one last night and one this morning. They were both friends of mine. Their bodies –" She choked up as she spoke and took a minute to quiet herself. "They were dressed in pink and black corsets and hose and heels and masks and had these dog collars –" Candy had to stop.

Fran put an arm around her friend's shoulders and drew her close. "Two? Rick said there was an attack. Oh my god, hon. Does Tom think it's personal? Does he think someone's after you?"

Candy nodded. She tried again. "They were strangled with spiked dog collars turned inside out. And they had these flowers. Pam, she had six flowers pinned to her corset, and Andrea had five, like the killer was counting down." Candy's hand went to her throat. "They were good people. Mothers. Nice women, you know? They didn't deserve this!"

Fran rubbed Candy's back and held her hand. "What in hell are you doing here, then?"

"Honestly? I don't want to be home alone."

"Of course."

The two women sat in the waiting room quietly for quite a while before the doctor emerged, looking for Fran. "Miss Simone?"

"Yes, that's me. How is Rick?"

Fran and Candy both stood up.

"I'm Dr. Sam Kaul. I've been taking care of Rick. We were able to bring his blood pressure down, which was a good thing. It was 180 over 157," the doctor began. "The left arm was shattered in two places. The surgery was long, but it looks good. It may be months, possibly even a year, before the arm makes a full recovery. He has a large hematoma of the lower leg, but it's not bad enough to require surgery or drainage at this point. However, it does require careful watching. An infection or complication could be serious. He needs to use crutches for a while and stay off of it as much as possible, keep it elevated and in a compression bandage, and put ice to it four to eight times a day for at least 20 minutes until it can heal. He got it when his leg was pinned in the vehicle. There's also a smaller hematoma on the upper leg, but that should heal on its own."

"How long? How much time?" Fran asked.

"With the leg, maybe six to twelve weeks to get relatively back to normal, depending on how he takes care of it," Dr. Kaul said. "He's in pretty good shape and the injury is serious but manageable, as long as there are no complications. He got lucky. As for his arm, he could regain full and normal use of it in eight months to a year, but that would be beating the odds. Chances are he will have some problems from here on."

"His eye?" Fran asked nervously.

"That's still questionable. We have a very good ophthalmologist on loan from the Bascom Palmer Eye Institute in Florida. Rick couldn't be in better hands."

"And?" Fran waited for more information.

"It appears the damage spared the cornea and didn't go as deep as we first thought. We removed all foreign objects, but there's some nerve damage. We won't know for sure how his sight will be affected for a few days yet, or maybe even a few weeks." Kaul rested a hand on Fran's shoulder. "I've known Rick for a while. He's going to make it through this. That's one tough boyfriend you've got there."

"How do you know Rick?" Candy asked.

"I was a medic in Iraq when Rick was stationed there," Kaul explained.

"When can I see him?" Fran asked.

"He's in recovery now, sleeping off the anesthetic. As soon as he's awake and we check his vitals, we'll move him to a room. You can see him then."

"Thanks, doctor." Candy took Fran's arm and pulled her back into the seat. "He's going to be fine, you know that, Fran. He's tough."

"He's also left-handed," Fran said.

"So?" Then Candy remembered the shooting lesson. "That's his gun arm. Damn."

"I'm sure he can handle a gun with either hand, right? Aren't guys like him trained that way?" Fran asked.

"Probably. Honestly, I have no idea."

"Look, as long as Rick's going to be here for a few days, why don't you stay at my place?" Fran asked. "It's a nice neighborhood, lots of security, and no one needs to know where you are. Besides, I don't like being alone, either." She offered a weak smile.

"How are you with a gun?" Candy asked.

Fran started to laugh. Maybe it was the fatigue, or the stress, or the insanity of the situation, but she started to laugh and had a hard time stopping. When she finally caught her breath, Fran squeezed Candy's hand. "I'm sorry," she said as she wiped laugh tears from her cheeks. "You would not believe how ironic –" She laughed some more and inhaled deeply. "A while back, when I was having nightmares, I woke up one night and pulled my gun out and was shooting at shadows in the house. Tom walked in, pissed as hell, and took the gun away from me."

Candy nodded. Tom had shared that story with her, but she didn't need to tell Fran that.

"I'm actually not a bad shot," Fran said. "I just gotta get my gun back. And to tell you the truth, I have a lot fewer nightmares with Rick around. I don't know why. I just do."

"You feel safe with him, that's why."

Fran leaned back in her seat, closed her eyes a minute, and imagined Rick's arms around her. "Yeah, I do."

"I like the idea of staying with you," Candy said, "but I have a meeting tonight first, with the three surviving members of my group."

"You think that's a good idea? Maybe it would be better if they stayed away from you for a while and you all laid low."

Candy sighed. "You may be right. I need to let them know." She pulled her phone out and sent text messages to her girls; she canceled the meeting, warned them that they were being stalked and were in danger, and said a detective wanted to talk to them. "This isn't going to be easy for them. The whole idea of working with me is to keep it all quiet, not to let the whole world know."

"Somebody knows. Somebody wants them dead, and probably you, too. You – and they – are just going to have to deal with the fallout."

Candy checked her cell phone for the time.

***

Tom didn't know why he had to talk to the Reverend Lawrence Blackwell again, but Sheriff Hodge insisted on it.

"Something about him I don't like," Hodge said.

"You think he's hiding something?" Tom asked.

Hodge shrugged. "Just talk to him. Check him out in his own environment. See if you can figure him out."

"Detective," Melissa Pearson said curtly as she pierced Tom's thoughts. She escorted him from the reception room into the minister's office.

Tom nodded politely at her and glanced around. The room was simple with inexpensive paneling on the walls, blue wall-to-wall carpeting, and tan curtains. Several over-stacked bookcases lined two walls. A small vinyl sofa was set to one side, and two almost-matching chairs faced a large but simple desk. The desk itself was littered with half-opened mail, a few files, and some writing materials. One wall was devoted to religious pictures including those of St. Francis De Sales and St. John Marie Vianney, a picture of Christ being whipped before the crucifixion, and one of Christ as a young boy. The four pieces surrounded a framed Bible quote: Galatians 5:24 – "And those who belong to Christ Jesus have crucified the flesh with its passions and desires."

Tom always considered himself a good man, but the display made him squirm.

"Ah, Detective Saddler," Blackwell said as he entered. "Melissa, some coffee for our guest," he instructed his secretary.

Blackwell was a tall man, around six feet, Tom guessed, and in his early fifties. He appeared in mud-splattered blue jeans and a dirt-smudged t-shirt. He was broad-shouldered and walked with a limp, and Tom noticed that he had dirt under his fingernails. Tom looked up to a smiling face with keen blue eyes, sandy hair, and high cheekbones.

"That's okay," Tom said. "I won't be long."

"Please, have a seat." Blackwell leaned the cane against a file cabinet and slid slowly and carefully into his chair as if every movement was painful. "Excuse the mess." He held up his hands. "We're replanting the garden. Melissa made some coffee for me; she might as well pour you a cup. How do you like yours?"

The secretary handed the minister a towel and he took a minute to wipe his hands.

Tom caved. "Milk only."

The woman nodded and scurried out of the room on her mission. Tom sat down and pulled out his notepad and pen.

"I have to confess, first –" Tom began.

"Confessing? Already?" The minister laughed. "Surely that's not necessary."

Tom grinned and started to relax. "As I was about to say, I need to confess that I'm not sure why I'm here. The sheriff thought perhaps you might know something that could help us, but I don't know where to begin."

"Perhaps the Spirit moved your sheriff to send you here for your own edification." Blackwell was still smiling, but Tom got the feeling there was a bit of disdain behind the pleasantries. "We can never do enough to rid ourselves of the vices of the mortal world. And it is such vices that bring you to my doorstep, is it not?"

Mrs. Pearson returned, put the coffee tray down on the desk, and stood by the minister like a sentry, her hands in the pockets of her calf-length skirt, her blouse buttoned to the top and adorned with a simple gold crucifix.

The minister sighed. "I was discussing the – er – murder with Melissa and her husband earlier. I don't know exactly what we can tell you except –" He glanced at his secretary for a moment. She nodded and he continued. "We overheard you speaking with the waitress, Missy, is it?"

"Yes." Tom took a drink of his coffee out of courtesy, then leaned back and listened.

"You asked her about a woman, if she knew this — What was her name, again?" he asked Melissa.

"Knight. Candace Knight," Melissa said. She tensed.

Tom noticed. "And?"

The minister nodded at his secretary to continue.

"About three years ago, our son was murdered," Melissa said. "He was twenty-eight. The police investigated, and that woman —" She hesitated a moment and Tom heard the anger in her voice. "That woman decided that it wasn't murder. It was — She called it something else — like an accident."

"Negligent homicide?" Tom asked.

"Yes, that was it. She said it wasn't on purpose, and our son's murderer walked free."

"Not exactly free." The minister patted her hand gently. "I understand he was given a split sentence with three years in jail."

"Our son is dead, and his killer is out," she said.

"How did he die?" Tom asked.

Melissa blushed a deep red and ran out of the room in tears. Tom, puzzled, turned his attention to the minister.

"I'm terribly sorry. It's very embarrassing for them. It's so sad when a child is misled by evil. His baser instincts were corrupted and –"

"Minister, none of that means anything to me. Do you know how he died or don't you?"

Blackwell, a bit irritated, cleared his throat. "Of course. I believe they call it homoerotic asphyxiation."

Tom frowned. "Do you mean autoerotic asphyxiation, when sex partners engage in breath play?"

"Is that what they call it when two men do it?"

Tom pursed his lips. "I see. So, your secretary's son died from this – er – activity, and she believed his sex partner should have been convicted of murder, but he wasn't."

"What he did was far worse than murder. He condemned poor Bryce to hell for eternity. Corinthians tells us that when a man lies with a man, he shall not inherit the Kingdom of God. If Bryce had lived, he could have repented his sins. He could have done penance. He could have saved his soul. But, dying like he did –" The minister looked up to the ceiling as if offering a silent prayer.

"I can't fix that," Tom said. "All I can deal with is earthly justice."

"Exactly. I've seen this kind of thing before. Young people become addicted to certain kinds of what you call sex play. It's a perversion of the natural order and a sin in the eyes of God." Blackwell examined Tom as if he could somehow see into the detective's soul. "Don't you think, detective, that if Dr. Knight wasn't one of THEM, that if she wasn't the devil's pawn, that she would have tipped the scales of justice differently?"

"One of them?"

"A member of the BDSM community," Blackwell explained. "Given her affiliation with the dead woman, I can only assume —"

"Did you see Dr. Knight at the restaurant this morning?" Tom avoided the question and the insinuation.

"No, I did not. But I didn't see the victim there until —" The minister shuddered. "I can only assume, given the victim's state of dress and given that she was friends with this Knight woman —"

"How do you know they were friends?" Tom asked.

"Again, just from what the waitress told you while we were there," the minister repeated. "I admit I'd seen them at the diner before, but I never really paid much attention."

Tom made a note.

"Don't you find it oddly suspicious?" Blackwell asked.

"Dr. Knight used to be head of the crime lab. I worked with her on numerous cases. I find it hard to believe she could kill someone."

"Kill someone?" The minister looked surprised. "Heavens, I wasn't going there at all! All I meant was — Well, how shall I put this?" He leaned back and rubbed his chin. "If Knight is willing to let someone walk for homoerotic asphyxiation, and she spends time with a woman who clearly has a BDSM fetish, that there's a connection, you understand, because she's one of them. Because she leads the innocents into hell."

"You don't know that Andrea Ortiz was into BDSM," Tom said. "The killer dressed her up that way. There's no indication –"

"Oh, please, detective. Don't talk to me like I'm ignorant of the ways of the world. I assure you, I have sinned plenty, and I have paid the price for it." He winced a little and glanced down at his coffee as if remembering. "We are all haunted by our pasts, are we not? But I have been saved in the Lord and have driven the evils of the flesh from me."

Tom didn't want to know how the minister had accomplished that. "Do you know for a fact that Ortiz was part of the BDSM community?"

"How would I? I'm not one of them."

"Them?"

"The prostitutes. Those who pervert the instincts of others, who twist them into evil addictions. Jezebel. Bathsheba. A witch."

Prostitute. There was that word again. Tom frowned and remembered how angry Candy was at him over breakfast. Tom clenched his jaw a moment to keep from yelling at the man. "Dr. Knight isn't with the lab anymore, so I'm not sure it's relevant."

"Yes, you mentioned she 'used to be' head of the crime lab. Why 'used to be'?"

"She took a job teaching at UNLV." Tom knew the minister's probable hunch, that Candy was forced out of her job because of her lifestyle, was correct, but Tom wasn't about to say so.

The minister nodded. "Well, that's really all I can add to what we said this morning."

Tom took one last sip of his coffee and stood up. "Thank you for your time."

The men shook hands, and Tom left the office. As he climbed into his car, he glanced back to see the minister and his secretary standing shoulder to shoulder and staring out a second-floor window at him. Below them, Jim Pearson was busy painting the red trim on the porch shutters. Tom nodded politely, got in his car, and drove off, happy to be away from them all.

Chapter 4

Early Monday Evening

Candy hung back in the doorway as Fran entered the hospital room.

"You can just press that button if you need anything, Mr. Brandt," a nurse was saying. She held his wrist as she checked his pulse.

"It's Rick," he replied.

The deep, soft vibration of his voice made Fran smile. He sounded good. He sounded like his old self. "Flirting with the nurses already?" she asked as she walked to his bedside.

The nurse stepped out of the way. She was young and pretty, and Fran felt a tinge of jealousy.

A curtain was drawn between Rick and the next bed, blocking his view of the window. He wouldn't like that, Fran knew, but he wouldn't complain. He never did. His left leg was elevated, his left arm was in a sling, he wore a neck brace, and bandages covered the left side of his face, including the eye. She swallowed down her fear and mustered a reassuring smile.

Rick opened his good eye. "Kiss me, woman."

Fran, keenly aware that both Candy and the nurse were watching, blushed warmly. She gripped the bedrail and bent to kiss him. Rick wrapped his powerful right hand around the back of her neck. His fingers tangled in her long red hair as he pulled her down into a hard kiss. When he finally let go, she glared at him.

"You did that to see if I was drinking," she accused him as tears stung her eyes.

"Yup." He met her look without apology. "And because I liked it."

"You don't trust me?" Fran spoke out of anger. She knew better, but a part of her wanted to get even with him.

"If I didn't trust you, I wouldn't be sleeping with you."

"You bastard," Fran muttered just loud enough for him to hear. "You slept with Toni de la Rosa, and she tried to kill you."

Rick blinked. It was the strongest reaction Fran had ever gotten from him regarding his former lover, and Fran knew she hit a nerve.

"You scared me to death." Fran lowered her eyes a moment, feeling ashamed for attacking him. All he ever did was look out for her, that and save her life a few times.

"I know. That's why I was worried. You're not Toni. You never were. I expect better from you."

The nurse quietly slipped out of the room as an aide walked in with a vase of flowers – orange, purple, and blue daisies. The aide smiled at Rick before leaving.

Fran glanced at the flowers and frowned. "Who would know you're here?"

Candy stepped into the room and checked the card. "Margo." She glanced at Rick and smiled.

"What are you doing here?" Rick asked.

"Well, hello to you, too," she snapped back. "I came to check on you. I didn't know that was a crime."

Rick scowled. "It's not safe–" he started to say.

"Tom brought me," Candy interjected. "If I knew you didn't want me to come–"

"That's not it and you know it. I have a vested interest in making sure you don't get killed."

Fran glanced at Candy and then back at Rick. "She's going to be staying with me for a while," Fran said.

"If you don't mind." Candy stood at the foot of his bed. "I don't want to throw you out of your house. I just figured as long as you were laid up, it might be better to go someplace, you know, where no one knows where I am."

"I don't live there," Rick said.

"He doesn't live there," Fran said at the same time.

"Oh." Candy looked confused but didn't comment. "Well, then –"

Rick took Fran's hand. "I'll be out of here soon. Will you be alright?"

"Of course," Fran lied.

"Candy, we need a few minutes of privacy," said Rick.

Candy backed out of the room and closed the door.

"Is there anyone in the next bed?" he asked.

Fran tugged back the curtain a little. "No. The bed's not made. Someone sleeps there, but he's not there now."

"Good. Come here."

When Fran returned to his side, he reached up and took her arm. "Someone is trying to kill Candy," he whispered. "I don't like the idea of her being with you. I don't want you in that kind of danger."

Fran curled her fingers around Rick's hand. "She told me. I'll be careful. I promise. We'll be careful."

"I mean it, boss. I can't run out and rescue you like this."

Fran saw the worry on his face. She brushed his cheek with the back of her hand. "What do you want me to do? Candy needs my help. No one has to know she's there. Tell me what to do and I'll do it."

He closed his good eye, leaned back in the bed, and sighed. "If I had my way, I'd lock you up somewhere safe until I can get outta here."

"That won't do much to help me dig my company out of the clutches of gangsters. If what Rupert Hawksworth told me is right, I either need to divest immediately or face racketeering charges. I have to do something."

"Oh shit. I forgot," Rick responded. "Get Candy to help you. She was head of the crime lab once. She knows how to get information. Just don't let her go wandering around in public, not yet. I don't know how long –"

Fran put her fingers gently on his lips to hush him. "You'll be home soon, but you won't be up and around for a while. You're going to need help."

Rick groaned and muttered, "I've got things to do."

"And me to help you do them," Fran added.

"Baby doll, I know you'll do your best."

Fran's heart ached when she left him. She slipped behind the wheel of her silver Mercedes, with Candy in the passenger seat. The air was hot and stifling. Fran turned on the AC and wiped her eyes with the back of her hand. Then she reached for the radio. Jamie O'Neal crooned "Like a Woman" as Fran fought back tears.

"Hey, he's going to be alright," Candy said. "You heard that cute doctor. He was lucky and he's tough. He'll pull through just fine. You'll see."

"It scares me how much I need him, and I don't think he even realizes it," Fran admitted. She reached into her purse, pulled out some breath mints, and popped them into her mouth. "Just about the time I think I'm fine, that I'm past all the shit in my life and I can stand on my own two feet, then bam, something happens, and I panic."

Candy just nodded, listening.

"My place or yours, first?" Fran asked as she dropped her purse into the backseat and started the car.

"Mine. I'd better get some things."

"I need your help." Fran put the car in gear and pulled into traffic.

"What kind of help?"

"I found out this morning that I inherited some stocks from my father in a company called Max-Mil Enterprises."

"The real estate group?"

Fran chuckled. "Well, you already know more than I did. I was told there's a board meeting on Friday, that I own the majority shares, and that my dear old dad and the current CEO were using the company for illegal activities."

"What kind of activities?"

"Hell if I know."

"How much of a majority?" Candy asked.

"Fifty-one percent. Why?"

"I take it you've never done anything like this before."

Fran shook her head no. "First time."

"What do you need from me?"

"I need to find out what the hell I've gotten myself into, and what the hell I can do about it."

Candy smiled. "I've still got contacts in the organized crime unit. Let me dig around and see what I can find out. What's this CEO's name?"

"Jax Saynte."

"Oh." Candy inhaled deeply. "Yes, I've heard of him. I hear he's charming, dangerous, and slippery as hell. And handsome too. We got our work cut out for us."

***

Lois Devost sat uncomfortably in the small police conference room while her husband waited in the lobby. He was joking with someone. She could see him but not hear him, but the fact that he seemed to be relaxed and in a good mood irked her. Tom Saddler had called her to say he needed to question her regarding the deaths of two friends of hers, Pamela Mayhew and Andrea Ortiz. Lois took the news hard. She hadn't checked her messages. She had no warning. She felt as if a horse had kicked her in the chest and left her abandoned at the side of the road.

Yes, she would come down. Of course, she would help, if she could, even if she had nothing to offer, even if the news left her unable to breathe. Her husband was home for lunch and getting ready to leave for work when he saw her turn pale and sink into her chair. He was worried about her, and he drove her to the station.

Now, the 65-year-old grandmother of three pulled her cardigan tightly around her large body and fingered the cross that dangled from a chain at her throat. She came as she was – stretch pants, sneakers, an oversized tunic splashed with large yellow roses, and her gray hair fresh out of rollers. She didn't bother with make-up.

Tom Saddler stepped into the room, smiled at her, and tried to put her at ease. "I promise this won't take long," he said as he sat down. "I take it your husband doesn't know about your relationship with Candace Knight."

"No." She blushed.

"I've known Candy for quite a while, so don't be worried about talking to me." Tom set the file down, folded his hands together, and leaned forward. His voice was calming. "I'm not here to embarrass you or make this more difficult for you than it already is. What you choose to tell your husband about this meeting is up to you. I'm trying to solve two murders, and I'm trying to prevent yours."

"Mine?" Lois flashed him a frightened look. No one had suggested that she was in danger. She tensed. "What do you mean?"

"Two of Candy's girls are dead. They were killed with a collar, like a dog collar, spiked, turned inside out and used to strangle them and slash their throats." Tom's hand went to the file. He had initially planned on showing her the photos of the victims; now he thought better of it. "When they were found, they were dressed in BDSM clothing." He took a minute to watch her react. "I think the killer is targeting Candy's girls, her students, that is, including you. And when he's done, he'll go after Candy. That's what I think."

Lois looked like she was about to throw up. She clasped her hands tightly together and squeezed them to keep them from trembling. "I don't know what to tell you. My husband doesn't know. I never told him about the group. I wanted to – "

"It's okay, Mrs. Devost. I understand," Tom said, although he wasn't sure that he did. "I want to know if you saw anyone suspicious before, during, or after your meetings. Was anything out of the ordinary in the last few weeks? Did you notice a stalker?"

"No, nothing like that. It's a good group, good people. We don't talk about it, of course. I mean, with the rest of the world, except maybe Pam. She talked about everything with her husband." Lois smiled momentarily. "They were cute together, but otherwise, I can't imagine – "

"So, no one knew about the group or who was in it except for the members and Pam's husband?" Tom asked.

"As far as I know. I can't believe Howie is behind this. He only came to one meeting, and he was so sweet." She stopped as if she'd said too much.

"What are you thinking?" Tom asked.

"Well, there was a guy there once. I never really met him. He didn't stay. He stopped by to talk to Candy, but she wouldn't let him inside. Then he left. I don't know who he was."

"Can you describe him?" Tom asked.

"I don't remember much. I know he was young, and he was well-dressed. He looked like a businessman, a suit type. Otherwise, I didn't get a good look at him. It didn't seem important at the time."

"Did he say anything? Did they argue? Did he appear upset?"

"They didn't exactly argue, but he didn't look happy," Lois responded. "Candy was upset, though. She just told him it was a bad time, something along those lines, and he left. Then the meeting started."

"And no one else ever showed up?"

"Not that I saw. I didn't make every meeting, though. Have you talked to Mistress Candy?"

Tom caught his breath a second. It was the first time he'd ever heard Candy referred to as "mistress," and he wasn't sure how to process it. "Yes, I spoke to her. She's helping us."

Lois smiled meekly. "Can I go now?"

"Yes, you can go." Tom stood up and escorted her to the door.

"Please don't tell my husband," she whispered as he opened the door.

"I'm trying to solve a murder, ma'am, not make your life more difficult," he reassured her.

She nodded and left.

Tom closed the door behind her and sat back down at the table. He opened the folder and laid the crime scene photos of the dead women in front of him. Leaning forward, he studied them carefully and murmured to himself, "What aren't you telling me, Mistress Candy?"

***

"Damn." Candy threw several small suitcases into the back of Fran's car and checked her phone.

"Problem?" Fran had grabbed a lemon soda from Candy's fridge and now gulped it.

"Nothing that can't wait." Candy slipped into the car.

Fran had left the car running, and it had cooled down. She slid behind the wheel and tucked the drink into one of the cup holders. "I'm supposed to have Lauren for visitation this weekend." Night was creeping up on them and she turned on the headlights. "I hope you don't mind."

"Of course not. She's how old now?" Candy pushed her bangs out of her eyes and looked out the window.

"Thirteen," said Fran. "Her step-mother lets her come every weekend."

"So, why isn't Rick living with you?" Candy asked.

"Didn't we just talk about this at the hospital?"

Candy shook her head. "Probably. I'm sorry. I have so much going on in my head."

"It's such a mess with Rick killing Paul and all that." Fran shuddered, remembering the day her ex-husband had lost it and taken his stepson hostage in the hospital cafeteria. Rick came to the child's rescue, but at a price. Paul was dead, and his stepson was probably traumatized for life. As for Lauren, "She can't even talk to Rick, yet. It's been hard on her, losing her dad that way."

"I bet." Candy nodded. "Can we stop at the store? I need to pick up a few things."

"What kind of store?"

"A mini-mart is fine."

"Good, I should get some gas while I'm at it."

Candy's phone rang again. She glanced at it and put it back into her pocket with a growl.

"An admirer?" Fran asked jokingly.

"Something like that. It's Allyson."

"Allyson Stone? The deputy D.A.? I'm impressed. When did you start dating him?"

Candy sighed. "I'm not. We had one afternoon of drinks and talking, ONE afternoon. He's been calling me ever since. He's getting to be a pain in the ass."

"Does he know?" Fran asked.

"About what?" Candy asked innocently.

"You know what. About your attic of toys."

Candy gave Fran a strange look. "You've seen it?"

Fran never mentioned the trip to Candy's house, or how Rick had suggested she check out the attic. She blushed. "When you were in the hospital last time, I went to feed the cat and –" she started.

"And you just had to look."

Fran couldn't read whether or not Candy was pissed at her. "Look, if that's a problem, I'm sorry. Rick told me what was up there and – By the way, how would Rick know what's in your attic?"

"Maybe you should ask Rick," Candy said with a grin and a wink.

"Aww! Come on! That is SO not fair!" Fran argued. "You know how I feel about Rick. I'm curious! He told me he wasn't one of your – er – well, if you'll excuse the expression – boy toys." Her blush got deeper. "So, I was wondering."

Candy couldn't hold back the laughing at this point. "Okay. He came to the house to serve a subpoena, and one of my so-called 'boy toys' answered the door and let him in. He thought Rick was there for a session, so he brought him up to the attic." She shook her head and looked out the window, remembering. "You know, nothing rattles that man. He looked around, nodded, said something like, 'This is interesting,' and handed me the subpoena. Before I could respond, he was gone. And that was that."

"Oh." Fran was almost disappointed that the story wasn't more titillating.

"Of course, the 'boy' who answered the door had to be severely punished after that." Candy grinned.

Fran shook her head, picturing it. "You're right. Nothing much rattles Rick. I imagine he's been in a few similar places in his time."

"Probably at the other end of the whip," Candy said.

"You think so? When we talked about it, about your attic, he didn't seem really interested."

Candy shrugged. "Well, for some people it's a game, and for others, it's a lifestyle. As far as I know, Rick was never in the lifestyle, and he's not the gaming type, at least not anymore. Who knows what he was like when he was younger?"

"You got a point," Fran conceded.

Candy's phone rang again. "What the fuck!" she yelled, looking at it. This time she answered it. Her voice was suddenly smooth as silk. "Yes, Allyson, what can I do for you?"

Fran glanced at her, surprised at the sudden change of tone.

"Oh, I'm sure, Allyson. That's so sweet of you, but I'm fine, really. No need to worry." Candy was silent for a minute.

Fran could hear what sounded like an argumentative voice on the other end of the phone, but she couldn't make out the words. Suddenly, Candy's tone changed again, this time from sweet to dictatorial.

"I told you," she said quietly and firmly. "I'm fine. I don't need your help. Now leave me the hell alone." She hung up the phone.

"What the hell?" Fran spotted the mini-mart and pulled into it.

"You didn't hear that," Candy said with a sigh. "Need anything while I'm inside?"

"Yeah, scotch, but Rick would skin me alive and enjoy every minute of it."

"He's still got you drying out?" Candy asked with surprise.

"I had to choose--him or the booze." Fran parked the car and looked at Candy. "It was easier to give up the booze."

"Licorice. It helps. Trust me on that one." Candy crawled out of the car and headed to the store as Fran dug out her credit card for gas.

"Licorice," Fran mumbled to herself as she filled her tank. "And here I was thinking dark chocolate."

She stepped up to the pump just as an ocean blue BMW coupe pulled to the other side. A tall, pleasant-looking man in an expensive suit got out, glanced at her, offered up a quiet smile, and began to pump his own gas. Across the street, Allyson Stone put down his phone and focused his camera. The man with the BMW finished and was gone before Candy exited the store.

Chapter 5
Monday Night

"I have a very active imagination, but I never thought my fantasies would get someone killed."

Candy flipped open the lid of one of her suitcases on the spare bed at Fran's house and pulled out a handful of clothing including several elaborate lace corsets, some silken lingerie, and an elegant lace mask. Some carefully folded suits, still on their hangars, came next. Casual clothes – mostly skinny jeans and funky tops – followed. Finally, she unpacked the retro dresses Tom was accustomed to seeing her wear. The next suitcase had shoes, boots, gloves, hats, and a feather boa.

For the first time since moving to this house, Fran appreciated the spare bedroom's large closet and two empty dressers. She sat on the edge of the bed and arched her eyebrows as she watched Candy unpack. When Candy said she needed to pick up a few things at her apartment, Fran expected a gym bag or maybe an overnight bag. But for Candy, a few things meant two suitcases plus a cosmetic case and a small black bag of "miscellaneous" items yet to be revealed.

"Someone has it in for you," Fran told her friend. "It wouldn't matter what you were doing, that person would find a way to use it against you. You can't blame yourself for that."

Candy shook her head. "My grandma tried to warn me. She was always running to church and praying for my soul. I was dabbling in the devil's workshop, she said. No good could come of it." Candy's voice mimicked her grandmother's stern warning. "Not that she gave a rat's ass about me anyway. Not that any of them did."

"You never talk about your family."

"With good reason."

Fran frowned. "What do you think is going on here? Why are you a target?"

Candy sat back on the bed, a handful of fine lingerie in her lap. She picked at it as if it might bite her. "I wish I knew. I have ideas, but none of them make any sense."

"What kind of ideas?"

"Maybe I'm being punished for my sins," Candy said.

"Yeah, well, I doubt that. What else?"

"Well, for one, Allyson might be behind this. He's got this thing for me. Sometimes I think he wants to own me, and other times I think he wants to give me grief. It's like an obsession. In his twisted little mind, he might be jealous of my girls and, the thing is, I don't think he's the type to pull off this shit. He's too damn self-righteous. He's always spouting off about crime in Vegas like it's personal to him. I think he's politically ambitious. If I thought for one minute that he murdered any of my girls, I'd put a bullet – POW – right between his eyes. I swear I would." Candy's dark eyes filled with tears, and she held her hands as if pointing a gun at Allyson. "Then there's Alex."

Fran's heart seized up. "Alex de la Rosa? He adores you! He's like your lost puppy dog. Why would he do anything to hurt you?"

"I don't know that he would, but I know his sister would. She tried to kill me once. Why not twice? And it wouldn't be the first time Toni got into Alex's head and twisted it around."

"Toni is in prison and will probably be there the rest of her life," Fran said. "She's a crazy, homicidal maniac. Right now, she can't touch anyone. I think Alex has got at least six months left on his sentence. He's not going anywhere either."

"But he's so quiet lately. Haven't you noticed?" Candy leaned back on the bed and tossed the lingerie aside. "He used to be so outspoken, a flirt, a tease. He was always laughing and joking, a regular smartass. Don't you remember when he ran for mayor? He's not that man now. That mess with his sister broke him someplace deep inside. I never see him smile anymore."

"You've visited him in prison?" Fran asked.

"Of course."

Fran glanced at her hands. "To be honest, Candy, I've been so wrapped up in my own stuff that I haven't been to see Alex."

"You haven't wanted to see him, you mean." Candy tried to keep the bite out of her voice.

Fran nodded. "Maybe you're right. I feel like he betrayed us, betrayed me. He would do anything to keep his sister safe, and that almost got us all killed. I don't think I'm ready to deal with those emotions yet."

"You used to be in love with him."

Fran felt an unexpected rush of grief. "Used to be – a long, long time ago." Maybe still was, a little, someplace deep inside.

"And now, all of that is gone?"

"It's not that all my feelings for Alex – or for Tom, for that matter – are gone. It's that those feelings don't matter anymore. Rick changed all that. I can't even explain how or when or why. He just did." Fran smiled softly, lifted the black lace mask, and examined it as Candy continued to unpack.

"I didn't like him at first. I thought he was rude, arrogant, pushy, and too machismo."

"Alex?" Fran asked in surprise.

"No, Rick."

"What changed your mind?"

"Did I say I changed my mind? He is still rude, arrogant, pushy, and too machismo. Maybe I've just grown to like him despite all that." She grinned. "He was willing to sacrifice so much for Toni. It was…" She thought for a few moments. "…noble – stupid but noble."

"And?"

Candy looked at Fran. "The way he was willing to put his life on the line to save you. You hear about guys like that. You don't often actually meet one."

Fran felt a warm glow through her body. "I just wish Cheryl and those damn social workers saw it that way," Fran complained. "All they see is Rick, the tough guy – tattoos and bullet scars and someone they can't control. They don't like that."

"Cheryl?"

"My ex-husband's widow. She has Lauren for now."

"Of course," Candy agreed. "That's not how those people work. Everything is about what's best for Lauren, and if living with Cheryl is best for your daughter, nothing you do will fix that."

"How can it be better than living with me?"

Candy raised an eyebrow.

"Okay," Fran conceded. "I drink too much – drank. I've been sober for months now."

"And you work long hours. And you deal with criminals in your law practice. And you're sleeping with the man who killed Lauren's father," Candy said. "Sorry, hon. It's going to be one hell of a hearing."

Fran groaned. She needed to change the subject before she got depressed. "I like nice things." She picked up some red silk lingerie and fingered it. "I just never thought of having quite so many of them." She picked up one of the corsets next. The fabric felt soft in her hands. "Doesn't this restrict your breathing?"

"It can if you don't wear it right. You need a quality corset with the right style and shape for your body. It's not a toy, and you can get hurt wearing it if you don't know what you're doing." Candy took the item from Fran's hand and smiled. The corset had a rose pink, leather-like underlayer over steel boning, with a black lace decorative fabric finishing the look. The laces were rose pink velvet. "This one is Alex's favorite. You want to try one on?"

Fran blushed. "Maybe another time."

"Don't be shy, sweetie. Everyone is a virgin sometime."

"I'm not a —" Fran started to say.

"I mean with corsets." Candy opened the little black bag. Fran stared as Candy unpacked some velvet-covered hand and ankle cuffs, a couple of vibrators, a black blindfold, half-dozen scarves, a couple of paddles, and a few other unidentified items.

"No whips?" Fran teased.

"They're in storage." Candy winked and sat on the bed. "This is your chance. Ask me anything."

"Are you kidding? I don't know where to begin!"

"You're not a kid, Fran. You've been married and had a child. I'm sure you've seen this stuff before if only on the Internet. Why haven't you ever tried it?"

"Rick told me that sex toys were like triggers for arousal." Fran tried to remember exactly how he put it. "Some people need more triggers –"

"Or different kinds of triggers," Candy corrected.

"Okay, more or different kinds of triggers, than other people do. I don't think I've ever needed anything like this and, to tell you the truth, I find it – well – intimidating."

"Why?"

Fran hesitated a few moments as the memories came flooding back. She took a deep breath as she prepared to dive into murky waters. "My father molested me when I was 12 years old." Fran lowered her eyes. As fast as the memories came, she locked them back in her Pandora's Box. "He forced himself on me for nearly a year before I was able to get away from him. My mom found out, and they fought. She started drinking and ended up dying in a car wreck."

"Molested or raped?"

Fran didn't answer.

Your mom never went to the police?" Candy asked in surprise.

Fran shook her head no.

"I'm so sorry." Candy reached for Fran's hand and squeezed it.

"I ran away when I was thirteen, right after my mom died. I went to live with my mom's sister. That didn't last long. By the time I was sixteen, I was on my own. The only reason I got into college and law school was because my mom left a trust account for me. I got it when I turned eighteen. It saved my life. So, this stuff–" Fran picked up one of the vibrators with two fingers as if afraid it would bite her. "This isn't something I ever wanted to be familiar with."

"We seriously need to talk," said Candy. "BDSM – or for that matter, using any kind of sex toys whether or not you're in the lifestyle – isn't about force, isn't about abuse, isn't about someone taking advantage of you. That part is all roleplay to get into the mindset. The whole idea is to pleasure both parties, especially the recipient, what we call the submissive. It's hard to explain unless you're doing it, but –" She looked at Fran for a moment, thinking. "When Rick makes love to you, what is it about him that turns you on?"

"Everything." Fran laughed. "The way he holds me, the way he strokes me, the way he kisses me, the way he—He has this way about him, a kind of 'take no prisoners' attitude about sex. He just knows what to do and does it. It's a relief in a way. I don't have to explain anything to him, and that's unusual. Most of the men I've been with have no idea how to make me feel that way. He does it without thinking."

"Oh, trust me, he's thinking. He's thinking a lot," Candy said. "But he's also very experienced. You're lucky that way."

"Tom was good at pleasuring me, but it was different. With him it was more like putting on a warm sweater, comfortable, easy. Natural."

"But not with Rick."

"No. Rick is not 'comfortable.' That's not the word I'd use. He's more –" Fran struggled to put words to it, and Candy didn't interrupt. "He's more sure of himself. He's more – well – demanding, in a way. I don't mean he makes me do anything that I don't want to do. It's just that Rick seems to know how far he can push me. He knows what I like, even if I don't. He makes me feel – damn, I can't explain it."

"Sexy?" Candy asked.

"Hell, yes. Definitely sexy. Definitely horny. And definitely loved. And definitely turned on. And definitely – definitely." Fran was blushing more now. She covered her face with her hands as if she wanted to crawl somewhere and hide from embarrassment. "It's just different. I've never had a lover like him before."

"And you probably never will again. He's one in a million, Fran." Candy picked up one of the vibrators and held it in her hand. "What would you like to do to let him know how much you appreciate the way he makes you feel?"

"Oh my god, I never thought of it that way." Fran examined the lace panties.

"I suspect Rick is a one-girl kinda guy or at least a one-girl at a time kinda guy. He's not going to wander off unless you decide to leave him. Although if you left him, I doubt you'd get a second chance." She hesitated a moment. "That being said, he's still only a man, and he's a man that other women find attractive. A little appreciation goes a long way toward keeping him in your bed."

"You think using these toys or fancier lingerie will help?"

"I'll tell you a secret." Candy lowered her voice and grinned. "It's not about the toys. Stroke a man's ego, and he'll follow you anywhere." Candy held one of the paddles in her hand and looked down at it. The lighthearted smile disappeared. Her hand tightened around the grip.

"Hey, hon, you okay?"

"Goddamn son-of-a-bitch!" Candy yelled as she threw the paddle into the wall. "Damn him to hell!"

Fran sat straight up. She waited for Candy to calm down.

Candy curled into a ball on the bed. "It's all my fault. If I hadn't – Those women didn't – They came to me. I should have known. I should have realized something bad would happen."

Fran stretched out next to Candy. She gently stroked Candy's arm. "None of this is your fault. Some idiot out there –" Fran started to say.

"You don't understand. It was just a game to them, a pastime. They had no idea what they were getting into, and I didn't tell them. For people in the lifestyle, it's so much more. It's all about the submission, the power exchange, the addiction, the intoxication of it all. I couldn't teach that to these girls. They didn't come to me for that. They read some silly book and they wanted a thrill. I should have warned them. There are a lot of creeps out there. You can't trust people. You've got to be careful who you get mixed up with."

Fran ran her fingers gently through Candy's hair. "Any asshole can find an excuse to hurt or kill a woman. If you weren't involved in BDSM at all, it still could happen. You don't know –"

Candy turned her head into the pillow to stifle her tears. "It just seemed so harmless. I didn't take them to any clubs. I didn't invite anyone in. It was our secret. A chance to explore and learn. A pre-school of sorts." She shook her head. "I don't get it. I don't."

Fran pulled Candy into her arms to comfort her.

The two women were curled up together just as Tom walked into the room. Startled, they looked up at the shocked expression on Tom's face.

"I don't want to know," Tom said as he turned red.

"You always walk into a house without knocking?" Candy wiped the tears from her face and offered up a weak smile.

Tom held up a key. "I used to live here."

"For god's sake, Tom, it's not what you think," said Fran.

"What time is it?" Candy asked.

"Almost nine," Tom told Candy. "I know it's late, but I have to talk to you." He offered the key to Fran. "I probably should give this back to you."

"No, you shouldn't. You're always free to come and go as you please." She felt the old ache well up in her chest. The breakup was sudden but not unexpected. Part of her still missed him.

Candy glanced from Tom to Fran and back again. "Any news?"

"No one died today," he said, his face somber. "I'll wait for you ladies in the kitchen." He turned and walked away. Fran's shoulders slumped.

"Do you still love him?" Candy asked.

"In a way. Just not in the way he needs."

Candy nodded. "Good."

"Good? How is that good?"

"Because you won't bitch when I take a shot at him."

"You? Since when?"

"Mm, I've had a bit of a crush on him for a while now," Candy admitted. "Of course, when he sees my toys, he runs like a scared rabbit. But I think I can cure him of that."

"Tom will never be –" Fran searched for the right word.

"A boy toy?" Candy asked.

"Something like that."

"No, he never will be, and I don't expect him to be. That doesn't mean I can't have some fun with him."

Fran was still trying to picture Candy and Tom as a couple when they gathered in the kitchen. Tom was leaning against the sink and drinking a cup of coffee. Fran admired his athletic build, his square jaw, the way he seemed so relaxed with a gun holstered at his side. She caught Candy grinning at him. Tom smiled back at Candy, and Fran felt a twinge of jealousy. She poured her own coffee.

"So, what's the latest?" Candy asked, leaning against the table in an imitation of Tom, her hands resting on the tabletop.

"I interviewed Lois," Tom said. "Nice lady. She's pretty upset about the whole thing, but she didn't have much to offer except for one thing."

"What's that?" Fran asked.

Tom's eyes never left Candy. "She said you had an unwelcomed visitor one night, a relatively young man in a business suit. She said you were not happy to see him and sent him away."

"Damn, that would be Allyson," Candy said. "I completely forgot about that."

"Allyson?" Tom asked.

"Allyson Stone, the assistant D.A.," Fran explained. "He has something of a crush on Candy."

"How big of a crush?" Tom's eyes were still on Candy.

"I don't know if I'd call it a crush, exactly. He's a royal pain in the ass. At first, he just wanted to go out, so we went out, once. You were there, remember? You and Rick stopped to talk to us, and you ended up taking me home."

"I remember," Tom said.

"I didn't want to leave with him. He was too intense, too possessive, right off the bat. Later it was all about looking out for me, making sure I was safe, that sort of thing. Hovering." She shivered.

"Stalking?" Tom asked.

"Not exactly, but close," Candy admitted. "The thing is he's got this law-and-order vibe going. He's all about cleaning up Vegas as if that hasn't been tried before. I think he's on track to be the next D.A. At any rate, he's a damn control freak."

"He keeps calling her," Fran added, now a bit irked that Tom wouldn't look at her.

"How often?" Tom continued to drink his coffee.

"Three times just in the ride over here," said Fran.

"Yes, but that's because I didn't answer," said Candy. "Once I answered and told him to leave me alone, he stopped calling."

"What does he drive?" Tom asked.

"I don't know," said Candy. "Why?"

"I'm going to find out and let you know. I want you both to keep an eye out for his car, okay? Just to be safe."

They nodded.

"You think this guy's a threat to you?" Tom asked. "He sounds like a stalker, and stalkers usually up their game sooner or later. It's the way they operate. Once the thrill wears thin, they do something more threatening and more –"

"I know how that works," Candy stated. "I've been stalked before – a couple of times."

"If he's got that kind of a problem, he's probably done it before. We can always check his history," Fran said.

"Yes, I can." Tom acknowledged her statement with barely a glance at her. "In the meantime, I still haven't been able to catch up with Juanita St. Francis or Meghan King."

"I think Juanita is away this week," Candy said. "She said something about visiting family in New York. Meghan should be around, though. She works for a dentist in Paradise. I can give you that information. They haven't responded to my messages." She stood up. "I need my purse. I'll be right back."

Fran pulled out a chair and sat down in front of Tom. She looked up at him as she drank her coffee. Tom turned, refilled his cup, and then wandered over to the kitchen window to look outside. The silence stretched between them like a taut bungee cord.

Fran cleared her throat, and he turned around. Before either of them could speak, Candy returned. She dumped her purse on the kitchen table, fished around and found a business card, which she handed to Tom. "There you are. That's the dentist. You should be able to find her there."

Tom glanced in wonder at the contents of her purse. "Do you eat at the Yellow Hen often?"

"Eat? Not really. I go for coffee there about once a week, or I did, with Andrea. She had a thing for their banana cream pie." Candy choked on her words and took a moment to compose herself. "She was only about five or six years older than me, and we had a lot in common. And it was good to get out."

"Do you know a Reverend Lawrence Blackwell?" Tom asked.

"The name sounds a little familiar, but I can't be sure. Why?"

"He was the one who called the police. He was eating breakfast with his secretary and her husband, a …" Tom stopped and pulled out a small notepad, glanced at it, and looked up. "…Melissa and Jim Pearson. Do you know them?"

"Melissa Pearson." Candy frowned. "Why does that ring a bell?"

"You headed up the forensic investigation into her son's death about three years ago – autoerotic asphyxiation," said Tom.

Candy's eyes widened. "Yes, I remember that case. Very heart-wrenching."

"Yes, well, apparently they weren't satisfied with the outcome of the case."

"They weren't," Candy agreed. "They wanted their son's lover charged with first-degree murder, but we didn't have enough evidence to make that stick. The D.A. ended up striking a deal."

"What does that have to do with these murders?" Fran asked.

Tom glanced at Fran a moment as if surprised she was still there, then he turned his attention back to Candy. "They seem to think – or at least the minister seems to think – that you are responsible for the deal, that the boyfriend wouldn't have gotten off if you weren't in the lifestyle. From there, it was just one more step to them believing you are responsible for Andrea's death." He said the words slowly and without inflection, trying to keep the impact as neutral as possible.

"That's insane!" Candy said. "How the hell did I do that?"

"By seducing her with your wicked ways," Fran said sarcastically. She had guessed where Tom was going.

"Something like that." Tom set down his coffee cup. "Blackwell called you Bathsheba and Jezebel. You were friends with her, so you must have shared her dark and evil lifestyle, which resulted in her murder." He stopped to clear his throat.

"I don't need this!" Candy yelled, bursting into tears. "I don't need this, Fran. I told you it was all my fault. I was right. I shouldn't have –"

"Hey!" Tom interrupted. His quiet demeanor was gone. He grabbed Candy by the arms to calm her down. "I'm not the one saying that. NO ONE is saying that."

"Except –" Candy began.

"Except some asshole who doesn't know you. Look, they're very religious. They got ideas. Their ideas, their opinions, don't amount to squat. You are not to blame for someone else deciding to commit murder. That would be like blaming Fran here for Toni deciding to strangle you. It's not rational."

"If I hadn't dragged them into my lifestyle, they'd be alive today," Candy argued.

"And someone else would be dead. Maybe Fran, or Alex, or me. Whoever is out to hurt you would find a way to do it. YOU didn't choose the victims. HE did."

Tom was tense as he let her go. "There's still a lot of ground to cover. I assume you'll be staying here for a while?"

Candy nodded. "I thought it would be safer than being alone."

"If you go anywhere else, let me know."

"Of course." Candy looked confused. "You don't think —"

"I don't know enough to make any assumptions, and I won't speculate. You two ladies have a good day and lay low — especially you." He indicated Candy. "Until I find out what's going on, you could both be in danger."

Tom turned and walked out the door without saying goodbye. Candy was worried, and Fran was fuming. When Fran went to the sink to rinse out her coffee cup, she found Tom's house key sitting on the counter. She picked it up and angrily threw it across the room.

Startled, Candy jumped, unaware of what had triggered Fran. "What the hell?"

Fran marched into her bedroom and slammed the door behind her. She collapsed on her king-sized bed and cried herself to sleep.

Monday had been an exhausting day – from the battle in court, to meeting Hawksworth, to the revelation of the murders, to Rick's car accident, and Candy moving in, and finally to the argument, if one could call it that, with Tom. They had been apart several months already, but the breakup had happened almost as an afterthought. First, Tom stopped living there because Rick had moved in temporarily. Then they stopped dating. There wasn't an official breakup until he left the house key on the kitchen counter without comment.

Fran didn't quite understand her grief over it. Maybe it was because she was already so stressed out. Or maybe it was the finality of the gesture. Or maybe it was because, at some level, she still loved him, even though she knew she could never be the wife he wanted. She wasn't wired that way. And when she thought of Rick, every other man in her life disappeared like the steam from boiling water. She sighed and rolled over in bed.

***

"You called?" Charlie stood in the doorway of Rick's hospital room. He'd swapped his American eagle t-shirt for an army green one with the New Hampshire slogan "Live Free or Die" written on it. He had to abandon his cigar at the hospital entrance, but he still reeked from the smell of tobacco. One of his large hands was curled around the handle of what would otherwise be an inconspicuous, small, silver case – if anyone else had been carrying it.

"You're a sight for a sore eye," Rick joked. He pushed a button to adjust the bed so that he could sit up.

"You look like shit." Charlie walked in and placed the case on the tray table.

"I've been getting a lot of that lately." Rick glanced at the case but didn't look inside.

Charlie motioned toward the bandages on Rick's left eye. "You gonna be able to use that again?"

"Maybe."

"You're a lucky son-of-a bitch. I saw the Jeep. You should have died in that crash. Speaking of crashes, did I mention that Burrows is getting the Medal of Honor?" Charlie glanced around the room and shook his head.

"You kidding me?" Rick chuckled. "Damn, well I guess he earned it. How's he doing anyway?"

"Good, for a man with one leg and only half a brain. I guess we were lucky we got out when we did."

Rick nodded and fell silent. There were some things about the war that he still wasn't comfortable talking about. "Hey, you remember Sam Kaul? The medic?"

"Wasn't he from India or something?" Charlie asked.

"His dad was. He's a Jersey boy. He's working here. He's my doctor."

"That's cool." Charlie pointed to the case. "So, what happened to yours?"

"Disappeared from my Jeep after the accident. I got my phone, my wallet, even my leftovers from lunch that were in the back seat, but the .45 didn't turn up. Somebody got her."

"You reported her stolen yet?"

"Not yet." Rick rubbed his chin with his good hand. "If I don't get a shave soon, I'm gonna start looking like you."

"Beards are good for the soul," Charlie said with a grin. "Did you know there's a red beard club? They even have contests and stuff."

"You don't have anything better to do with your time?" Rick glanced at the case again. "How much?"

"I gotcha a deal. Only 375."

"New?"

"Only the best for my buddy." Charlie glanced at the door to make sure they weren't overheard.

"Thanks. I'll stop by with the cash in a couple of days. I just need to get my ass outta this bed."

"I trust you. I got too many guns for you to stiff me," Charlie laughed.

"And too much history between us," Rick admitted.

"Speaking of history – you and Candy?" Charlie asked.

"Hell, no. I got a cute little redhead at home."

"A redhead. Damn. Good luck with that."

"You gonna keep an eye on Candy and Fran for me while I'm laid up?" Rick asked.

"Fran?"

"My little redhead."

"Oh, THAT Fran. Sure thing. I like keeping an eye on her, er, on them." He winked as he waved and walked out the door.

"Why are you asking about Candy?" Rick yelled after Charlie, but the man was already gone.

Rick reached for the tray table and pulled it closer. The case had a combination lock on it. Rick unlocked the lid and slowly lifted it. His good hand stroked the grip of the Smith & Wesson M&P45. He shut and locked the case before any of the hospital staff saw it. He felt naked without his gun, and not in a good way.

An aide entered, smiled, and closed the shades for the night. "Can I put that somewhere for you?" She reached for the case.

Rick gripped the handle tightly. "It's fine where it is. I got some work to do." The last thing he needed was her taking it out of his reach or realizing how heavy it was.

Startled, she withdrew her hand. "Anything else I can get for you?"

"Yeah, when's that physical therapist supposed to be here?"

"Soon," she said as she slipped out the door, shaking her head.

Rick exhaled.

Chapter 6

Tuesday Morning

Fran fell asleep on top of her bed with her clothes on. The curtains were closed, and the room was dark when she woke. Startled, she sat up and brushed the hair out of her eyes with her hand. There was a soft knock on her bedroom door. Fran jumped a bit and then remembered that Candy was still in the house.

"Are you up?" Candy stuck her head in the room.

"Yes. What time is it?" Fran looked around for her cell phone. "What did I do…? Oh."

"Do what?"

"My phone. I left it in my purse."

"It's nearly seven. I let you sleep. I think you needed it," Candy said.

"In the morning?"

"Yes, in the morning. Tom's here."

"Already? Why?" He was the last person Fran wanted to see at the moment.

"He wants me to go downtown with him and answer some questions. I thought maybe I could use a lawyer."

"Of course!" Fran followed Candy into the living room. Tom was wearing his nylon jacket over his holstered gun, and his car was running outside. The room was dimly lit with a single lamp, the sun peeked through the curtains, and, given how she looked just getting out of bed, Fran considered the darkness a blessing.

Tom glanced at Fran, nodded, and looked at Candy. "Ready?"

"I'm going with her." Fran glanced down at her rumpled clothes and bare feet and realized she hadn't brushed her hair or put on makeup. "I need a minute to freshen up and I'll be right out."

"Why?" Tom asked.

"Because I look like hell," Fran said.

"No. I mean, why are you coming with us?"

"Because I'm her lawyer."

Tom sighed. "Why don't you guys meet me down there then. It'll save me having to drive you back."

"Like that's such an inconvenience?" Fran snapped. "You would have driven Candy back anyway."

Tom frowned. "Look, I've been on this case since four YESTERDAY morning. I barely got four hours of sleep last night and I'm tired – hell, I'm exhausted. I got the sheriff breathing down my neck because I haven't questioned Candy yet, and I got three dead women –"

"Three?" Candy yelped. "Who's the third?"

Tom scowled. He didn't plan on letting that information slip until they were at the station. "Meghan King. She was found about two hours ago. Same MO."

Candy backed up and fell into the sofa. "No. No, no, no, no, no!" She screamed as she slammed her fists into the cushions. "Shit, no! This can't be happening! No!" She buried her head in her hands.

Fran sat down and pulled Candy into her arms. "Damn, Tom, did you have to be so blunt about it?"

"Do you think this is easy on me? I'm the one who has to go to the crime scenes. I'm the one –" He stopped. "I'm sorry, Candy. I didn't want to tell you this way. I need you to come downtown. We're going to go over this inch by inch until we figure it out."

Candy nodded and picked up her head. "Yes, of course."

"We'll be right behind you," Fran said.

"I thought you were going to 'freshen up' first," said Tom

"I just need to throw on some clean clothes. I have makeup and a brush in my purse. I can do it in the car."

"While you're driving?" Tom asked.

Fran glared at him. "Does it matter, Tom? Get out of here. We'll be down there in a few minutes."

Tom turned on his heel and walked out, muttering under his breath.

Fran changed into her new peach suit and a pair of matching pumps. She took time to fix her hair and do her makeup. "If you're going to do it, do it right," she told Candy while clamping a hairpin in her teeth before inserting it into her hair. "Right?"

"Right." Candy had already changed into a navy pantsuit.

When Candy and Fran arrived at the police station, Sheriff Hodge was waiting for them. He ushered them into a small conference room and took a seat across from them. A thick file sat between them and, on top of that, a dark wig.

"Tom told me you lawyered up," he said to Candy.

She glanced at Fran and then back at Hodge. "I want to help in any way I can. What I don't want is to get tricked into making incriminating statements. I love – loved – my girls. I never hurt them, and I sure as hell didn't kill them."

Hodge grunted. "I don't have much use for your lifestyle. I admit that. It was always a problem for me. You're a bright woman. Bright and educated and – hell, Candy, I used to think highly of you. For you to stoop to this – this – lifestyle as you call it, is beyond me. You should know better. But right now, I got bigger things to worry about than your poor choices."

"You're just pissed I didn't choose you," Candy snapped.

Hodge bit his upper lip a moment before continuing. "This ain't about you or me. This is about those dead women, all of them friends of yours. Now, you may think you'd never do anything to hurt them, but my guess is they've each gotten some pain from you, one way or another."

Candy's face flushed in anger. "I have never hit any of those girls, not even in play. If you don't believe me, check their medical records. Check the damn forensic report. You won't find a scratch on them that has anything to do with me."

"Maybe. Maybe not. Each of those women – including Pamela – was wearing a black wig designed to look like your hair. Each of those women was raped with some foreign object. Each of those women was beaten and then strangled, their throats ripped apart with a spiked collar. Now, tell me that has nothing to do with your lifestyle?"

"What about the sweetbriars?" Candy asked.

"Four on this one."

Candy covered her mouth as bile burned its way up her throat.

"That sounds more like a sadistic, homicidal serial killer," Fran interrupted. She gripped Candy's hand and squeezed it. "Now, if you have a legitimate question for my client, say it. But don't sit there and play mind games with her. It's not her fault that they were tortured or raped or killed. She didn't do it."

"Just because she wasn't the one who did it doesn't mean she's not responsible," Hodge barked back.

"We've had enough." Fran let go of Candy's hand and stood up. "You have questions? We'll answer them. If you called Candy in just to give her more grief than she's already going through, you can shut the hell up and let us go."

Hodge leaned back, took a deep breath, and studied each woman. "Don't think for a minute that this case isn't completely about you," Hodge said to Candy. "The killer dressed these women up to look like you – right down to the wig."

"Let me see the pictures." Candy's hands trembled under the table.

Hodge opened the file and laid out the crime photos. He kept his eyes on her. If he was looking for a dramatic reaction, he didn't get it. Candy shelved her emotions to the side and studied the photos as if she was still a forensic investigator.

"Well, for openers, I've never worn an outfit like this." She indicated the photos. "This is someone's idea of what I might look like as a dominatrix, not what I actually look like. Second, I have never used a dog collar or anything closely resembling one. Those are usually reserved for the Goth community. My collars are lightweight and discrete, something you would mistake for a choker or some kind of jewelry. Third, I need to see the corsets up close to know what they are and where they came from. Maybe that will help you find your killer." She pushed the photos back at him.

Fran sat down.

Hodge signaled to the one-way window and put the pictures away. "Someone is stalking you."

"I know that," said Candy. "Allyson Stone is. He has been for months. But I don't believe he's the type to pull off something like this."

"Allyson Stone? The assistant D.A.? What the hell is that all about?"

"He's a royal pain in my ass. Every time I turn around, he's there – or calling me, or texting me, or hounding me. I keep putting him off, and he keeps coming back. But he's so focused on this law-and-order thing that I have a hard time believing he'd risk his career just to make my life miserable."

"I'll be the judge of that," Hodge said. "Anyone else have a beef with you?"

Candy frowned a minute. "Tom said something about a couple whose son died three years ago. I was the forensics investigator on that case. They weren't happy with the result. But that was three years ago. If they didn't do anything then, why would they do something now?"

Hodge checked his notes. "That would be the Pearsons. Their son's killer got out of prison recently."

"They overheard Tom asking about me at Andrea's crime scene." Candy choked a bit on her friend's name but kept going. "Their pastor told Tom about the case. He said a few other choice things that you might actually agree about. I'm sure you can check Tom's notes."

"Maybe this is someone with a grudge against the crime lab," Fran said. "Maybe you should check those cases. Who is out there? Who has been recently released from prison? Who has a history of rape and violence against women? That sort of thing."

"The only person I know of who is out of jail and who even remotely fits that description is Alex de la Rosa," Hodge said.

Fran gasped. "Alex is out? How the hell did that happen? WHEN did that happen?"

Hodge shrugged. "He made some kind of deal with the D.A. The thing is, his relationship with you…" Hodge indicated Candy. "…has been anything but hostile. As far as I can tell, he's got no beef with you, not that I wouldn't love nailing that bastard for something."

A tirade of words flooded Fran's mind. "When did he get out?"

"About a week ago," Hodge said. "Are you telling me he hasn't contacted either of you, yet?"

"Not me," said Candy.

"Me neither," said Fran, "but he was pretty angry with me. I'd be surprised if I heard from him."

"I'm surprised that I haven't," said Candy.

"Well, he made it to the prison to visit his sister," Hodge said. "At least she's still behind bars, and probably will be for life. That bitch –" He stopped and took a deep breath. "If either of you hear from De la Rosa, let me know. In the meantime, I'll check the case files from Candy's time here and see if it correlates to any recent releases that match our MO."

"Is Tom still handling this case?" Candy asked.

"Yes. I sent the poor bastard home to sleep. He looks like a damn zombie."

Someone knocked on the conference room door, and Hodge yelled for them to come in. Edgar Mitchell lugged in an evidence box, put it on the table, and smiled briefly at Candy before walking out. Hodge opened the box and removed a sealed plastic bag containing a black leather corset.

"Do I need to take it out of the bag?" he asked Candy.

"Let me see it. Maybe I can tell –" She took the bag and felt around, moving it carefully and examining it. "It's definitely not one of mine. Inferior quality. The stays are weak, not steel." She pulled it a bit through the bag until the tag showed. "This is what you need. It's a relatively common brand, but I only know one store that sells it in Vegas. It's probably only been worn this one time." She stopped for a moment. "Are the others identical?"

Hodge nodded. "As far as we can tell."

"I can't imagine a store not wondering why some guy would buy five or six of these at once, or even within a tight time frame. Somebody out there saw this guy. Check with the store."

"And what store would that be?" Hodge asked.

A place called LL&W, Leather, Lace and Whip, Whipped for short."

Hodge made a note. "Anything else you can tell me?"

"These are cheap. They're more for costume wear, like Halloween or maybe a stage play. They aren't the real thing. Again, this is someone who THINKS they know what BDSM is, but who doesn't have a clue, which means this person is not in the lifestyle," Candy explained.

"Another reason to rule out Alex," Fran added.

"Unless he, or she, IS in the lifestyle but is pretending not to know any better," said Hodge.

"Convoluted thinking," Candy stated.

"Okay, ladies. If you think of anything else, you know how to find me."

"I do have one thought." Candy leaned forward and frowned. "This Reverend Blackwell guy, is he a regular at the diner? I don't recall seeing him there. Maybe we just go at different times."

"You know what he looks like?" Fran asked Candy.

"No, but I don't recall seeing any clergy there at all."

Hodge slid a photo over to Candy. "That's the guy."

Candy picked it up and studied it for a few minutes. "He does look familiar, but I'm not sure why. It could be I saw him at the diner or –" She thought for a minute. "Maybe it was the Pearson case. I just feel like I've met him before."

Hodge retrieved the photo. "You ladies are free to go."

Fran and Candy walked into the reception area and were accosted by Allyson Stone.

The attorney frowned. His tie was too tight. His shirt was wrinkled. He grabbed Candy by the arm to pull her aside. "What the hell is going on? Are you alright? I heard about the murders."

Candy yanked her arm away and backed up. "What do you think is going on? You get the police reports. Are you investigating? Or are you just sitting on your ass and watching me squirm?"

"That's not fair, Candace," Allyson snapped back. "All I've done is look after you and make sure you're okay. I'm out there every day busting my ass to clean up this city from the likes of –" He stopped mid-sentence.

"From the likes of me?" Candy asked, eyebrows raised. "Is that what this is about? What are you trying to do, Allyson, save my soul? Well, you're too damn late."

"I'm worried about you; that's all. When you didn't return to your apartment last night, I thought he got you, too."

"Is that supposed to make me feel better?" Candy frowned. "How do you know I didn't go home last night? You went to my apartment?" She was already stressed and upset, and now she was mad. "How the hell do you know where I live?"

"I asked. I'm the assistant D.A. It's one of the perks of my job. If I want to know something, I just ask."

"Well, you can stop asking! I'm not staying there for a while. I'm staying –" she stopped a moment and thought about her answer. "I can't tell you where I'm staying, and I don't want you asking."

"She's staying at a safe house Rick arranged for her," Fran cut in.

"I just want to make sure you're okay," said Allyson.

"Then check with Tom Saddler. He will tell you if I'm okay or not."

"Saddler? The cop? The last time you and I were out, he came up and offered you a ride home."

"The only time we went out," Candy clarified. "And I asked him for a ride home."

"And you went with him," Stone stated.

"Yes? So?" Candy looked at him quizzically. "What's it to you who takes me home? He's a friend and he's a cop. I trust him. That's all you need to know."

"You probably do more than just trust him," Stone argued.

"How fast do you want to lose your license to practice law?" Fran stepped between Stone and Candy.

"Lose my license? For what? I didn't do a damn thing wrong! I'm only trying to make sure she's safe. I'm a prosecutor. That's my job."

"You wouldn't know your job if it bit you in the ass," Fran countered as her anger grew. "You're stalking this woman, and that ends today, or I'm going to beat your ass until you're not fit to be wiped off her shoes!"

"Are you threatening me? I wouldn't go there if I were you, Miss Simone."

"It's not a threat. It's a warning. You don't follow her, you don't call her, and you don't show up at her home or work."

"My job –" he started to say.

"This is a matter for her friends and the police. Not you! You come anywhere near her again, you call her, you harass her, anything, and I'll get a restraining order and sue you until you can't walk straight. Got that?" It was all Fran could do not to hit him.

"You are way out of line, Simone. You threaten a prosecutor, and you'll find yourself in jail, and no judge in Clark County will let you walk out."

The commotion drew a small crowd. On the one hand, several officers wanted to break them up. On the other, Fran was a loud-mouthed defense attorney and Stone was the assistant district attorney. The officers, arms crossed, decided to wait it out and see who came out on top.

"Oh, we are SO gone!" Fran announced. She grabbed Candy by the arm and dragged her out the door before the argument could continue. Fran shoved Candy into the car as Stone followed them into the parking lot.

"Go away!" Fran yelled at him as she jumped into the driver's seat, started the engine, and roared out of the lot, turning the opposite way from her home. She kept her eye on the rearview mirror to see if he was following her. When he didn't move, she relaxed. Her heart pounded hard in her chest. She was panting. "What the fuck was that all about? He scared the shit out of me!"

"Wow. That was something," Candy said. "He's a pain in the ass, but I never thought he'd commit murder. You, on the other hand –"

Fran fired a warning look at Candy. "You already know what I can do." Fran took a deep breath to calm down. "Well, if he's got your address, then he's probably got mine. We should talk to Rick."

"He's supposed to be resting," Candy said.

"This will wake him up."

***

The hospital ward was quiet when Candy and Fran approached Rick's room. It was almost nine a.m. Their pumps clicked softly on the highly polished tile floor as they marched side by side down the hall. The charge nurse looked up from her computer.

"Rick Brandt," Fran said softly. Something about the atmosphere made her feel like whispering.

"Oh, of course." The nurse returned to her work as the women approached the room.

"I need to use the lady's room," Candy said. "I'll catch up with you in a minute."

Fran nodded.

The door to Rick's room swung open silently. It was designed to be extra wide to allow for gurneys, beds, and wheelchairs. The blinds were drawn and the room itself was dark except for a small light over Rick's empty bed. The bed next to his was vacant and neatly made. Fran frowned until she heard the sound of a toilet flushing followed by the soft squeak of a faucet turning on and off. She stepped back, and a few minutes later the bathroom door swung open, and Rick emerged.

He was walking with a crutch, slowly, painfully, his bad arm in a sling around his neck. The neck brace was gone. He stepped up to the side of the bed and turned to sit down. He was shirtless and his arms and chest were heavily tattooed. His back showed the scars of an eventful and painful life. He wore loose pajama pants with one leg cut to the knee. The leg was heavily bandaged.

When Rick saw her, he tried to smile through the pain. Fran felt as if she was standing at the edge of the ocean, the waves brushing up against her ankles and trying to drag her into the water, the sand shifting and sliding out from under her feet until she was dizzy and about to fall. Everything was moving. Nothing was stable. Fran realized she was panicking. She leaned on Rick so much; the idea that he would be this helpless scared her.

She gripped the door handle and smiled back.

Rick sat down on the bed and put the crutch to the side. "I wasn't sure you'd make it this morning."

"A lot is going on." Fran walked up to him. She tenderly cupped his face in her hands, bent down, and kissed him. "Where does it hurt?"

"Everywhere," he admitted, pressing his forehead to her belly. "My head, my neck, my back, my hips, my legs. Hell, the only things that don't hurt are my balls."

Fran chuckled, hugged him close, and fought down her fears. She was still standing quietly and holding him when Candy walked in.

"Oh, sorry." Candy started to back out of the room.

"It's okay. Come on in." Fran looked down at Rick. "Get back into bed."

He grinned at her. "You wouldn't get away with ordering me around, woman, if I wasn't so damn beat up."

"I know." Fran kissed his forehead, careful to avoid the bandages on his face.

"Damn, you look good enough to eat," Rick said.

Fran blushed deeply and took his hand. "We have a problem that you might be able to help us with."

Rick grunted in pain as he slid back into the bed and clicked one of the buttons. The head of the bed rose up to meet his back. "What's going on?"

"A couple of things. There's been a third murder. We just came from the police station. Hodge grilled Candy and had the audacity to imply that she was somehow to blame for all this shit."

Candy stood at the foot of the bed looking pale. She was still angry.

"While we were there," Fran continued, "Allyson Stone showed up and started harassing Candy. He's been stalking her. He's mad that she moved out of her apartment and didn't tell him."

"He said he's only trying to protect me," Candy told Rick.

"You think he murdered those girls?" Rick asked her.

"I don't know. He can be intimidating and annoying as hell, but he's on this rampage to clean up the city, and by clean up, I think he means me. He's just so political. I can't imagine he'd throw his career away to kill a bunch of housewives."

"They wouldn't be just housewives to him. They represent something, perhaps something he hates, perhaps something he fears, perhaps something he can't have, like you." Rick turned to Fran. "What do you think?"

"I don't know what his problem is, but I told him I would get a restraining order against him if he tried any more bullshit. I think he took it to heart, although he threatened to throw me in jail."

"She told him a hell of a lot more than that," Candy said. "You would have been proud."

Rick smiled.

"When we pulled away from the police station, he didn't follow," Fran added.

"Of course, he didn't," Rick said. "First, he knew where you were going. He now knows Candy is with you. Second, he's a prosecutor. If he wonders where you are, he just asks, and someone tells him. But I'm more worried about a third possibility."

"Which is?" Fran asked.

"He can put a transmitter on your car or trace your cell phone GPS signal. He can even get a warrant to have someone follow you. He's got those kinds of resources," Rick explained. "If he wants to, he can find you when you're not at home, when you're alone and not safe."

"Damn." Fran gripped the hospital bed rail. "So now what?"

"Candy, you still got your gun?" Rick asked.

She nodded.

"I take it you and Charlie are on good terms?"

"Yes, of course. Why?"

"I'm going to call him. I want him to stay at the house until I can get there. Once Stone, or anyone else for that matter, sees you have a guard dog, they'll back off, at least for now. Got it?" Rick pushed himself up a bit in the bed and winced.

"I'm sure the man has a life," Candy said as she started to object.

"He'll do it for me. He owes me. Besides, I think he's sweet on you."

"That I DON'T need!" Candy sputtered. "One more man sweet on me!"

Rick laughed. He looked at Fran. "I should be there."

"You will be soon." She squeezed his hand. "I miss you."

Rick slipped his hand out of her grasp, reached up, and stroked her cheek. "Soon. Now be good and do what I say."

"Everything on your terms," Fran said, a bit of sarcasm in her voice.

"And don't you forget it. What are your plans for today?"

"I have to teach this evening," Candy offered.

"We haven't even had breakfast yet," Fran said. "I have a deposition at one, a short hearing at three, and then I want to research that Max-Mil Enterprises thing. Idle hands and all that."

"Sounds like a busy day for both of you," Rick said.

As they were speaking, an aide walked in carrying a potted miniature rosebush with a card. She set it on a shelf near the window, avoided looking at them, and walked out.

"Have you been harassing the staff?" Fran asked with a grin.

Rick drew his hand over the back of Fran's neck and pulled her into a kiss. "I'm a miserable bastard without you."

Candy snickered. "I thought you're always a miserable bastard."

Rick ignored her.

"And here I thought you were all hot with the ladies," Fran said.

Rick shrugged.

Fran walked up to the plant, took the sealed envelope, opened it, and read the card within. "Oh my god."

"What is it, babe?" Rick asked. "Let me see it."

Fran handed him the card. It read, "How much do you love her?"

"Candy, give us a minute," Rick directed.

"Sure thing." Candy was getting used to him ordering her out of a room, and that bothered her, but she left anyway.

"Give me that." Rick pointed to the briefcase on the floor near the nightstand. "Then come to the other side of the bed."

Fran positioned herself so she could look across his bed and into the hallway. Rick took the case, laid it on the edge of the bed nearest Fran, and opened it, keeping the lid side closest to the door in case he had to quickly close it again.

Fran looked down at the .45 and tensed. She reached out and drew her hand along the barrel of the gun. As she withdrew her hand, Rick closed the case, locked it, and slipped it under his blankets.

"I'll call Charlie. I want him to stay with you, and I want him to get you a gun."

Fran met Rick's eyes. "Alex?"

"Nah, not his style. I've made more than a few enemies, darling. It's one thing when they threaten me directly, but when they threaten you, I take it personally."

"The whole rose thing. That's like a trademark. There's even been roses found on the dead bodies of Candy's friends – sweetbriars. Do you think it's all connected?"

"A trademark for murder?" Rick asked. "Interesting thought."

Fran felt that drowning sensation again. She looked down to make sure the floor wasn't moving under her feet.

"Fran?" Rick's soft voice pierced her thoughts.

"Mexico is looking pretty good about now," she joked. "Who's going to take care of you while Charlie is taking care of us?"

"That's why I want you to know I have that. I want you to know I'm okay. I can handle it."

"You saw this coming. How? Why?"

"I spent six months on the run with Toni de la Rosa," Rick said. "You learn something when you live with a homicidal maniac. You learn to be prepared for anything."

"You didn't just live with her, Rick. You loved her," Fran said gently.

He didn't respond.

"Alex is out of jail," Fran said.

"He is? Fuck. Is he bothering you?"

"I haven't seen him yet. No one's seen him."

"I'm not afraid of Alex. We got bigger problems." Rick patted the case under the blanket. "This baby is all I need for now."

"Rick, I –"

"You asked me once what I wanted from you," he said. "I told you – everything. "I'm going to take care of this, and I'm going to take care of you. Count on it. What about Lauren? Wasn't she supposed to visit this weekend?"

"Yes. You don't think I should cancel, do you? I hardly see her enough as it is."

"You really want her in the middle of this?"

Fran's shoulders slumped. "You have a point."

"Go home. We'll talk more later. Maybe we can work something out."

Fran kissed him slowly before she left. She was always afraid that any kiss could be the last kiss.

Chapter 7

Tuesday Mid-Morning

Fran stood in her office with the heavy, brown leather sofa she'd inherited from her former boss, Alex De la Rosa. The arched window looked out onto the side alley. The leather-bound books and the antique-looking Persian rug that framed her oversized mahogany desk were all his once. She asked herself, "Why am I still doing this?"

The Max-Mil thing came as a shock to her. More than once she considered calling the feds, but what would she tell them? That she inherited an outlaw corporation worth millions and wanted to turn in the board of directors and CEO based on some old man's word? The feds would seize everything, employees would be out of work, investors would lose their shirts, and Fran would make headlines, again, for all the wrong reasons.

Her whole career was about getting justice. She was challenged by the work. She took her role as an officer of the court seriously, and she was proud of it. It was her way of getting revenge against the father who had molested her. But he was dead now, and thanks to her inheritance, she never had to work again. Yet here she was, standing by the large, upholstered office chair, looking out over her domain, questioning all the stress, heartaches, and mundane atrocities of her job, and facing incarceration.

Fran had a headache. She reached into her desk and pulled out a small bottle of painkillers. She took two without water.

She could hear her secretary, Margo, in the front office, chatting with Candy, and it occurred to Fran that if she closed the law office, Margo would have to find another job. Fran sat down and rifled through the stack of messages on her desk only to find that quite a few were from various charitable organizations trying to hit her up for money. She groaned.

She had enjoyed working for Alex. He had handled the daily management of things. The only thing she did was focus on the law, and that was fine for her. But this?

"Margo!" Fran called out as she walked across the hall to the conference room that doubled as a library. "Lock the door, put the phone on hold, and join me, please!"

Candy was the first to walk through the door. She was carrying a cup of coffee and a notepad and pen. She smiled and slipped into one of the chairs. "I assume you want me, too?"

Fran grinned. "Yes, of course."

Margo had gone orange that day – her hair, that is. She wore a Girl Scout brown dress to match with orange pumps. Fran was always amazed that Margo could accomplish so much and still be so wonderfully childlike in her approach to life.

"Ladies, I have a situation and I need your help." Fran sat at the head of the table. "I've inherited the mansion, which is being sold. I've inherited over seven million dollars. And I've inherited a compilation of stocks and bonds, most of which I don't even begin to understand. So, what do we do with it all?"

"We?" Candy asked.

"Sure, why not? It seems this money is going to affect all of our lives. Should I keep the law practice going? Maybe open a law clinic for low-income clients? Should we create a nonprofit corporation to help, say, victims of domestic violence? Should the money go into real estate investments or the stock market?" She looked from one lady to the next as they stared at her. "What do you think? I can't do this alone, you know."

Margo chuckled. "Thank you. I've been biting my nails that I was going to end up out of work."

"What do you want to do?" Candy leaned forward and gripped her cup of coffee with both hands.

"Something meaningful and kick-ass," Fran said. "Something – honorable. Something that will create a legacy."

"For you?" Candy looked surprised. "I never thought of you as someone who thought about a legacy."

"I inherited this wealth from Max, and as you both know, he was a bastard extraordinaire who screwed half the people in this town. I suspect he stole half of what he ended up with. I want to do something good with it. Something to redeem the family name. Something worthy of honorable men."

"And women," Margo chimed in.

"Yes, and women," Fran added with a laugh. "Any ideas?"

"Wow," Margo said. "I feel like I'm in one of those fantasies where you hit the lottery and now you want to know what to do with it."

"Speaking of which," Candy interjected, "there's Max-Mil Enterprises. Could we PLEASE start by changing that name? It's a horrible name."

"Unless I sell it. I may have to dump it just to keep the feds from sending me to jail. Were you able to look into what's happening there?" Fran asked Margo.

"Be right back!" Margo dashed out of the room and a few minutes later returned with a handful of large files. "These are copies of what's on file with the court. The CEO of Max-Mil, Jax Saynte, is handling the cases. He's an attorney himself but he's working with Barry, French and Michaelson. They represent the company. Three of these cases are in mediation – two personal injury cases and one damage to property case."

"My property?" Fran asked.

Margo shook her head no. "There was some kind of car accident in a parking garage. One of the victims is claiming the garage was improperly designed and therefore you, or the company, are liable for injuries. They're suing for $1.3 million."

"That's one hell of a vehicle unless someone was hurt," Fran said.

"It was a flatbed truck carrying three antique vehicles. The cars aren't worth that much by themselves, but they are also seeking punitive damages," Margo explained.

"What the hell is a flatbed truck doing inside a parking garage? Okay, continue."

"Two more: there's a boundary dispute in negotiation but the complaint hasn't been filed with the court yet. And then there's a hearing set in November for a question of clear title."

"Clear title?" Candy asked.

"Yes. Max-Mil may have sold property they didn't actually own," Margo said.

"Or which had a cloud over the title," Fran noted. "And Friday's meeting?"

"According to the agenda…" Margo pulled out a couple of papers from the top file and spread them on the table, "…the official business is to determine how the lawsuits will be handled but, based on some of the attachments – including an inventory of properties, an internal audit, and memos regarding the lawsuits – there's a move to divest the liabilities and keep the assets."

"Interpret, please," Fran said.

"If I had to guess, and it's only a guess, I'd say they want to saddle you with the lawsuits and walk away with the properties, free and clear, in order to salvage the company and save their investments," Margo explained.

"Why me?"

"You're the patsy with the money," said a man's voice.

Shocked, all three women stared at the doorway.

Alex de la Rosa smiled back. "May I come in?" His large brown eyes focused on Fran.

Fran felt the old tingle go through her body, and she just as quickly looked at Margo.

"I locked it! I swear!" Margo said.

"She did." Alex pulled a key out of his pocket. "Vestiges of another life, when this was my office." He placed the key on the table in front of Fran. "I locked it behind me."

Candy broke into a grin. "You're out of jail!" She jumped up, ran to Alex, and gave him a warm hug. "Why didn't you call me?"

"I missed you, too, mistress," Alex whispered in Candy's ear as he hugged her. "I heard about your girls. I've been worried about you. I wanted to see you but..." He shrugged. "...there just didn't seem to be a good time."

"I'm okay," Candy lied. She smiled and kissed him on the cheek.

"You understand this stuff?" Fran asked as she stared at her old boss.

"Only on the surface," Alex said. "I get the big picture, but we need a corporate attorney type to paddle us through the muddy waters." He glanced at the files on the table. "And these are very muddy."

"You look good, boss," Margo said, then quickly backpedaled. "I mean —"

"It's okay," Fran said with a soft sigh. "She's right, you do look good, Alex. You might as well join us."

Alex always looked good, Fran thought, with his dark Italian looks and impeccable clothes. Prison didn't change that. Fran caught herself remembering better times between them — before everything went south. Before he almost got her killed. She took a minute to shove the old feelings back into their box and then turned the key in the lock.

Margo jumped up and got more coffee for everyone as Alex sat down. He ran his fingers through his thick hair and looked at Fran like a child seeking approval from its mother.

"I didn't mean to crash your party." Alex removed his navy blazer, tossed it aside, and loosened his tie. "I came by to ask you a favor, but that can wait."

"Ask." Fran crossed her arms and leaned back in her chair.

Alex accepted the coffee from Margo. "I worked out a deal with the district attorney. I'm out so long as I can be working."

"How can you work? Didn't the bar association suspend your license?"

"They officially disbarred me, although I can appeal, and I probably will, but you're right. I'm not going to be walking back into court any time soon."

Fran folded her hands and leaned forward. "We were just discussing what we should do with the law firm. Should we disband? Start something new? I want to put Max's money to work doing something good for a change."

"That would be a change," Alex said. "He was up to his neck in criminal activity."

"You knew?" Fran asked.

Alex frowned. "You didn't? You're the one who kept telling me how terrible he was. I was the one who defended him on a murder charge, remember?"

"He was a child molester. I just suspected he was –" Fran took a deep breath and calmed down. "Politics and money – I should have known he was up to no good. Now I get to find out how dirty he really was."

Alex ran his fingers over the conference table. "You're a damn good lawyer, Bella. You're passionate about it, good with clients, smart. You can stand toe-to-toe with the best of them. I'd hate to see you give that up." He smiled. "You remember when we picked out this furniture? We had big dreams. We were ready to take on the whole world."

Fran felt a slight flush at the use of his nickname for her. "I remember."

"I can't see you giving that up."

"Old history. The question is, what do we do now?"

"Hire me. You know I'm good. You know I'll work my ass off for you. I can get to the bottom of this stuff. I know enough about Max to know where to look, who he associated with, what kind of things he was into. I know things you can't find out anywhere else now that he's dead. Give me a second chance, Bella. Please."

Fran caught her breath. She glanced at Margo and Candy. She knew they wanted him back. She was the breaking point. She held the power. Would she accept Alex back into the fold after all the hell he put her through? Was it worth the risk?

"I'll think about it," she said finally. "In the meantime, what do you know about Max-Mil Enterprises?"

Alex glanced at Candy and grinned. "Other than I also hate the name? I know Jax Saynte. I've dealt with him before. He's a heavy hitter. Smart, savvy, and very dangerous, with possible ties to organized crime. But then, you like dangerous men, don't you Fran?"

Only one, Fran thought. She closed her eyes a moment, pictured Rick, and smiled.

"Maybe you should follow in your father's footsteps and run for mayor," Alex suggested with a wink.

Fran groaned. "Please, not mayor!"

Everyone laughed.

"How about district attorney, then?" Candy suggested. "You have enough money to fund your own campaign."

"As tempting as that sounds, and it does sound tempting, the seat isn't open for another year or two. In the meantime, I need to clean up this mess."

The discussion turned back to Max-Mil and Jax Saynte.

Later, when the group broke up, Alex followed Fran into what had once been his office. He stood in the middle of the room and took a deep breath as if he could inhale everything he lost and somehow restore it to life.

Fran moved to the window and looked out, her arms still crossed. She frowned. "You put me in one hell of a spot in there. You know how Candy and Margo feel about you, despite everything that happened." She turned to look at him. Yes, there was a flutter. She had to admit it, but she was damned if she was going to let him get to her again.

"I know, Bella. I'm sorry. I was –" He stepped closer to her.

She cut him off. "I don't want any of your excuses anymore," Fran said sharply. "You used really poor judgment, and you nearly got Tom and Candy and me killed. You helped your crazy sister hide from the police when she was trying to kill me. She shot Tom. She tried to strangle Candy. Candy still has nightmares about it. All you had to do was turn her in. That's all. At least Toni's behind bars now. That's something. By all rights, you should be sitting in a jail cell and rotting away."

"I wasn't the one who helped her escape. Rick was."

Fran stiffened. "Fortunately, he came to his senses before she killed us all. Toni put a gun in his mouth. Did you know that? She put a gun in his mouth and threatened to blow his head off! I hope she burns in hell."

"I know. I was there, but I never intended to hurt you or anyone. I didn't know she'd go that far." Alex rested a hand on her arm. "When I realized –"

Fran raised her eyebrows, and he stopped. He dropped his hand.

Fran took a deep breath. "I need to talk it over with Rick. I won't make this decision without him."

"It's your law firm, Bella. You can do what you want with it," Alex argued.

"Everything I do impacts him. This gets filtered through him, first."

Alex leaned back on his heels and studied her for a couple of minutes. What he saw was someone very different from the frightened and insecure woman he had known in the past. This was a different Fran, and he wasn't sure how to handle her. "Rick it is, then. I'd like the opportunity to persuade him. How do I reach him these days?"

"He's in the hospital at the moment. He was in a car accident yesterday. He should be home tomorrow. Once he's home, you can talk to him there."

She never said it, but she knew she meant her home.

"Thanks, Bella," he said softly.

"You might want to get used to calling me boss."

Alex smiled, nodded, and left her standing in the office where it all began.

Feeling weak, Fran sank into her seat, picked up the phone, and called the hospital. She felt Rick deserved a fair warning.

"Hi, sweetheart," he said when he recognized her number.

"I have a question to ask you," Fran said simply.

"Sounds serious. What is it?"

"Exactly how mad are you at Alex?"

***

Tuesday Night

The air smelled like rain.

Charlie was parked in front of Fran's house when Fran and Candy arrived at 10 p.m. His burly body was resting against the hood of a weathered pickup truck. His thick dark beard and curly hair made him easily recognizable, even in the dim light of a streetlamp. He was wearing his now familiar brown bibbed overalls and a khaki-colored tee-shirt that displayed the name of his store across the front. His feet were encased in heavy, well-scuffed boots, the steel-toed kind that reminded Fran of construction workers. He had a gun holstered to his hip, but Fran didn't know enough about guns to tell what kind, only that it was big.

He was totally out of place in the exclusive, upscale community. Fran loved it.

"I heard you need a hero?" he said with a grin. He was chewing on tobacco and took a second to spit some out before giving Candy a hug. "I thought Rick had that job?"

"I'm hoping he'll be home in a day or two. In the meantime, we're having a couple of problems."

"You must be the cute little redhead he told me about. I'm Charlie Cook."

"Fran. Fran Simone. Nice to meet you, Charlie. Thanks for coming." She felt heat crawl up the back of her neck and flow to her cheeks. She liked being thought of as Rick's 'cute little redhead.'

"We have a stalker, alright," said Candy. "Possibly two."

"And in the meantime –" Fran started to say.

"I know," Charlie interrupted. "He told me about the death threat. Not good."

"So, how long have you known Rick?" Fran asked as they settled into the living room. She instinctively turned to the bar to pour a drink and then realized she had nothing to offer. Another one of Rick's rules. "I'm afraid I'm out of booze. Will coffee do?"

"Coffee's fine," he said. "We were in the Marines together in Panama in '88 with Operation Just Cause and then later in Iraq." He leaned back and got comfortable to relate the long tale. "Rick won't talk about it much. Things happen in combat, things you'd rather forget, and he had his share of it. But there was this one time, in Panama —" Charlie grinned from ear-to-ear and stopped only a moment as Fran handed him his coffee.

She took a seat next to Candy and listened. There were so many things about Rick she didn't know, and so many she wanted to know.

"It was near the end of our tour there, and it was a rough one. Folks don't know that much about it, but Panama was hell back then. Anyway, we were out celebrating. Had a few drinks, picked up a few – er – young ladies. We were getting ready to come home, stateside, that is. Anyway, we went out in the jungle for a little R&R with the ladies and, hell, if we didn't get lost." He chuckled, put down his coffee, and rolled up his pant leg, revealing an ugly scar. "That's when I got this. Rick saved my life. Wasn't the first time either."

"What happened?" Candy asked, now intrigued by the story.

"Well, Noriega was in charge back then, and there was a lot of tension between us – the U.S. forces stationed there and the local bigwigs. Noriega had combined his military with the police. He called them the PDF, the Panamanian Defense Forces. There weren't many of them, but they were tough. Then they had this thing called the Dignity Battalions, groups of out-of-work troublemakers who acted like a kind of local militia to fight what they called American aggression." Charlie stopped a minute as if remembering something.

"Go on," Fran encouraged.

"Well, in '88, Noriega was indicted in Florida for racketeering and drug trafficking. This didn't do much to help things in Panama, which had a big drug trade going on at the time." Charlie stopped for more coffee before continuing. "Anyway, Rick and I had taken our 'dates' for a nice stroll in the jungle when we ran into some members of a local Dignity Battalion. The long and the short of it is words turned into insults and insults turned into a fist fight and a fist fight turned into an incident, and some asshole took a chunk of my leg with a machete." He leaned down and patted the scar as if it was an old friend, and then he rolled his pants down over it. "We were left for dead, and I have no idea what happened to the ladies, although I suspect they were sent to lure us into a trap. Anyway, I would have bled out but for Rick. He was hurt pretty bad, but he still managed to stop the bleeding and bandage me up tight. He dragged my sorry ass out of the jungle and back to headquarters."

"Wow." Fran realized she was staring at him through the whole story.

"Fuck, we were kids then, 20? 21? Still wet behind the ears. What the hell did we know? We were just damn lucky to get out alive, and we nearly got our asses court-martialed for it." Charlie smiled. "Like I said, it wasn't the first time he saved my sorry ass, or the last." He looked at Fran and then Candy. "So, tell me about your stalker."

"Stalkers." Candy took a deep breath. "I have this group of ladies that I meet with once a week. Five of them. And, well, you know about my lifestyle," she said with a small smile.

He nodded.

"A few days ago, the ladies started turning up dead." Candy's head lowered, she grasped her hands together and looked as if she was going to be sick.

Fran held Candy's hand and picked up the explanation. "Three of the five of them have been murdered. They've been found dressed up in BDSM regalia, raped, beaten, and strangled."

"And each one had a cluster of flowers with the body – six flowers on the first body, five on the second, four on the third," Candy said.

"Are you one of the five?" Charlie asked, eying Fran.

She blushed. "Hell, no. I mean –" She looked at Candy. She didn't want to insult her friend. "It's just not my cup of tea, so to speak."

Charlie nodded, looked at Candy, and frowned. "This shithead is after you then. It's personal."

"That's what Tom thinks," Fran said.

"Tom?" Charlie asked.

"Tom Saddler, the detective on this case," Fran explained. "He's also a friend of ours. But that's not the whole story. There's the possibility that this creep is an assistant district attorney."

"Or there are two stalkers," Candy cut in.

Charlie raised an eyebrow, waiting.

"Assistant D.A. Allyson Stone," Candy added, "I don't know if he's dangerous or just a pain in the ass. He's got this thing about cleaning up Vegas. Political, I think. I suspect he'll run for D.A. next."

"Oh, so THAT'S why you want me to run," Fran noted.

"Run?" Charlie asked.

"For D.A.," Fran explained. "Politics."

"Did either of you confront him?" Charlie asked as he scratched his beard.

"Yes," said Fran. "And he went ballistic. He insists he's just trying to make sure Candy is safe, but the jerk gives me the creeps."

"Maybe he has kept her safe, whether he intended to or not," Charlie said thoughtfully.

"What do you mean?" Candy asked.

"Well, if some other fucker is trying to kill you, maybe he can't get to you 'cause lover boy is always hanging around." Charlie shrugged. "Just a thought."

Candy felt a chill go down her back.

"Shit," Fran muttered. She stood up and paced the room. "So, keeping Allyson away only puts us in more danger."

"Maybe," Charlie agreed, "assuming he ain't the killer. Now, if he is, that's another story."

"Damn, I wish Rick was home. Nothing personal, Charlie. I just – I just miss him." Fran stopped pacing and pressed her hand to her head to drive away a headache. "Now what do we do?"

"Now, you let me handle it," Charlie said.

"But you have a business to run," Candy interjected. "You can't be babysitting us all day."

"And I've got a law practice to get back to," Fran stated.

"Hon, you're a millionaire. You don't have to keep the practice going," Candy said. "Why are you always talking like you're going to go broke?"

"I've had my days of sleeping on the streets. It was a long time ago, but I remember."

"You don't forget that shit," Charlie agreed with a nod.

"I recently got an inheritance from my dear old dad, Max Simone," Fran told Charlie.

"The former mayor?" Charlie asked.

"Yes," Fran acknowledged.

"Shit, lady. You're already living dangerously. That bastard was into everything. Does that mean you own Max-Mil Enterprises, too?"

"Am I the only person in Las Vegas who does NOT know anything about that company? Yes, I own controlling shares of Max-Mil, but I have no idea what that means. I just found out about it, and there's a board meeting Friday." Fran's heart skipped as she spoke. "What can you tell me about it?"

"Well, for one, you're in the middle of at least three lawsuits involving injuries or damage on the properties, a boundary dispute involving an apartment building, and an argument over a piece of property you sold – that is, that your company sold."

"How do you know all that?" Fran asked.

"Promise you won't hate me?"

Fran crossed her arms and stared down at him. "Spill."

"I'm suing you over property I bought from the company."

Fran almost choked.

"What does that mean?" Candy asked.

"I got some land northwest of the city. Nice spread with an old farmhouse. I call it my camp. When I bought the piece, someone else thought they owned it. Now they're trying to get it back or get me to pay them for damages. My title insurance company dragged Max-Mil into the court battle. It's been one fucking nightmare, complete with midnight phone calls and death threats."

"Geez," Candy said.

Fran sat down again and let out a sigh. "It just figures."

Charlie checked the clock on the mantel. "It's late, girls. I think anything else can wait for morning. You ladies get on to bed, and I'll take the night watch. We'll figure the rest tomorrow."

"Good idea." Candy stood up, stretched, and yawned. "Thanks, sweetie." She gave Charlie a kiss on the cheek and headed down the hall to bed, dragging Fran behind her.

"But I want to know more," Fran objected as she was pulled along.

"And you will, after we get some sleep," Candy said. "Now get to bed before I tattle on you."

"You wouldn't dare!"

"Try me!" Candy responded with a grin.

About an hour later, Fran woke up screaming. She thought she was done with the nightmares. Thinking about Max, talking with Alex, it brought back so many bad memories. The nightmares disappeared when she started dating Rick and he forced her to quit drinking. Still, if he wasn't in her bed, she slept with the lights on and her phone close to her. But now, with him in the hospital, the gruesome images came flooding back. Blood, death, agony surrounded her. She pulled the trigger on an imaginary gun. Someone screamed again and again. Blood ran under her blankets and saturated her sheets. She aimed and fired at a demon only she could see.

Fran's bedroom door flew open, and Candy rushed in with Charlie right behind her. Candy had thrown a short, silk robe over her otherwise naked body, but Charlie was still dressed and still armed. He looked about as Candy ran up to Fran and put her arms around her, holding and rocking her.

"It's alright. It's okay. It's just a dream." Candy spoke softly into Fran's ear. "You're fine, hon. You're safe."

Charlie, confused, stood in the doorway and watched. "Is she okay?"

Candy looked at him and nodded.

"Fuck," Fran muttered as she pulled out of Candy's arms and wiped away her tears. "I could use a scotch."

Charlie chuckled.

"No scotch," Candy scolded. "No scotch, no bourbon, no wine, nothing. You know what Rick said. I was there, remember? You want to lose him?"

"Grrrrrr!" Fran growled, pounding her heels into the bed like a child throwing a tantrum. "If I wasn't so fucking head over heels for that man, I'd bash his fucking teeth in!"

Charlie stopped laughing, quietly backed away, and disappeared down the hallway.

"Can you white-knuckle it or do you need some help?" Candy asked.

Fran forced herself to calm down. "It's not physical. I haven't had a drink now for over three months. It's psychological. I know that. I know I can do this. I just get so damn –" She growled again.

"I have a little weed," Candy offered.

Fran nodded. "Okay, but just a little. I have to get some sleep."

Candy went back to her room and reappeared a few minutes later with a joint and a lighter. She lit the joint and passed it to Fran. "This should calm you down for a bit."

The two women sat and smoked and talked quietly for about a half hour until Fran couldn't keep her eyes open anymore, then Candy curled up under the blankets with Fran and held her until they fell asleep.

Outside, a patrol car drove slowly through the neighborhood without stopping.

Chapter 8

Wednesday Morning

Tom rang the doorbell to Fran's house as he eyed the rusted brown truck parked at the curb. He was startled when Charlie answered. The big man in the doorway looked down at Tom and scowled.

"Yeah? Whaddya want?" Charlie asked with a deep and threatening tone to his voice.

Tom's eyes went to the holstered gun on Charlie's hip. "Detective Tom Saddler, here to see Miss Candy Knight," he announced. He showed his badge. He felt odd enough knocking on Fran's door instead of just going in. Seeing Charlie blocking his way only made things worse.

"Ah, you're Tom," Charlie said in recognition. His stance relaxed as he smiled and backed up. "The girls were up late. Let me wake 'em."

"And you are?" Tom asked.

"Charlie Cook." Charlie offered a firm, quick handshake. "Rick asked me to keep an eye on the ladies while he's laid up."

Tom felt his chest tighten a little. Rick, of course. Rick would know a guy like Charlie Cook. Tom glanced at the man's t-shirt. "L&L Cook's is your place?"

"Yeah, sporting goods. You know, camo, guns, knives, bows, whips." Charlie grinned and winked, and Tom had this strange sensation that he'd fallen down Alice's rabbit hole.

"I heard about the whips," Tom admitted with a slight blush.

"Tom!" Candy yelled as she poked her head out of her bedroom. "I'll be right there! Just let me throw some clothes on!"

"You don't have to get dressed for me, girl," Charlie joked. He turned to Tom and saw the detective wasn't laughing. "Well, she DID have a robe on, last I checked."

Charlie was about to usher Tom into the living room, but Tom stepped into the kitchen instead, opened the cupboard, and pulled out the coffee. He rinsed the pot and turned on the coffeemaker.

Charlie leaned against the door frame and watched. "You know your way around this house."

"I used to live here. Or didn't Rick tell you?"

Charlie shook his head no.

"Fran and I –" Tom started to say. He poured the water into the coffee maker and slipped the pot into place. "Well, Fran and I." He stabbed the on button.

"Oh," Charlie said.

"I keep trying to cure what ails him, but he won't let me, yet." Candy stepped next to Tom and gave him a kiss on the cheek and a slap on the ass. Her hair was still damp from a shower, and she was wearing fresh makeup. She had slipped into one of her retro dresses. It had a soft tan color with pink piping and a little bow at the collar.

"Don't do that! Or I'll charge you with assaulting a police officer!" Tom closed his eyes a second and inhaled the scent of her shampoo.

"Sooner or later, my dear, I'm going to win you over to the dark side," Candy said.

"Damn. You'd better be careful there, man," Charlie warned. "That woman is dangerous."

"All the women in my life are dangerous." Tom slipped an arm around Candy's waist and gave her a warm hug. "Is Fran getting up or are we on our own today for a change?"

"She had a rough night." Candy gave him a quick kiss on the lips.

"More nightmares?" He turned out of her embrace and pulled the cups from the cupboard. "Coffee anyone?" He glanced at Candy and Charlie.

They both nodded. Candy got some milk from the fridge and set it next to the sugar bowl on the table. Then she pulled out some spoons and put them down as well.

Tom waited for the pot to finish filling. He poured as he spoke. "I thought she was over those."

Candy sighed. "She's been through a lot."

"We all have," Tom countered as he handed her a cup. He poured one for Charlie and then for himself.

The three sat down at the small kitchen table, and Candy rested a hand on Tom's arm. "So, what's the reason for your visit?"

Tom covered her hand with his warm one. "No one's dead if that's what you mean. I talked to Juanita this morning. She's staying in New York a few more weeks to give us a chance to figure this thing out. She should be safe there."

"And Lois?" Candy asked.

"She and her husband decided this was a good time to see family in Arizona." Tom ran his thumb over her hand. "It's just us babe, you, me, and a homicidal maniac."

"Sounds like old times," Candy said with a nervous smile. "How long will you be around today?"

"I'm all yours. I put in so much overtime this week that the union is getting antsy. Hodge ordered me to take the day off." He turned to Charlie. "If you have things to do?"

Charlie nodded. "Yeah, I gotta get back to the store. I'll check in with you later." He gulped the last of his coffee and pushed himself up from the chair.

Candy glanced at the small chair and felt sorry for it.

The two men shook hands, and Charlie gave Candy a wink as he headed out the door.

"A friend of Rick's, huh?"

"And mine, actually," Candy said.

Tom looked at her quizzically. "You never cease to surprise me."

"I'd like to surprise you more if you'd just give me the chance." Candy looked warmly into his eyes.

"I'm not sure –" he started to say.

"I know, you're on the rebound." Candy's voice dropped to nearly a whisper. "And I know you don't share my sexual proclivities. But underneath all this leather and lace is just an old-fashioned girl looking for an old-fashioned guy. Is that such a terrible thing?"

Tom felt himself growing warm again.

"I promise I won't bite," she said.

"What, no punchline?" he asked.

Candy put her fingers to his chin, turned his head to face her,

and kissed him. "Give me half a chance. I'm not used to asking."

"I know." Tom pulled his eyes away from hers. "Damn, I know."

***

Rupert Hawksworth leaned against the windowsill and looked out at the view from the conference room at Max-Mil Enterprises. The sky above Las Vegas was overcast, and the rising sun was hidden behind a dense layer of clouds. Foreboding, Hawksworth thought. An omen of things to come.

He was tired. He'd served on the board of Max-Mil for nearly thirty years, and in all that time he was loyal to the board and its appointed representatives, until Monday when he stepped out of character and warned Fran Simone of the upcoming board meeting and the attempt to steal her company from her.

He felt compelled to do something since the board, led by Max Simone, had decided to hire Jax Saynte to serve as CEO. The man's unbridled thirst for power and nefarious connections frightened Hawksworth, and Hawksworth hadn't felt frightened in a very long time. He had to stop Saynte, but his only weapon was an alcoholic attorney who didn't even know she owned the company. He shook his head in thought. Fran had no idea what she was walking into. He wondered if his warning would be enough.

But Hawksworth knew something else about Fran Simone, something Saynte would find out in time. Rupert Hawksworth knew that Fran had partnered with Rick Brandt, and Brandt had a reputation that made men nervous. Saynte would never find a way to manipulate Fran so long as Brandt stood in the way.

Hawksworth refocused his eyes until he could see himself in that window. An old man looked back at him – shiny bald head rimmed in fluffy white hair and topped with a long dark spot that looked a little like the country of Chile, the familiar bow tie that he now needed help to put on, and the slight body now bent and weak. Friday would be his last day on that board. He already wrote his resignation but didn't tell anyone. He had to maintain as much leverage as possible until the very last moment.

Jax Saynte walked into the room, and Hawksworth turned, a placid smile carefully in place.

"Ready?" Jax asked.

"For Friday? Yes, I guess I am. I'm still not sure it's a good idea, but I've read the legal opinions, and they support your position."

"Max Simone made a number of bad moves, which cost this company millions and tied us up in the courts," Jax said. It was a good argument, solid and unimpeachable. It just had nothing to do with the truth. Jax walked up to the window, stood next to Hawksworth, and looked out on the panorama. "Cutting his heir out of the company will allow us to settle a few of the lawsuits."

And get rid of potential threats to your network, Hawksworth thought. "But it will result in Francesca Simone being stuck with her father's liabilities." He eyed the younger man in the window.

"She can afford it. Besides, we're all better off this way."

Jax was nearly six foot six, with broad shoulders and an imposing stance. His black hair was trimmed close to the scalp and his blue eyes sparkled. He wore an expensive gray suit. Everything about his clothing was conservative and expensive. He dressed to impress but acted like he didn't have to.

Hawksworth looked away. "She should be warned."

"She's a Simone. If she doesn't know by now –"

"Maybe you should talk to her," Hawksworth suggested.

"Meet the lioness in her den? That would be interesting."

"Carrots are cheaper than sticks, and we don't need to draw more attention right now."

Jax crossed his arms and looked at Hawksworth as if examining an insect. "Maybe."

"What could it hurt?" Hawksworth asked.

Jax grunted softly to himself and walked away, leaving Hawksworth hanging limp and useless. Hawksworth licked his dry lips. He was being forced out to pasture by circumstances beyond his control, but he could still leave the battlefield with one more victory under his belt. He would take down Jax Saynte one way or another.

***

Wednesday Mid-Morning

Fran overslept. She rolled over in her bed, pulled a pillow into her arms, and moaned. She could smell coffee coming from the kitchen and, every so often, she could hear a bit of laughter. Frowning, Fran forced herself to sit up and listen. Yes, she was right: it was Candy and Tom. Fran checked her cell phone for the time and wondered if Charlie was still there. Then she pulled the covers back over her head and crawled into her cocoon.

It was Wednesday. She didn't have court today, that part she remembered. She stretched and wondered about the rest of her day. Turning over, she picked up the phone and called the office. Margo answered with her usual cheery voice.

"How do you manage to do that?" Fran asked.

"Do what?"

"Sound so damned happy and awake at such an ungodly hour."

"It's almost 10. You ARE coming in today, right?" Margo asked.

Fran moaned. "Why? Do I have to?"

"I just got a call from Jax Saynte."

Fran sat up in bed. "What does he want?"

"To meet you. I told him one would be good. Was I wrong?" Margo waited patiently on the other side of the phone.

"No, one is fine. I'll be there. Just do me a favor, all those files on Max-Mil we had out last night, make sure they're in my office by the desk. I don't want them lying around the conference room when he gets there."

"Why?" Margo asked.

"Just trust me on this. I got a gut feeling he thinks I'm still in the dark. I want him to keep thinking that until I can size him up. I'll meet him in the conference room."

"Alex is going through the papers now, piece by piece."

"That's fine," said Fran, somewhat relieved. "Just make sure they get moved before Saynte gets there."

"Okay, boss. See you soon."

Fran hung up and sunk back into the bed. She stared at the ceiling for a few minutes and started to think about Rick. He was up by now. He probably ate. Maybe he even saw his doctor. Fran felt a shiver go up her back as she rolled onto her side and closed her eyes. She could feel Rick's strong hands on her body, touching and stroking her. She moaned again as her body started to react. "Damn," she muttered.

Fran forced herself to sit up again and swung her legs to the floor. She picked up the phone and called Rick's hospital room. When he answered, she said, "I need you."

She could almost hear his smile over the phone.

"Rough morning?" Rick asked.

"Not rough enough, you bastard." Fran untangled her long hair with her fingers. "You ruined me. What am I going to do now?"

"I can think of a few things."

Fran laughed lightly. "Are you coming home today?"

"I'm waiting to find out. The doctor is making the rounds, but it may be a while. They said I should know by noon."

"I have a meeting at one with the CEO of Max-Mil," Fran told him. "I need to get to the office and prep for that. When you're ready, call me. Either I'll come for you or I'll send someone. I want you home. My home. My bed. The sooner, the better."

"You know I'm on pain meds, right? I got an arm in a sling? I'm not sure I'll be much use to you."

"I'll figure something out. Just let me know."

"I'll call," Rick said. "Be careful, boss. Don't commit to anything. Don't sign anything." He was quiet for a moment. "I shouldn't have to tell you this, right? You're smart. You know what to do."

"Thanks for caring and for believing in me," Fran said softly. "I'll see you soon."

She hung the phone back up and decided a cold shower was in order.

***

Rick hung up his phone and looked at Charlie. "That bad, was it? Maybe Tom had the right idea. Maybe she shouldn't have a gun, after all."

Charlie nodded. "What's causing the nightmares?"

Rick glanced at the empty bed next to him and indicated that Charlie should shut the door. Once they had some privacy, Rick explained.

"Fran's father was Max Simone, the former mayor, and a real piece of work," Rick said. "About a year ago, a guy named George Elliott kidnapped Fran's daughter and was using the child to extort money from Max. One thing led to another, and, in the end, Fran shot and killed Elliott. Then about four months ago, Fran's ex-husband took his stepson hostage at the hospital. He ended up shooting Fran, and I ended up blowing him away. It wasn't pretty."

"Shit. She can shoot?"

"Apparently, although I've never seen her do it. I should have taken her out to the range years ago."

"I take it the cops didn't charge her with what's-his-name's death?"

"They didn't have to. Max took the blame for the Elliott shooting, and then Max turned around and died of cancer.

Of course, everyone knew he didn't shoot Elliott. For openers, it was my gun," Rick explained. "But Fran had several people in law enforcement on her side, including Candy and Tom. They covered for her."

Charlie moved over to the window and looked outside. "What's the story with Tom?"

"Story?"

"He came by the house to talk to Candy today," Charlie said. "He mentioned something about him and Fran. I thought, maybe –"

"Yeah," Rick interrupted. "He was in love with her, even asked her to marry him. She said no. I think he still has feelings for her, though."

Charlie shook his head. "You sure know how to pick 'em." When Rick didn't respond, Charlie turned to look at him. "You really fell hard for this girl, didn't you?"

"I've known Fran about ten years, probably longer. I worked for her, and I had her back. She always trusted me, and I never let her down, until I got mixed up with Toni de la Rosa, and you saw what that cost me." He hesitated a few minutes, shook his head, and added, "I really should have known better."

"And what about this character?" Charlie asked, indicating the potted rose bush.

"I don't think he'll make a move while I'm in here." Rick's hand rested on the lump under his blankets where his gun was hidden, still in its case. "It's obviously personal. In the meantime, I'm more worried about what will happen when I get out of here, or what will happen to Fran if I don't."

"Are you living with Fran?" Charlie asked.

"No. I'm not sure I will be. There are – complications."

"Complications?"

"Her daughter," Rick explained. "She has some issues with me and, quite frankly, she's right to have them. I need to build some bridges there."

"What kind of issues?"

"I killed her father. That was the hospital shooting."

Charlie's jaw dropped open a minute. "Oh, THOSE kind of issues. Well, you can't go home like this, man. You're in no shape to save your ass if these fuckers show up."

"You have any other bright ideas? I've got to get outta here; the sooner the better. No ifs, ands, or buts."

"Yeah. Come out to the camp. We can set you up out there and no one will find you."

"The camp? You still got that place?" Rick asked, surprised. "I thought the feds took it."

"Just a little tax disagreement," Charlie said with a laugh. "We worked it out."

Rick nodded. "I think the camp will work. It's outta the way and easy to defend. I'm not sure how Fran will feel about it. She wants me home, in bed, with her."

Charlie chuckled. "Yeah, I just bet."

"What? You don't see me as a great lover?"

"You? You're damn lucky a broad would look sideways at you – once!" Charlie countered. "You're one lucky son-of-a-bitch. If I looked as shitty as you do, I'd never crawl out into the light of day."

"Well, she must like something about me, if it ain't my damn looks," Rick said with a grunt.

"Don't give me that shit, man. I've seen you naked. Remember Panama?" Charlie was grinning.

"Oh, fuck! You didn't tell Fran that story, did you? What the hell, man!"

Charlie shrugged. "She seemed to like it. In fact, I think she'd like to hear every story I got about you."

"Even some you've made up."

A nurse stepped into the room to check Rick's vitals, and the men quietly watched, Charlie with a smirk on his face and Rick looking annoyed.

"The doctor will be here in about twenty minutes," the nurse said. "Do you want lunch before you go home?"

"Not unless I can get a real steak."

When she left, Rick looked at Charlie. "So, there's your answer. I'm a free man again. How much time do you have?"

"Just enough to get you back to your sweetheart," Charlie said.

"Good. I won't have to call her for a ride then. She's got her hands full today." Rick stretched his back, closed his good eye, and thought about Fran and her warm hands.

***

Assistant District Attorney Allyson Stone marched past the sheriff's secretary and into Joe Hodge's office without stopping. He pulled back a chair and plopped down, then tossed a handful of papers onto the desk, just missing a tuna fish sandwich. "What's this all about?" Stone asked.

"Morning, Al," Hodge said, his voice heavy with sarcasm. He moved the sandwich out of the way. "Come right in. You don't need to knock. It's not like I'm busy or anything." Hodge closed the file he was working on and tossed it onto a large pile.

"What are you doing about the Knight matter?" Stone stretched his legs out.

Hodge leaned his thin body back in the large office chair and tapped his fingers on his desk. "The Knight matter? Which one? The one where three of her friends are dead or the one where you're stalking her?"

Stone scowled and leaned forward. "You know damn well I'm not stalking that bitch. I'm talking about the murders. Is she or isn't she a suspect?"

Sheriff Hodge frowned. "I thought you were all gung-ho on protecting her. I was there when you and Knight and Fran Simone got into that screaming match in the foyer. They were accusing you of stalking Knight, and you were all about saving her ass. Or did I hear that all wrong?"

Stone glared at the sheriff. "That's my point. Does she have someone trying to kill her or not? Or is she a serial killer?" Aggravated, he took a deep breath. "Three of her so-called girls are dead, she's the common denominator, she has no alibi that anyone has reported, and you got her damn lover investigating the case. Is there something I'm missing?"

"Her lover? Who the hell is her lover?"

"Tom Saddler. Detective Tom Saddler, or didn't you know?"

"Shit, he's not her lover." Hodge relaxed a bit. "Alex de la Rosa was, but that was, I don't know, four? Five years ago?"

"I don't know where you get your information from, Sheriff," Stone argued, his eyes flashing, "but those two, Saddler and Knight, have been a couple for a while now."

Hodge leaned forward and groaned. "I'll look into it, but this is the first I heard."

"Look, you're the one who got Knight to quit the lab. I know you had a good reason. Her lifestyle –" Stone started to say.

"You don't have to go there," Hodge conceded. "I considered her lifestyle a threat to the integrity of the lab. I made her an offer, and she took it. Done and done. But I don't see what that has to do with these murders. Candace Knight might be the common denominator but calling her a suspect is pushing it. She has no motive and no reputation for violence."

"She's a BDSM dominatrix, for god's sake. Isn't that a reputation for violence?"

"You sound like Lawrence Blackwell," Hodge muttered. He took another folder and opened it in front of him.

"The minister?" Stone leaned forward, grabbed the folder, and shut it in Hodge's face. "I want answers. I want to know who you're going to assign to her case and when I'll get an affidavit that I can act on." He took the papers he brought in and put them on top of the folder.

"How do you know Blackwell?" Hodge asked.

"I know a lot of people in my line of work."

Hodge picked up the papers in front of him and glanced at them. "What's this?"

"The final report on the death of Roger Elliott," said Stone. "Remember him?"

"Yeah, I remember him. He was a child rapist and serial killer. He's dead. Died before I even got this job. What's your point?"

"Blackwell and the Pearsons accused Candy – er, Knight, that is – of screwing up a case because of her biases, right? So, I decided to look into a few other high-profile cases of hers including the murder of Roger Elliott."

"I wouldn't exactly call it a murder," Hodge said. "Elliott kidnapped Max Simone's granddaughter and Max shot him dead. Open and closed."

"Did you read Dr. Knight's report on the shooting?"

"Of course not," said Hodge. "It was before my time. Mayor Randall was sheriff then. Max Simone confessed to the killing, and then he died of cancer a few weeks later."

"Two points of interest. No, three," Stone said. "First, there were three people in that room: Max Simone, Roger Elliott, and Fran Simone. Second, the gun used to kill Elliott belonged to Rick Brandt, Fran Simone's boyfriend. Third, there's no report of gunshot residue found on Max Simone. Given that Tom Saddler and Candy Knight were involved in this case, and given their friendship with Fran Simone, you don't find that the least bit suspicious?"

"They didn't test Max Simone for GSR? Or they tested him and didn't find any?" Hodge asked.

"They didn't test him. At least, there's no report that they did."

Hodge smirked. "You're implying there was a conspiracy in the lab to cover up a crime. Why would they have to cover up a crime that Max Simone admitted to doing?"

"Because maybe, just maybe, he took the heat for his daughter, they helped him, and Fran Simone got away with murder."

Hodge groaned. "Okay, let's just pretend for a moment that all of that is true, what the hell does it have to do with the Knight killings? Those women were friends of Candy's, ordinary people, housewives. Candy isn't at the lab anymore, and I can't imagine Tom not trying to find their killer. So, again, what's your point?"

"My point is that if Knight and Saddler lied to protect Fran Simone, they'll lie to protect each other," Stone said. "I, for one, want to see justice done. Candace Knight dragged this lab through the mud at least once. She let two killers walk free: Fran Simone and the boyfriend of Bryce Pearson. She's dirty. I know it and you know it. So, I'm asking, is she or is she not a suspect in these killings?"

"She's a suspect." Hodge leaned back, looking defeated. "I'm not going to touch the Max Simone case. He confessed and the D.A. bought it. That case is closed. I have Angela Simmons investigating the Pearson matter. If she turns up something, I'll let you know. I'll question Tom Saddler about his relationship with Candace Knight. If that's a problem, I'll assign someone else to the case. Happy?"

"Happier than when I came in." Stone stood up and picked up his papers. "Have a good day, sheriff." He marched out the door.

Hodge waited for him to leave before opening the drawer to his desk and digging around for his antacids. He took a couple of tablets, glanced at the bottle, took a couple more, and then chased them down with black coffee. Then he picked up the phone and called Tom Saddler. "We got a problem. Get your ass in here and bring the murder files. Stone is making waves."

Chapter 9

Wednesday Afternoon

Fran arrived at the office out of breath. She thought long and hard about her meeting with Jax Saynte. She researched him online, checked the company profile, and even called Rupert Hawksworth for a thumbnail sketch of the man. What she got was brash, arrogant, smooth, intelligent, and dangerous, very dangerous. She knew the type.

The parking lot was only half full. It was almost 12:30 and people were at lunch. She looked around for a vehicle that presented itself as belonging to Saynte, something subtle and yet showy. Nothing quite fit. Except her Mercedes and Alex's Corvette, the cars were standard, middle-income, made for mileage types in mundane colors.

Fran crossed the lot and entered the air-conditioned building. Her high heels clicked on the tile floor and the satin lining of her new peach suit rustled as it brushed against her silk hose. She had considered wearing a navy suit, something that would meet the approval of the "dress for success" types who considered navy to be a power color, but peach had always been the color that made her feel most confident. Besides, a man like Saynte would know if she dressed to impress him rather than having the power to dress for herself.

She slipped off her heels and ran up the stairs. She had overslept that morning and didn't have time for her daily run. This was going to have to do. At the top of the stairs, she put her heels back on. Fran stepped into the office, set her valise on Margo's desk, and locked the main door. Margo's bangs were a shade of yellow over her black hair, and she wore a fifties-style suit of yellow with a white shell underneath.

"He's not here yet, right?" Fran asked.

"Not yet. Are we locking him out?"

"No. Is Alex here?"

"He's in the file room digging through closed cases. Something about finding some old research notes."

"Did you show him how to use the new filing system?"

"Yes, ma'am."

"That's fine. Grab him and meet me in the conference room. We have to go over logistics before Saynte arrives." Fran knew she was rattled. In the old days, she would have reached for the scotch to calm herself, but since Rick had her on a no-booze diet, she was going to try something different. Staging the meeting would help, she thought.

A few minutes later, Margo appeared in the conference room. Alex, carrying several file folders and a notepad, was right behind her. He had ditched his suit jacket and rolled up the sleeves of his shirt to just below his elbows. His tie was loosened. Even dressed down, and this was as down as Alex usually got while at work, he looked good. For a moment, Fran's mind flashed back to the days when she worked for him instead of the other way around. She felt a constriction in her chest. Closing her eyes, she let it go.

"Okay, this is the drill," Fran said as if marshaling forces for a military assault. "I'm going to be sitting at the end of the table, here."

The conference table was rectangular, its length running parallel to the far wall with its large, heavily framed window. The room was flanked on either side by bookcases, but the bookcase on the left was cut to leave enough wall space for a large painting. Fran had chosen a powerful, impressionistic piece by a local artist. It was bold, with streaks of gold, silver, and red. Depending on how you looked at it, you could perceive fields of poppies or a bloody battlefield. Fran didn't like the painting at first, but it grew on her.

She was configuring the meeting so that she would sit directly under the painting. It rose behind her much like the back of a throne.

"If Saynte sits here," Fran indicated the opposite end of the table, "then, Alex, I want you to sit here..." She pointed to the center of the table nearest the window. "...as if you are mediating between us. You're my shield. I want him to psychologically believe he has to go through you to get to me." Fran moved around to her end of the table and placed her hand on the chair to her right. "If Saynte sits here, if he tries to cozy up to me, then I want you to sit directly opposite from me," she directed Alex. "That will give the table a sense of being off-balance. He will be forced to turn away from me to talk to you and we will, in effect, bookend him."

Alex nodded.

"Margo, once we're seated, I want you to bring in a tray with coffee, cups, and the sugar bowl. Place it in the center of the table and pour coffee for Alex and me, but not for Saynte. I will suggest that he help himself. I don't want him to get the impression that he's a guest or that we are waiting on him. Technically, he works for me. Got it?"

"Got it."

"After the coffee is laid out, I want you to bring your digital recorder and place it next to you. You'll have a pad and pen for keeping notes and you will use them. If Saynte sits next to me, sit on the opposite side of the table, in the middle, where Alex would have sat. That will help with keeping things off balance. If he sits on the end, then sit facing Alex. Any questions?"

"I don't think so. I guess I'd better start the coffee."

"I take it you're doing all the talking," Alex said to Fran.

"You're more business savvy than I am," Fran admitted. "I'll do my best, but if you see a hole, feel free to plug it."

"Your objective?"

"To rattle him. To send him back thinking he underestimated me." She moved toward the door. "When he gets here, engage him in the front office for a few minutes. Introduce yourself. I want to be seated at this table before he walks into the room."

Fran disappeared into her office and collapsed behind her desk. She needed something for her nerves. No booze, no pot, nothing that would give her away. She fished around in her desk and found the bottle of painkillers from when she was attacked by a dog while out jogging. They were a few months old, but one or two might just do the trick. She quickly took them without water and dug through the Max-Mil files Margo left by the desk. Fran was buried in them when Margo buzzed her. Without answering the phone, Fran picked up her files and notes, tucked a pen behind her ear, and headed to the conference room. She had just sat down when Alex arrived with Jax Saynte in tow.

Despite her research, Fran was unprepared for the effect Saynte had on her. She had seen photos of him – good-looking, charming, well-dressed – but none of them captured his powerful and sexual essence. Fran always thought of Alex as a handsome man with his dark, Italian looks and deep brown eyes, but Jax was another cut. Everything about him exuded confidence, charm, and power. Fran's skin tingled. She suspected he had that effect on a lot of women. She also had the sensation that she'd seen him before, but she couldn't remember where or when.

"Welcome," she said calmly, grateful she'd found the pills. "Won't you have a seat?" She remained in her chair.

As predicted, he chose to sit opposite her at the table. He set his briefcase down in front of the chair and then came back to her to shake her hand. He had thought it all out himself, she realized. He had predicted her game plan. Well, no matter. The battle was now engaged.

"Jax Saynte."

"Yes, Mr. Saynte. Please make yourself comfortable. I understand we have a lot to talk about today." Fran accepted the outstretched hand. It was firm, warm, and dry, with the kind of handshake you would expect from someone who could reassure you that all was well.

Alex took that moment to circle the table and sit in front of the window. Margo brought in the tray of coffee and put it down. She poured some for Alex and gave it to him black. Alex smiled. Then Margo added sugar to Fran's and passed it to her. Alex raised an eyebrow but said nothing.

When Margo didn't serve Saynte, he looked up from his chair and asked, "Do you mind?"

"Oh, of course not. Help yourself," Fran said.

She motioned to Margo who slid the tray closer to Saynte so he could reach it. Margo then pulled out the digital recorder. She set it on the table next to her, took a seat, and jotted down a few things on her notepad.

"You're recording this meeting?" Saynte asked.

"Of course," Fran said. "The way I see it, I own controlling shares of Max-Mil Enterprises and you're the CEO. That means you work for me." She took a sip of coffee but kept her eyes on Saynte. "It was my understanding that you were going to fill me in on what is happening with the company and with the lawsuits. I don't want to miss anything."

Saynte shrugged. "Well, if it makes you feel better, by all means."

"Where would you like to begin?" Fran leaned back casually in her chair and sipped her coffee.

She felt slightly light-headed, and she wasn't sure if it was the pills or the adrenalin getting to her. She couldn't dismiss the idea that she was reacting to Saynte. Fran knew how dangerous sexual chemistry could be when she was trying to focus on business.

She glanced down into her coffee a moment, closed her eyes, and pictured Rick in his hospital bed. She smiled. It was only chemistry, she told herself. It didn't mean a damn thing. It would pass. If only the feeling of déjà vu would also pass.

Saynte took his coffee black. He smiled and copied Fran's body language. "As you know, we have a meeting on Friday to discuss options for resolving a number of lawsuits."

"Yes, about that," Fran interrupted. "I will be asking for the meeting to be rescheduled to a later date, say, sixty days from now."

Saynte paused for a moment to consider what she said. "Based on?"

Fran could see his shoulders tense slightly. "Based on lack of notice. This meeting was scheduled months ago, and I just learned of it yesterday. I'm only beginning to delve into the matters before the board, and I need time to review the lawsuit materials with my attorneys."

"The secretary made reasonable efforts to contact you." Saynte leaned forward and frowned slightly as if he was about to reprimand a child.

Alex followed suit and leaned forward as well, breaking up the space between Fran and Saynte. "I would hardly call using an old address to be reasonable. Fran is a well-known attorney with an established law practice. A few phone calls or a five-minute Internet search would have easily found her, and yet no one bothered to do that." Alex tilted his head a bit as he looked at Saynte. "Why?"

Saynte gripped his cup tighter. He glanced at Alex, barely acknowledging him, and then refocused his attention on Fran. "We need to address these lawsuits as soon as possible. I'm afraid sixty days is too far along."

"Sixty days," Fran said deliberately. "Unless my attorneys advise differently." She set her cup down, picked up a file, and leaned forward. "Now, about these lawsuits. Please summarize."

Saynte was quiet for a moment. He heard the word "please" but he recognized the tone as that of an order. He put the coffee down, clasped his hands together, locked his eyes with hers, and spoke directly to her.

"We have six different suits, all rising from misconduct on the part of your late father," he began.

Both barrels, Fran thought. She smiled. "Allegedly. Go on."

"Two are personal injury cases, one of which is a slip and fall, and the other has to do with a loose roof tile that struck someone in the head. Neither person was seriously injured at the time. Both cases are in mediation and are expected to settle for reasonable amounts."

"When did mediation start? How far along are we in the process? When is the next court date?" Fran fired off questions and relied on Margo to keep up.

"We met twice for mediation on the slip and fall, twice for the head injury case, and once for a property damage case. Future mediations have yet to be scheduled. The next court date is November 13th for a discovery motion on the title issue."

"Make sure I'm free for court on that day," Fran told Margo. "I understand the property damage case involves a flatbed truck, some antique cars, and our parking garage," she added without looking at her notes.

"Yes. They want $1.3 million," Jax began.

Again, Fran interrupted him. "What in hell was a flatbed truck doing inside a parking garage? One million in punitive damages, right?"

"Right." His eyes widened slightly.

177

"Then there's the title issue regarding L&L Cook's Sporting Goods. What is the basis of the claim?"

Alex and Margo both looked at Jax and, for a moment, he seemed lost, then he refocused. "Yes, the Sylvester estate matter. The former owner, that is, the man who sold the property to us, may have owned only a life estate in the property, not title in fee simple."

"How did that happen?" Alex asked. "Wasn't a title search done for insurance purposes?"

Jax nodded. "Our lawyers discovered that the old man had written a deed transferring the property to the children of his late son and reserving a life estate to himself, but he never perfected the transfer. He filed it in the land records without having it witnessed or notarized. Our attorneys determined that, without a perfected transfer, the heirs had no claim on the estate, so when Sylvester turned around and sold the property to us, we took it in fee simple."

"That seems relatively open and shut," Fran said. "There's no apparent dispute regarding the facts, so it comes down to a legal issue. Have we filed for a summary judgment?"

"Yes, on that issue," Jax said. "We don't have a decision back from the court yet."

"Why would we lose the case?"

"Because there's a second issue. The heirs are also claiming that Max took advantage of Sylvester's ailing health to unduly influence him into transferring the property to us."

"Ah." Fran leaned back and tapped her finger on the side of her cup. "That's a whole other matter."

"And, finally, there's the matter of the boundary dispute on the apartment building," Jax said.

"Fill me in," Fran directed.

"We bought the property about 15 years ago and finally put up the building. At the time of purchase, the land was part of a larger development that included 140 lots." Jax hesitated a moment to see if he'd be interrupted again, but when he wasn't, he continued. "It turns out that there was an error in the original survey for the development. The third lot in, closest to the southwest boundary of the development, was off by six feet. We're not sure why, although we expect it was a typo or a misprint; someone may have read the number seven as the number one. That error affected every lot after it on that side of the road, 60 lots."

"We didn't create the development, right?" Alex asked.

"No, we didn't," Jax said with an edge in his voice. He didn't look at Alex. He seemed irritated that Alex had somehow joined the conversation.

"And title insurance doesn't cover that error?" Alex asked.

"The issue goes beyond that," Jax said. "Because the boundary is six feet off, the apartment building does not meet the zoning setback requirements. In short, the neighbors want us to tear down the building or move it, something very expensive."

"But –" Alex started.

This time, Jax looked directly at him. "There are no buts. The zoning board has stated, and they are probably right, that we should have surveyed that individual lot again before the structure was built rather than relying on the existing plot map on file with the city."

"And we didn't," Fran said.

"We didn't," Jax affirmed. He turned his attention back to Fran.

"Who did the construction?" Fran asked.

"Another one of your father's companies. Golden Sunrise Construction, Inc."

Fran closed the file in front of her and frowned in thought. "Assuming for a minute that the mediated cases settle, and we lose in court on the others, where does that leave us financially?"

"Bankrupt," Jax said.

"But we can't declare bankruptcy in the middle of a lawsuit to avoid paying the plaintiffs. That's illegal," Fran noted.

"Correct," Jax agreed.

Fran handed Margo her cup, and Margo refilled it for her.

"Would the Sylvester family take the property back to settle?"

"No. We tried that, but, of course, Cook is fighting it. He has invested a lot of money in that property and doesn't want to lose it. Besides, the grandsons really don't want the property, which is why I think Sylvester finally sold it to us in the first place."

"And the sales price, what Sylvester got for it, was probably part of his estate. So, his grandsons have already inherited the value of that property," Fran added.

Jax raised an eyebrow. "I hadn't thought of that," he admitted with a small grin. "Of course, that doesn't take care of the punitive issue of the case for supposedly exerting undue influence."

"No, but it's a start." Fran took a sip of her coffee and scowled. "What if we sold the properties and just paid everyone off. Start from scratch. What would we have left?"

Jax stiffened, and Fran realized she hit a nerve. "We can't do that. That would mean divesting the company. This is a privately held corporation. The board members would lose their shirts."

"Yes, but they would also lose their liabilities," Fran said.

Jax adamantly shook his head. "They'll fight you on this. I'll fight you on this."

Fran studied him for a moment. He intrigued her. He also puzzled her. She knew he was hiding something, but she didn't know what. "Mr. Saynte, you're a smart and educated man. Surely, you're not worried about being out of work? There's enough money for a healthy severance package."

"You looked at the numbers?"

"Of course, I have. I own 51 percent of the company. I damn well better know the numbers."

His jaw tightened. "I'm trying to save the company."

"Are you sure you're not trying to save the board, and yourself, from jail?"

He stared at her and didn't respond.

"Is that why you suggested that the other shareholders buy me out at thirty cents on the dollar?" Fran pulled a copy of a memo from her file and handed it to Margo who passed it on to Jax.

Jax didn't look at it. "I was advised by counsel –"

"Whose counsel? Yours? And they told you that it was cheaper to screw me over than to settle the lawsuits." Fran leaned forward. "If you're going to give me hush money, Mr. Saynte, you can offer me a helluva lot more than this."

"If we buy the shares from you, you will have more money in your pocket than you will if we settle outright. The shares still have some value. Once the lawsuits come to a head, the value tanks. Right now, we could buy from you at 30 cents, sell at 50 to 75 cents, write off the loss and use the revenue to bail out the company. We would have no cash flow and show no income for this year, but we would retain the properties."

"That would break every law in the book," Fran said.

"It would keep the company solvent, appease the investors, and keep your pretty little ass out of jail."

"And my pretty little ass will be out how much?"

"If you do it our way, you would be out about $2.15 million. If you sell the property outright and settle, you will probably break even, but the assets will be gone, and the company will be dissolved."

"But the sale would be above board. And that, Mr. Saynte, is why I need at least sixty days to look this over." Fran closed her file. "I want to thank you for taking the time to enlighten me, today. I'm sure you can show your pretty little ass out the door. I look forward to seeing you on Friday."

Margo stood up.

Jax, finding himself summarily dismissed, rose to his feet. "As do I, Miss Simone." He grasped his briefcase and walked out the door without shaking her hand.

Once he was gone, Fran slid back into her chair, tipped her head back, and closed her eyes. "Damn. What a rush."

"I thought that went well," said Alex, watching her.

"Did you see that?" Margo asked when she returned. "What the hell was that all about?"

"That's what I want to know." Fran opened her eyes and sat up.

"What did I miss?" Alex asked.

"Our Mr. Saynte is up to some very unsaintly shenanigans. It shouldn't matter to him if we sell off the assets or not. He gets his paycheck and a severance package, and he moves on, but he is clearly willing to break the law to hang onto those buildings, and I want to know why."

"Sounds like a job for our favorite investigator," Margo said.

Fran smiled. "Yes, it does, if he's up to it."

"Why don't you ask him? He's in your office."

Heat flooded Fran's body and she jumped up, grinning. "Why didn't you tell me?"

"And ruin the show?"

"I don't want to be disturbed!" Fran ordered.

"For how long?"

"At least an hour." Fran kicked off her shoes and ran into her office.

Chapter 10

"That bitch is going to be a problem." Jax Saynte paced the floor of the three-story parking garage. He had parked his blue BMW next to a navy Lincoln.

A man and a woman stood by the second car. The woman driver's hands were in the pockets of a long, navy coat. Under the coat, she wore a uniform-styled pantsuit that matched the color of the car. Her skin was silky and dark. Her black hair was pulled back into a knot at the nape of her neck, and her eyes were hidden behind sunglasses. Her posture was rigid and tense, the look of someone expecting trouble and ready to deal with it.

The passenger was older, Caucasian, and tanned. His graying blond hair peeked out from under a straw Panama hat. He wore loose-fitting slacks, loafers, and a long, white Hawaiian-style shirt. He also wore sunglasses over his gray eyes. Unlike his driver, he was relaxed.

"You're over-reacting, Jax," the man said in a calming tone with a New Zealand accent.

"I went there to charm her, to win her over, Mr. Ant," Jax stated.

"To seduce her, you mean. That's what you usually do with women like her, isn't it? Charm them, seduce them, then use them until there's nothing left?"

Jax continued to pace. "She had me on the defensive in three moves. She grilled me about the cases. She wants to know why the buildings are so important that I'm willing to break the law and throw away her money to keep them."

"Smart woman. Good questions. Maybe she's more than you can handle. What does she want to do, then?"

"She wants sixty days to go over the lawsuits with her lawyers."

Ant nodded. "That's not bad. That gives us sixty days to prepare a strategy for what might come."

"A strategy?" Jax stopped pacing. "We had a sweet deal going on here for the last year thanks to Max Simone, and except for that nosy Rupert Hawksworth, no one on the board even bothered to look at our numbers. And even Hawksworth can't make heads or tails out of them."

"You're smart with the books," the New Zealander said. "I'm sure you have all the figures safely tucked away and legitimately explainable."

"Yes. We had that audit recently and the accountant found nothing suspicious, but then, he didn't know where to look."

Ant patted Jax on the shoulder. "I trust you to do the right thing, here. Keep that woman in line. If she gets out of line…." He shrugged. "We'll deal with that problem when and if it happens. No need to draw attention to ourselves if we don't have to."

"There are good uses for a woman like Fran Simone," Jax said with a smirk.

"Don't get ahead of yourself, Jax. You've been a good employee. I'd hate to see something happen to you over some piece of ass."

"And what about the other one? Knight?"

"As long as De la Rosa does what he's told, you don't have to worry about her, do you?"

"If it were only that easy. She's never alone, and half the time the assistant D.A. is on her tail," Jax grumbled.

"If we need to, we'll deal with that problem when the time comes, too. As long as she's in our sights, De la Rosa is on a short leash."

"He thinks we killed those women."

"Let him think that. It works in our favor." The New Zealander got into his car.

***

Fran slipped into her office with the idea of surprising Rick, but she found him stretched out on the sofa and apparently asleep, his good leg on the floor and his injured one on the cushions. His eye was closed, and he looked more peaceful than she'd seen him in a while.

Fran walked quietly up to him. She slowly lowered herself to the floor and then rested her head on the cushion by his arm. She just wanted to close her eyes for a few seconds, to feel safe and warm and close to him. It was all she needed.

His arm moved and his hand stroked her hair.

She smiled and looked at him. "Rest," she said.

Rick nodded and closed his eye again.

The next thing Fran knew, she awoke with a start and realized the painkillers must have been stronger than she thought. She was on the sofa, covered with a blanket. She yelled Rick's name and sat up.

"I'm here, boss," he said softly. He was seated behind Fran's desk and pouring over her Max-Mil files.

"How long have I been sleeping?" Fran brushed her long hair out of her eyes with her fingers.

"Two hours." Rick looked across the desk at her. "I figured you must've needed it."

"How'd you get me on the sofa with your broken arm?" Fran stretched her legs.

"You can thank Alex for that."

Fran stood up and walked over to the desk. She slipped behind Rick, rested her hands on his shoulders, bent over, and kissed his neck.

He reached up and took her hand. "Keep that up and I won't get any work done."

"You've been at this the whole time?" Fran looked over his shoulder at the files. She tried to concentrate, but her mind kept going back to the warmth of Rick's body. "How's the eye?" She circled him to study the bandages that ran along the side of his face.

"Too soon to tell." Rick turned to face her. "Should we move to the conference room? There's probably more room on the table. We can spread out there."

"The files or us?" Fran bent over and kissed him fully on the lips, and his hand quickly went to the back of her head, pulling her in harder.

Alex picked that moment to walk in the door. He started to say something, thought better of it, backed out, and shut the door behind him. Rick and Fran were still kissing, but they both started to laugh. Rick finally let her go.

"I never told him. Did you?" she asked.

"About us? No, babe, I didn't," Rick said with a smirk.

Fran blushed. She liked that Rick referred to them as "us." She drew her fingers along his jawline. "I'll get Alex to move the boxes. We don't have to rush. We have all day tomorrow."

"Not if I'm going to get to the bottom of this." He tapped the files. "An audit was done recently, and it didn't show any irregularities, but you know how auditors are, they only look inside the box. There's a lot of out-of-the-box shit going on here."

"Like what?" Fran sat on the edge of the desk.

"Well, let's start with the personal injury case. Saynte said the guy was hit in the head and his injuries weren't that severe at the time, yet the guy is suing for the maximum amount plus punitive damages."

"We're in mediation with that one, right?"

"Sort of," Rick said. "There's been two mediation sessions, but the mediator never got involved. According to one memo, the parties spent a lot of their time outside, haggling. The same thing happened the second time."

"Who wrote the memo?" Fran asked.

"The mediator. The only person with no skin in the game, at least as far as I can tell." Rick flipped through a few more papers. "The question I have is this: Why would a minor injury case lead to –" He stopped a moment, thinking.

"What?" Fran asked.

"I think our plaintiff has something on the company."

"By something, you mean leverage."

"Yes. There's more to this case than a bump on the head, otherwise, it would have settled months ago." Rick pulled out a second file. "Now this case is even more interesting."

"The slip and fall one?" Fran asked.

"Yes. In this case, the original plaintiff is dead, and his son took up the suit, claiming we're responsible for his father's death."

"What the hell? I didn't see in there where he's dead." She started to pick up the file, and Rick gently slapped her hand. "I got this organized so I can find things. Don't mess it up."

She went to cuff him in the head but thought better of it, considering his recent injuries. Instead, she pouted.

Rick didn't have to look at her to call her on it. "That's enough of that."

"Where does it say in the file –" Fran started to ask.

"It doesn't. I called the court to get some information, and the clerk told me about it. I do have my uses, you know."

Fran chuckled. "That's putting it mildly. So, how was the guy injured?"

"He apparently slipped and fell out a fourth-story window. He died from pneumonia after being in a coma for three months."

"He died? Jax Saynte said the injuries weren't serious."

"He lied. It's unclear from the original complaint what caused the fall. There was some discussion of a possible suicide, but the police weren't satisfied with that answer. However, they couldn't find evidence of foul play, either. The case is marked unsolved."

"And you got all of that from the clerk's office?"

"No. After she told me about the plaintiff dying, I called the sheriff's office and got the rest of the story." Rick looked up at her. "This is what I mean by running out of time. I gotta put in some leg work on this."

Fran looked down at his leg. "Can you walk on that?"

"With a cane, slowly, and not a lot," Rick admitted. "But I can get by for now."

"Take Alex with you," Fran suggested. "Just in case."

Rick scowled. "Of all the people I want to take with me, he'd be my last choice."

Fran looked down at her hands a minute before speaking again. "You never did tell me how you felt about Alex working here. You said you'd think about it."

Rick tossed a file onto the desk and leaned back in his chair, his fingers knitted together. "I don't trust him, Fran. He put you through hell and almost got you killed. I don't need that." He looked back up at her. "But he's also smart and he knows the ropes. I know you need the help, more help than I can give you."

She nodded.

"He can stay for now. But I swear, Fran, one false move and he'll be lucky to walk again."

With anyone else, the threat would have been for show, but Fran knew that Rick meant it.

"Thanks." She kissed him on the forehead, gently this time. She moved her lips to his ear. "I want to make love with you," she whispered.

"I'm not going to be very good in bed like this." Rick indicated his sling.

"You could just lie back and let me do all the work." Fran slipped her hand under the desk and brushed against him.

"Damn, woman! Stop distracting me!" Rick's voice was stern, but he smiled.

"If you insist." Fran stood up and headed for the door. Turning, she added, "Just think about it. We have all night."

When she was gone, Rick exhaled.

Fran found Alex and Margo sitting in Margo's office and chatting. "This is how we get work done?" Fran asked with a smirk.

"Like you should talk," Margo quipped. "Alex was just asking me–"

"Hey, I didn't –" Alex tried to interrupt.

"What were you asking her?"

"I just didn't realize that you two…" He made a motion that encompassed Fran and Rick, who was still in her office. "…were, you know, together."

"Yes, well, things happened." Fran frowned slightly as her eyes met Alex's. "Rick said you can stay for now, so you'd better be good to me. You don't want to piss him off." Her tone was light, but Alex tensed. He heard the message beneath the message.

Margo seemed oblivious to it. "Alex is always good. Aren't you?" she teased.

"Did you need something?" Alex asked Fran.

"Yes, I need you to move the Max-Mil files into the conference room so Rick and I can finish going over them," Fran said. "Then I need you to head over to vital records. Rick will fill you in. I want the death records and any related information for one of the plaintiffs in a case. I'd also like you to stop at probate court and find out if there's a will."

Alex nodded. "Will do." He slipped on his jacket. "I'd better get to vital records and probate first before they close."

"It's going to be a late night. Get us some takeout. Something good," Fran added.

"Sure thing."

"Raw meat for Rick?" Margo asked with a laugh.

"By the way, Cheryl Burns called. Isn't that your ex's widow?" Alex took the message from Margo's spindle and handed it to Fran. "Is Lauren staying with her now?"

"Hey! That's my job!" Margo yelled.

"If it's bad news, you don't want this job," Fran said flatly. She went to the conference room and dialed the number from heart. "You called?"

"Yes, about visitation –" Cheryl began.

"You're canceling." Fran was unable to keep the bitterness from her voice.

"I'm afraid it can't be helped," said Cheryl. "Lauren's friend Amy is having a sleepover for her fourteenth birthday. The girls are very close and, well, Lauren insisted on going."

Fran sighed. She wanted Lauren to come home more than anything, but given the problems with Rick and Candy, perhaps it was best if Lauren stayed where she was for the weekend. "Alright," Fran said reluctantly. "But I want her home next weekend, the whole weekend, Friday night through Sunday, no excuses."

"That'll be fine." Cheryl sounded relieved at not having to argue with Fran.

Fran hung up the phone and looked out the conference room window. She had a tightness in her chest that she couldn't get rid of. Work, she thought. Work would cure it.

She went back to the front office. "Has anyone heard from Candy or Tom?"

Margo shook her head no.

Fran sighed. "I wonder what the hell those two are up to."

***

Wednesday Late Afternoon

"Candy! Stop! I can't do this!" Tom was trying very hard to sound playful if only to be polite, but he also meant it. He gently shoved her back from him.

"It's just a kiss, Tom. For heaven's sake, loosen up!"

The two of them stood outside Candy's apartment building. It was late afternoon, and the street was busy with traffic. A few pedestrians wove around them and gave them a snarly look until they moved closer to the building.

"At least come inside with me," Candy said. "I won't be long, and I promise not to try and seduce you."

"Just stop, Candy. I'm in enough shit as it is."

"What are you talking about?" she asked, backing up, a pout on her face.

"The sheriff called me into his office. Stone's making trouble for me – for us," Tom explained. "He told Joe that we are sleeping together. I was happy to be able to look the sheriff straight in the eye and say no, but if Stone is stalking you like we think he is, he'll have photos of us kissing. And if that happens, I'm off the case. Got it? You will have to deal with someone else, someone a lot less sympathetic."

"Stone is a freaking pain in the ass." They stopped while she picked up her mail. "First he's telling me he's going to protect me, and next he's trying to screw up the investigation."

"According to Joe, Stone thinks you may be guilty of killing your friends."

Candy's eyes teared up. "I refuse to let that bastard get to me. I'm innocent. You know that. There's no way in hell –"

"I know."

"Is this just about Stone?" Candy asked after she cooled down. "I know you're still in love with Fran." She flipped through her stack of mail and then looked up at him. "It will pass, you know. You will get over her."

Tom frowned and looked like he wanted to hit something or someone.

"You're still mad at her," Candy stated.

"If Rick didn't show up when he did –"

"Nothing would have changed. The breakup would have just been later in coming." Candy turned to face him. "This isn't Rick's fault. He didn't steal your girl."

Tom raised an eyebrow in disbelief.

"How many times did you ask Fran to marry you?" Candy asked.

"You know the answer to that," Tom snapped. "Three."

"And how many times did she say no?"

"Three." Tom shifted uneasily and looked away from her.

"And that was before Rick came back from Mexico." Candy shook her head. "The end was coming, dear. You just didn't want to see it."

Tom sighed. "I had this whole life planned. You know, house, kids, or at least her daughter. A life."

"Does Fran strike you as the picket fence type? Really?"

Tom chuckled. "Yeah, you got a point."

Candy gave him a peck on the cheek. "I like you. You know that. I hate seeing you in this funk. I just want us to relax and have some fun together without Fran, or Allyson Stone, or anything else hovering over your head all the time."

Tom forced a smile. "It's not that I don't appreciate –"

Candy interrupted him again. "Appreciate, hell! I don't want your appreciation. I want you to fall madly, wildly, deeply in love with me, sweep me off my feet, and drive me crazy!" Candy laughed and headed up the stairs to her apartment.

Tom watched her go. He did appreciate her – the cute smile, the way she challenged him, even the way she dressed in her retro skirts and simple pumps. If it wasn't for Fran, who knows what would have happened in the moment Candy kissed him. Tom followed her up the stairs and watched as she put the key in the lock and turned it.

Candy screamed.

Tom yanked her back from the apartment door and drew his gun. He nudged the door open and stood clear of it.

Getting shot once this year was once too many, he reasoned. He froze a second as the memory caught him.

Tom yelled, "Who's there?" No one answered. He glanced at Candy. "Who did you see?"

"I didn't see anyone, just –" She waved her hands frantically. "Everything. Paint. Graffiti. Trash. Broken stuff. Everything."

Tom put a hand on her arm to quiet her. He stepped into the room.

The once calm and orderly space was torn apart. A print of purple, blooming crocuses was ripped from the wall and sliced into ribbons. The cushions on the print sofa and upholstered chair were slashed, their stuffing falling out like guts. Red paint was splattered everywhere, including on the wall, where a huge cross, dripping blood, dominated the room. A small cabinet of dishes was overturned, and the glass was shattered across the floor. The coffee table was spray painted with the word "REPENT," and the windows were painted over as well, giving the entire room a hellish red glow.

"Stay here." Tom left Candy in the hallway. He made his way through the tiny apartment before rejoining her. "The rest of the place is untouched. It looks like whoever did this is gone."

Candy leaned against the wall, dizzy, angry, and in shock. "If I'd stayed at home –" She started to say.

"You would probably be dead," Tom finished. He holstered his gun and hugged her. "You wanted to get a few things, right? Do that now. I'm going to call the lab and get someone up here to process this place."

"Are you kidding? No one's dead. There isn't a body. They don't have time for this." Candy shook her head.

"Three women are dead," Tom reminded her. "All friends of yours, and I'm willing to put money on this being the same person. Whatever clues we find here could solve the other murders."

"Of course." She tiptoed through the room, over some broken glass, and into her bedroom.

Tom got on the phone. When he was finished, he joined her and watched as she pawed through her closet. "Looking for something special?"

Candy's shoulders slumped and she turned around. "I was. I wanted something to wear out. Something, well, sexy but not overpowering. Something feminine." She glanced down at her dress. "Something contemporary."

"Do you have something like that?"

Candy turned around. She chose four dresses from the closet and put them on the bed for him to see. "Tell me what you like," she said, her voice shaky.

Tom put up his hands. "Oh, no! I don't pick out clothes for women. I wouldn't begin to tell you what to wear."

"Just tell me what you like. It's not a big deal."

"I like everything you wear. Besides, if it's not a big deal, then you do it."

Candy put her hands to her eyes and trembled.

"Hey, hey." Tom held her. "We'll just take them all, okay?"

Candy buried her face in his chest and sobbed. "Damn, him. What the hell? Why do this to me? Who would do this to me?"

Tom shook his head. "I'll take you back to Fran's place. It's going to be alright." He wiped a tear from her face and kissed her cheek. "The forensics guys should be here soon. I'll let them know how to find us."

"I don't like this, Tom. I don't like being the victim. I don't want to be. I won't let this guy do this to me."

"You'll just have to take a whip to him," Tom said, trying to make her feel better.

"Either that or a thirty-eight," Candy said sharply.

Tom escorted her out of the ravaged apartment, holding her close to him and carrying the dresses over his arm.

***

Allyson Stone marched across the street, an arrow bent on the target of Alex's Corvette. Alex saw him coming. He started the engine, but Stone grabbed the door handle, pulled it open and flashed his badge.

"Who the hell are you and why are you following Dr. Knight?" Allyson demanded to know.

Alex stepped angrily out of the car. He towered over Allyson. "Maybe I'm not following Candy. Maybe I'm following you. The real question is who the hell do you think you are and why are YOU following Candy?"

"I want to see some identification now," Stone said.

"Go to hell. You think I haven't seen you following her? Taking photos? Videos? Stalking her? I'll tell you exactly who I am – I'm her friend. Remember? Or doesn't your brain reach back that far?"

Stone scrambled to remember, and then it hit him. "Alex de la Rosa. What the hell are you doing out here? I thought you were in prison!"

"Someone's trying to kill Candy, and I'm going to find out who it is and stop him."

"That's my job," Stone argued. "You stay out of this."

Alex took a threatening step forward and Stone backed up. "You are way in over your head," Alex said. He then got in his car and drove off.

Stone was left standing in the street and gawking at the Corvette as it disappeared.

Chapter 11

Wednesday Early Evening

The sky clouded over and began to drizzle as Candy and Tom drove toward Fran's home in Henderson. They never made it. Ten minutes out, Tom got a call from Sheriff Hodge.

"I have to stop at the office," he told Candy after he hung up. "We seem to have a problem with the Pearsons."

"Who are the Pearsons?" Candy was too upset to focus. She gripped her dresses to her chest as if they were a baby she was cuddling.

"The couple that's pissed at you over your investigation of their son's death," Tom reminded her. He glanced at her and saw she was fighting back tears. "How about I leave you at Fran's office while I take care of this business?"

"Is she still there?" Candy checked her cell phone for the time.

Tom picked up his phone and dialed Fran's office number. He got Margo. "You guys working late?"

"It's going to be one of those nights," she said.

"I want to drop Candy off for a bit. I need to go to work. I won't be long."

"Sure, no problem. I'll meet you downstairs and unlock the front door."

"It's locked?" Tom asked, surprised.

"Yes. Rick received a threaten note when he was in the hospital, so we're being cautious," Margo explained.

Tom frowned. He wondered if the office was a safe place for Candy after all. "You sure it's okay there?"

"Alex just got back, and Rick is here, and the building is locked up tight. We're fine."

"Alex?" Tom asked in surprise.

"Yup."

"I'll get back to you."

"What about Alex?" Candy asked when Tom hung up.

"You didn't mention that he was out of prison," Tom said.

"Oh, that. Yeah. Fran agreed to hire him back on a trial basis, as long as Rick approved it," Candy explained.

"And Rick said yes? I didn't see that coming."

Candy nodded.

Tom looked at Candy. "I don't want you at the sheriff's office because that might make this situation with the Pearsons worse. But Margo said Rick received some kind of threat when he was in the hospital, and now they have the office locked down. What do you think?"

"I think I'd rather be with you." Candy held her dresses tighter.

Tom called Margo back. "I'm going to take Candy with me, after all. Someone broke into her apartment and vandalized it. I need her to make out a statement." It was a weak excuse, Tom knew. He could have Candy make out the statement anyplace and anytime, but an excuse was an excuse.

"Okay," Margo said. "See you guys later."

Tom hung up and leaned back further in his seat. He couldn't keep up with all that was going on. Candy was being targeted by some nutcase, her apartment was trashed, three of her friends were dead, and her forensics work was in question. Now Rick was in danger, of course. Rick was always in some kind of danger. That's how he ran his life. Tom shook his head as he thought of Fran and how she fell so hard for Rick.

"What?" Candy asked.

"Oh, nothing," Tom said, not wanting to upset her. "Just one of those days."

She nodded and didn't press him. If his concerns didn't affect her, she didn't want to know right now. It was all she could do to hold herself together.

When they arrived at the police station, Tom put the dresses on the backseat of his car. He removed his nylon jacket, held it over her head to keep her dry, and escorted her into the building.

"There's a coffee room –" he started to say as he shook the rain from his jacket.

"I know where it is, Tom." She shivered and rubbed her goose bump-covered arms with her hands.

"Wait for me there. Once I get done, I'll look for you." He wrapped the jacket over her shoulders.

Tom found Sheriff Hodge in the conference room with Reverend Lawrence Blackwell and the Pearsons. The minute Tom walked into the room, he felt the tension crackle around him. The parties were hunched over the table like football players in a huddle. The file on Bryce Pearson's death, complete with graphic photos, was spread out across the table, along with Blackwell's ever-present cane. They all looked up as Tom entered as if he was somehow carrying the answers in his pocket. He took a seat next to Hodge and nodded a greeting to everyone.

"The Pearsons want the investigation into their son's death reopened," Hodge began. "They feel that Dr. Knight was biased in her assessment of the evidence."

"Biased? How?"

Blackwell folded his hands together and spoke to Tom. "It's our opinion that Bryce's killer would have been charged with first-degree murder if Dr. Knight had cared more about processing the evidence than about protecting a member of the BDSM community."

Tom frowned. He didn't like Blackwell the first time they met, and now his feelings toward the man just got worse. "I assure you, Dr. Knight would never do that." He glanced at Hodge and could tell the sheriff wasn't so sure.

"This isn't just about justice for Bryce," Blackwell insisted. "It's about this poor boy's soul!" He glanced at the Pearsons before continuing. "He was a good boy, a loving boy. He couldn't possibly have agreed to this. It's – it's a mortal sin, it's unnatural, and he was a believer. Don't you understand? He bears no sin if he's a murder victim."

"It's more than that," Jim Pearson interrupted. The older man took his wife's hand and held it. He had come straight from his work at the church and had only stopped to put a lightweight jacket over his jeans and soiled plaid shirt. Paint was splattered on his cuffs and pants. His hands were rough and calloused, his head was nearly bald under a Wranglers' cap, and he wore thin-rimmed glasses. When he spoke, crooked, broken, yellow teeth appeared. "We believe that the young lady found at the diner would still be alive if she wasn't friends with that woman."

"By 'that woman,' you mean Dr. Knight?" Tom asked.

Pearson nodded.

His wife, who was quick to speak when she was alone with Blackwell and Tom at their previous meeting, now said nothing. Instead, she kept her eyes down except for an occasional glance at Blackwell.

"We're going to look into this matter," the sheriff said, "if only to make sure that Dr. Knight did her job right."

"I have a question for you," Tom told the couple. "When did you find out Candace Knight was into BDSM?"

The Pearsons both turned and looked at Blackwell.

"I heard about it through a parishioner," Blackwell said. "Then we were having breakfast one day and she –"

"By 'she' you mean Dr. Knight?" Tom asked.

"Yes. Miss Knight. She came into the diner and Melissa recognized her."

"This parishioner, who was it?" Tom asked.

Blackwell frowned. "I'm really not sure I should –"

"Worried it will ruin her reputation?" Tom asked.

"He doesn't have a reputation to ruin," Blackwell said curtly. "He's dead. But there's no reason for his wife or children to know –"

"That he used Candy's services," Tom concluded.

"God, no! He would never have done that. It's just –"

"Just what?" Hodge leaned forward, now curious. "If this guy is dead, why not just tell us?"

Blackwell shifted in his seat, glanced at the Pearsons and back at Hodge. "Paul Burns," he said finally.

Tom's eyes widened and he leaned back abruptly in his chair. "Fran Simone's ex-husband told you Candy was into BDSM?" he asked, just to be sure.

"Yes, about five months ago, just before Rick Brandt murdered him," Blackwell said, his face tense.

"It was not murder. It was self-defense," Tom shouted.

Hodge tensed and glared at Tom.

"So they say," Blackwell responded.

"So I say. I was there." Tom indicated Hodge. "We were both there." His hands balled into fists.

"That's enough, detective," Hodge warned.

"That's not the way Paul's widow tells it."

"His widow? Cheryl Burns would be dead now if Brandt hadn't—" Tom began.

"Enough," Hodge barked.

Tom turned on the sheriff. "Burns tried to kill his own son. He shot Fran. We were both there. This is nuts."

Hodge raised his hand to quiet Tom. "Enough," he repeated.

Blackwell looked at Hodge. "I realize you work together and that this is complicated. I considered hiring a private investigator to look into the matter, but, for now, I'm relying on your sense of professionalism."

"Worked together," Hodge reminded Blackwell. "Dr. Knight doesn't work here anymore."

Tom slowly exhaled. He felt a knot form in his chest. He couldn't imagine Candy throwing a case because of her personal involvement, and then he remembered that Fran killed Roger Elliott, and that he and Candy had covered up the evidence. Max took the blame. The case was closed. Or was it? Heat rose up the back of Tom's neck. He deliberately forced his shoulders to relax.

"Whatever you decide," Tom told the sheriff through clenched teeth.

Blackwell and the Pearsons stood up and said their goodbyes. Tom noticed how Blackwell gripped his heavy cane tightly and moved slowly out of the room. When they were gone, Tom leaned back in his chair and felt a headache building up. "Shit. He's friends with Cheryl Burns? She's trying to get custody of Fran's daughter. Damn, I should have known he had an agenda. I wonder how cozy they are."

"I know you're friends with Knight, close friends," Hodge said. "It's bad enough I've got you on the BDSM murder case, but I'm going to give this one to Angela Simmons. I want you to talk to her and tell her everything you know about the Pearson matter. If Candy Knight killed those girls, you'll give me all the facts, right? Despite what Allyson Stone says, I think you're a good cop, but lately you seem to be on the verge of being derailed. Keep your distance from Candy. Keep your objectivity. Got it?"

"If I'm not on the Pearson case, why am I here?" Tom asked.

I wanted you here to meet the Pearsons and give me an assessment. What's happening here? What's this all about?"

Tom shook his head. "Blackwell's connection to Cheryl Burns worries me. There's a lot more to this story than Bryce Pearson's death."

Hodge nodded. "Keep working on the Ortiz case and the other dead girls. I want all the T's crossed and all the I's dotted."

"Yes, sir," Tom said.

"Will you be seeing Knight today?"

"She's upstairs right now. She was with me when you called. I was taking her to Fran's office, but apparently they have their own problems."

"Anything I need to know about?" Hodge asked.

Tom thought a minute. "Two things. Candy's apartment was heavily vandalized. I think it's related to the three homicides, so I'm having the lab guys go over it. I was also told that Rick Brandt received a possible death threat while he was in the hospital. I don't know anything more about that, yet, but I was going to stop at Fran's office and talk to him."

Hodge scowled. "What is it with these people? They attract trouble."

"Especially Brandt," Tom noted.

"Talk to them. I want more details," said Hodge. "And don't let your feelings for Fran Simone color your judgment on this one, either."

"Excuse me? What does –"

"Everything," Hodge answered. Leaving Tom feeling exposed and uncomfortable, Hodge turned and walked out of the room.

Tom went up to the coffee room where Candy was sitting at a table with Edgar Mitchell. Mitchell smiled at Tom.

"All done?" Candy asked.

"Just beginning. We've got problems. I need to go back to Fran's office and have a serious heart-to-heart with her and Rick. Can I drop you off somewhere?"

"Alone? Like hell. I'm not leaving your side until I absolutely have to."

"Let's go then."

The drizzle had turned to a heavy rain by the time they got to the parking lot. Candy was still wearing Tom's jacket and hugged it around her.

"Stay here and I'll bring the car around." Tom made a mad dash for the car and managed to get wet in the process.

The air was still warm in the car, but the dampness gave Tom a chill. He turned on the heat and drove to where Candy was standing. She scrambled in. A fog developed on the windshield but disappeared. The wipers slapped and swished against the rain.

"So, anything exciting happen?" Candy asked as they headed towards Fran's office.

Tom sighed. "It's the Pearsons."

"Yes, you mentioned that. What else? What do they want?"

"They think you screwed up their son's case, and they want to reopen it."

"Of course, they do. They've been saying that for the last three years. What makes now different?"

"Now they know you're in the lifestyle." Tom glanced at her.

Candy tugged the jacket tighter around her like a security blanket. "What does that have to do with anything?"

"They think you covered up for Bryce's killer because they were engaged in BDSM play when Bryce died," Tom explained.

"That's nonsense. I wouldn't do that."

Tom was silent.

Candy shifted in her seat. "I know what you're thinking. We covered up for Fran when she killed Roger Elliott, and I probably shouldn't have sided with Alex when he was accused of killing Carol McEnroe."

"I'm not worried about the McEnroe case," Tom said. "I admit, Alex was a friend and maybe we should have had someone else handle it, but in the end, he was innocent. With Fran, however –"

"We can't go back and change that now. Max Simone took the fall for Elliott's murder. The sheriff and the prosecutor were happy with the result. Max died of cancer a few weeks later, and there's no turning back those pages. Besides, what good would it serve? We both know Fran killed Elliott to save her daughter's life. No jury would convict her, anyway."

"That's true," Tom agreed.

Candy leaned back and closed her eyes for a few minutes. "I wonder if they're right."

Tom glanced at her and frowned, then turned his attention back to the road. "What do you mean by right?"

"If I wasn't in the lifestyle, if I wasn't a mistress, would I have looked at the evidence differently? Would I have found something else, something, anything that would convince the prosecutor to go with a first-degree murder charge instead of negligent homicide?"

"You're second-guessing yourself."

"Anything else I should worry about?" Candy asked.

Tom thought about Blackwell's assertion that Candy's "girls" wouldn't have died but for their association with Candy. Tom decided not to share that thought with her, either. She had enough on her mind, especially with the apartment being vandalized. And she was already beating herself up over the Bryce Pearson case. No, Tom thought. That little tidbit of shit could wait for another day.

"Yeah, one more thing. The Reverend Lawrence Blackwell was friends with Fran's ex, Paul Burns. He's also close to Cheryl Burns, and Cheryl is after custody of Fran's daughter."

"Damn," Candy muttered.

Tom picked up his cell phone and called Fran's office again. "Still there?" he asked when Margo got on the line.

"Yes. We're working on the Max-Mil cases," she said.

"What's that? No, don't tell me. Candy and I will be there soon. I need to talk to Rick." And Fran, he thought.

"I'll let him know," said Margo. "Just call when you get here so I can unlock the door."

Tom hung up and felt the knot in his chest return. Just once, couldn't Fran settle down with a nice guy and stay out of trouble? Why in hell did she have to get mixed up with Rick Brandt?

Tom stopped on the front steps of the office building and looked down. A potted rose plant with a note tucked into it had been left by the locked door. Frowning, he picked it up. The clay pot was heavy and smelled of rich, fresh soil. The note was made out to Rick. Tom was holding the plant when Margo unlocked the door.

"For me?" she asked, smiling. "Or did you bring Fran flowers? You gonna kiss and make up?"

"Sorry, no. For Rick. They were left on the front step. I didn't have anything to do with it."

"Ditch the card and tell Fran they're from you, anyway," Margo suggested with a wink.

She took the clay pot in her arms as Tom locked the door behind them. A few minutes later, Margo put the small rosebush on her desk and ushered Tom and Candy into the conference room.

Fran, looking tired, was seated at the head of the table. She'd lost her suit jacket, kicked off her heels, and untucked her white blouse. Her earrings were tossed to the side and folders and papers littered the workspace. She had unpinned her long red hair and it fell softly over her shoulders.

Rick sat next to her, knee to knee, with his back to the window. He was straining to see through his good eye. His cane and leather jacket were on the chair next to him. Alex was on the far side of the table, opposite Fran. The sleeves of his shirt were rolled up to his elbows. His tie hung loosely around his neck, and his head was buried in papers. He didn't look at Tom, but he smiled at Candy. She walked up behind him and hugged him. The table was covered with remnants of Chinese takeout. The room smelled like soy sauce.

"Hi, there, stranger." Fran tried to sound light. She was still angry with Tom, but she was determined not to let it show.

"Why is it every time I see you, you look like shit," Tom said to Rick. Tom knew about the accident but was still surprised at how bad Rick looked, especially with half his face bandaged up.

Rick grunted. "Trojans bearing gifts?" he joked on seeing Candy. He gave her a warm smile.

"I don't bear gifts," Tom said with a grin.

"Except for the rose bush," Margo added.

"What rose bush?" Rick asked as he and Fran both looked up.

"Someone left a potted rose bush by the door downstairs," Tom said. "Margo took –"

Before Tom could say anything more, Fran jumped up and ran past him.

Rick screamed after her, "Fran! No!"

But she was too fast for him. She seized the plant and ran to the open stairwell in the middle of the large hallway. Leaning over the railing, she dropped the potted plant straight down, past four floors, all the way to the basement. She turned to run back to the office just as the explosion hit.

The building rocked, and Fran went sprawling onto the tiled floor.

"Shit!" Tom screamed as he ran after her. He grasped her arm, pulled her up, and rushed her back into the office as the hall started filling with smoke. He slammed the door shut behind them.

"Fire escape – my old office," Fran panted. She grabbed her shoes but left the jacket behind.

Rick limped to her side and grabbed her arm. "Damn you, woman!" he barked.

"My files! My cases!" Fran yelled. She tried to pull out of Rick's grasp and go back to the conference room, but he wouldn't let her go.

"Leave 'em! Get out, now!" Rick yelled.

"But I'll lose them!" she argued.

"Now!" he ordered.

Margo, who managed to grab the women's purses, ran past Fran and out the fire exit door. Alex, folders in his hand, held the door open as the others filed out of the building and into the rain. Rick brought up the rear. He leaned unsteadily on the iron railing and looked down.

The building shook again and everyone yelled and grasped the railing to hang on.

"Get down on your ass!" Tom, now on the ground, yelled up to Rick. "It'll be easier!"

Rick nodded, sat down, and slid down the stairs as quickly as he could with Alex behind him. When they neared the bottom, Tom held the ladder for them, and Rick used his good arm to lower himself down without landing hard on his injured leg. He was muttering obscenities when he hit the ground.

"Get away from the fucking building!" Rick yelled at everyone.

Alex fell to the ground and quickly got up.

Tom slipped an arm around Rick and helped him walk as they hurried to the far end of the parking lot.

By now, smoke was pouring out of the lower windows, and everyone was soaked from the rain. Alex stuffed his files under his shirt. Fran's eyes stung and she coughed. Sirens approached. People driving by slowed down to look.

Rick limped up to Fran and grabbed her arm tightly. Water poured down his hair and face. His voice shook as he yelled at her. "What the hell were you thinking?"

Fran stared him down. "I wasn't thinking! There wasn't time to think! There wasn't time to argue, or strategize, or any other shit! I just acted!"

"You could have died!" Rick fired back.

"We all could have died."

"Damn, woman. You scared the shit outta me." Rick, still panting from the near escape, pulled her tight against him and kissed her hard.

Fran held him tightly around the neck and whispered in his ear, "I love you, too."

His grip on her tightened.

Firemen gathered on the scene and ushered them further from the building.

"I'm going to need a new cane," Rick said as he leaned on Fran for support.

"I'll find you a good one," Tom said. "Like that fancy, carved thing the Reverend Blackwell has."

"Ain't seen it," Rick said.

"It's big and heavy and wooden and perfect for clobbering people over the head," Tom explained with a grin.

Rick looked down at Fran. "Now, that sounds like something I could use."

Chapter 12

They were lucky, and they all knew it. Fran escaped the explosion with some bumps and bruises, and Rick managed to aggravate his existing wounds but nothing that required medical attention. The rain let up. The sun peeked through the clouds.

The deepest pain, from Tom's point of view, was watching Rick and Fran kiss. In their relief to be alive, in their obvious passion, and in their total lack of awareness of anyone around them, they had yelled at each other, they had embraced each other, and they had kissed. Tom's hands tightened on the steering wheel of the car as the image played out in his mind. He knew they were now a couple. He'd known it for months. He didn't realize how much it would hurt to actually see it.

Candy didn't say a word as she sat next to Tom in the car. Her eyes shifted from the road to Tom and back again. She saw the pained expression on his face, and she knew what he was thinking. Some part of him had been in denial, she was sure. As long as he never saw Rick and Fran as a couple, Tom could always imagine her coming back to him.

Tom parked the car at the curb in front of Fran's house and turned the engine off. He sat there for a moment without speaking until Candy rested a hand on his arm.

"I wish there was something I could say."

Tom shook his head. "Me, too. I didn't realize –"

"That they were really a couple," Candy interrupted.

"No, not just that. More. That there was so much – so much –" He had trouble finding the right word. Or maybe it was just because he didn't want to use the right word. "In all the time I was with Fran, she never kissed me like that," he admitted, turning away. "Not like that."

"Passion." Candy said. "They're in love."

Tom wiped rainwater from his forehead. "I suppose we should go in and dry off."

Inside, Fran, a large bath towel wrapped around her shoulders, stood by the front door and looked out the window at Tom and Candy. She couldn't hear them, but she had an idea about what was being said. She had seen the look on Tom's face, too, when Rick finally let her go.

There wasn't time to talk, or think, or analyze it. The firefighters showed up and all they thought about was going home. Without a word to each other, everyone migrated to Fran's house. No matter where else they lived, that was home.

Rick approached Fran and looked out the window at Tom's car. Then he looked at Fran. He brushed the wet hair from her face and kissed her.

"We smell like smoke," Fran said when he finally released her lips. She shivered.

"I have a cure for that." Rick smirked.

"Get a room!" Margo teased as she walked past them. She was carrying several hot cups of coffee.

"Do you have anything else to drink in the house?" Alex asked from the living room. He'd found some garbage bags and some blankets and spread them on the sofa so they could sit down without getting the upholstery wet.

Ricks focused on Fran as he spoke. "No booze in this house. Not anymore. You gotta settle for tea or something."

Fran smiled. Rick took her hand and led her down the hall to the den.

"Hey! Where're you going?" Margo yelled after them.

"Taking your advice," Rick yelled back.

Rick was limping and he was operating one-handed with his left arm still in a sling, but he quickly folded out the sleeper sofa and gently pushed Fran down onto it. He kicked the door closed and stretched out on the bed.

"Now, young lady," he said to Fran. "When we were at the office, you said –"

"Shouldn't we shower first?" Fran asked.

"We can shower later."

"I know exactly what I said," Fran told him. "Now lie down and shut up." She undid his belt and slid off his wet shoes and slacks. Then she unbuttoned his shirt and carefully slipped it off of him and over his cast. Finally, she stripped off her own soaked, smoke-filled clothes. Fran stretched out next to Rick, rested her soft hand on his strong chest, and kissed him. "Keep me warm." She was still trembling from the shock of the explosion.

He pulled her close and kissed her softly. "We're safe. Everyone's okay." He pulled a blanket around them both. "I'm sorry I yelled at you, babe. I don't want to lose you."

Fran's eyes drifted to his lips. She pulled herself up and kissed him again, this time pressing down hard. "God, I need you."

Tom and Candy joined Margo and Alex in the living room. They were somber and exhausted. Their nerves were frayed, and their clothes reeked of smoke.

Tom looked around the room. "Where's Fran and Rick?"

"They needed some alone time," Margo said.

Tom winced.

"I'm going to shower, bag these smelly clothes, and stick them in the garage." Candy glanced at Margo. "I've got some sweats you can wear if you want."

"Great idea," Margo nodded. "Where's the shower?"

"Fran's room." Candy noticed Alex sitting on the sofa with his head tipped back and his eyes closed. She walked up to him, leaned down, and gave him a kiss on the cheek. "You okay?"

He opened his eyes and nodded. "That was close. That was one hell of a blast. I wasn't expecting that. Are you okay?"

"I will be."

"Aren't Fran and Rick in her room?" Margo asked.

"They're in the den. That's sort of Rick's unofficial official room here. Come, I'll show you where the bathroom is." Candy took Margo's hand.

"Fran has some of her ex's old clothes in her bedroom closet if you want to change," Tom told Alex. "I think they'll fit you.

Alex followed Tom and the girls down the hallway.

Fran hadn't bothered to make her bed that morning. Her clothes were strewn across a large chair and a pile of files littered the floor next to her nightstand.

Tom used his foot to sweep a pair of high-heeled shoes out of his way as he turned on the lamp, walked across the lush rug, and drew her curtains closed against the encroaching night. He slid open the mirrored door to the closet and pulled the small suitcase from the top shelf. He then opened it on Fran's unmade bed. "Help yourself," said Tom.

"Thanks." Alex pawed through the clothing. "I should probably shower too." He smiled at the ladies as they slipped into the bathroom. "Is there room for three in there?"

Candy laughed. "Use the one across the hall, boy!"

"Ouch," Tom remarked. For the first time since the explosion, he smiled. He glanced at Alex, a million questions in his mind about Alex's relationship with Candy.

"You, on the other hand –" Candy made a motion to Tom to join them.

"Ah, I don't think so," Tom said. "If Alex ain't going, I ain't going."

"Then we'll take both of you!" Candy said.

Tom felt heat crawling up the back of his neck as he scurried to the safety of the living room.

"Damn, this is sweet." Margo looked around at the luxurious bathroom. She ran her fingers over the marble countertop and stopped to sniff at the candles in their tall glass containers. She frowned and looked at Candy. "You think we're safe here?"

"I was just wondering about that." Candy leaned against the sink and watched as Margo turned on the shower and shrugged off her clothes. "I was thinking we should call Rick's friend Charlie."

"Charlie? Who's – Oh, yeah, he was at the office. He brought Rick back from the hospital." Margo stepped into the large open shower. "Check with Rick first. I think he might have called him already." She glanced back over her shoulder. "Care to join me?" She tipped her head back and let the water run over her hair and down her toned body.

Candy smiled. "Ah, hell." She stripped down and joined Margo.

Tom heard the women laughing. He wanted to be a fly on the wall. He wanted to know all their secrets. The more he associated with this group, the deeper he fell into Alice's rabbit hole, and he wondered if he'd ever get out. One thing he knew, he needed fresh clothes. As Alex stepped out of the spare bath, now showered and changed, Tom grabbed his car keys. "I'll be back. Shall I pick up something to eat?"

"Good idea." Alex dug out his wallet and handed Tom a wad of cash. "Knock yourself out. Margo is vegetarian, and Rick likes meat – raw, I think. As for the mistress, anything that tastes good – steak, fish, seafood, chicken – whatever. I'll eat anything. Oh, and a bottle of something – scotch, maybe?"

"I can do all but the scotch. Rick has a no alcohol policy around Fran. He's got her dried out and intends to keep her that way, and since I'm not suicidal, I don't want to piss him off."

Alex nodded and said, "His house, his rules."

Tom caught his breath. It wasn't that long ago that he considered this his house, not Rick's. The comment had a truth to it that he didn't want to face. He headed out the door.

The rain had stopped, leaving puddles on the sidewalk. Tom barely stepped up to his car when a large, banged-up pickup truck with a leaping buck detail on each door pulled up to the curb, the headlights nose to nose with Tom's unmarked cruiser. Tom, one hand on the handle of his car, shielded his eyes and watched as Charlie Cook killed the engine, turned out the lights, and slid out of the cab.

Despite the truck's size, Charlie made it look small. He hit the ground in battered work boots and was wearing denim overalls over a camouflage print tee shirt. His long, curly dark hair was tossed in the breeze, and he had crumbs on his bristly beard from eating a burrito. Tom was not surprised to see Charlie's ever-present pistol strapped to his side.

"Detective!" Charlie said with a grin. Then he stopped. "You smell like shit. You been swimming in them clothes? What the hell happened?" He laughed, his features lit up by the front porch lights of Fran's house and a nearby streetlamp.

Tom leaned back against his car and crossed his arms. "Some asshole blew up Fran's office. Didn't Rick tell you? Isn't that why you're here?"

Charlie finished off the burrito in one bite and brushed off his beard. "Nope. Yup. Sorta," he said with a grin. "Rick said some shit happened. Didn't say what. He weren't big on specifics, you know. Just said to get my ass over here. Anyone hurt?"

Tom shook his head. "Nothing serious. It didn't help Rick's other injuries much. He's having a sore time of it, although you wouldn't know it at the moment." Tom glanced at the house. His voice had an edge to it that caught Charlie's attention. "Is it really just me?" Tom asked, looking up at Charlie. "I'm I the last normal human being left in the world? Or am I the crazy one and they're all – Hell, they are NOT normal!"

Charlie laughed. "What the fuck you talking 'bout?"

Tom sighed deeply before speaking. "We're in a building. It gets blown up. Everyone could have died."

"But they didn't," Charlie interrupted.

"Right. They didn't. But they could have. What do they do? They all come here."

Charlie shrugs. "So?"

"So, Rick and Fran are – well, they're doing what Rick and Fran do these days, I guess. And Candy and Margo –"

"Margo?" Charlie asked.

"Yeah. Fran's secretary. The one with the funky hair," Tom explained.

"Oh, yeah. She's a cutie," Charlie said with a grin.

"Anyway, Candy and Margo are now in the shower, together, laughing their asses off like we're on some kind of vacation."

Charlie's eyes widened as he thought about that image.

Tom ignored the look and continued. "In the meantime, Alex de la Rosa is wandering around the house like someone hit him with a two-by-four and he forgot he wasn't dead." Tom stopped to catch his breath. He dug the toe of his boot into the pavement as if he could somehow kick the Earth and make it right again.

"Sounds normal to me," Charlie said. He pulled a wrapper out of his pocket and opened it up. Inside were several sticks of beef jerky. He offered one to Tom, who turned it down. Charlie then took one and stuck it between his teeth like a cigarette while he wrapped up the package and put it back in his pocket.

"How the hell is any of that normal?" Tom asked. "Normal should be crying, screaming, upset, something. Anything."

"Well, this is how I see it. The girls are celebrating being alive. They're giddy. Your buddy Alex -"

"He's not my buddy," Tom corrected.

"He's in shock. I'd worry about him. As for Rick and Fran...." Charlie hesitated a moment when he noticed how tense Tom got at that second. "...Rick is probably doing what he does to get Fran through it, to get her past the shock. He's distracting her." Charlie chewed on his jerky a bit.

Tom opened his car door. "Yeah, well–" He started to say. Then he stopped. "I still feel like I'm in some Alice in Wonderland nightmare." Tom wondered if Charlie was the Cheshire cat.

"Look, bud," Charlie said, "I know you had a thing for that girl. I know this has got to be hard. And it ain't no secret that Rick's had his share of women – hell, more than his share. But in the twenty-plus years I've known that guy, I've never known him so damn crazy about a broad like he is about this Fran woman."

"That's supposed to make me feel better?" Tom asked.

"You care about her, right? You should know it's for real. He'll take good care of her. That should make you feel better." Charlie tipped his head a bit and patted Tom on the shoulder. "So, where you headed off to?"

"I'm going to try and secure Fran's legal files from the office, assuming the building is still standing and stable enough for me to walk around in it. Then I'm going to go home, shower, change clothes and get back here." He slipped his hand into his pocket for his keys and rubbed up against the wad of cash from Alex. "Oh, and get food. Everyone's going to be starving."

"Here." Charlie pulled out his wallet, rummaged around, and found a battered and soiled business card. "Call these guys. They're cheap. They can load up any stuff from the office and stick it wherever you want it. And I happen to know they're free right now 'cause they just finished a job for me earlier today."

"At this hour?" Tom glanced up at the night sky. There was no sign of clouds and the stars twinkled overhead. For once, the world seemed a calm and peaceful place. He took a deep breath and let the night air clear out his lungs.

"You wanna leave that shit there overnight? God knows who'll get into it," Charlie said.

"You have a point." Tom looked at the number and pulled out his phone. "I'll see you in a bit, then."

Charlie nodded and headed to the front door.

***

Tom was almost to Fran's office when he called Sheriff Hodge and brought him up to speed. "I'm headed there now to look around."

"The fire is out," Hodge told him. "It's not as bad as I thought it would be. Hell of a blast but concentrated on the first floor. A lot of smoke and water damage, but the upper levels look good. Still, I wouldn't throw a party in there. The music could bring the whole damn thing down."

"You've been there?"

"Of course. The forensics guys got the place taped off. Not much to do there. They did find some remnants of the clay pot the bomb came in. Nothing exciting. Nothing to say where it came from."

"Probably Home Depot or some such thing," Tom said. "Someplace where they sell a dozen a day and have no idea who bought it."

"Yeah. You okay?"

Tom pulled into the parking lot at Fran's office and parked the car. "A bit shook up, but it'll pass."

"Need anything?" Hodge asked.

Tom thought for a minute. "No, not really. I need about a dozen things, but nothing you can help me with right now unless you feel like making a food run."

Hodge laughed. "You know what time it is, detective? I'm home having supper and I ain't leaving. Call if anything comes up." The phone clicked off.

Tom got out of his car. A white paneled truck was parked near the side of the building and three men were standing next to it. Two were young and strong, just the kind of guys needed for this type of work. Tom nodded to them.

"Harry Gervais," the older one said, offering a handshake. "These are my boys, Tim and Matt."

Tom nodded and shook hands with the man. "Detective Saddler. You can call me Tom."

"You're all wet," Gervais noted.

"We got caught in the rain. I need to go home and change soon."

"What have we got?" Gervais asked.

"Third floor, law office. Most of the files are in the file cabinets and were untouched as far as I could tell. We made a rather hasty escape earlier. Think it's safe enough to retrieve them?"

"Yeah. Looks like it. It's gonna be a mess, but we can get in and out quick like."

"There's papers all over the conference room. I need them boxed and kept separate. They're part of a large lawsuit," Tom continued.

"Anything else?"

"I'm headed up with you. I'll let you know if anything strikes me as important. I'm mostly worried about the files." Tom looked up the fire escape stairs to the open door to Fran's old office and realized he was never going to be able to clean out her office and get groceries at the same time. "I'll be right up," he told the guys.

Tom stepped under a streetlamp and made a call to a local grocery store. "You deliver?" he asked. A few minutes later, he'd given them a large order and his credit card number, closed the phone, and pulled himself up the three flights of clanking iron stairs to Fran's office.

Gervais set up some battery-operated flood lamps to light the space. The men went from room to room. They emptied the file cabinets into boxes and lowered the boxes down the fire escape stairs. Then they gathered the papers from the conference room, boxed them and did the same.

The flood lamps created as much shadow as they did light. Tom felt as if he was walking through some kind of carnival. Everything took on a different shape. Familiar objects became strange and looming threats. He got a flashlight from Gervais and ran his hand over the bookcases. Most of Fran's research material was online, so she didn't have the traditional row upon row of law books. There were a few good ones there, however, but Tom was more interested in personal things – a photograph, a piece of art, a figurine, and her earrings. He opened her desk drawer and pulled out her bottle of painkillers. Frowning, he slipped them into his pocket. He collected her spare clothes from the closet and grabbed her suit jacket. The clothes were soiled and smelled of smoke, but they might be salvageable, he thought. At least, that was a decision for Fran to make.

In one of the closets, he found a tall, thin statue of a cat. He recognized it as the one that Alex got from his sister, Toni, a long time ago. Tom held it in his hand for a moment. He remembered Toni from "the good old days," before she lost her mind and tried to kill everyone. He wondered if she was behind this bombing now. Toni wanted to murder Fran; Alex and Rick stopped her. Now she sat in prison, awaiting trial. Tom put the statue back.

"We got it all?" Gervais asked.

Tom nodded. "Yeah, looks like it." He followed them down the fire escape stairs.

"Where do you want it?" Gervais asked.

Tom handed Gervais some cash and wrote down Fran's address for him. "Just put it in the garage for now. We'll sort it out later."

Gervais nodded, loaded up his boys, and was gone.

Tom called Margo.

"Yes?" she answered in her usual, bright tone.

"There's a truck on its way to Fran's," Tom told her. "It's got the files from the office. Can you unlock the garage doors and make sure there's place to put the stuff?"

He heard Candy laughing in the background, and then he heard Charlie's booming voice, but Tom couldn't make out what Charlie was saying.

"Yeah, sure," Margo said. "The groceries arrived. Thanks. We're cooking now. See you soon?"

"Soon." It wasn't until he hung up that Tom realized he didn't want to go back to Fran's house. He wanted to go home. He wanted to take a nice, long, hot shower and put on clean clothes. He wondered if the explosion made the news. He wondered if his mom was worried about him. He dialed her number.

Maryanne Saddler was quick to answer. "Oh my God. I've been sitting here, wondering –"

"It's okay, Mom. No one was hurt."

"That's what the news reporter said. Only minor injuries. But I didn't hear from you."

"I'm fine. I'm going to clean up and head to your place. It's not too late, is it?"

"Not for you, dear. Come home. I bet you're starved."

"I am." Tom remembered what Candy said to him: 'I'm just an old-fashioned girl looking for an old-fashioned guy.' He wondered if she meant it.

***

Candy stood in the doorway and looked out on the front porch. She was watching Alex. Of all of them, he seemed most affected by the bombing. He sat on the top step, his hands clasped around his knees, his eyes staring at the starlit sky.

Charlie startled Candy when he came up behind her and asked, "Is he okay?"

"I don't know." Candy stepped onto the porch and sat next to Alex.

He smiled weakly at her.

"Hey, pet." She shoved him gently with her shoulder. "What are you doing out here?"

He was looking at her as if he was trying to memorize every part of her. Then he looked at the ground for a bit until his eyes went back to the stars.

"I did some work for Max Simone once," he said. "A long time ago. You remember?"

"Vaguely," Candy admitted. "Max died almost a year ago. Why think about him now?"

Alex looked back at her. "I think this bombing is related. Max hired Jax Saynte to run the company. They were both dirty, and both into god knows what. Now Fran inherits the company, Jax is trying to force her out, and, the next thing she knows, she's in the middle of more crap than she can fathom, and someone is trying to blow her up."

"I thought, being a rose bush and all, this had something to do with your sister," Candy said.

Alex shook his head. "I know Rick thinks that, but Toni's head is scrambled with all the medication they give her. One minute she's on suicide watch; then she's not. She tried starving herself to death, but they force-fed her. She's so messed up she couldn't tie a pair of shoes much less plot and orchestrate a bombing."

"I'm sorry."

Alex closed his eyes for a minute. "I know Fran and Rick are in danger. I know everyone around them is in danger." He looked at her. "Including you. And it's got nothing to do with Toni and everything to do with Jax Saynte."

Candy took his hand as she talked to him. "If that's the case, why was the rose bush sent to Rick? Why not to Fran?"

"Can you think of a better way to get to Fran than through Rick? What they have isn't just love. It's co-dependence. That bomb was a warning. Rick knows that, but Fran seems to be oblivious to it. I think – I think he doesn't tell her things. I think, in his own way, he tries to protect her."

"They'll work it out, I'm sure. Rick's smart. Just tell him what you know."

"Candy, what I know is that someone may be trying to kill Rick, and you may be caught in the crossfire. It's bad enough you have your own problems. You don't need this, too." His hand tightened around hers.

She waited for him to continue.

"When I first got out of prison, I came to see you. In fact, I came to your apartment three or four times." He looked apologetically at her. "You were the only one who stuck by me through all of this, the only one who called me or wrote to me or came to see me. I wouldn't have made it through everything if it hadn't been for you."

"But you did make it through," Candy said.

"Anyway, I came to see you, and each time I either got cold feet or I saw Allyson Stone there, watching your place."

Candy tensed. "You knew he was watching me, and you didn't say anything?"

"I was specifically told not to meet with you alone. It's a condition of my release. I was afraid he'd tell someone. Afraid I'd end up back in jail. But I just had to see you." He cleared his throat. "And then today Allyson confronted me outside your apartment."

"Why were you at my apartment? Hell, why was Allyson at my apartment? I told that son-of-a-bitch to back off!"

"I was there to warn you. I needed to talk to you alone, when no one else was around, but you're never alone, not anymore."

"What are you trying to do, Alex? Why did you really come back to the office?"

"I think Jax Saynte is after Rick and Fran, and I'm worried you're in his way. You're with Fran all the time. Attached at the hip. If he comes after her, you could end up dead."

Candy frowned. "You came back to Fran's office to protect me?"

"Yes." Alex turned to face her. "I know these people. I know Jax Saynte. This guy is dangerous, and I don't mean in a small town, bad boy kinda way, I mean very dangerous. As long as you're around Fran, you're in danger. We all are. I don't know that Jax has anything to do with what's happening to your girls. It's not his style. But he's the kind of guy who would use it to his advantage. If that's the case, then you're going to get hit from two ends, and I don't want that to happen."

"You're scaring me, Alex."

"I hope so." He caressed her cheek. "You might not be my mistress anymore, but I still care about you. And I'll always be your friend."

"What should I do?" Candy took his hand. "Staying with Fran and Rick is protecting me from a serial killer. But according to you, staying with them also puts me in danger from this Saynte character. I can't stay and I can't leave. Now what?"

"You and Tom weren't supposed to be at the office today. That bomb was meant for Rick and Fran, not you."

"You need to talk to Rick," Candy told him again.

Alex glanced over his shoulder at the house. "Maybe tomorrow. They're busy right now."

"Why can't you be alone with me?" Candy asked.

"The deal was that I would stay out of jail if I was working and working with Fran was permitted. But my private life is another matter. It was a condition of my release that I stay out of the BDSM scene because I was convicted of a violent crime – aiding and abetting in the escape of a murder suspect. If I saw you alone, at your place, and they knew it –"

"You'd be violating parole." Candy leaned her head on his shoulder, and he put his arm around her. "I rather miss being your mistress. You were very good."

"So were you."

Chapter 13
Wednesday Night

Fran thought the nightmares were over. Rick was back. She felt safe again. She no longer saw the bullet-riddled body of her daughter's kidnapper grinning at her when she woke in the middle of the night. She no longer saw her father's emaciated ghost when she crossed a street or had to visit city hall. Fran killed Elliott and got away with it, and Max Simone died of cancer. Fran thought she was done with death until the day her lover shot and killed her ex-husband during a hostage situation.

The image of Paul Burns' brains splattered over the concrete post in the hospital cafeteria jolted Fran from her sleep. She sat up in bed and her hand went to her gut. She felt the scar where Paul shot her. Rick saved a lot of people that day, including her, but at a price.

Fran turned over in bed and found Rick watching her.

He reached up and caressed her cheek. "Bad dreams?"

She wondered how many men those hands had killed. She curled up next to him. "It's nothing."

"Tell me," Rick ordered.

Fran closed her eyes and shuddered. "I was dreaming about Paul, about the day he died."

Rick tipped her chin until she had to look at him. "You shouldn't have been there for that. You shouldn't have seen it."

"I know what it's like to hold a gun, to aim at a man's heart, to fire, to watch the life leave his eyes," she said.

"I know." Rick stroked her hair.

"Do you ever get nightmares? The people you killed, do they ever haunt you?"

"Some of them," he admitted.

"When it's over, do you always look back and know you did the right thing? That you were justified?"

Rick frowned. He looked at her quietly for a few minutes. "No. There have been times when I wasn't sure. Times when I thought later that I could have done different, and maybe some stupid kid would still be alive." He looked up at the ceiling and remembered.

"How do you deal with it?"

Rick met her eyes. "How do you?"

Fran sighed. "Elliott had it coming," she said defensively.

"I agree."

"I didn't have a choice," she continued.

"Yes, you did," he said softly.

"Fuck." Fran buried her head in his chest.

"You can't lie to yourself, babe. It don't help."

Fran stretched her body against his as her thoughts went from death to the way Rick made her feel alive. He slid down, lowered his head, and gently bit her breast. Fran moaned.

Rick looked up at her. "You deal with it by living every day, in every part of your being."

Fran tensed as his lips went to her belly and his hand cupped her ass.

"Am I a bad person?" Her arousal grew.

"Right now, babe, I sure as hell hope so," Rick said with a warm smile.

***

Thursday Morning

"What time is it?" Fran rolled over in bed and shielded her eyes against a slit of sunlight that made its way through the bedroom curtains.

"Nine." Rick, groaning, pulled her into his warm, strong arms.

"At night?"

"No sweetie. In the morning. You slept right through supper. I figured you needed it." He brushed her tangled red hair away from her face.

"In the morning? Shit!" She sat up quickly in bed. "Damn, you bastard! Why didn't you wake me up! I've got that board meeting this morning, and I smell like smoke and I gotta –"

Rick yanked her back into the bed and planted a heavy kiss on her lips to silence her. "It's Thursday," he whispered when he pulled away. "The board meeting is tomorrow."

"Oh, crap." Fran covered her face with her hand. Her heart was racing, and it took her a while to calm down.

Then the memory of the explosion hit her, and she felt the grief well up like a tidal wave inside her chest and head.

Rick pulled her close as she sobbed. "We're okay. You're okay. Tom went over last night and got the office files. They're in the garage. Candy and Margo cooked up a nice spread last night, and it smells like they're at it again this morning. Everyone is going to be fine, boss. Well, everyone except Alex, but then he never was quite right." He held her until she stopped crying.

Fran looked up at him, her cheeks stained with tears. "You got up and ate supper?" She took a sniff. "And showered too. And I slept through all of that?"

With his good arm, Rick pulled himself up and sat on the edge of the bed. "Why don't you shower now, and we'll get breakfast?"

Fran jumped out of bed, her red hair streaming down her bare back as she hurried past him and bent over to gather up her clothes. Rick took the opportunity to swat her on the ass. She jumped up, squealed, and blushed. She held the clothes to her breasts and turned to face him. For a moment, he just looked at her, then he reached up and tugged the clothes out of her arms.

"Turn around," Rick said softly.

Fran obeyed, pivoting on her toes until she came full circle. The blush covered her whole body. She wondered if she'd ever get used to him, and she wondered if she even wanted to.

"Beautiful," he said. "You can go now."

Fran didn't know whether to laugh or scream at him, but she gathered up her clothes and made a dash for the bathroom. She could hear him chuckle as she fled.

Rick pulled on his sweatpants and limped over to the mirror. He needed a shave and was almost due for a haircut. The bandages on the side of his face were slightly soiled from the smoke from the explosion and fire. They were loose in one spot from his shower. He slipped the sling over his shoulder and winced as he slid his arm into it and flexed his fingers. As he examined his still-muscular body with its splattering of scars and tattoos, an old country song came to mind.

"I ain't as good, but I ain't bad," he muttered to himself as he padded barefoot into the hallway.

Margo and Alex were chatting in the living room while they watched the late morning news. A reporter stood outside of Fran's office building and talked about the bombing. Rick nodded to them, went to the kitchen, and got a cup out of the cupboard. He found Charlie and Candy in the kitchen, huddled around the table and conspiring.

"Let me get that for you." Candy jumped up. She wore a cute dress covered in ladybugs over a pair of white sandals.

Rick grinned and backed away. He sat next to Charlie. "This is the life, ain't it?" he asked with a wink.

Charlie was eyeing Candy as if he wanted to lick her. "Oh, yeah."

"Behave yourselves, boys," Candy snapped with a grin. "Or I'll have to change into leather and pull my whips out of storage."

"Is that supposed to turn me off?" Charlie teased.

Rick laughed. He leaned back in the chair and waited until Candy brought him coffee. Then he reached over and gave her a gentle pat on the ass.

"Hey! Save that for Fran!" she yelped.

"Save what for me?" Fran walked into the room like a spring breeze – smelling good and looking better. She had changed into light green pants and a matching cropped top. Her wet hair was pulled back with a couple of clips, and she skipped the cologne that Rick didn't like.

"Your boyfriend can't keep his hands off my ass," Candy stated.

"He's in one of those moods," Fran snickered.

"Caught me," Rick admitted.

Fran walked over to him, cupped his chin, tipped his head back, and gave him a long, slow, wet kiss until Charlie let out a whistle. "Do I have to get jealous around you?" Fran asked when she finally let Rick go.

"Damn, woman, you'd better." He stared at her until his concentration was broken by his phone ringing.

"Is that mine?" Candy asked, looking around.

"Mine." Rick pulled the cell phone from his pocket. "Hello?" He dropped his hand and let Fran slip away. He listened for a minute and then whispered to Fran, "It's Sheriff Hodge."

She nodded and poured some coffee.

"Yeah, I think you're right. We should meet," Rick told Hodge. "About an hour? Make it two. We're just getting going here." He watched Fran as Hodge continued to speak. "Fine, I'll meet you there." Rick hung up.

"Meet him where?" Fran asked.

"At the office building to talk about the explosion." Rick watched her face for any reaction.

Fran bit her lip and slid into the chair next to him. "I guess I'd better find some new offices."

"Well, you were considering a change," Candy noted. "When the opportunity knocks –"

Fran's hands shook as she lowered the coffee cup to the table. She jumped when the doorbell rang.

"I'll get that," said Charlie, pushing his massive body out of the kitchen chair.

"Breakfast?" Candy asked Rick and Fran. "I've got ham and eggs for the meat-eaters and oatmeal and yogurt for us civilized folks."

"Oatmeal sounds wonderful," Fran said. "I haven't had that since – "

"Hey, Rick, get over here," Charlie interrupted from the front doorway.

"Yeah? What is it?" Rick was unwilling to pry himself from his chair.

Sweetbriar roses – a large handful of them, cut and displayed in a clear crystal vase – had arrived at Fran's home via a floral delivery truck. No one outside of the residents of that house would have thought twice about it. But considering Rick had received a potted rose plant with a note threatening his life and, considering the second potted rose plant had blown a large hole in Fran's office building, Charlie was having none of it. He wasn't even aware of the sweetbriars left on the bodies of three of Candy's friends.

"Where did those come from?" he asked the delivery girl.

She was maybe twenty and very petite, dwarfed by Charlie's size and width, and clearly intimidated by the gun holstered at his hip.

"Ah, er. I –" She stammered, "I don't know." She stretched out her arms to offer up the roses and stepped back in shock when Charlie immediately turned the vase upside down and dumped the flowers across the lawn.

He examined the vase carefully until he was convinced it wasn't concealing anything dangerous. He even sniffed at the water but was hesitant to touch it. Still, what wouldn't kill a dozen roses would likely not kill a man his size. He scratched his thick red beard and called into the house. "Rick! Get your goddamn lazy ass out here!"

Rick ignored the cane and limped out of the kitchen. When he showed up at the front door – shirtless, tattooed and with a black patch over his injured eye and his left arm in a sling – the delivery girl looked as if she was seriously considering another job.

Charlie handed Rick the vase and pointed to the roses on the ground. "We had a delivery." He spat some of his chew.

Rick hefted the vase a few times, scowled, and looked at the girl. "What's your name?"

"Marie."

"Well, Marie, you heard the man. Where'd they come from?" Rick asked sternly.

The girl, trembling, pointed back at her paneled van with the florist's name and number on the side.

Rick almost grinned. He was enjoying her discomfort, but he was also relieved that the roses weren't trying to kill him this time. "Who sent them?"

The girl shrugged. "There was a card." She bent over, fished it out of the wet dirt, wiped it off on her slacks, and handed it to Rick.

He handed the vase back to Charlie, took the card, and studied it a moment, front and back. All it said was, "For Mistress Candace."

Rick sighed. He reached into the pocket of his jeans and the girl jumped back a bit, not knowing what to expect. With a smirk, he handed her a tip. "Tell your boss, no more rose deliveries here for a while. Got it?"

"Yes, sir!" She spun around, jumped into her van, and headed down the street.

"Poor kid. We scared the shit outta her," Charlie said, one hand resting lightly on the grip of his gun.

"Really? You feel sorry for her?"

"Sure. Well, don't you?"

"Then why the silly grin on your face?" Rick teased as he picked up some of the roses and headed into the house.

Candy took one look at the flowers in Rick's hand and fell back against the kitchen counter. "Get them out of here!" she screamed.

Rick stopped. He glanced at Fran for an explanation, but she had already jumped up, seized the flowers, and thrown them outside.

"Fill me in," Rick said as he and Charlie stared at the women.

"That's a sweetbriar rose," Fran said. "Candy's girls – the killer – he left them on the bodies. Six for the first victim, five for the second, four for the third."

"Allyson," Candy muttered as she fought to catch her breath. "It's got to be Allyson. Who else would know I'm here? Who else would send those, of all flowers?"

"You don't know that it's him," Fran said. "If he's innocent, it was a damn stupid move. He's the assistant D.A. He knows about the murders. He knows about the flowers. What do you think? He'd do this as some kind of sick joke?"

"What happened?" Alex made his way into the kitchen. "Are you alright?" he asked Candy.

"Someone sent a vase of flowers – sweetbriar roses. The same –" Fran started to explain.

"Shit," Alex muttered. He took Candy's hand. "It could be Jax trying to scare you. I told you he'd pull something like this. He finds a weakness and he plays on it."

"Jax Saynte?" Fran asked. "What the hell? What does he have to do with any of this?"

"What the fuck are you talking about?" Rick demanded to know.

Candy nodded at Alex. "We were talking about Jax Saynte last night," she told Rick. "Alex thinks – well, speculates – oh, hell." She took a deep breath. "I told him to talk to you."

"Oh?" Rick asked.

"You were busy," Alex said in his own defense.

"Well, I ain't busy now, so talk."

Alex cleared his throat. "I think the bomb came from Jax Saynte. I think he's trying to rattle Fran by hurting you. The card – the rose bush – was for you. If you're out of the picture, if you're dead, Fran is vulnerable."

"Okay. I follow that," Rick said. "But what does that have to do with this?" He nodded toward Candy.

"I told her that Jax might try and take advantage of the serial killings to spook her. It's the kind of thing he would do – send her flowers like the kind used by the killer."

"You're nuts," Rick said. "Why would he do that? What's she got to do with anything?"

Alex started to speak and then stopped. The flowers weren't a warning meant for Candy, and he knew it. They were meant for him. Jax was reminding Alex that Candy's life was in his hands. "It's just the way he thinks."

"My money is on the actual serial killer," said Fran. "He's trying to spook Candy. He gets his jollies off of it. I'm sure."

Rick nodded. "That makes more sense." He looked at Candy. "And this Allyson Stone character? You think he's killing your girls?"

"No," Candy said.

"Maybe," Fran said.

"Whoever it is, he's letting Candy know that she's vulnerable, even here." Fran put her arms around Candy and held her.

Alex shook his head but didn't add anything.

"Don't worry, sweetie," said Charlie. "We got your back. You ain't never gonna be alone."

"Tom never came back last night," Candy noted. She almost said he never came home, but she caught herself. "I hope he's alright."

"We need to tell him what happened," Margo suggested. "He can trace the flowers."

"He probably went home to shower and fell asleep," Fran offered. "It was a rough day."

"For all of us," Candy added.

"Tomorrow is going to be rougher," Rick said.

"The board meeting. Yes. It's going to be hell." Fran sat at the table and rested a hand on Rick's arm as if she was about to apologize in advance for something. "I want to take Alex with me to the meeting. He understands all this corporate stuff better than I do and –" She hesitated a moment when Rick looked up at her like he wasn't completely buying it.

"And I don't fit the corporate model?" he asked with a slight grin.

She gently pressed her fingers to the bandages on his face.

"You don't, and you know you don't." Fran grinned back and ran her fingers over the stubble on his chin. "But more importantly, I want to save you. I want just the right moment to introduce you to Saynte. I want you to blow his damn socks off."

"You're always thinking, boss." Rick relaxed, took her hand, and kissed it. "Okay, you keep this old junkyard dog in the background 'til you're ready, but I expect a bite outta this guy. Got it?"

Fran smiled warmly at him. "Always."

"In the meantime –" Rick began.

"In the meantime, you guys have your hands full taking care of Candy," said Fran. She pulled out a chair for Alex and patted it. "Sit."

Rick grinned into his coffee and said nothing as Alex sat down. Alex was wearing a pair of creased, new jeans and a fresh shirt. Even dressed casually, Alex looked like he was posing for a magazine spread.

"Rick said Tom got the files from the office. They're in the garage. Can you sort them out for the meeting tomorrow? I'll need a summary and talking points." Fran leaned forward, one hand still on Rick's arm, as she spoke to Alex.

"Sure thing. I need a place to set up."

"There's a long, folding table in the garage, and we can always get another one if we need it. I'm sure Charlie can give you a hand. There's also an AC unit in there. I'm not sure how well it works, but it's worth a shot."

"If we're gonna do that, we'd best get started," Charlie said. "I need to get back to the store for a bit." He looked at Candy. "If you wanna come with me, sweets."

"A little later. I want to get my car. I feel stranded here, relying on everyone all the time."

Rick nodded. "We'll be by later," he told Charlie.

"We will?" Fran asked.

"Yes, darling. We will," Rick said with a wink.

***

The morning sky was cloudy, and a long, black veil of rain could be seen on the horizon just beyond the city. Rick stood on the front step of Fran's house and finished his coffee as he watched the sky. The door shut behind him and Fran joined him. She slipped a warm arm around his bare waist and rested her head on his chest.

"We're going to get hit again," she said.

"You certainly gathered a motley band of fellow travelers around you," he commented as he wrapped his strong arm around her shoulders and held her.

"You disapprove of my friends?" Fran had to admit, between Candy with her sex toys, Margo with her purple – or was it green today? – hair, Alex with his stiffly ironed demeanor, and mountain man Charlie, they were quite the bunch.

"Oh, maybe just one or two of them."

"Gotta go, guys." Charlie walked past them, a slice of toast hanging from his teeth as he fished for his keys. "Gotta business to run."

"I need to get some shooting in," Rick said. "We'll come by a little later to use the range."

Charlie nodded and climbed into his beat-up truck. His engine turned over on the third try, and he pulled away from the curb with a wave.

"I like him," Fran said.

Rick gave her a quizzical look. "Do I need to be jealous?"

Fran laughed. "I wish to hell you were, but you know better." She kissed him on the nose.

Candy was the next to emerge. "Are you guys taking off?" she asked. The little red ladybugs on her white dress seemed to dance as a breeze suddenly blew in.

"Front coming." Rick looked back at the sky. "We're gonna get hit again."

"I just said that," Fran teased.

"I want to get my car. Can you take me by the apartment?" Candy watched the rain move over the city.

Rick nodded.

"I better get a sweater." Fran turned toward Rick and drew a line down his chest. "And you, my sexy lover, had better put on a shirt, as much as I hate to have you cover this up."

"Sure thing, boss."

A few minutes later, dressed and ready to go, they got into Fran's car.

Margo ran out to the car a moment to talk to Fran, her hair blowing wildly in the wind. "I'll have the office calls transferred here for now." She yelled to be heard above the encroaching storm.

"Do whatever you need to do. Let's get these cases wrapped up."

Margo dashed back into the house.

"Speaking of getting things wrapped up," Rick said, as Fran pulled away from the driveway, "I gotta check on my wheels. I only had liability on that thing. I need to shop around for a truck or Jeep or something."

Fran was driving. One hand brushed up against Rick's thigh as she shifted gears. These days, it seemed she always wanted to be touching him somehow, even in the slightest of ways.

"I could buy you a car today if you want," she said.

Rick chuckled. "That you could, darling. But I do have my own resources, you know."

Fran wasn't going to argue with him. She wondered if it bothered him, the way it bothered Tom, that she was the one with the deep pockets.

Candy sat in the backseat and watched the rain as it turned from a sprinkle to a drizzle to bullets of water against the windshield. She bit her fingernail. She didn't know what she'd find at her apartment. More roses? A killer? A dead body? The police had been there. The place was sealed up. She didn't know how long it would be before she could paint over the hateful graffiti or move into her own home. Maybe never, she thought. Maybe it was time to find a new home, a more permanent one.

"I've been thinking about Arizona," she said out of the blue.

"Arizona?" Fran glanced at Candy through the rearview mirror.

"I know someone with an intentional community there. I would have a safe place to live. I'd be able to practice my lifestyle openly. It would be a nice change. They even like cats."

"Have you talked to Tom about it?" Fran asked.

"Yeah. He's not too keen on the idea," Candy said with a grin. "I think he'd miss me."

As they turned down the street to Candy's apartment, the rain turned into hail.

"Shit!" Rick yelled. "Anyone check the forecast this morning?" He ushered the women out of the car and toward the apartment building as bean-sized balls of ice pelted the car and dented the hood. The three of them crowded under the overhang. Candy slipped the key into the main entry door.

Before she could unlock it, an older woman opened the door for them and ushered them into the building.

"Get in here!" the woman ordered. "What in the world are you doing out in that weather?"

"Sorry, Mrs. B." Candy bent over and shook the hail out of her hair. "I just need to get my car keys from the apartment and pick up a few things."

The neighbor lady nodded.

Fran pulled chunks of ice out of the collar of her shirt. Rick brushed her long hair forward over her shoulders and removed more ice, then shook out the hair with his hand. The bits of hail clattered to the floor.

"That was nasty," Fran said. "I didn't hear anything about a tornado warning."

They heard the hail pound against the walls and windows.

Rick pulled out his phone and called Alex. "You getting it?" he asked, without explanation. He nodded silently to Alex's reply. "Well, batten down and stay away from the windows. We'll be back when we can." He then called

Hodge. "Canceling our meeting, sheriff." Rick was quiet for a moment. "Okay. Just call me when you do."

"Shall we go up?" Candy asked. She didn't want to go up. She didn't want to face the vandalism or the words written in paint. She didn't want to come face to face with her nightmare.

"Oh, that nice young man from the police is up there," the neighbor woman said with a smile.

"Tom?" Fran asked in surprise.

The woman shook her head. "No, that's not his name."

"What does he look like?" Fran asked.

"Oh, well, let's see, he's got a nice suit on, and a bit of a receding hairline. Sweet smile."

"Allyson," Candy spat. "That son-of-a-bitch."

The neighbor looked surprised. "Miss Candy, I –" she started to say.

"Sorry, Mrs. B. He's an old boyfriend I can't seem to get rid of," Candy explained.

"Oh. I didn't know. I mean, he showed me his badge," the woman stammered.

"The badge is legit," Rick cut in. "He's with the D.A.'s office. I'll take care of it."

Rick took Candy's arm and guided her up the stairs as Fran and the neighbor trailed behind. When they arrived at the door, they found the police tape cut and the door unlocked and ajar. Rick reached behind him and pulled his

.45 out of his back holster. He nodded to the women to step back, and then he quietly pushed the door open.

The hail worsened and the spray-painted window shattered in Candy's apartment.

Standing in the middle of the trashed room was Allyson Stone.

"What the hell!" Allyson yelled on seeing the .45. "Brandt, you put that damn thing down now or I'm having you arrested!"

"What the fuck are you doing here?" Candy charged ahead of Rick and pounded on Allyson.

"Investigating, you little –" He caught himself.

"You're damn lucky the neighbor warned us you were up here." Rick dropped the gun to his side but didn't holster it.

Candy swung wildly at Allyson.

Her neighbor yelled, "Miss Candy! Don't do that! You'll hurt him!"

Rick holstered his gun and grinned. "Not like he don't have it coming."

"I told you to leave me the fuck alone!" Candy screamed at Allyson, who blocked her blows with his arms. "You come here again, and I'll blow your fucking brains out!"

"Get this crazy bitch off of me!" Allyson yelled at Rick.

Rick didn't move, but Fran grabbed one of Candy's swinging arms and pulled her back. "Enough. He gets the point."

Candy stepped back. "Why the fuck did you send me those flowers?"

Allyson stared at her like she was going out of her mind. "What are you talking about?"

"The flowers, you idiot. The sweetbriars. I know they came from you. What were you thinking!"

"Look, I have no idea what the hell you're yelling about. If I'm going to send flowers to anyone, it'll be to someone I actually like," he yelled back.

"I told you to stay away from me!"

"We'll get a restraining order as soon as we get outta here," Fran promised Candy.

Candy was still yelling. "I swear to god, Allyson! You come near me one more time and I'll kill you!"

Allyson straightened out his jacket and scowled. "I'm doing my job."

"You got cops for this," Rick said. "If I was you, I'd take the woman's advice and get out. Now."

Allyson stomped past Candy and Fran and came nose to nose with Rick. "Be careful there, Brandt. You'll be damn lucky if I don't charge you with threatening an officer of the court!"

"You really want to take THIS…" Rick indicated Fran, Candy, and Allyson, "…into a court of law? Seriously? Because I'm game if you are."

Allyson marched past the neighbor woman and down the stairs.

"Get out and stay out!" Candy shouted after him.

Fran grabbed her friend and stopped her from chasing Allyson into the street. "That's enough. He's gone. It's over."

"Listen to your friend, Miss Candy," the neighbor said. "He's gone now. No need to go shooting anyone." She wrung her hands and hurried to her apartment.

Rick put his hand on Candy's shoulder to calm her down. "Look at me," he ordered.

Still trembling in fear and rage, she obliged. She stood petulant, arms crossed, prepared to bite him.

"I know you didn't mean that," he said quietly, "but you can't go around threatening to kill anyone, especially not him. Next time, I expect you to keep that thought in your head. Got it?"

Candy glowered at him. She wasn't accustomed to taking orders from a man, and she wasn't about to change that now, but she knew he was right. She nodded her understanding.

"Besides, if anyone is going to do any killing around here, it's going to be me," Rick smirked.

"Okay, okay!" Candy snapped. She grabbed her keys from the counter. "I'll meet you at the police station. One way or another, I'm getting that man off my ass."

Chapter 14

Thursday Afternoon

The hail had stopped when Tom entered the Yellow Hen Diner and took a seat at the counter.

"You're that detective guy, aren't you?" Missy Barber smiled and poured Tom a cup of steaming coffee.

The diner was still busy. The lunch crowd had delayed leaving until the storm was over. Outside, the wet parking lot glistened with beads of ice.

Missy was slim and tanned and, at a distance, could pass for 24, but when Tom looked closer, he saw the crinkles at her eyes and the taut skin. He wondered if she was merely older than she looked at first blush or whether she was younger but too much sun and too many cigarettes had left their mark. He didn't ask her age, of course.

"Yes, ma'am. I am. I was hoping to catch you. Have you got a few minutes?"

The waitress looked around and caught the attention of another employee. Missy spread her fingers to indicate she needed five minutes and Tom noticed she wasn't wearing a wedding band. He put some cash down for the coffee and poured milk into it, then followed her through the noisy kitchen thick with its heavy scent of frying onions and the loud sizzling of burgers, fries, and today's blue plate special. A black metal door led to the delivery entrance and swung shut behind them.

"Mostly, I'm following up. There are some questions I have that, well, didn't occur to me until I met with some witnesses the other day." Tom scratched the back of his neck, feeling unexpectedly uneasy.

"Like what?" Missy leaned against the back of the building and lit a cigarette while she listened. She was wearing a little pink skirt and blouse covered by a red and white checkered apron. A red motif of a steaming cup of coffee adorned the bib. Long, slender legs ended in white oxfords with rubber soles.

"Well, for one, did you know Candy was into BDSM?"

Missy's eyebrows went up in mock surprise. "She is? I didn't know that." She winked and blushed a little, hinting at the lie. The way Missy looked Tom over reminded him of Candy's interest in a pair of chaps.

"Did you ever talk about her to the minister? He said you went to his church."

"Hell no. I don't go to that guy's church. I mean, I think I went there once, maybe twice, with a friend of mine. But I ain't much for church-going and, honestly, I wouldn't want to go to any church where he'd be anyway."

"You don't like him?"

"He gives me the creeps," Missy said.

Funny, me too, thought Tom. "Do you know if he knew Andrea or knows Candy?"

The waitress nodded and took a long draw on her cigarette. She tucked a stray strand of hair behind one ear and shooed away a fly that was buzzing around the battered blue trash bin. The area next to the bin was still cordoned off with yellow police tape. Tom could picture the body of Andrea Ortiz lying in the dirt. He looked away from the spot and took a deep, cleansing breath.

"Yeah, he knows Candy. Not sure about Andrea," Missy said.

"So, he talks to Candy then?" Tom felt like he was dragging every ounce of information out of her, and it occurred to him that she might be stalling to avoid going back to work.

"Talk? Nah. He never talks to her. But I know he knows her." Missy stepped away from the wall and leaned toward Tom. Her smoke rose between them as she gazed into his eyes.

Tom stepped back a little. He sighed and took a drink of his coffee. He made a face. He was still adjusting to going sugarless. "How do you know?"

Missy frowned and brushed some ashes from the bib of her apron. Her movement drew attention to her pert breasts. "He asked me once if that's who that was. You know, is that so and so? And I said yes, and after that, he just kinda looked at her funny, you know? Like he was trying to decide if he was gonna condemn her to hell or save her soul." She laughed.

"Does Candy know him?" Tom grew more curious.

Missy shrugged. "I don't think so. I told her he asked about her once, but she just blew it off. I think her head was someplace else."

"So, she wouldn't know the minister, then."

"Hell, I didn't know he was a minister, not for a long time. He never shows up in them funny collars or anything. He's usually got jeans on or something like that. Then I heard him talking to that lady friend of his – the one who comes in with him."

"Melissa Pearson?"

"Yeah, that one. The old lady. Anyways, they were talking about something going on at the church, and I kinda put two and two together, you know?" Missy dropped her cigarette butt to the ground and stomped out the tip of it with her shoe. "I didn't ask after that 'cause I don't wanna get dragged into any religious stuff." She stepped forward and ran a finger down Tom's arm. "I have my own kind of religion if you know what I mean."

"Do you know if the Pearsons recognized Candy?" Tom asked as he tried to ignore her touch.

"Yeah, I think so. I think that's why the preacher asked about her. They said something to him."

"And that didn't concern you?" Tom looked at her quizzically.

Missy shrugged. "It's Mistress Candy." She winked again as if sharing a big secret. "Everybody knows who and what she is, you know?" She leaned in and whispered. "Do you like Candy? Are you into whips?"

Tom cleared his throat. "Yes, I know her." It had never occurred to him before that Candy was something of a local celebrity. "Whips aren't my thing."

"What is your thing?"

Tom handed Missy the empty coffee cup and said goodbye. One more itch scratched, he thought to himself – investigative itch, that is. He was forced to ignore the other kind of itch, but it was hard to get the image of Candy and her whip off his mind.

The Reverend Lawrence Blackwell had lied to him, or at least didn't fully tell the truth. Maybe it all meant nothing. Or maybe it all meant something. But right now, other than Allyson Stone, it was the only lead Tom Saddler had.

Rick, Fran, and Candy were at the police station when Tom arrived. He had the Ortiz file in one hand and his jacket thrown over his other arm.

As much as he wanted to deny it, Tom felt his heart skip on seeing Fran. She turned to look at him. Her eyes flashed an angry blue as if she was bent on some mission from hell. Her red hair swirled around her shoulders. He wasn't in denial anymore. He'd lost her and it hurt. But at least it was over, he kept telling himself. No use dragging out the pain. He glanced at Rick who at least appeared not to notice Tom's discomfort.

And then there was Candy, and the itch got stronger.

"Something I should know about?" Tom asked as he walked through the door and saw them gathered in the lobby.

"I'm getting a restraining order against Allyson," Candy said. She was pacing the floor, a tight scowl on her face, her arms crossed.

"What happened?" Tom asked.

"Where do I begin?"

"He sent flowers," said Fran.

"We don't know it was him, and he denied it," Rick interjected.

"Alex thinks Jax sent the flowers," Candy reminded them.

"Bullshit," said Rick.

"What kind of flowers?" Tom asked.

"Sweetbriars," Candy said. "A vase of them, to Fran's house."

Rick, his hands buried in his pockets, spoke again. "We went to Candy's place to get her car, but the hail was comin' down hard, so we went inside and found Allyson Stone in her living room. He said he was investigating the break-in, but –" He got cut off by Fran.

"I told that little piece of shit to stay away from Candy, her home, or her work. He's got selective hearing and a damn selective memory. I'm getting a restraining order and –"

"You know that's going to hurt his job, right?" Tom asked. "If he has an RFA order against him, he can't carry a gun.

But as a prosecutor, he's a law enforcement officer. Not that he ever carries a gun that I know of. But I can see where there'd be a problem."

"I really don't give a shit," Candy said. "I want him to stay the hell away from me, and I'll do anything to make that happen."

Rick gave her a warning look.

"Okay!" Candy yelled at Rick. "Anything LEGAL. Happy now?"

"Well, getting a judge to issue a restraining order against a prosecutor is going to take some doing," Tom said. "You're going to need a lot of evidence. And from what you're saying, you can't prove he sent the flowers."

"I got emails, texts, phone messages." Candy held up her cell phone. "I kept them all just in case."

"Can you look into the flowers?" Fran asked Tom.

He nodded.

A policewoman led the ladies away as Tom motioned for Rick to join him in a small conference room. Rick obliged. His limp was worse, and he grimaced in pain as he walked.

"What's up?" Rick lowered himself slowly into a chair and stretched out. His lower leg throbbed, but he was hesitant to take anything for it.

"I went back to the scene of the Ortiz murder and spoke to the waitress out there. She said Blackwell knows who and what Candy is, but the waitress doesn't know how he found out."

"Oh? And?" Rick sat up.

"When I questioned Blackwell, he denied knowing Candy, but he knew who she was because, get this, Paul Burns told him." Tom waited for a reaction.

"Burns? Fran's ex?" Rick frowned. "Shit. Is that –? Do you have a picture of him?"

"Yeah." Tom opened the file on the table and pulled out photos taken of the crime scene by the diner while the witnesses were present. "This guy," Tom said, tapping the photo of Blackwell.

"I know him," Rick said. "Not well, but we've met."

"When?"

"Back when Paul Burns flipped out on us and disappeared with that kid of his – Matthew? I was looking for Burns, trying to get him to turn himself in. I went to his church and talked to this guy. Blackwell, yeah. That's him. Reverend Lawrence Blackwell."

"Burns told Blackwell about Candy's – whatever you call them." There was that itch again.

Rick chuckled. "Yeah, whatever."

"I don't know when, but Blackwell made the connection recently when the Pearsons recognized her at the diner. That's when he found out that our Candy was Dr. Candace Knight of the crime lab."

Rick looked up at Tom. "You think he's got something to do with these murders?"

"Maybe. I don't know. I know I don't like him, but Candy hasn't had any run-ins with him, and I've got nothing to go on but a gut reaction."

Rick groaned as he leaned forward and adjusted his arm in its sling. "I was thinking of taking the girls outta town for a bit. Charlie's got an old farmhouse where they can stay. Nice place. I'm worried I can't protect them like this." He lifted his bad arm slightly, indicating the cast and his other injuries.

Tom nodded. "That's probably a good idea. What do they think about it?"

"I haven't talked it over with 'em, yet. Fran's got this big corporate meeting tomorrow. We'll see what happens then. In the meantime, Charlie is spelling me now and then so I can get some rest."

Tom leaned against the table and studied Rick. No matter how hard he tried, he couldn't dislike the man. "Okay. Just let me know when and where. I need to stay on top of things."

"You got it." Rick pulled himself to his feet and limped out of the room.

"You should have that looked at again – tonight," Tom told Rick.

Rick nodded dismissively.

***

"Tom's right. You should have the doctor look at that right away," Fran said as she watched Rick squirm uncomfortably in the car.

"You were eavesdropping," Rick said.

"Damn straight."

Candy had taken her car and was headed to Charlie's store, leaving Fran and Rick alone to squabble over his injuries.

"I just overdid it." Rick looked out the passenger window of the car to prevent Fran from seeing the pain in his face.

"Rest, ice, compression, elevation." Fran repeated what the doctor had said. "You haven't even been using crutches. What's wrong with you?"

Rick scowled at her.

Fran pulled the car over to the side of the road and threw it into park. Both hands gripped the steering wheel. Tears burned in her eyes, and she didn't dare look at him. She hated making Rick mad, not because she was afraid of him. It never occurred to her that he could hurt her – at least not that way. She was more afraid that one day she'd go too far, say the wrong thing, piss him off, and drive him out of her life.

"I – love – you," she said slowly and deliberately. She finally turned to look at him and saw him staring back at her. "You think I can't tell when you're suffering? You think I don't know when you push too hard? When you care too much? When it hurts like hell? I can read every blink of your eye, every twitch of your muscles, every curve of your lips. I can tell, Rick. I know. And all your macho bullshit and all your sacrificing for my sake – for OUR sakes – doesn't change that. I know you're hurting. And when you hurt, I hurt." Fran's lower lip trembled, and she tore her eyes away from him as she waited for the backlash.

Rick sat silently for a few minutes. He kept staring at her as if there were things he had to say but he couldn't find the words to say them. Finally, he reached out, rested his hand on hers, pried her fingers away from the steering wheel, and pulled her hand down to his lap. "I know."

She wiped the tears away as the traffic sped past them. "I'm not trying to make things harder for you."

"You're not. Hell, you are, but not like that," he chuckled.

"When something happens to you –" she began.

Rick interrupted her. "You're right."

"I'm right?" Fran looked surprised.

"Yeah, you're right. I ain't used to –" He stopped and thought a minute before continuing. "I ain't used to having someone give a shit," he finally said. He forced a smile.

Fran relaxed. "I don't want to piss you off. I know what you are – how you are. I'm not trying to change you. But, damn it, Rick, you nearly died in that car crash. You're still hurting. You have got to take care of yourself. I don't want to lose you."

"I ain't going anywhere, baby. And don't worry about pissing me off, either. Now, I catch you drinking again, or you decide to run off with some jackass or put yourself in danger, THEN I'll be pissed. Got it?"

Fran nodded and smiled.

Rick leaned over and kissed her firmly on the lips. "Okay. You want me to see a doctor? Let's see a doctor and get this shit over with."

Warmth spread through Fran's body as she put the car into gear and pulled back into traffic.

***

The leg ached with a throbbing, deep, burning sensation that got worse with every step. Rick felt the pain seep up the muscle and into the knee, weakening it. He leaned against the wall as he limped into the emergency room. Fran, watching him carefully, grabbed his arm and helped lower him into a chair in front of the receptionist.

"What can I do for you today?" the woman asked.

"I was in a car crash. They treated me here Monday. I got a problem." Rick looked down at the battered leg and saw a soft red patch forming on his pants. "Shit," he muttered. He felt dizzy.

"It's a hematoma," Fran cut in. "It's gotten a lot worse. He can't stand up."

"On a scale of one to ten," the receptionist started to ask.

"Fifteen," Fran said.

"Eight," Rick said. He clawed the arms of the chair and tried to shift his weight as the pain spread up to his thigh. "Okay, ten," he admitted.

The receptionist called for a triage medic from the ER and took the rest of his information as Rick tried to stop his head from swimming. He could feel the trickle of blood oozing down his leg and foot. Within minutes, the medic was wheeling him into an examining room.

"Can you get onto the table?" the medic asked, raising his voice.

"Jeez. He's not deaf," Fran snapped. She tried to offer Rick an arm to help him, but he shrugged her off.

"No offense, sweetheart, but I'm gonna need more help than you got to give." He looked at her with a weak smile.

It was then she saw the blood. "Shit." She turned to the medic.

His eyes followed hers and he immediately called for help. A couple of minutes later, Rick was on the table and divested of socks, shoes, and slacks. A warm, white blanket was thrown over his lap, mostly for modesty's sake, but he felt chilled and pulled it up his chest. Waterproof pads were slid under the leg as blood soaked through the bandage. A tourniquet squeezed his upper leg.

"Fuck!" Rick yelled through clenched teeth.

"What happened?" Dr. Kaul asked as he walked through the door. He was dressed in greens and a face mask hung around his neck like a bandana.

"It was aching like hell and now this." Rick shivered from the cold and pointed to the bloody mess.

"Damn, I hate tough guys," said Kaul. "You've been walking on it, haven't you, Sergeant? After I told you not to? What the hell's the matter with you? What's your blood type?"

"AB Negative," Rick told him.

"Nurse! I need blood in here, and a drip, and –" He looked at Rick. "Can you handle Dilaudid?"

Rick nodded and grimaced.

Dr. Kaul pressed his fists to the table and leaned over Rick to make sure he had his full attention. "Look, I'm going to start you on Dilaudid, but until it takes hold, this is going to hurt like hell. The hematoma has ruptured and you're hemorrhaging. The tourniquet will slow it down, but I've got to stop it. Then I've got to pack it and wrap it back up. With any luck, there won't be any infection. If there is, we're talking a wound pump and six months on your ass, unless you don't care about saving that leg."

With anyone else, the doctor's tone would have seemed harsh, but Fran knew it was just the tone that Rick needed. It was the voice of a medic used to operating on a battlefield, and that was something Rick understood.

Rick nodded. "Go for it, Sam."

The doctor had a wound cart wheeled in and began to remove the existing bandages by cutting them away with snub-nosed scissors. As the bandages peeled back, deep red blood flowed over the table and pooled in the pads beneath his leg.

"Fuck!" Rick's fingers dug into the thin mattress beneath him.

Fran waited by his side, one hand gently on his shoulder. "Do you remember that little adventure you had in Panama with Charlie?" she asked, trying to distract him.

Rick grunted. He heard her over the pain. He knew what she was doing. He just wanted the drugs to kick in. As Kaul sliced away the last of the bandages, Rick felt as if he was being hacked open with the burning hot blade of a machete. "Yeah, I remember. It hurt like hell then, too."

"Look at me, sweetheart," she said softly. "We can get through this."

"Speak for yourself, woman," Rick snapped. He grit his teeth as the pain burned deeper, but he turned to look at her. He saw the deep worry in her blue eyes. "I'll be fine, babe, but I swear to god, if you say anything like 'I told you so,' I'm gonna whip your ass 'til you can't walk."

Fran smiled. "Candy giving you lessons, again?"

Rick tried to smile but couldn't. He put his head back and closed his eye as the room began to spin around him. The burning sensation subsided a little and his grip loosened on the mattress. A few minutes later, he was out cold.

***

Candy sighed with relief as she unlocked the door to Fran's house and stepped in. She had planned on going straight to Charlie's place, but she wanted to pick up her gun first. She dragged the gun case out from under her bed and headed for the front door, but when she opened the door to leave, Allyson Stone stood in her way.

"Oh my God! What the hell are you doing here? Get out!" Candy screamed.

She tried to hit Allyson in the head with the gun case, but he snatched it from her and tossed it aside.

"What's wrong with you, Candy?" Allyson pushed his way inside. "I'm trying to protect you! Don't you see that? Or do you want to end up like your girlfriends?"

"Get away from me, you psychopath!" Candy tried to push him back out the door.

He hit her hard across the face with an open hand, and she went reeling into the wall behind her. She came out punching. Allyson grabbed her hands and pinned them over her head as he pressed her into the wall.

"You think I don't know what you're doing? You can strut around in the leather and whip outfit all you want, but what you need is a real man to protect you and take care of you and teach you how to be a real woman."

He kissed her hard on the lips. She screamed and kicked him in the groin with her knee.

His grip loosened just as two strong hands grabbed him from behind and tore him away from Candy. Alex yanked Allyson back onto the porch and threw him down the stairs. Allyson staggered to his feet with fire in his eyes.

"You're done, De la Rosa! This is the last straw. You're going straight back to jail to rot!"

"Fuck you! Get out of here! Now! You bastard!" Candy screamed at Allyson as she ran up to Alex and clung to him. She was trembling.

Allyson stomped to his car, got in, and drove off.

Alex relaxed and asked, "Are you alright?"

"What are you doing here?" Candy asked.

"I'm working on the papers in the garage. I heard you screaming." He held her tightly.

"Oh my god." Candy pressed her head into Alex's chest. "What is wrong with that bastard? Why the hell won't he leave me alone?"

"It's okay, Mistress. He's gone," Alex assured her. "You aren't supposed to be alone, remember? Someone should be with you."

Candy nodded. "Thanks. I was just going to get my gun and head to Charlie's for some target practice."

"Tough lady with a gun, huh? What, a whip wasn't enough?" He kissed her on the forehead. "You need to tell Tom what happened."

"I will. I just want to get out of here first."

"You call him, or I will."

"Okay, okay. I'll call," she said.

"And call me when you get to Charlie's, so I know you're safe." He kissed her gently on the lips.

She gave him another hug before heading into the house. She pulled her phone out of her purse and dialed

Tom's number. When she got his voicemail, she left a message.

"Allyson attacked me at Fran's. Alex showed up and took out the garbage. I'm okay. I'm headed to Charlie's. Call me, please." She hung up, rescued her gun case, and headed out.

Allyson tried calling Candy as she drove to Charlie's store. She let the calls go to voicemail the first three times, then she shut off her phone. She was so shaken that she could barely drive. She didn't want to think about him or about what happened. She kept looking in her rearview mirror and wondering if she was safe.

***

Rick woke up in a regular hospital room with his left leg heavily bandaged and a compression pump on the right one. "Fuck, what now?" Rick muttered as he looked around.

The room was quiet except for the monitors hooked to him. The curtains were drawn against a bright afternoon sun. Fran's purse and a blanket were tossed into a chair that sat in the corner of the room. Her shoes were tucked under the chair, but she was nowhere to be seen.

Rick closed his eye and felt a twinge of panic. He didn't have his gun with him. No one here knew about the death threats or the bombing. Fran could be anywhere.

He barely processed those thoughts when Fran and Tom walked into the room. Rick heard their steps and opened his eye. He felt relief wash over him, but he was determined not to let it show.

"I wondered where you'd gotten your ass off to," he said with a smirk.

Fran grinned and leaned over the bedrail at him. "Well, you're just no fun when you're unconscious. Feel any better?"

Rick nodded. "Yeah, some." He turned his attention to Fran's old boyfriend. "What's up?"

"I can't find Candy," Tom said. "The last time I saw her was at the police station when you were there. I got a panicked message from her saying there was a problem with Allyson Stone. I tried calling back but there wasn't an answer. I finally went to your house – Fran's house. Alex said she was there, but Allyson showed up and there was some kind of fight. He thought she was headed to Charlie's, but she's not picking up her phone. Any ideas?"

Rick thought for a minute. "Yeah, she probably went to Charlie's. If they're using the range, she might not hear her phone. Did you check her apartment, too?"

"It's worth a shot," Fran said.

Tom nodded. "Okay, I'll head over to the apartment and then Charlie's and see if I can find her. In the meantime, if she shows up or calls you, I have to talk to her immediately."

Once he was gone, Rick reached up and took Fran's hand. "My piece?"

"I have it in my purse safe and sound." She lifted his hand to her lips and kissed it.

"I gotta get out of here." Rick glanced at the monitor and its smattering of cords, and he felt as if he was in a Dr. Who episode.

"You're not going to be able to walk on that leg for a while," Fran said.

"Then I'll use crutches, but I gotta get out of here."

There was a restless tension in Rick's eyes that worried Fran. "What is it? What are you thinking about?"

"I had a death threat and an explosion. Someone is trying to kill me – or us. I don't know who and I don't know why, but right now I'm a sitting duck."

Fran glanced at the door as some people walked by. Then she turned her attention back to Rick. "Shall I get someone in here? Charlie, maybe? Or Tom? Do you want to be moved to a different room? Tell me what to do, Rick."

"Charlie has some property not too far from here, about a forty-five-minute drive from the city. It's a ranch with an old farmhouse, and about a hundred or so acres and a small stream. I was thinking it would be a good place for you and Candy to be while I figure out what's going on."

Fran squeezed his hand. "You're in no shape to tackle this alone. I can help. Candy can help. Don't pack me up and send me away. I won't be able to handle it, especially if I have to be out in some no man's land worrying about you."

He wanted to argue with her. He wanted her to be safe. He also felt that no matter where she went, she was safer being close to him. But in his current condition, he wasn't up to waging much of a war.

"Besides," Fran added. "Tomorrow is the big day, remember? Corporate meeting? Max-Mil Enterprises? I can't miss that one."

Rick felt his chest tighten. "You're taking Alex, right?"

"Yup." Fran smiled. "Why? Are you jealous?"

Rick scowled at her. "That's enough of that outta you, woman." He grabbed her arm and pulled her into a kiss. "I may be in rough shape, but I can still kick his ass if I have to – and yours!"

Fran giggled. It was an unusual sensation for her. She wasn't accustomed to giggling, but something about Rick brought it out in her. His hand tightened on the back of her neck, and she realized he wasn't just kissing her. There was an urgency to it as if he expected their world to blow up any minute. She didn't feel like giggling anymore. Fran slowly pulled herself away from him and nodded.

"I'll be careful. Go ahead and call Charlie. I have to make this meeting, but anything else you decide, you know I'll do it," she said.

"Anything?" he asked with a wink. "You don't know just how twisted I can be, sweetheart."

"I have a feeling I'm going to find out." Fran was smiling as she left.

Chapter 15

"That son-of-a-bitch attacked me!" Candy shouted as Charlie tried to calm her down.

"It's okay, darling. You're safe here. Just take it easy and tell me what happened."

Candy paced the wooden floor in the store. "Stone. Allyson Stone. He pushed his way into Fran's house and hit me, then he kissed me and – Oh, God, I don't know what would have happened if Alex wasn't there!"

Charlie stopped her and held her chin in his hand. He turned her face toward the light. "Yup. He landed a good one. Your jaw will be sore a day or two, but you'll be okay." He could see the red, hand-shaped mark on her cheek. "Did you call the cops?"

"I tried calling Tom, but he didn't answer so I came here."

"Got your gun?" Charlie asked.

Candy nodded. "What the hell am I going to do, Charlie?"

"Well, I think you're gonna text that Tom fella and tell him where you are, and then you're gonna stay put and let Pete and me look out for you." Charlie nodded to his stockman.

Candy took a deep breath. A few minutes later, Charlie had her on the firing range behind the sporting goods store, working off her adrenalin until Tom arrived.

Tom leaned against the door frame and quietly observed her for a while, then he joined her. She was still a bit unsure of herself with the gun, but he could see her gaining confidence with each round. Candy was surprised when Tom took the position next to her and started firing. She smiled. Just seeing him made her feel safer.

"Allyson Stone is swearing out a warrant for Alex's arrest. Stone says Alex violated parole by beating him up," Tom said between rounds.

Candy lowered her gun and stared at him. "No way in hell! Did you get my message? Stone would have raped me if Alex wasn't there!"

"I talked to Hodge. He's going to see what he can do." Tom went another round and then looked over at her. "You want to file a complaint against Allyson?"

"Hell, yeah." Candy pointed and fired.

"You're making a dangerous enemy," Tom told her as he reloaded.

Candy's eyes flashed with fire. "As far as I'm concerned, Allyson is the one with the dangerous enemy – me!"

Charlie came up behind her and rested his large hands on her shoulders. "Take a break, sweetheart." He nodded at Tom.

Candy took a deep breath and felt herself relax. "What do I need to do?" she asked Tom. "Should I write out something here? Or do we need to go back to the station? How do you want to do this?"

"I just want to make sure you know what you're doing. You know he'll say you're lying. He'll dredge up your lifestyle. He'll say you were hitting on him. Hell, he'll say just about anything."

Candy frowned. "Well, I did apply for a restraining order against him this morning. That says something. And I got all his messages and emails to me, including my responses, which border on the 'go to hell' theme. Fran and Rick were at the apartment with me. They know how upset I was. And Alex pulled him off of me."

"And you got this." Charlie tipped her head so Tom could see the mark on her face.

"Ow," Candy said.

Tom pulled out his phone and moved her toward the light. "Let me get a photo of that. That's gotta hurt."

"I underestimated him. I didn't realize –" Candy had a lost look in her eyes. "He got worse and worse, and I ignored it. Then I got those damn flowers and – Hell, I don't know if he sent them. But if he didn't, who did?"

"Where did he touch you?" Tom asked.

Candy took a deep breath. "I was headed out the door, and he pushed his way in. He slammed me up against the wall and pinned my wrists over my head." She stopped and hugged herself. "Then he shoved his body into mine and started kissing me, hard. I kicked him in the balls. Not real hard, but enough to make him back up a bit. That's when Alex grabbed him and threw him out the door. He fell down the front stairs to the sidewalk. When he got up, he was swearing at Alex and threatening to send him to jail."

"Did you notice if he was aroused?"

"What are you after?" Candy asked.

Tom glanced down a moment, a bit uncomfortable. "Was it just a physical assault or was he trying to sexually assault you?"

"Other than kissing me, he didn't touch me that way," she admitted. "But I'm sure he got off on it."

Tom ran his fingers through Candy's hair and pulled her into a hug. "I'm going to take care of this. I promise." He kissed her lips, hesitated a second, and kissed her again, slower, taking his time. He savored the taste of her. Tom called the sheriff.

"Sadler here. Did Stone get that warrant against De la Rosa, yet?" He listened and nodded his head. "Yeah, that one." He waited. He smiled at Candy as he spoke. His fingers wove through her hair. "Can you block it? I'm with Candy now. Stone tried to rape her, and Alex stopped him. If we are going to arrest anyone, it should be Stone."

Tom listened for a while as he continued to hold Candy. She looked up at him. She wondered if Allyson was actually trying to rape her or if he was just trying to scare her. She didn't interrupt.

"Yes, we have enough evidence. Among other things, he hit her pretty hard," Tom was saying to Hodge. "We'll be in soon. I'm getting a statement from Candy, now. Thanks." Tom hung up the phone. "You know Allyson is going to lie about you."

"Of course. What are you thinking?"

"I just want you to keep that in mind when you're writing up your statement."

***

Candy never wanted to be in this position. She never wanted to be a victim. She never wanted to make accusations against a man for hurting her. She never wanted to stand on the other side of a one-way mirror in the police station and listen to some man lie about her.

She knew the routine. She worked forensics too long to not know it. Men like Allyson Stone would say anything. And when it came to Candy, there was a lot to say, and a lot of it was true.

It was true she went out with him – once. It was true she was a flirt. It was true she was in the BDSM lifestyle. There were even some, like Rev. Blackwell, who would say that Candy had it coming. If you're going to live in sin, you're going to pay the consequences.

Candy sat in the police department and shivered. She arrived on Tom's arm, and he put her in a small conference room to write out her statement. Now she picked up the paper and read it through for the fifth time. Was it enough?

She had applied for the restraining order. Witnesses heard her tell Allyson to stay the hell away from her. She had copies of his harassing messages. Alex made a statement about pulling Allyson off of her. She even had the handprint on her cheek where Allyson struck her. It should have been enough. But Tom was right, Allyson would lie, and Allyson was the assistant district attorney.

Candy took a deep breath and looked up as Tom walked into the room.

"You want to listen in on the interrogation?" he asked as he picked up her statement.

"I don't feel well," she admitted.

"I know. You'll be okay. It's just nerves. He can't get to you." Tom offered her his hand and pulled her up. "I'm not sure who will end up handling this case. Probably Detective Simmons. She's good at this sort of thing."

"Why not you?" Candy asked.

"I seem to have a conflict of interest." Tom kissed her uninjured cheek.

Allyson Stone faced off against Sheriff Hodge in the interrogation room while Tom and Candy watched from the other side of the glass. Stone was cocky and nervous at the same time. His tone was sarcastic and demanding, but he couldn't sit still, and he kept clasping and unclasping his hands.

"This is insane!" Allyson yelled. "You know that bitch would say anything to keep her pet out of jail!"

Hodge nodded calmly and eyed Stone like some curiosity. "That's one hell of a bruise she's got on her cheek. Mind telling me how she got it?" Hodge asked.

"How the hell should I know? Probably De la Rosa hit her to make it look good. Those two are –"

"I know exactly what those two are." Hodge leaned forward. He shoved some papers toward Allyson. "You know what these are?"

Allyson glanced at him and got quiet for a second. "Looks like text messages."

"From you," Hodge said. "Let's see what they say: 'What are you trying to do to me? Don't you dare ignore me! Why haven't you returned my calls? You think you're too good for me. You need me in your life.' Hmmmm. Interesting."

"Bullshit," Allyson said. "Anybody could have sent those to her."

"True, anybody could have, if all we had were the transcripts, but we have her phone, and your phone, and we can track those messages." Hodge leaned back. "You knew she was in here earlier to get a restraining order against you. Why in hell would you follow her to Fran's house?"

"I just wanted to talk to her," Allyson said. "The whole restraining order thing was a misunderstanding. Her apartment was a crime scene. I went there to check it out. She walked in and started hitting me. Put that in your damn report! She hit me! And then she threatened to blow my brains out. Her and what's his name."

"Alex?" Hodge asked.

"No, no, the other one," said Allyson. "You know – with the patch on his eye."

"Oh, Rick Brandt. Yeah, that makes sense. Let me get this straight: Candy screams at you, hits you, and threatens to kill you, then applies for a restraining order, and you call that a misunderstanding?"

"All I did was talk to her. I swear," he said.

Candy leaned toward Tom and said quietly, "I have an idea."

"Oh?"

"If he was that aroused attacking me, he probably had to jerk off before he came here, right?"

Tom raised an eyebrow. "I'm not sure where this is going, but I think you worked forensics too long."

"I bet he ejaculated on his clothing. You turn off the lights, spray a little Luminol –"

"I wonder if I need a warrant for that?" he asked.

"He's being investigated for sexual assault. Do you need a warrant to seize his clothing?" Candy asked.

Tom smiled and picked up his phone to call Hodge. "How long can we hold him?"

"Why?" Hodge asked.

"I'm getting a warrant for his clothing. It should prove interesting." Tom glanced at Candy and signaled her to be quiet.

"Go for it," Hodge said.

Tom hung up.

"You didn't tell him about the semen," Candy said.

"We'll surprise him. Besides, if we're wrong, we won't look like idiots. Any trace evidence of you on him will be suspicious."

She nodded and leaned against him. "He's not going to leave me alone, is he?"

"Right now, he's looking good for the murders."

Candy stiffened. "I need to know. How do we find out?"

"I'll add a few things to the warrant application. Once the judge knows Allyson's been stalking you, he'll let us search his place for photos or other evidence."

Candy took a deep breath. "I need to go home. I've seen enough."

***

Fran parked her car in her driveway and found one of the garage doors open. Alex's black Corvette was parked in one bay. In the other, two large, folding tables were erected and piled with boxes and papers. Alex had set up several fans on chairs near the garage entrance. They were turned to blow the warm air out. Alex, wearing blue jeans and a light blue shirt, was sitting at one of the tables. His sleeves were rolled up to his elbows. He was bent over his work. He didn't even look up when Fran's heels clicked on the concrete floor, the sound lost in the whirring of the fans.

"Hey," she said softly as she rested her hand on his shoulder.

Alex jumped, looked up, and smiled. "Damn, I thought you were Allyson coming back, or maybe the police."

"What happened?"

"Allyson showed up here and went after Candy. I threw him out, but he threatened to have me arrested. That was the last I heard," he told her.

"And you're still here?"

"You think running would help me any?"

"Is Candy alright? Where is she?"

"She went to Charlie's store," Alex said.

"And Allyson?"

Alex smiled. "I don't think he'll be back."

Fran tried to remember the last time she saw Alex smile. It had been months – long before he was arrested for trying to help his sister escape capture, long before Rick and Tom turned against him, long before Fran chewed him out for endangering her life. Another adventure ago, she thought. A long, long time ago.

"What's this?" Fran indicated a rectangular box on the table.

Alex shrugged. "A delivery man dropped it off. Said it was for you. It hasn't blown up yet, so I figure it's safe."

The joke was lost on Fran. She tapped the box thoughtfully and looked around. "The air conditioner idea didn't work?" she asked.

"Not good enough, Bella," he said, using his old nickname for her. "This isn't great, but it'll do for now. The meeting is tomorrow, right? We just need to get through this."

"Yes, and I need to find more office space." She removed her hand and pulled up a folding metal chair. It scraped along the concrete floor. "Where's Margo?"

"Running errands. We don't have notepads, pens, staples, a printer, or anything else," Alex explained.

The cell phone on the table rang and he picked it up. "Law office of Francesca Simone." He listened for a bit before continuing. "Can I get your number and have her get back to you? We're moving and the office is closed for a week or two, but I can have her call you." He nodded as he picked up a piece of scratch paper and jotted down a name and number. "Thanks for calling." He hung up and stuck the note on a spindle. "Do you really want to stop practicing law?" he asked Fran. "You're good at it, you know. You have a reputation in this town."

"I agree; I have a reputation. I'm not sure it has anything to do with practicing law, though." She smiled at him. "Was that for me?"

"I made that mistake once, and Margo made me pay for it. All messages go through HER first, then from her to you. That's how she knows what's going on."

"Probably a good idea." Fran picked up the spindle, read the note, and put it back down. "Do you miss being an attorney?"

"Yes. I knew what I was doing, then. I mean – with my life. Who I was." He ran his hand along the table as he remembered. "We had some good times, you and me.

Some tough times, but some good times." He chuckled. "Remember when you were so mad at me that you locked yourself in the gas station bathroom and wouldn't come out?"

Fran felt a tidal wave of emotion coming at her. Yes, she remembered. She harbored fantasies about him then. She looked down and blushed slightly. "Find anything interesting?"

"Nothing more than we discussed at our last meeting. You're going to have to question Jax Saynte about omitting the part where the plaintiff died." He scowled. "Be careful with him, Fran. He's up to no good."

A sharp breeze blew through the garage door and ruffled the papers a bit. She put her hand on a stack to keep it from blowing away and Alex did the same, his hand covering hers. They laughed and she pulled her hand away.

"I may be stating the obvious, but you own a real estate investment firm. Any chance there's a building in your inventory that we can move into?"

Fran looked up in surprise. "Damn. Why didn't I think of that? Of course, after tomorrow, I may no longer own the company. See if you can get an inventory of the properties today."

"I'll call," Alex said. "We don't have a fax yet."

"He can e-fax it."

"The board won't be able to accomplish anything tomorrow," Alex told her. "Pushing for those sixty days was a good idea on your part, and I'm sure they'll buy it. In the meantime, any luck finding out what's going on with the properties? Has Rick had a chance to look into it?" He averted his eyes as he asked the question and began sorting through the paperwork.

"He can't do everything," Fran said. "Maybe we should make a trip ourselves, tonight, before it gets dark."

Alex frowned. "What's going on? You two have a falling out?"

"You wish," Fran joked. "No. Rick's back in the hospital. He started hemorrhaging, and they had to work on his leg and bandage it back up. He should be home tomorrow, though."

"That's not good. What about the bombing?" He tapped his pen on the table. "It's too quiet. Something should have broken by now. Or Rick should have gotten more threats. I don't like it."

"Some people think your sister is behind it," Fran said quietly.

"By some people, you mean Rick," Alex snapped. "If you saw her, Bella, if you went there, you would know she can't do that. She's in no condition to plot against you or Rick. They have her heavily medicated, more often than not in isolation, and half the time she's on suicide watch. I'm the only one who's been to see her except Candy, and she only went once." He shook his head. A heavy sadness weighed on him. "She's dying, Bella. I go there and I watch her die, a little at a time, and it's all his fault."

"His fault? You mean Rick's fault?" Fran asked, surprised.

"I'm sorry. I didn't mean that the way it came out –" he started to say as he rubbed his eyes.

"It's not Rick's fault that Toni wanted me dead," Fran argued.

"That's not what I meant."

"Then what exactly did you mean?" Fran asked.

"If Rick had stayed with her in Mexico, if he stopped her from coming back, if he just did what he set out to do, none of this would have happened. He betrayed her and –"

"You saw what she did to Candy! You were there! Toni nearly strangled her to death!" Fran yelled. "She's insane, Alex. She kills people. If Rick had stayed in Mexico, if he'd kept her there –" Fran felt her heart suddenly seize up. "She simply would have killed him first."

Alex shook his head. "Well, she's not trying to kill you now."

"She wants me dead. The bomb came as a potted rose bush. What else could I think?"

"That someone is setting her up? That someone is using her as a distraction? That someone is taking advantage of what happened?" Alex grew more irritated. "We're not doing this."

"I didn't suggest that YOU were, but I need your help. If someone is using the roses to make us think Toni de la Rosa is behind this when she isn't, then you should want to find out who's doing it, too. Don't you? You almost died in that explosion. Your life is in danger just as much as mine or Rick's."

"She's not behind this," he stated again.

Fran sighed. "I haven't heard from Hodge about the bombing either, and if Tom knew anything, he would have said so. I'll give them a call in a few minutes. I don't like it. I worry about Rick in the hospital. He's still recovering from the car accident, and he's vulnerable right now. If someone is after him —"

"Of course, you're worried about Rick. In the meantime, Toni is dying, and no one gives a shit about her," Alex said bitterly.

Fran stared silently at him until he couldn't look at her anymore.

"And what about Candy?" Alex asked. "She's got Stone after her, and someone trying to kill her, and now she's caught in the middle of all this." He threw up his hands, indicating the files in front of him. "She almost died in that explosion, too. Why should she die because someone's trying to kill Rick?"

"Did you say she went to Charlie's?" Fran asked.

"Charlie Cook. Yes, that one. Now, he's a piece of work." Alex rolled his eyes.

"I like Charlie. He's salt of the earth. I trust him." She gave Alex a curious look. "Jealous?"

Alex avoided the question. "I'm sorry, Bella. I'm not trying to pick a fight. Toni's my sister. I'm worried about her. I just feel so damn helpless." He leaned back into his chair and looked at her. "I know Toni's not behind this. I know someone is targeting Rick. I know Stone is after Candy. And what am I doing? Shuffling through papers like a damn office clerk. I want you to know how much I appreciate this chance to be working again. I'd be sitting in jail today if it wasn't for you. I just – I just feel like I should be doing more."

"I know." She squeezed his arm. "This doesn't mean I'm done being pissed at you."

"Can I ask you a question?"

"Sure. I may not answer it, but you can ask."

"Why Rick?" Alex asked.

"Why Rick what?"

"Of all the men in all of Las Vegas, why are you with him? Why not with Tom? Or me? Or someone more –" He stopped. He was trying to determine how he wanted to phrase the question.

"You know why I'm not with you," she told him. "I'm not a dominatrix. I don't do BDSM. I'm not Candy, and I don't want to get tied up. That pretty much sums up my sex life."

"I know. That wasn't what I meant."

"Then what did you mean?"

"I just think you could do better. I could see you with someone – well – better educated, for one. Someone who speaks English correctly, who makes a good living and drives a nice car. Someone –" He sighed. "I like Rick. I always did. If it wasn't for this mess with Toni – but that's beside the point. He's a redneck. He comes from the wrong side of the tracks. His education was the streets. He sleeps with a loaded gun and, for all I know, eats his meat raw." Alex chuckled a bit. "At least that's what Margo says. The point I'm trying to make is that you and he are about as different as you can get. I don't understand it. Why Rick?"

Fran leaned forward and smiled. "Rick is exactly the man I need in my life. He knows me. He accepts me. He pushes me to be better. He doesn't put up with my bullshit, but he's always there to pick me up. He catches me when I fall. He tells me what he really thinks. He keeps my secrets. He saved my life. He's loyal to me. And when he kisses me, I swear Alex, the world stops. He makes me feel in ways I haven't felt before, right down to the marrow of my bones. Are those enough reasons for you?"

"Bella, you're a smart and beautiful woman, and a millionaire heiress. You could have anyone."

"I don't want anyone. I want him." Fran stood up and brushed some dust from her slacks. "And while we're talking about relationships, what's the story with you and Autumn?"

"She filed for divorce. It looks like I'm back in Vegas for good."

"You don't look particularly unhappy about it," Fran noted.

"Maybe I'm not," he admitted. "Hollywood was not a good place for me. I didn't fit in. Besides, I missed you."

"You mean you missed Candy. I'm going to fix myself something to eat. Do you want anything?" She picked up the box and tucked it under her arm.

"You're cooking? Should I be scared? Sure, anything you got is fine."

Fran turned and headed to the kitchen. A part of her was angry with Alex. How dare he question her relationship with Rick? Now, as she entered the house, she was also faced with remembering that someone was trying to kill the man she loved.

Fran put the box on the kitchen counter and opened it carefully, half expecting it to blow up in her face and at the same time knowing it wouldn't. When she finally slid open the top, she was holding a bottle of Bowmore 25-Year-Old Single Malt Scotch Whiskey. She had to smile. "What, couldn't go for the Camas an Staca, Jax?"

Fran realized she should dump it out. She thought about giving it to Alex, but both would be a waste of a $400 bottle of scotch. She took a deep breath and decided to put it away for a special occasion. Just because she couldn't drink it, didn't mean someone couldn't. Fran went to the sink, knelt down, opened the cupboard, and pulled out some cleaning supplies. She then slipped the scotch way in the back. Not the best place to store it, she thought, but at least it wouldn't be out in the open.

She licked her lips, put the cleaning supplies back, and called Charlie.

"Yeah, Tom was here. He took Candy to the police station. That D.A. guy attacked her," Charlie told Fran over the phone.

"Alex just told me. Rick is back in the hospital. The hematoma on his leg ruptured and started bleeding all over the place. They have him pieced back together, but he probably won't be out until tomorrow. I'm worried about him, Charlie. He's got his .45 but, still, this isn't good."

"I'll check on him. You see what's happening to Candy and let me know, okay?"

"Got it." Fran hung up the phone and was about to leave when she remembered she hadn't eaten or gotten anything for Alex. At the very least, she owed him lunch. She quickly warmed up some leftover lasagna and took it out to him.

"Thanks," Alex said as he sniffed at it. "Looks like Margo's cooking. Good job."

"Things just got interesting," Fran said as she leaned on the table. "Candy's at the police station with Tom. Charlie said something about them going after Allyson."

Alex sat back in his chair and stared at her. "Well, don't just stand there, Bella! Get going!"

Fran bolted from the garage and was quickly driving away. She picked up her phone and called Rick. "You'll never guess what just happened," she said.

Chapter 16

Late Thursday Afternoon

"What are you going to do?" Rick asked after Fran gave him the news about Candy. He was talking to her on the phone while a nurse checked his monitors. He tried to smile politely at the nurse, but he didn't want to be there. Everything about the situation made him restless. He felt the grip of his .45 pressed against his thigh under the covers.

"I'm going to head down there and find out what's going on." Fran talked to him as she drove, her eyes watching out for patrol cars. "I'm wondering –" Fran's voice drifted off as she got caught up in her thoughts.

"Don't leave me hanging, boss."

"I'm wondering if Allyson bugged Candy's apartment. That would explain why he was there. And we know he's been stalking her. He might even be behind the murders, for all we know."

"If it was bugged, it probably ain't now." Rick nodded at the nurse as she left.

"Maybe. It can't hurt to look."

"You are NOT going over there alone," Rick barked.

Fran's hand tightened on the steering wheel. "It won't take that long, and Allyson's still in custody, at least for now, and–"

"Hell, no, woman! We don't know who's behind all of this yet. I told you, you put yourself in danger and I'll be pissed!"

Fran slowly exhaled. Everything inside of her screamed for her to go to Candy's apartment and search it for bugs. It just made sense. She could do it without telling Rick. He didn't have to know.

"I can hear you thinking, and I don't like it," Rick said. "Either you go to the police and tell Tom what you think, or you come here. Right here, right now, where I can keep an eye on you."

Fran sighed. "I'll go to the police station. I just think —"

"Fran, don't do it. Don't take that chance. Don't end up dead."

Fran heard a heavy, plaintive sound in his voice. It wasn't like him to beg for anything, and she doubted he would call what he was doing now as begging. It was more like manipulating her, showing her his vulnerable side to get her to listen to him. All of this and more went through her head as she thought about her options.

"Okay," Fran finally said at last. "I won't go." She hung up without saying goodbye and drove to the police department.

Tom and Candy were both in the front lobby when Fran arrived. Candy stood with her arms crossed. She'd been crying and her eyes were red and puffy. Tom stood with his hands on his hips, listening to her. He was nodding his head. He looked worried. Fran walked to them. They both looked up at her as she approached.

"I just heard. What's happening?"

"Allyson's with his lawyer now." Candy gave Fran a hug.

"We got a warrant for his clothes and to search his home," said Tom. "Simmons is taking a team over there in a few minutes."

"Are you okay?" Fran asked Candy.

"I've been better. I was damn lucky Alex was there."

"I'm surprised he made a move on her at your house," said Tom. "That took a lot of nerve."

"Alex has his car parked in the garage. Allyson probably didn't think anyone was home," Fran explained.

"I need you guys to stay out of this one," said Tom. "This guy is the assistant D.A. I shouldn't have to tell you how delicate this is going to be. The press will be all over it. If you or Rick or any of your crew go off half-cocked on this thing, it'll blow up in our faces. I have to do this by the book."

"I'll let Rick know," Fran said.

"I'm more worried about Alex," said Candy. "You should have seen the look on his face. Oh my god, I thought he was going to kill Allyson."

"If anything happens to Stone, you're all suspects," Tom said.

"You, too," Candy told Tom.

He grunted. "I think Allyson could be the BDSM killer, but if I'm going to prove it, I need you to stay away from him."

"Rick and I were wondering if Allyson bugged your apartment," Fran said to Candy. "Maybe that's why he was there this morning. Maybe he went back to get his bugs."

"I'll check with the lab boys and see what they found," Tom said. "Simmons is handling that end of the case, but I haven't talked to her."

"So, Candy's free to go, right?" Fran asked.

"Yes," said Tom.

Candy looked like she was about to hug Tom when he took a step back.

"Not here. Not now," he said quietly.

She stopped.

Fran took Candy's arm. "I have to go. I want to see Rick at the hospital. He's rather pissed at me at the moment."

"I need to pick up my car and let Charlie know I'm okay," said Candy. "Why is Rick pissed at you?"

"I argued with him."

Tom grinned and Fran playfully slapped him in the arm.

"You argue with everyone, all the time. He should be used to it," said Candy.

"What did you argue about?" Tom asked.

Fran scowled. "Well, if you MUST know, I wanted to go to Candy's apartment and check it for bugs, and he ordered me not to. He said it was too dangerous." She took a deep breath. "I'd give anything for a drink right now."

"Rick is right. You shouldn't go there. If someone comes after you, too, I'll never forgive myself," Candy said.

"It's not your fault. None of this is your fault," Fran told Candy.

"For once, I agree with Rick. Too risky," said Tom. "We just don't know enough yet."

Candy picked up her phone and made a call. A few seconds later, she said, "Hi. I just wanted you to know Fran is here and I'm okay. She's headed to the hospital now." Silence. "I'll be fine. I'll see you later." She hung up.

"Charlie?" Fran asked.

"Rick," said Candy.

Fran's eyebrows went up. "Why did you call Rick? Charlie's the one waiting to hear what happened."

"Because no matter how you feel about it, Rick's right. He needs to know that we're safe."

Fran felt hot anger crawling up the back of her neck, but she said nothing. Candy didn't have any right interceding between her and Rick. What happened between them was between them, Fran reasoned. She decided not to share those tidbits with Candy in the future.

"I'll run you to Charlie's to get your car," Tom told Candy. "Wait here. I'll be right back." He headed out to the parking lot to get his cruiser. The two women stood by the door.

Candy called Charlie next. When she hung up, she turned to Fran. "You know, if I didn't like Tom so much, I might consider Charlie." She smiled.

"For what? A pet?" Fran knew the remark was the result of being angry with Candy for calling Rick, but Fran couldn't catch the words before they escaped her mouth.

"Fran, I've had a really shitty day," Candy said in a slow, quiet voice. "I don't need any more from you. So shut up."

Fran pursed her lips together and frowned. Candy was right, of course. Maybe that's why Fran was so mad. She hated it when other people proved her wrong. "Fair enough," she finally said. "But the next time I confide anything to you about Rick, you don't go running to him like a schoolyard tattletale."

"Deal."

**

The hospital staff was delivering supper trays when Fran walked into Rick's room. She was still upset with Candy and worried Rick would be mad at her for hanging up on him. Candy was right: Fran argued with everybody, all the time. It wasn't like she didn't warn Rick, she told herself. She was stubborn and willful and had a mind of her own. He knew that. Few things would piss him off, but her walking into a dangerous situation was one of them. She stopped before the door to his room, cleared her throat, and entered.

Rick stood looking out the window. He wore a sleeveless undershirt over baggy pajama pants, with the left pant leg cut to the knee. His fists were white-knuckled as they gripped his crutches. He didn't turn around right away, and she read the tension in his shoulder muscles. Fran sighed.

Rick dropped his head a bit and turned to face her. The doctor had removed the bandages from his face and eye. Stitches remained in random patterns down his temple, cheek, and jawline, and he still wore the patch over one eye. Fran felt her heart ache for him. She chided herself for being petty. Why should she be mad because he was trying to protect her? What was wrong with her?

"Am I forgiven?" she finally asked.

Rick frowned. "Did you go to the apartment?" He moved slowly toward the bed and sat on it.

"You know damn well I didn't. Candy called you." Fran stepped closer. She wanted to comfort him, but she didn't know how. "What's the word on your eye?"

"They did some tests. We'll see." He lowered the crutches into a nearby chair and looked back at her. "You got one hell of a temper, woman."

"Yeah, well, on that score, we're even."

For the first time since she walked in, a smile crossed his lips. The tension eased in her body. She ran her fingers through his hair. "I'm used to doing things my own way."

"So am I." He wrapped his hand snuggly around the nape of her neck and drew her close for a long, deep kiss. When he finally let her up, he said, "If I have to, I will fight you at every turn. You take too many risks. You don't think before you act. I know you mean well, but –"

"I sound just like you."

"I don't want to lose you, Francesca." Rick leaned back, pushed himself onto the bed, and grimaced in pain.

"Should I call a nurse?" Fran asked.

"Hell, no. They just want to give me more meds and dope me up. I can't afford that. Too dangerous."

"Speaking of dangerous –" Fran sat on the edge of the bed and took his hand.

Rick looked quizzically at her. "Whatcha gonna spring on me now, boss?"

"I was talking to Alex about moving our offices, and he suggested we move into one of the buildings I own under Max-Mil. What do you think?"

"You decided to keep the Max-Mil properties?"

"I don't know what I'm going to do yet, but I'm leaning toward opening another law office, something that helps the victims, a way of making restitution for my father's sins. I want your opinion."

Rick tilted his head and squeezed her hand. "Sounds good so far. Go on."

"I told Alex we should get an inventory of the properties that I own and go check them out – tonight – me and Alex." Fran waited for a reaction but got none. "You don't look surprised."

"I'm not. Alex called about that earlier."

"What? Must everyone butt into my business?"

"Only 'cause we love you, boss."

Fran sighed and shifted a bit on the bed. "So, what did you men decide was this poor woman's best course of action?" Fran asked, her anger flaring.

"That you should do just that – go with Alex to look at the properties, only do it tomorrow, after the meeting with the board of directors."

On the one hand, Fran was happy that Rick was agreeing to her plan. On the other, she was irritated at having any constraints on her. "Why tomorrow?"

"Alex said he heard back from the accountant and the inventory of the properties won't be ready until tomorrow, around noon," Rick explained.

"Oh. I just thought –"

"I would object to you going out at night, to properties that might be used in criminal activities and getting your heads blown off?" Rick held onto her hand.

Fran blushed. "Okay, you made your point."

"Come here." Rick pulled her down next to him in the bed and wrapped his arm around her. "Look, you've got a lot to bite off these days, and I'm not there standing behind you to make sure you're okay. I don't like it."

"And I don't like Alex or Candy running to you every time they don't like what I want to do. I'm not a child."

"No, you're not." He looked down into her eyes. "You're a beautiful woman, and we all love you, and we want to protect you."

She reached up and gingerly touched the stitches on his cheek. "When are you coming home?"

"Sometime late tomorrow morning. When's the board meeting?"

"Ten," she said. "Maybe I'm wrong. Maybe you should be there."

"No, you were right the first time. You need to go with Alex. The two of you will get more out of them than me." He chuckled. "I tend to intimidate people."

"No! Really?"

He leaned down and kissed her firmly. "Yeah, I don't seem to scare you much, though. I gotta work on that."

Fran smiled and wrapped her arms around his neck. "Trust me, sweetheart. You scare me plenty." She pulled his head down and cradled it. "Think the nurse will be pissed that I'm in bed with you?"

"Fuck her." Rick's whole body relaxed as he melted into her, held her, and let her soothe him.

***

Edgar Mitchell packed up his things at exactly 5:15 p.m. from his desk at the Las Vegas Forensics Lab. His files were all neatly organized by case number. He lined all his pens and pencils up in his drawer and placed all the garbage in the trash can next to his desk.

"Headed out?" Tom Saddler asked Edgar.

Tom, as usual, was in a hurry and, as usual, was on overtime.

"Yes, there's a special evening paleo art exhibit tonight at the natural science museum." Edgar hung up his neatly pressed lab coat and threw his raincoat over his arm. "Have you seen it?"

Tom shook his head. "I don't have much time for museums these days. Do you have the results on that luminal test on Allyson Stone?"

"Yes, I emailed them to you. Didn't you get them?"

"I didn't see them. Maybe they went to junk. I'll check later. In the meantime, send them again, will you?"

Edgar looked at the expensive, antique watch he always wore. "Tonight?"

Tom smiled. "Tomorrow is fine. You said the test was positive for semen, right?"

"Yes, detective," Edgar said with a smile. "Plus, I have some trace evidence for you. It should prove interesting. Now, if you don't mind, I don't want to be late."

Tom stepped aside as Edgar hurried out the door.

About twenty minutes later, Edgar was sitting at his favorite coffee shop, sipping cappuccino, and reading the latest edition of the Las Vegas Tribune. He folded the newspaper and checked his watch again. The watch was a gift from his father, and he preferred using it to check the time on his cell phone. He didn't have time for supper, so he purchased another cappuccino to go and hailed a cab.

The morning's stormy weather gave way to a beautiful evening. The sun was low, and a ribbon of gold shone over the horizon. The few, wispy, remaining clouds were a pastel blue and pink.

The entrance to the museum was large and solid, its adobe-like walls decorated with faux fossils. The lobby was cool, and the tile floor muffled the multitude of footsteps. Edgar paid the entrance fee and obtained a small map of the museum. He hurried to the paleo art exhibit with the sense that someone was following him.

He realized he was being paranoid, but six months of working in the crime lab left him with the feeling that evil-minded criminals lurked in every corner. He turned slowly. He observed the exhibit while at the same time looking for his shadow. A chill went down his back and he shrugged it off.

Several teachers herded a handful of students whose voices echoed in the large halls, a Cub Scout troop on an outing filed past, an older couple pressed their respective noses up to the information plaques to read what was on them, some teenagers giggled in the corner and looked more like they belonged in a mall, and a young woman with a pad and pencil busily sketched from the exhibit.

Nothing to fear, Edgar told himself. He moved to the next section of the exhibit.

The feeling of being watched persisted. Frustrated and worried, Edgar decided to call it a night. The exhibit was drawing to a close, and at least he'd be safe at home. He called a cab and then followed the Cub Scout troop and the elderly couple out the door and into the parking lot. The sun had set, and the air had cooled. Edgar waited patiently at the entrance until the cab appeared.

The elderly couple reached for the cab door at the same time as Edgar.

"Oh, I'm sorry. Is this one yours?" asked the man. He was slightly bent, and his clothes and shoes were well worn. He had a Wranglers' cap perched on his head and his hands shook. The woman Edgar took for his wife offered a shy smile. Her blouse was buttoned tight against her neck and adorned with a small gold cross on a chain.

"That's alright," Edgar said politely. "I can get another one." He could already see the second cab pull into the parking lot.

"Sweet boy," the woman said as she patted Edgar on the arm. A few seconds later, they were gone.

Edgar got into the second cab, gave his home address to the driver, and glanced over his shoulder. He still had the feeling he was being followed, but the darkness and blinding headlights prevented him from making out any single vehicle. Eventually, he gave up looking.

When he arrived at his townhouse, Edgar got out and paid and tipped the driver. He looked left and right, seeking out any suspicious vehicles, but he didn't spot anything. Turning, he walked up the stairs to his door. His hand trembled slightly as he fought with the key. He could feel his heartbeat increase. Just a few more steps and he would be safe.

Edgar walked through the door and shut and locked it behind him. He took a deep breath and reached for the hall light. A strong hand tightened around his throat. Edgar screamed and thrashed about, trying to knock the assailant off of him. The grip tightened and Edgar felt dizzy. He kicked harder. His fingernails clawed at a gloved hand.

"Repent!" a man screamed in his ear. "Repent, you sinner! Do you hear me? Repent and be saved!"

Edgar thrashed and clawed until he was able to turn partially around. He couldn't see who was attacking him. He only knew it was a man. The assailant wore a black hoodie and mask and smelled like fresh dirt. Edgar fought until his fingernails finally hit skin just above the man's glove, but by then the damage was done.

The man screamed in pain, smacked Edgar hard across the face, and grasped his throat again. "Repent and be saved!"

Edgar gasped and lost consciousness.

The assailant bent over Edgar's motionless body and swore. He turned on a flashlight, fished around in the kitchen for a paring knife, and used it to clean under Edgar's fingernails. Then he took out a spiked dog collar and wrapped it around Edgar's throat, the spikes digging into the soft flesh. When that was done, he pulled Edgar's pants down to his knees and used the paper towel dowel from the kitchen to angrily sodomize the young man. Finally, he stood up, stretched, and pulled three sweetbriar roses from his pocket. He dropped them on the body and let himself out the kitchen door.

***

"Do we have to meet in person? I don't like it. What if someone sees us?" Alex shifted from side to side in the dark, unfinished apartment of the empty building and stared out the window. Night had fallen and a streetlamp sent an eerie glow that spread Alex's shadow along the wall and floor.

"Were you followed?" Jax Saynte stood behind Alex and blocked the open doorway.

Alex turned to face him but couldn't see the man's features in the dark. "Of course not. Fran is at the hospital with Rick again. Candy is off with Tom somewhere, and Margo went back to her place." Alex's voice was bitter. "As far as anyone knows, I'm just a good little boy, working hard and doing what I'm told."

"That's exactly what you are. You left a message for me. What's the problem?" Jax stepped into the tomb-like room. He was dressed in an evening suit, complete with cufflinks on his shirt and polished shoes that reflected the light when he walked. He smelled like money.

"Fran wants to view the properties. She wanted to do it tonight, but I managed to get around that. She'll push to do it tomorrow, though," Alex said.

"All of them?"

"All of them." Alex glanced back out the window at the streetlamp. He had parked his car just out of reach of the light. Now he wondered if that was a good idea. He didn't trust Jax, but he didn't think the man would try and kill him either. At least, not yet. "She asked her accountant for an inventory of everything Max-Mil owns. I dragged my heels getting the request to him. When he got back to me, it was late, and he didn't have time to look everything up. He said he'd do it tomorrow, and I said that was fine."

"You finally did something right." Jax verbally patted Alex on the back. "I'll handle Simone at the board meeting tomorrow. She won't be a problem."

"You don't know Fran. She's tougher than you think, and she's always a problem." Alex faced Jax. "So why the one-on-one? I could have told you all of that over the phone."

Jax stepped closer, facing off against Alex. "I'm worried about you. We have a deal. You haven't been keeping up your end of the bargain."

"Is that why you sent the flowers to Candy? To warn me?" Alex stepped back a bit. "I did what you asked so far. I got you the Max Simone files, didn't I? I told you what everyone was up to, where they were going, what they knew. I even did your dirty work at Fran's office. Scared the hell out of me."

Jax frowned and stepped toward Alex again. "So far, you fucked up the one thing I really wanted done. You didn't take out Rick Brandt. If I'm going to move on Simone, he's got to be out of the picture."

"You promised no one would get hurt. You'd get me out of jail if I'd go back to work for Fran and be your eyes and ears in the office. I did that."

"And you thought that would be it?" Jax asked.

"I swear, Jax, if you hurt one hair on Candy's head –" Alex began.

"Don't worry. Your little mistress will be fine as long as you don't cross me. You don't want her to end up like her girls, do you?"

"Then why send the pictures? And where did you get them, anyway?"

"I have a – a contact in the department." Jax grinned.

"A woman," Alex said.

Jax raised an eyebrow. "Astute."

"Are you killing those girls?" Alex asked directly. His chest tightened as the question came out. He wasn't sure he wanted the answer.

Jax chuckled. "No, but I admire the work. And if you don't keep your ass in the game, you can bet your precious Mistress Candy will meet a similar fate."

Alex ran his fingers through his hair and glared at Jax. "I was just supposed to rattle Rick's cage, that's all – just put some distance between him and Fran, if only to protect her. If he knows he's endangering her, he'll push her away. That's the way he thinks. You didn't say anything about blowing up the whole damn building. How much explosive was in there, anyway? We could all have died – including me."

"Sloppy work. Brandt was supposed to get that bomb, not Saddler. You left too much to chance."

"Why kill Rick?"

"I need Simone to sign those properties over to me. She'll never do it as long as Brandt is in the picture. With him gone, she'll fold. I can get her to do anything."

"He's her strength," Alex admitted.

"And her greatest weakness," said Jax. "You don't see the bigger picture, do you? We need to hang onto that property. A lot depends on it."

"How much?" Alex stepped back again until his back was pressed against the spackled wall.

"Don't push it." Jax, his hands planted deeply in his pockets, took one step closer.

"Fran thinks Toni's behind the bombing. I told her no. I told her it was personal to Rick."

"Which is true. The only people I know with a personal grudge against Rick Brandt are you and your sister." Jax shook his head. "You've built this guy into some kind of legend, and you're scared of him. Maybe you should be, I don't know. I've yet to meet him. One thing I do know, if you're more afraid of Rick Brandt than you are of me, we have a problem."

"I'm not afraid of Rick," Alex lied.

"Then we have no problem, do we? You do your job and get him the hell out of my way. You keep working for me, and I don't hurt your mistress. I get the properties, and we both go home happy, right?"

"Leave Candy out of this!" Alex yelled.

"You do what you're told, boy, and she'll be just fine." Jax turned on his heel and marched out of the building.

Alex stood alone in the dark, his heart pounding. As the tension left his body, he braced himself against the wall. "Damn." He glanced out the window and watched Jax drive away. For the first time, it occurred to Alex that if Jax didn't kill him, Rick would.

Chapter 17

Friday Morning

Fran pressed up against a sink counter of gold and black granite in the ladies' room of Max-Mil Enterprises and studied herself in the mirror. She was prepared for this, she told herself. She did her homework. She even dressed the part. She pulled her normal tangle of long red hair back into a neat bun with a few stray curls to soften the effect. She bought a new suit for the occasion, giving up her normal "good luck" peach for something a little different, a blend of ivory and apple green. The jacket topped a silken blouse with a low, cowl collar. She wore a simple necklace of pale green garnets and a matching bracelet. Her shoes were closed-toe ivory stilettos that clicked delicately on the tile floor as she walked. Under her arm, she carried an ivory, leather portfolio.

Yes, she was ready, except for the fear in her gut, but she could work with that.

She added a touch of concealer under her eyes, washed her hands, and walked back into the spacious hallway where Alex was waiting for her.

She smiled at him as she straightened his tie. "Seen Jax yet?"

"Not yet. Shall we head to the conference room?"

She nodded. She half expected Saynte or Hawksworth to meet her at the door, but this was her company, and she was free to come and go as she pleased. Or was she?

The conference room was encased in glass, from the glass wall that fronted the hall to the large windows that overlooked the Las Vegas vista. The table was silver granite on mahogany pedestals. The chairs were thickly upholstered. A cart with coffee and assorted muffins stood in the corner, and a young woman in a navy suit was serving everyone at the table.

The table itself was strategically stacked against Fran, much as she had stacked her table when Jax visited her office. At the head was the man himself, leaning back, his feet protruding under the table, his jacket tossed into a nearby chair. He was claiming his territory, Fran realized. The rest of the board members, consisting of five men and one woman, were seated on either side of him. At the opposite end of the table was a folder with the meeting's agenda, placed at the chair that Fran was expected to take. Max had been the chairman of the board, Fran realized. But she didn't know who held that title now, and she wasn't sure what her role would be. It was Fran against the board of directors. That was the layout. Jax smiled at her.

Fran picked up the file and circled the table. She sat next to the last person on Jax's left and motioned for Alex to sit opposite her. Jax's smile waned slightly as he watched her. Hawksworth smirked. The others glanced at Jax and at Fran. They were accustomed to dealing with Max Simone, who had been in league with Jax. This, they realized, might be a different experience.

Jax pulled out the agenda from his folder. "Before we begin, I want to welcome the newest member of our board, Fran Simone. Miss Simone recently inherited her father's ownership interest in Max-Mil."

A subdued murmur of welcomes drifted in Fran's direction.

"Excuse me," Fran said as politely as she could. "It's rather unusual for the CEO to run the board meetings, isn't it? Who's the chairman of the board?"

Shoulders tensed. Heads turned towards Jax and then Rupert. The old man cleared his throat.

"That would be me. I recently surrendered that post, and we have yet to pick a new chairman. For now, Mr. Saynte is, shall we say, facilitating the meeting."

"I see." Fran found the situation both annoying and confusing. "I'd like to introduce my business associate, Alessandro de la Rosa."

A less cordial welcome followed, and Fran noted that Jax never acknowledged Alex.

"Before we begin," Fran said, "I am here to ask the board to continue the matter of resolving the outstanding lawsuits for at least sixty days, to allow my attorney and accountant to analyze the material I received regarding the company and to make a recommendation to me as to whether I shall retain or divest my holdings."

She could tell that the news was not unexpected. A few people leaned back in their chairs as if preparing for a long and tiring meeting. A couple of others became more attentive. Hawksworth, his nearly bald head glistening as the late morning sunlight filtered through the window, cleared his throat to get attention.

"Yes, Rupert?" Jax asked.

"I want to state for the record that I support Miss Simone's position. The lawsuits require a thorough review. We have a large liability here. If Miss Simone, who is also a lawyer, can shed some light on these cases, it can only help us. And given our current court schedule, I believe sixty days is a reasonable amount of time."

"And we do need to consider all our options when dealing with the fatality," Fran added.

A number of board members suddenly turned to look first at Fran and then at Jax.

"Fatality?" one asked. "What fatality?"

"Our slip and fall case." Jax leaned forward and pressed his fingers together. He glared at Fran as if she'd ambushed him, and she had. "The gentleman in question suffered complications following a stroke and died after being in a coma for three months. I was only made aware of this a few weeks ago, and we didn't have a board meeting until now."

"So much for not being seriously injured," Fran said.

She wondered if she should call attention to the fact that Jax had omitted the victim's death when he briefed Fran at her office only two days before. She decided against it. There were enough issues on the table today.

"The police report indicated he slipped and fell out a four-story window," Fran said. "The police ruled out suicide but still have not solved the case. In the meantime, a family member has stepped in to continue the suit and the pleadings have been amended to include…" She opened her portfolio and glanced at her notes. "… a wrongful death claim."

She pulled her eyes away from Jax and studied the rest of the board. The tension level in the room shot up.

"Like I said," Hawksworth interrupted, "it would be wise to continue this for sixty days to allow Miss Simone to study the cases before us."

Most of the board members nodded their heads in agreement. The one woman at the table looked to Jax for direction.

He seemed reluctant at first, but then he leaned back again and nodded. "Agreed. Sixty days. But no more, Miss Simone. We can't afford to drag our heels on this."

Fran wanted to remind him that he worked for her, and that she could do anything she damn well pleased, but she decided against challenging his authority outright at this meeting. "Thank you," was all she said.

The remaining meeting passed quickly until the portion for new business. Rupert Hawksworth pushed his frail body up from his chair and reached into his inside jacket pocket. Leaning against the table for support, he handed a letter to Jax.

"I am hereby submitting my resignation from the board, effective immediately." Hawksworth looked around at those seated at the table. "I have served this board for over forty years, and I have fought the good fight. Now, it's time for someone younger and stronger to take my place." He smiled at Fran. "I have been retired for the last fifteen years. This board kept me active in the community and, I might add, young at heart. But you reach a point when being young at heart isn't enough. You have to have the physical stamina to handle the position and its related stress." Hawksworth straightened up and pointedly looked at a couple of the senior board members. "This is a young man's – excuse me – a young person's game. It's time for me to move on." Hawksworth offered a weak smile and slowly sunk into his chair.

Jax glanced at the resignation letter before him and then passed it along for the other board members to see. "Well, we will certainly miss your spunk and your humor at our meetings." Jax looked at the others. "May I have a motion to reluctantly accept this resignation?"

"So moved," said the one woman there.

"Second," said one of the gentlemen.

"All in favor say aye," Jax directed.

All but Fran gave the obligatory agreement.

Fran spoke up. "I wish to abstain from this vote as I don't feel qualified to make a determination regarding Mr. Hawksworth."

"Very well," said Jax. "Six ayes and one abstention. The ayes have it. Rupert Hawksworth's resignation is hereby reluctantly accepted." Jax turned to Hawksworth. "It's been an interesting year for me, sir. I hope we see each other again soon."

"Speaking of which," said Hawksworth, "there will be a soiree at my home tomorrow night, six p.m., semi-formal. All board members and their significant others are invited to attend." He stood up again and nodded as the board members clapped and offered well wishes. A few minutes later, Rupert Hawksworth was gone, and Fran was left holding the proverbial bag.

The meeting came to an end. Fran found herself back in the hallway with Alex. She waited patiently until Jax left the conference room. He deliberately engaged in small talk with several board members in order to make her wait, but when it became obvious that she wasn't leaving, he finally walked out to greet her.

"Miss Simone," he said with a nod. He ignored Alex.

"I will be receiving an inventory of Max Mil-holdings this afternoon. I intend to view the properties for my own edification," Fran said.

"Of course. You can get the keys from the receptionist. I'll call down and let her know you're coming."

"She doesn't know who I am?"

The question seemed to catch Jax by surprise. "I'm sure she does. Why?"

"Since I own the controlling interest in this corporation, I shouldn't need permission from you to get the keys," Fran noted.

Jax smiled. "Of course. I just didn't want there to be any problems."

"There won't be. Will there?" Before he could answer, Fran turned on her heel and, with Alex in tow, headed for the elevator.

***

Candy sat in the diner booth she had once shared with Andrea Ortiz. With Fran and Alex at the meeting, Rick in the hospital, and Tom at work, Candy found herself alone at Fran's home. Alone anywhere was not a good experience for her these days, and she really wasn't up to going to Charlie's store. Somehow, the familiar diner seemed comforting.

The sky was slightly overcast. The diner was quiet. Soft pop music played over the speakers as a couple of waitresses in checkered aprons made the rounds. Candy ordered the banana cream pie. It was her own mini wake, a tribute to the woman who had been her friend. The pie was Andrea's favorite, and they often split a slice.

The waitress set the pie down with two clean forks and then sat down in the facing seat. Candy looked up, surprised.

"Missy, isn't it?" Candy asked. Andrea had been better at names.

"Yeah. I'm sorry about your friend. She was a nice lady."

"Yes, she was." Candy pulled the pie to her and took a bite.

"I just want you to know that that lawyer guy came in here every day looking for you for a while," Missy said. "I wasn't sure if it had, you know, anything to do with Miss Andrea."

"What lawyer guy?"

"Stone? The one with the girl's name."

Candy felt her gut wrench. "Yes, Allyson Stone."

"He stopped when I told him you didn't come here anymore."

Candy smiled. "Thanks for that. He turned out to be a real ass."

"Yeah, he kinda gave me the creeps."

"I guess I should tip you extra for that one." Candy took a drink of her coffee and handed the second fork to Missy.

Missy leaned forward and whispered. "Are they all like that? I mean, your clients? You know, stalking you, and wanting you to do things to them, and all that?" She took a bite of pie.

Candy stifled a laugh. "Well, first off, he's not a client. But, to answer your question, no, they are not all like that. Some want to be mothered. Some just want someone to talk to. Most want someone to talk to. The call girls I know say the same thing. The guys like the sex. They get off on it. But they want to feel like someone gives a damn, like someone is listening to them."

"But some just wanna get beat, huh?"

"More like spanked. I'm not a sadist, and my clients don't tend to be pain sluts. I leave those for the specialists."

"So why is this character following you around all the time?" Missy kept eating.

"I don't know. I wasn't scared of him at first. Maybe I should be."

A bell chimed as a tall, handsome, and well-dressed man walked into the diner.

"Damn, I want a piece of that," Missy whispered as she wiped her mouth with a napkin and got up to wait on him.

He flashed a smile at the two women before he took a seat at the counter.

"Lucky girl." Candy took one more forkful of pie. "For you, Andrea." She washed it down with some coffee.

Candy left cash on the table to cover the bill and a tip, slipped on her jacket, and stepped out the door and into the parking lot. She scanned the area and thought of Allyson. Had he been there? Had he followed Andrea there? Had he been watching them the whole time? Candy shuddered.

She glanced back at the large picture window to wave goodbye to Missy, and she caught the man at the counter looking at her. He smiled and then went back to talking to the waitress.

Feeling safe, Candy got into her car and started the engine. That's when she saw the single sweetbriar rose on the passenger seat. She looked around to assure herself that no one was lingering nearby. Swearing under her breath, Candy drove off.

***

Friday Afternoon

"We're missing something on these murders." Sheriff Joe Hodge leaned back in his office chair and looked at Tom Saddler. "I've been over the statements, the reports, the trace evidence, the forensics, everything – and I got nothing. I'm willing to bet that we saw something or heard something that we're missing."

It was nearly noon and Tom had been working since four that morning. He'd skipped breakfast and now was starving and exhausted. His nylon jacket was draped over one leg as he sat across the desk from Hodge and felt the bite of a pending headache.

"I was very thorough in my report." Tom leaned forward in the chair and rubbed his neck. He hoped to log off his shift and get some rest, some real rest, for a change. But the sheriff was right. They must have missed something, and Candy's life was still in danger.

"Talk to Candy again."

"Again?" Tom asked, skeptical. "What good will that do?"

"Just talk to her. We're missing the obvious. I'm sure of it. If there's any evidence at all that Allyson Stone is behind those murders, we have to find it now. Sit down and go over it with her."

"But there's still the bombing case out there. I've been working 'round the clock. Maybe Simmons should talk to Candy this time. You said –"

"Simmons can't get these people to open up to her, but maybe you will. Besides, I assigned her to the Stone sexual assault case. You have the inside angle with Candy. Talk to her. Figure it out." Hodge closed the file in front of him and waved for Tom to leave.

Tom pushed himself out of the chair and slogged out the door. Food and sleep. So much was going on and none of it made much sense: bombs in potted rose plants, dead women in leather and collars, vandalism in red paint, and a stalking prosecutor. Tom's head was swimming. Maybe talking to Candy was exactly what he needed to do. She seemed the only person inclined to listen to him these days. He rubbed his aching temples.

On his way to his desk, Tom ran into Jeanette from forensics.

"Have you seen Edgar? He was supposed to email me some reports today, and I haven't seen or heard from him yet," Tom said.

"He didn't come in this morning," she told him. "I think he took a personal day, but I'm not sure. I'll check if you want."

"Please do that. I've got to get that material ASAP. What about you? Got anything?"

"I have all kinds of things, detective. What are you looking for?" Jeanette asked him.

"Let's start with Fran Simone's apartment. I'm looking for listening devices, surveillance items, anything like that," Tom said.

"Fran Simone's apartment?" Jeanette looked confused.

"Damn, I mean Candy Knight's apartment. Sorry. Tired."

"Well, we found one listening bug, but it wasn't in her apartment. It was in his pocket."

"Whose pocket?"

"Attorney Stone's. When we seized his clothing in the assault case, we found a number of interesting things, one of which was the bug in his pocket."

"What can you tell me about it?" Tom crossed his arms and listened.

"Standard issue. Typical police type. Has some red paint on it. I included it in my supplemental report. I can email that to you now."

"Great! What else?"

"We lifted hair from Stone's jacket. Pretty sure it's Dr. Knight's, although the DNA isn't finished yet. But it's her type and color. We also took a print of his hand which matches the mark on Dr. Knight's face."

"So far, so good. Anything else?"

"Well, yes, but –" Jeanette looked a little uneasy.

"What?"

"I may have done something a little, well, outside the rule books," she confessed.

Tom perked up. "That would be a nice change. Talk to me."

"Attorney Stone had several of Edgar's files, but he's temporarily suspended while Dr. Knight's complaint is investigated. So, when Edgar didn't show up today, I went to Stone's office and went through his desk to find the files." She pulled out a large, clear bag. "That's when I found these."

Tom took the bag and glanced at the contents. "A key – probably for a padlock – and some receipts, from the looks of it." He raised his eyes questioningly at Jeanette. "Analysis?"

"You're right. The key appears to be from a padlock. But where would one use a padlock?" Her smile widened.

"Enlighten me," Tom said with as even a tone as he could muster.

The smile dimmed but only slightly. "There are two kinds of receipts in there. One group is for coffee shops, mini-marts, and gas stations. I arranged and cataloged them by date. The earliest ones are for establishments near where Dr. Knight used to live. The latter ones are for establishments near her current apartment. And the last three are for establishments near Miss Simone's residence."

Tom's gut tightened. "It's not conclusive, but it's a damn good start."

"The other receipts are for a storage unit near Henderson. All paid in cash, or so that's what the receipt says," she finished.

It was Tom's turn to smile. "And you'll email me this info?"

"Yes, sir, detective."

"Good job. Thanks. Let Hodge know."

"I thought you only had a warrant for Attorney Stone's home," Jeanette said.

"Yes. I'll have to get one for the storage unit."

Tom started to leave, but Jeanette called him back. "Detective, one more thing."

"Yes?"

"I'm worried about Edgar. Maybe someone should check on him."

"I'll look into it." Tom hurried to his desk.

A minute later, Tom was arguing with the medical examiner on the phone. "Just send me a copy of the reports. Email me a PDF. That'll work. I can pick up the originals later." He was quiet for a minute. "I KNOW you gave reports to Detective Simmons. She's assisting me. I need my own copies, and I don't have time to track her down." Tom slammed the phone down.

Sleep and food. He needed both.

Tom picked up the phone and called Candy. "Where are you?" He skipped the 'hello' part.

"At Fran's. Her and Alex are back from the Max-Mil board meeting. They're talking legal strategy. Why? You want to rescue me?"

Tom smiled. "I need lunch, and I need to talk to you about the murder cases. How about I pick you up in, say, forty-five minutes?"

"What should I wear?" Candy asked.

He could almost hear her smile over the phone.

***

"I had this bad dream about my mom last night," Tom said.

He was sitting across the table from Candy at a small restaurant near the strip as they waited for their meal. He didn't know why he felt the need to open up to her now. Maybe it was the exhaustion. Maybe it was all the death he'd seen lately. He was having trouble sleeping, and the dreams had taken over. A couple of painkillers helped his headache, but not much. Food was the answer.

"Tell me about it." Candy leaned into the table and propped her chin on her hand. She wanted to tell him about eating pie at the diner, about Allyson Stone, and about the rose in her car. She needed to tell him those things, but right now, she had the sense that she needed to listen to him more. Besides, he'd be upset that she was out alone.

Tom cleared his throat and continued. "She was confused and lost and had wandered into a homeless shelter. The people who ran it wouldn't let me go in, because they protected the people who were there. I had to give the doctor all kinds of information on her meds, her condition, her friends, etc., to make sure she was okay."

"How is your mom?" Candy asked.

The waitress set their drinks down and disappeared again.

"She was pretty shaken up after Toni de la Rosa shot me. It took something out of her. It's hard to explain. She's not that old, but when she thought I was dying, somehow it made her older inside."

Candy nodded. "It was awful, Tom. It scared the shit out of me, too."

Their eyes met for a few seconds, and Tom felt himself growing warm. He looked down at his mug. Maybe he should have met her at the office, he thought. It would have been less intimate. He felt her legs move under the table, and he pulled his feet back.

"I guess I worry about what will happen to her if I'm not around." He took a drink from his coffee. "I almost didn't make it. Next time –"

"We can't worry about the next time." Candy watched him, studied him, read him. She saw the tension in his shoulders and the fatigue in his eyes. "What are you thinking?"

"I'm thinking I might want to consider another line of work." The revelation surprised even him. The thought had nagged at him since he was shot a few months before. He'd lost a kidney. The physical recovery was quick, but the emotional one was taking its sweet time.

Candy frowned. "I never thought of you as anything other than a cop. Well, that's not true, I have thought of you in leather chaps." She grinned.

Tom choked as he laughed. "Well, now that you're not at the lab, I can't accuse you of sexual harassment anymore," he said with a grin. He put down the coffee. "I want to talk to you about –"

Before he could finish, their lunch was served. Tom waited for the waitress to leave before looking at his plate. He got the 24/7 breakfast with steak and eggs and toast and pancakes on the side. Starving was putting it mildly.

Candy, as usual, was more selective. She jabbed her fork into a Caesar salad and smiled. "Just what I needed."

Tom began again. "I want to talk to you about the murder cases. Detective Simmons is helping me, but the sheriff is growing impatient, and he gave her the Allyson Stone case, so he wants me to pick up some slack. I had the lab boys and the ME send over all their reports. I thought, when we were done eating, we could look at them together."

The minute the suggestion passed his lips, he knew he was asking for trouble. He wanted to be alone with her. He wanted to forget about being a cop, and about Fran, and about people being killed.

"Oh?"

Tom grinned. "I guess I'm looking for inspiration."

Candy stifled a laugh. "I've been accused of a lot of things but being an inspiration has not been one of them."

Tom shrugged. "You always inspired me." He shifted a bit in his seat.

Candy leaned back and their eyes met again.

"Okay, I'll bite. What have you got?"

Tom looked at his food. "After lunch. I'm too hungry and too tired to think about death while I eat."

Candy put her fork down. "I have a confession to make."

Tom looked up in surprise. "If it involves whips or murder, I'm not sure I want to hear it." When he saw how serious she was, he leaned back and studied her. "What happened?"

"I was alone today, at the house. Fran and Alex were at the Max-Mil meeting. I have no idea where Margo was – home, I think. And Rick's in the hospital."

"Go on."

"I didn't want to be there alone after what happened with Allyson, so I decided to go out for a bit." When Tom didn't say anything, she continued. "I went to the Yellow Hen Diner. I had a banana cream pie. It was Andrea's favorite. I guess I just wanted to remember a good moment with her."

"Did anything happen? Are you okay?"

"Yes and no. The waitress, Missy, sat with me and we talked. She said Allyson Stone was in there a lot looking for me, but he stopped coming after she told him I didn't eat there anymore."

Tom breathed a sigh of relief. "That's good. I mean, it's not good he was looking for you, but it's good he stopped going there."

"Then Missy got up to wait on this guy, and I paid my check and got in my car." She stabbed the salad but didn't eat.

Tom tensed.

Candy pulled an envelope out of her purse and put it in front of Tom. "I found this in the front seat of my car."

Tom opened it up, tipped it, and watched as a sweetbriar rose fell to the table. "Shit." He looked at her. "You didn't see anyone suspicious?"

Candy shook her head. "There was the guy at the counter, but it wasn't Allyson and, well, he seemed nice enough. Good looking, suit type. He and Missy were talking. Otherwise, just the usual crowd."

Tom used the end of a knife to brush the rose back into the envelope, then he slipped the whole thing into an evidence pouch and put it in his pocket. "I'll have Edgar look at this later. I'm wondering if two more people are dead, and we just haven't found them yet."

"You want to go back to the police department to talk?" she asked.

"Not really. I put in my shift, and if I show up there they'll drag me into something else."

"I don't want to go back to Fran's house, and I can't go back to mine."

"Which leaves my place," said Tom. "You haven't been to my place yet, have you?"

She grinned. He forgot, she realized. She'd stepped into his place late one night when he wasn't home. She'd gone there to drop off some evidence for him, but she had taken advantage of the moment to look around. She told him eventually, but that was nearly a year ago. She thought about the lamp table near his bed and the little drawer that held his secrets. The grin widened.

Their moment was interrupted by a phone call from Hodge.

***

"What have you got?" Tom arrived at the police department out of breath and with an urgency to his walk. He had left Candy at his place. Sheriff Hodge met him at the door.

"You know that key and those receipts Jeanette got from Stone's desk?" Hodge held up a key with a tag dangling from it.

Tom frowned. He didn't have time for games. He wanted to shake the information out of the sheriff before another sweetbriar rose victim surfaced. "What is it?"

"We believe it's a key to a storage unit," Hodge explained. "I'm headed there now to check it out. Coming?"

"Let's go." Tom was already halfway out the door.

A forensics team was waiting for them at the storage unit, housed in a massive warehouse with tall, metal walls and stained windows. One man held bolt cutters in his hand.

"I don't think we'll need those." Hodge put the key into the padlock. He turned the key and the lock fell into his hand. Hodge smiled. They walked into the nightmare that was Allyson Stone's mind.

Several long, folding tables were pushed against opposite walls. One was covered with personal items of Candy's, everything from a Christmas snow globe to a pair of fuzzy pink handcuffs to a photo of her white cat. The wall behind that table was covered with fish netting. Pinned to the netting were photos of Candy at work, in court, in the courthouse public restroom, in a diner, at a club where she was dancing, in her bathtub and in her bed, and even one inside her makeshift dungeon at her former home. Many photos included the people around her – Fran, Rick, Charlie, Alex, Missy the waitress, a court officer, Sheriff Hodge, and, finally, Tom. In the photo, Tom and Candy were kissing in his cruiser.

Tom reached for the photo, but Hodge beat him to it.

Hodge quietly slipped the photo into his jacket pocket. "Let's not muddy the waters," he said.

There were also people in the photos whom Tom didn't expect to see: the Pearsons, Lawrence Blackwell, and a man he couldn't identify but who looked familiar.

Tom grunted and turned around. The table behind him was covered with electronic surveillance equipment and three laptop computers. Allyson had eyes on every place that Candy went and everyone with whom she interacted even in passing.

"Hey, sheriff! Got something," one of the forensic team members said.

Hodge walked across the small room to where the man had opened a large cardboard box. Hodge slipped on a pair of rubber gloves, dipped his hand into the box, and started pulling out duct tape, rope, rubber gloves, and a small, leather tool kit.

"Maybe Charlie and Rick were right," Tom said, watching the spectacle. "Maybe, in his own sick way, without realizing he was doing it, Stone was preventing someone else from getting to Candy."

Hodge nodded. "None of this stuff is related to the deaths of those girls. All of it indicates he intended to kidnap Candy."

"But didn't get to it," Tom said. "He was upping his game, building up his nerve."

"If that's the case, if he photographed everything about Candy's life, we may find evidence of who is behind the murders in all of this mess."

Tom turned on his heel and marched out of the unit. Hodge found him about ten feet away. Tom leaned weakly against a wall and looked pale.

"What is it?" Hodge asked.

"Candy went for coffee at the Yellow Hen today. She spoke with Missy Barber. You know, the waitress there?"

Hodge nodded.

"When she got back to the car, she found this." Tom reached into his pocket and pulled out the evidence bag. Inside was the envelope, and inside that was a single sweetbriar rose.

"Shit. You're thinking –"

"There's two more bodies that we haven't found yet, or there's gonna be soon."

Hodge shook his head. "No wonder you're all wound up."

"Sorry." Tom pushed himself up. "Some sick bastard is still after her. At least we got Allyson on attempted kidnapping."

"Maybe. He can still weasel out of that one. He'll just say this is some sick BDSM game they're playing. He'll claim consent." Hodge thought for a minute. "I want to get Rick Brandt in here."

"Why?" Tom asked, irritated. "I can handle this. Don't pull me off this case."

"I'm not doing that, kid. I want Brandt to go through those photos and put names to faces."

"Candy didn't think Stone could go this far, and I was stupid enough to believe her."

"You trusted her instincts. Besides, he might very well have been harmless to her. It was everyone else around her who was in danger."

"We don't know that. We don't have anything that pins him to the murders. If anything, it supports a suspicion I have," said Tom.

"Which is?"

"I think Jim Pearson has something to do with them. I can't prove it, but I have a feeling he knows more than he's telling. At this point, I doubt he'll talk to me though."

"Let's see what we can piece together. If we get enough for a warrant, we'll bring him in and find out what he knows."

Tom staggered back to the storage unit and started sorting through the photos.

"Leave it alone. We'll bring them to the station and go through them there." Hodge rested a hand on Tom's shoulder. "We'll figure this out."

"You're not going to pull me off the case?" Tom asked.

"Not yet. Why? Are you sleeping with her?"

"Not yet."

Chapter 18

Fran leaned against her silver Mercedes in the hot afternoon sun, shoulder to shoulder with Alex, both with their arms crossed, as they studied the dilapidated apartment building. They had shed their business suits in favor of jeans. Fran pushed her sunglasses up her nose and wondered if she should put on more sunblock. She wore a sleeveless white blouse and felt a burn on her arms.

It was a moment of normalcy – old friends on an excursion with a common goal. She missed that with Alex. It brought back old memories and emotions.

Before them stood a four-story quadraplex with a dry and unkempt yard littered with plastic toys, old tires, broken glass, and beer cans. An inflatable pool was half filled with muddy and leaf-covered water. The vinyl siding was battered and dirty. The building was across the street from a convenience store and located at the intersection of two busy streets. It was prime commercial land being used for low-rent housing. Inside the building, a dog barked fiercely, defending the castle from potential intruders.

Fran shuddered. She remembered how, a few months earlier, a German shepherd had attacked her during her morning run and left her writhing in pain on the sidewalk. "I hate dogs."

Alex chuckled. "Funny. You always liked me."

Fran poked him in the rib with an elbow. "If you're about to make a bitch joke about me, better stop now. I'm signing your paycheck, kiddo."

They were there to inspect the Max-Mil properties. It wasn't until Alex showed Fran his map, spread out on the hood of her car, that she realized how daunting the task was.

"Sixty-three properties, huh? Sixty-fucking-three properties," Fran muttered. "Saynte must have laughed his ass off when I asked for the keys."

"We have 14 keys, which open the primary doors for three buildings. We don't need a key for the parking garage." Alex held a small manila envelope that he emptied into the palm of his hand. "He must have thought you meant only the properties involved in the lawsuits."

"He knew damn well I wanted access to everything." Fran sighed. "Only four structures? From six lawsuits?"

"Want to go in?" He eyed the apartment building.

She shook her head no. "This property has zoning and setback issues. I don't want to know what's behind those doors. Don't want to; don't need to. It looks like a damn crack house. No wonder the neighbors want to tear it down. Hell, I want to tear it down."

"I went over our notes. Jax said six cases, but I only found references to five, and the two personal injury cases stem from the same property. I think he made a mistake," Alex explained.

"Jax Saynte doesn't make mistakes. If he says there are six lawsuits, there are six. He has a way of skipping the important details, like the fact that someone died. Check with him later. The last case could be out of state or in federal court or not even filed yet." She groaned. "I really don't like that man. He's slippery as hell, and he lies without blinking."

Alex slipped the keys back into the envelope. He glanced at the building; his own dark eyes shielded by heavy sunglasses.

"Do you think the company has a portfolio with all of these properties in it? Something with photos, descriptions, addresses, tax assessments, and the like?" she asked.

Even as she posed the question to Alex, she was on the phone to Rupert Hawksworth. "Mr. Hawksworth? Fran Simone. How are you doing this afternoon?" she asked pleasantly. Hawksworth had been the one shining light in the whole Max-Mil mess so far.

Alex leaned into her, listening.

She nodded and then asked, "Does the company have a portfolio of all the properties? With photos, tax assessments, blueprints?" She was interrupted mid-sentence. "Great! Fantastic! When can I get that?" She nodded and smiled as she listened. "Yes, yes. I'll be there. Thank you very much." She hung up with a broad grin on her face. "He's got it."

"Hawksworth?"

"Yes. When Saynte took over as CEO of the company, Hawksworth got nervous. He had several copies of the inventory portfolio made and he keeps one at his home. Shortly after Saynte started working for Max-Mil, the company portfolio conveniently disappeared. Hawksworth questioned Saynte's activities ever since but can't prove that Saynte did anything wrong."

Alex straightened up. "So, how do you want to proceed, Bella?"

"We might as well look at the other two properties we have access to. I'll meet with Hawksworth at his party tomorrow night and get a portfolio from him. We can go from there. We'll leave Charlie's place for last."

"Don't you have to pick up Lauren for the weekend?" Alex checked his watch.

"I wish that was the case. This is the second weekend Cheryl called and said Lauren won't be coming home. It seems she's been begging to spend a weekend at her girlfriend's house. Some kind of weekend sleepover with a bunch of girls. I don't know. On the one hand, I want to scream and jump up and down and say 'I'm her mom! I got first dibs!' On the other, I think, with everything going on, and Candy and Charlie in and out of the house, and someone trying to kill me and Rick, maybe it's a good thing she stays away. But I miss her."

"No one's trying to kill you, Bella." Alex rested a hand on her shoulder.

"You sound pretty sure about that," she noted.

"I think someone is after Rick. I think it's personal."

"They sent the bomb to my office, when we were all there, including you." Fran shrugged his hand off.

"True, but it was clearly meant for Rick, and we would have been collateral damage." He pulled the car keys from his pocket. "The initial threat went to Rick while he was at the hospital. Not to anyone else. Not even to you."

"Well, regardless, Rick will be back at the house, and it won't be safe for Lauren to be there."

Alex was quiet, too quiet. Fran turned to look at him. "What?"

"Nothing."

"Spit it out," she told him.

"We already had this argument, Bella. I don't want to have it again. Rick isn't the right guy for you. Period."

"Yeah, right," she said sarcastically. The moment between them evaporated.

"I don't want to fight with you, Fran."

"And yet you sure manage to do that a lot lately." She wondered if she should have hired him. Their history was too complicated, too interwoven with pain and betrayal. She turned to get into the car.

His hand rested on hers as they both went for the door handle. At that moment, Fran felt overwhelmed with grief, but she wasn't about to let Alex know. She slid her hand away and let him open the door for her.

Alex got behind the wheel of Fran's car and started the engine. "Where to next?"

"What's the name of the man who died?" She studied the map.

"Jamieson Kennedy, 31, a carpenter," Alex said as he drove away.

"A carpenter? Was he working on the building? Was there a disability claim or any –" She caught her breath. "Damn! Saynte didn't tell us shit!"

Alex's hands tightened on the steering wheel. "I'm still doing a written summary of the lawsuits. You should have that Monday or Tuesday. There's a lot to read through."

"I'm being set up, aren't I?"

"I told you that the first day. The company is looking at significant losses. Saynte is trying to transfer the liability to you and keep the assets."

"But he can't." Fran turned to Alex. "I'm going to fight him. I don't even want the damn properties. Hell, I'd be happy to sell them off, pay off all the claims, and let it all go, but the harder he pushes, the harder I want to push back."

Alex frowned and kept quiet.

"You never tell me what you're thinking anymore," Fran noted.

"You don't want my opinion."

"I'll be the judge of that."

Alex cleared his throat. "Okay, here goes. You suspect Jax of some illegal activity involving the properties. You can investigate that. You can get to the bottom of it. God only knows what you'll turn up. But, in the end, you'll probably wind up dead." He took a deep breath. "Guys like Jax don't play games. He's got a lot invested in those properties. You can find out why or you can get out, and I think you should get out. Sell the properties. Take your money. Start your new law clinic, or whatever the hell it is you want to start. Just get out while you still can. You don't know this man. You don't know what or whom he's mixed up with. I don't want you getting killed."

"I remember a time when you'd jump into a case with two feet, no matter how hot it was, because justice had to be done. What happened to you, Alex?"

He avoided her eyes. "Wasn't it Rick who once said that justice has a way of biting you in the ass?"

Fran smiled. Just thinking about Rick made her feel better. "That sounds like something he'd say."

"I've been bitten one too many times."

They rode the rest of the way in silence. By the time they got to the property, the sun was setting. The air had cooled. A slight breeze kicked up dirt around the three-story apartment building that was still under construction. The work was abandoned. The yard was mostly sand. Some building supplies were stacked up and covered with a blue plastic tarp held down with cinder blocks. Fran stepped out of the car and studied the structure.

Alex walked up behind her. "The roof tile fell during construction. The guy who was hit was a passerby. There were signs up to stay out, but he wandered in to look. He had a mild concussion, and he's alright now."

"But this is the same building where one of the workers fell out of the window and died, right?" Fran felt Alex was uncomfortably close. She took a step forward. "Let's go in."

The power was working. They turned on the stairwell lights and walked up to the fourth floor, then stepped into the apartment and looked around.

"Where?" Fran asked, referring to the spot where the victim had fallen out the window.

Alex took her arm and guided her to the living room, to the same window where he had stood with Jax Saynte only a night before. "Here. Be careful you don't fall." He released her arm.

Fran stepped up to the window. She checked the lock. She eyeballed the distance between the floor and the bottom sash. "The window was open?"

"According to the police report, the decedent, Jamieson, was installing the window when the accident happened."

"But the police didn't rule it was an accident." Fran focused her eyes to see the reflection of Alex and her in the glass. He did the same, and she caught him looking at her reflection. There was a sadness to his face. She turned to look at him. "What is it?"

"I'm worried about you. You take too many risks. You're in over your head. You don't want to mess with these people."

"You're worried about me? That's rich."

She turned to walk away, but he grabbed her by the arms and pushed her against the wall.

Startled, Fran let out a yelp. Her eyes opened wide as she glared at him.

"Damn it, Bella! Listen to me for once, will you? I made a mistake. A big one, and it almost killed you. I'm sorry. I can't change that. But you're going up against Jax Saynte, and I'm telling you, I'm warning you, don't mess with this guy. Please. Sign over the damn company. Give him what he wants and walk away."

Fran glared at him. "What did I ever see in you, Alex?" She knew it was a hurtful question, but right now she wanted to hurt him.

He released her arms. "I'm trying to protect you."

"That's Rick's job," she snapped.

Alex raged red, raised his hand as if to slap her and then stopped. He took a step back. He lowered his arm. "If you won't listen to me, talk to Rick, then. Talk to anyone! I don't give a shit who! You don't want to go head-to-head with Jax Saynte. "

Fran cringed when he raised his hand. In all the years she'd known him, she'd never seen him that angry. "Take me to the hospital," she said.

***

"I've done enough digging to know that she's in real danger." Alex stood at the foot of Rick's bed like a child about to be horsewhipped. "I tried talking to her, but she won't listen to me. You have to talk to her. You're the only one who can change her mind. She needs to let Max-Mil go and get the hell out of that mess before it blows up in her face. Either she's going to wind up dead, or she's going to wind up in jail on a RICO charge. Either way, it's not good."

Rick was quiet as Alex explained the situation. Rick knew how stubborn Fran could be. He also knew she was right not to trust Alex. But the more he heard Alex talk about Jax Saynte, the more concerned Rick became. "Where is she?"

"Downstairs. She wanted to pick up something for you from the gift shop."

"I'll talk to her."

"I know you and I aren't –" Alex began.

"Damn straight," Rick interrupted. He pushed himself up further in his hospital bed and glared at the nurse who came in to check on him. "I thought I was supposed to be outta here today!"

"Your doctor said one more day," she responded, as politely as she could, given the verbal assault. "He'll check on you in the morning."

"Damn it, woman. I got things to take care of." His hand rested against the grip of his .45 under his blanket.

"Well, Mr. Brandt, if you had followed the doctor's orders to begin with, we wouldn't be in this mess now, would we?" she asked.

Rick grumbled some obscenities, and the nurse left. "I promised Fran I'd be home today. I don't like her alone in that house."

"If she leaves Saynte alone, she won't have a problem. She's more worried about you, and I don't blame her. It's pretty damn clear someone is trying to kill you, and they don't care who gets caught in the crossfire."

Rick frowned. "What's your point?"

Alex glanced around the room quickly to make sure they weren't overheard. "Someone threatened you. Someone tried to blow you up and would have taken Fran and me and Margo and Candy with you. Anyone with you, anyone around you, is at risk, and that includes Fran." Alex caught his breath. "I know she loves you, and I believe you love her. So, I'm asking you – damn it, Rick, I'm begging you – stay away from her until this is over. She shouldn't end up dead because of you."

Rick's hand tightened into a fist. He wanted to scream. He wanted to beat the crap out of Alex. Rick was furious as hell, not because Alex was wrong, but because the son-of-a-bitch was right. An ache twisted his heart. "What else is going on with the Max-Mil shit?"

"We looked at a couple of properties. Nothing exciting. Fran found out that Rupert Hawksworth has an inventory of everything, and she's going to get it tomorrow night at some party he's hosting at his place. She didn't ask me to go with her, but I don't like the idea of her going alone."

"Okay. I'll talk to her. I don't know what she'll do, but I'll talk to her." Even as he said the words, Rick knew exactly what Fran would do; she would throw a fit.

"You'll talk to me about what?" Fran asked as she stepped through the door. She was carrying a small package wrapped in flowered paper and boasting a large ribbon bow.

Rick smiled. Just having her walk into the room made him feel good. "The nurse said I can't go home until tomorrow morning. I'm being punished for not taking care of myself."

"It's about time," Fran laughed. She sat down on the bed, set the gift aside, and gave him a big hug and kiss. "Damn, I miss you."

Alex turned away and looked out the window.

"I miss you too, boss." Rick brushed back her hair. His fingers ran down her bare arms. "Got a little sun, huh?"

Fran pushed herself up and smiled. "Yeah. We were out looking at the Max-Mil properties."

"Alex just told me." He nodded at the package. "That for me?"

Fran beamed. She handed him the gift and watched as he struggled with the wrapping. She didn't offer to help.

After a few minutes, his efforts revealed a box holding an electric razor. Rick raised his eyebrows.

"I thought, since you're left-handed and your arm's in a sling, that it might be easier than trying to use a regular razor." Fran waited for his reaction.

Rick set the package down on his lap and pulled Fran close to him. He held her tight, his lips kissing her ear and neck. "You did good, Fran." He squeezed her tightly, and Fran felt the tension in his body.

She pulled back a little and looked at him. "What is it?"

Rick nodded to Alex. "Can we get some privacy?"

"I'll be in the hall." Alex left and shut the door behind him.

"Remember when we talked about Charlie's camp?" Rick asked.

Fran's face clouded over. "I don't want to be sent away. Besides, I can't handle this Max-Mil matter from there."

"Someone is after me, and someone is after Candy. I want you both to be safe while I work this out."

"Rick –" Fran began.

He hushed her with a kiss. "Please, just for a bit. Just until I find out who's trying to kill me."

Fran frowned and tears came to her eyes. "I hate being away from you."

He drew a thumb gently down her cheek. "I know. And I have one more favor to ask."

"What's that?" Fran held her breath.

Rick lowered his voice, drew her close, and whispered in her ear. "Don't tell Alex where you're going."

Startled, Fran pulled back and looked at him. She waited for an explanation, but none came. Rick just looked at her silently, and she read the worry on his face. "Okay."

There was a knock on the door, and Alex entered. "Ready to go?"

"Yes." Fran kissed Rick one more time and stood up. "I'll be around to get you in the morning."

"Charlie is picking me up," Rick told her. "You have enough on your plate for now. I'll see you later."

She felt his fingers slip out of her hand as she walked away with an uneasy feeling in the pit of her stomach.

***

Early Saturday Morning

Tom didn't know when or how he fell asleep, but he woke up on his own sofa, a blanket thrown over his shoulders and a pillow stuffed under his head. It was night outside. The apartment was black. He didn't know where Candy was. They were discussing the murders when he put his head back once too often.

Tom picked up his cell phone from the coffee table. It was nearly two a.m., and he had to be back at work by four. He wiped the sleep from his eyes and wondered how Candy had gotten home. She'd been helpful. He had to admit that. She had a way of looking at cases that was different from his. He paid attention to what people said and how they said it. She read body language, and she picked up on things around her – the placement of a chair, an open desk drawer, a smattering of dirt on someone's clothing. She had an eye for detail, which made her excellent in forensics.

He was sorry she was forced out of the lab, but the more he knew her, the more he understood the sheriff's decision. Candy was a complicated woman.

Tom stepped into the bathroom and took a quick shower, dried off and headed for his bedroom. His eyes were adjusting to the dark, but he still flipped on the hallway light to make sure he didn't trip over his shoes. Framed in his bedroom doorway, he froze. There, naked and tangled up in the sheets on his bed, was Candy.

Tom licked his lips. He could just turn away, he realized. That would be the smart thing to do. She had flirted with him and teased him and toyed with him for months. He had imagined her in all kinds of situations, even this one, but he still wasn't prepared for how strongly he reacted or how quickly. He wished he was privy to her thoughts. Was she really interested in him? Or was she just looking for another boy toy?

He grabbed a pair of sweatpants from the floor and slipped them on. Then he sat down on the edge of the bed and rested his hand on her cool body. His hand drifted down her smooth arm to her waist and then over her hip.

She moaned and rolled over, exposing her breasts. He retrieved his hand.

"What time is it?" Candy brushed her dark hair from her eyes and stared up at him. She wasn't the least bit self-conscious. She acted as if being naked in front of him was the most natural thing for her to do. He admired that about her.

"Two-thirty. I have to leave for work in an hour."

Candy smiled, reached her hand toward his face, and cupped his cheek. "Don't just stare at me, honey. Come here."

Tom caught his breath and gently took her wrist in his hand. "I don't just sleep with anyone. I'm not wired that way. It's not the way I was raised."

"I'm not just anyone. Let me prove it to you."

The emotions he kept pent up inside of him since his breakup with Fran gushed out. It was wrong to use Candy on the rebound, he told himself, but at that moment, as she pulled him into a soft, long kiss, wrong felt so right.

"I can't be –" he started to object as he pulled away from her.

"One of my boy toys. I know Tom. Maybe that's one of the things I like about you. You're not groveling at my feet, and you never will be." She pushed herself up to her elbow and ran her fingers down his arm. "I can whisper a word and a half-dozen men will be at my door, and I don't want any of them. I know you're still hurting from Fran. Let me help. Please."

Tom sighed. "You told me –"

"I'm not used to begging." Candy finished his sentence.

"Yes. I know, and I don't want you to. This isn't about you."

"Please, Tom," Candy countered. "Don't give me the 'it's not you, it's me' talk. I know you like me."

"I more than like you," Tom admitted. His hand went back to her arm, and he brushed it with his fingers. "I've thought about this moment. Imagined it. Wanted it. I'm just not sure –"

She didn't let him finish. She put her arms around his neck and kissed him again, harder this time, and she didn't let go until he was on the bed, on top of her, his body snug between her thighs. She was cool and smooth like ivory. She didn't rush him. She knew how to break through his barriers. He had fought her advances for so long that it was almost second nature to him. She knew how much pain he was in. It nearly broke her heart to think about it.

What she didn't know, what she didn't realize until that moment, was how hard she was falling for him.

Chapter 19

Longing for Rick's scent and touch, Fran abandoned her own bed and slept in his, in the spare room he used when at her home. She woke in the dark with a deep yearning for him. She stripped off the nightgown that twisted around her body. Her soft hands caressed her arms, her breasts, her stomach, her inner thighs. She moaned and stretched like a cat in the hot sun.

She couldn't sleep. She thought about him sending her away. It was supposed to be for her own good. It was necessary to save her life. That's what he said, but she couldn't accept it. It went against every fiber in her body. She ached for him. He was her air. When he looked into her eyes, she saw the deep fear and worry there, and when he told her not to tell Alex where she was going, her heart seized up in her chest.

Rick knew something, or perhaps he just felt it. He was like that, working as much on instinct as on evidence. It was one of the things that intrigued her about him. Was this a gut reaction on his part? Or was there more? She wondered to what extent Rick's disdain for Alex played into his decision.

Fran heard a soft footstep, and she froze. She knew Candy was supposed to be in the house, but Fran didn't see her guest all evening. There was a soft rap on the door.

"Are you awake?" Candy whispered. The door moved open slightly with a gentle squeak. "What are you doing in here?"

"Yes." Fran sat up in bed and pulled the sheet around her naked body. "What time is it?" She swept the hair from her eyes and reached for her cell phone.

"Four-thirty." Candy stepped into the room and leaned against the door frame. Her shape took form in a streetlamp's soft glow that filtered through the slotted blinds. She was still fully clothed, right down to the knee-high boots that she wore over her jeans. "It's a damn good thing Charlie was awake. Otherwise, he might have shot me."

Fran reached for the lamp, but Candy stopped her.

"It's okay. I can see fine."

Fran put down her phone. "Where have you been? I was worried."

"At Tom's. He brought me here on his way to work," Candy admitted. She sat on the edge of the bed and smiled at Fran. "I came to ask for your blessing, or your forgiveness, depending on the mood you're in."

Fran smiled. "You finally got him into bed."

Candy grinned. "Mad? I know you still have feelings for him."

"You know damn well I have no right to."

"Yes, but –" Candy left the thought dangling in the air.

Fran lowered her head and closed her eyes for a few moments. She searched inside of herself for a spark of jealousy, and she found it. Despite Rick's loyalty to her, she harbored a fear of ending up alone. Tom remained her back-up plan. If something happened with Rick, there would always be Tom. It was selfish of her, she knew. She sighed, looked up, and smiled.

"So, I guess I have your blessing," Candy said.

"Yes, you have my blessing. Come here." Fran opened her arms and hugged her friend. "I know you're good for him. Better than I ever was. You'll make him happy."

"Hungry?" Candy asked.

"Have you noticed that whenever you get emotional, you cook?"

"Yeah, I noticed." Candy stood up and headed out the door.

"I'll be right there. I need to shower." Fran leaned back in the bed and held Rick's pillow close to her. She stroked it and cuddled it and inhaled the smell of it. There was something else she needed to do before she got up – some self-pleasure to wash the tension away. All she needed was a few more minutes.

By the time Fran was up, freshly showered and dressed, Candy had omelets and small fruit cups with yogurt and a sprinkling of trail mix for them, and pancakes and sausage for Charlie, and coffee. The aroma filled the house and drew Fran like a bee to lilacs.

"Hey there, little lady," Charlie said with a grin.

"I didn't hear you come in last night," Fran said.

"Ah, that's okay. You were sleeping like a baby, and I didn't want to wake you." Charlie smiled as Candy got him a large mug of coffee.

Fran sank into the kitchen chair. "I hardly slept at all last night. Oh, this is wonderful." Everything seemed so peaceful that she felt guilty. "I used to go jogging in the mornings, but after that dog thing –" She shivered. "I've been meaning to get a treadmill, but I haven't had time."

"We can do that today," Candy said. "I need to find another place to live. I can't leach off of you all the time."

"I like having you around, but you're right. It's not like this is your own place. You need that."

"Well, for now it's good you gals got a place together. I can't split in two," Charlie laughed.

Candy nodded. "So, how'd it go yesterday?" she asked Fran.

Fran's smile disappeared. "I had a fight with Alex."

"About what?"

"Alex thinks it's too dangerous for me to be around Rick. He really hates him, you know. He still blames Rick for that mess with Toni. Alex also thinks I should just give up on the Max-Mil property, take my losses and run. Maybe reopen the law office as a clinic to help people. He thinks Saynte is dangerous, too."

"What does Rick think?" Charlie asked with a scowl.

"Rick agrees. He wants Candy and me to stay at your place for a while until he figures out who's trying to kill him."

"Him? Not us?" Candy frowned.

"Well, him and you. Both he and Alex agree, surprisingly, that I'm not a target, at least for the rose bush killer. Saynte is another story." Fran sipped her coffee slowly and mindfully, savoring every drop.

"When does Rick come home?" Candy asked.

"I'm picking him up this morning," Charlie said as he stood up.

"This morning," Fran said at the same time. Fran looked up at Candy. "I argued with him, begged him, pleaded with him. I don't want him to send me away to God-knows-where. I don't want to be away from him, and I have too much going on to go into hiding. He's stubborn as hell. When he makes up his mind about something, the earth stops."

"Sounds like you," Candy noted.

Fran set her coffee down. "I decided we could go to Charlie's place tomorrow if you want to go. I can't force you, but tonight there's this party I need to attend."

"A party?" Charlie asked. "Must be one hell of a party to risk staying around here."

"Rick's worried about us getting killed, and you want to go to a party." Candy echoed Charlie's sentiments.

"Not just any party. Rupert Hawksworth is throwing it. He has information for me on the company's properties. Everyone will be there, including Jax Saynte." Fran rubbed her hands together excitedly. "Semi-formal, very ritzy. Politics, money, danger. I can't wait."

"Taking Alex?" Candy asked with a grin.

"No!" Fran said with a big smile. "I'm taking Rick."

"Shit. I'd like to see that," Charlie laughed.

Candy nearly spilled her coffee. "Does that man even own a suit?"

"I have a feeling he cleans up just fine." Fran leaned forward on her elbows and looked across the table at Candy. "Now, it's your turn. Tell me all about you and Tom."

"Okay. That's my hint. I'm outta here ladies. Call me if you need me." Charlie smiled and headed out the door, letting it slam behind him.

"First, I need to tell you about the sweetbriar rose," Candy said. "I had a late breakfast at the Yellow Hen yesterday morning…."

***

Rick was dressed and anxious to leave the hospital when Charlie showed up. The big man slogged into the room in soiled, heavy boots, battered jeans, and a sweatshirt with cutoff sleeves and a drawing of a snake with the words "Don't Tread On Me" printed on the chest. In deference to hospital rules, he left his gun in his vehicle but still wore the holster on his hip.

"They gonna finally let you go?' Charlie asked with a grin.

"He isn't going far," said Tom Saddler as he walked up behind Charlie.

"Don't tell me you gonna arrest my boy." Charlie said. "What the hell did he do now?"

Tom grinned a bit. "I could give you a list, but no, I'm not arresting him. Not yet anyway."

"What's up?" Rick asked as he leaned against the bed. He had tried and failed to put both shoes on. The foot on his injured leg was too swollen and he opted for a hospital slipper. He leaned heavily on his crutches and waited.

Tom stood in the middle of the room, his hands on his hips. "I have some bad news about our rose bush bomber. I received the lab report last night, but I didn't see it until this morning. There was no timer on the bomb." Tom glanced back and forth between the two men.

"No –" Rick stopped mid-thought. "That means – Fuck."

"Remote control detonation, probably by someone close by," Tom said.

Charlie pulled a wrapper out of his pocket, broke off some jerky and put it in his mouth, then pocketed the rest. "Trying to quit chew," he said by way of explanation.

Rick scowled. "How close?"

"Probably within forty feet, although we can't be sure yet."

"You think –" Rick began.

"The son-of-a-bitch waited until Fran threw the flowerpot over the railing," Tom finished.

"What are you saying there, detective?" Charlie asked, confused.

Rick answered the question. "Whoever detonated that bomb at Fran's office was probably inside the building." He lowered himself until he was sitting on the bed and inhaled slowly. "We need proof."

"Yes," Tom agreed.

"No guessing. No speculating. Proof. Solid and undeniable," Rick added, the anger building in his voice. "He wouldn't do this on his own. I know he wouldn't. And I don't believe Toni's behind it, but I could be wrong." Rick took a deep breath. "That son-of-a-bitch warned me."

"Who warned you?" Tom asked.

"Alex. He said it was personal. He said Fran was in danger if she was around me. He warned me to keep my distance from her, so she won't get hurt. I guess he knew what he was talking about." Rick glared at Tom.

"Where is Alex now?" Tom asked.

"Hell if I know. Working at Fran's maybe. He's trying to piece the Max-Mil case together for her." Rick pulled himself back to his feet. "Why? Are you going there?"

"I was planning on it, but I have to check on something first. Are you headed back to Fran's?"

"I was supposed to be. Now I'm not so sure," Rick said with a chuckle. "She wants to drag me to some damn party tonight. Some guy named Hawksworth."

"I heard about that," Charlie said with a smirk.

"The billionaire?" Tom whistled. "When that guy throws a party, it's a party. Do you have a tux?"

"Me? In a penguin suit? What the fuck is that woman thinking of?"

"I bet Jax Saynte will be there," Tom said with a frown. "If I know Fran, she's going to mix some fire with gasoline and see what blows up. And you, my friend, are the match."

Rick leaned against the crutch and laughed. "Damn, that woman's crazy." He took a deep breath. "Alex warned me about Saynte, too. Said he's dangerous as hell."

"Didn't Alex say them flowers in the vase was for Candy? To spook her?" Charlie asked. "Weird idea."

"Not so weird anymore," Tom said. "That would explain a lot. Jax Saynte could get to Alex by threatening Candy. That would explain the bomb. If Alex thought –"

"If Saynte is behind this," Rick added.

"I've heard rumors about him, but I don't have anything solid," Tom said. "I heard he might be mixed up with some mob boss – some New Zealander they call Ant. Ever heard of him?"

Rick stiffened. "Hell, yeah. Shit. I know him too well. Fran's gonna get her fucking ass killed. He's got a big network. The last time I saw him, he was operating out of Philly. That was almost 20 years ago. The feds have been trying to nail him for years with no luck." Rick groaned. "I planned on sending her away, getting her out of town 'til this shit blows over, but she's stuck on going to this party."

"Then she's probably smart to take you." Tom pursed his lips together and thought for a minute. "I think maybe I should be available, just in case you need back up."

"I could go," Charlie said, sensing a volcano was about to blow.

"No offense, Charlie, but you wouldn't exactly blend in," Tom said.

Charlie looked at Rick, who nodded.

"He's right. Hell, I don't even blend in, but I gotta feeling that's the point. Fran is one sneaky little broad." Rick grinned with pride.

"There is something you can do," Tom told Charlie. "You can keep an eye on Alex de la Rosa. I don't want him anywhere near this party or near Fran."

"You think he'll hurt her?" Charlie asked.

"No. If he wanted to hurt her, he would have by now. Nope, I just want to make sure I know where he is and what he's doing." Tom glanced at Rick. "I take it you'll be armed."

Rick didn't answer.

"Expect trouble, Rick," Tom said. "It's gonna be one hell of a party."

***

Saturday Early Afternoon

"Are you sure this is a good idea?" Tom turned to Rick, who balanced on his crutches as they stood outside the

Florence McClure Women's Correctional Center in Las Vegas.

"I gotta see her. Maybe she can help. Maybe she can't. Maybe this thing's got nothing to do with her. Hell if I know. I haven't talked to Toni since the day I got her arrested." He felt an old ache in his heart. He loved Toni de la Rosa once. Some part of him still did, even though she turned on him and tried to kill him and everyone he cared about, including Tom. "I just gotta look her in the eye and make sure."

"I can go in with you."

"I know how much she meant to you, to all of us. I can handle it alone."

Tom had called ahead, and the meeting was set up for a small interrogation room. A large metal door, locked from the outside, ensured security. An oversized window allowed a guard in the hallway to keep an eye on what went on in the room. Rick clearly was not there for romantic reasons. He wasn't about to help Toni walk free. He just needed to ask her a few questions and see what she would reveal. Toni would only talk to two people now – Alex or Rick. No one else existed in her life. She even refused to consult with her attorney. She was found competent, but she was also self-destructive.

The guard helped Rick to his chair and then removed the crutches from the room in case Toni found the need for a weapon. Rick groaned a little as the leg throbbed. He didn't bother to shave that morning and fatigue was heavy in his eyes. He looked up when Toni was escorted through the door.

She looked thin in the navy jumpsuit, but she had always been thin. Her skin was pale, and she walked slowly as if in pain. Her dark curly hair was still relatively short. When she sat down, he could see the effect of the drugs on her. Her eyes were unfocused. It took her a minute to recognize him. Then a small smile spread over her lips. "Hey stranger. Where the fuck have you been?"

Rick forced himself to smile back. His hands clamped tightly together. "You're looking good."

Toni laughed slightly. "Liar."

"Okay, well, you look better than the last time I saw you."

Toni put her hands on the table, leaned forward, and smirked. "What do you want, lover?"

"I just came to check on you."

"Liar! Liar! Liar!" she yelled. Then, just as suddenly, she calmed down. "So, you're shacking up with Fran Simone, now, huh?"

"Shacking up?" Rick looked surprised. It was a phrase he hadn't heard in years. "No. I have my own place."

"That's not what Alex says. He says you practically live at her house now. He says you two can't keep your hands off each other."

Rick's eyes narrowed. "We're involved, if that's what you mean."

"Involved, shit!" Toni leaned back again. "Damn you, Rick. If you wanted out, why didn't you just tell me? You didn't have to turn me in to get rid of me."

"That's not what went down, baby. You decided to kill Fran. I stopped you. I had to. You had no reason to hurt her."

"So, I take it you're not here to apologize."

"Apologize? I regret I couldn't save you from yourself if that's what you mean."

She scoffed at him. "If you ever loved me –"

"I gave up everything for you, Toni, and look where it got me. I only asked one thing in return, to spare Fran. She never did anything to you. She was just— "

"The one woman you always loved," Toni finished. A heavy silence hung between them. "You gonna testify against me at the trial?"

"They haven't subpoenaed me yet."

"They will, and you'll testify."

Rick looked down at his hands a minute, then back up at her. "Yes, I'll testify. Now I have a question for you. Did you ask Alex to kill me, or is he trying to do that on his own? 'Cause he's doing a piss poor job of it."

For a moment, her eyes cleared, and he read the deep pain and anger there. "Alex won't blow his nose without my say so."

"What do you have over him? How could you twist him like that? He's a smart man. He has friends, a life, a future if he wants it. Why would he throw all of that away for you? Why would you let him?"

"We're De la Rosa. We take care of each other." She stood up to leave. "I'm gonna take the stand in my own defense. By the time I'm done, you'll wish Alex had killed you – and your little sweetheart."

The guard saw her stand up. He unlocked the door and led her back to her cell.

Every bone in Rick's body ached. His head was swimming as he retrieved his crutches and hobbled back to the parking lot where Tom waited in the unmarked cruiser. Tom was sitting with the air conditioning running and was looking over his file in the Candy Knight cases. He looked up as Rick approached and got into the car. Tom put the file down, read the look on Rick's face, and didn't ask.

"I gotta stop at the drug store and get some pills," Rick said. "I'm gonna need them to get through tonight."

"You need more than painkillers. You need clothes." Tom glanced down at the hospital slipper. "And real shoes."

"You don't need to be my damn chauffeur," Rick muttered.

"Consider me your bodyguard for the day. If anything happens to you, Fran will kill me."

"What about Candy?" Rick asked.

"She said she has something she needs to do." Tom scowled. "You don't think she's sneaking around with Charlie, do you?"

"Why? Would it matter to you?"

Tom didn't answer.

"Damn!" Rick said suddenly.

"What?" Tom asked.

"Fran bought me an electric shaver, and I left it at the hospital."

"Another reason to stop at the drug store. One electric shaver coming up."

Rick picked up his phone and called Fran. "Hi, boss," he said, his voice soft. "I'm gonna be late. I'll meet you there." He was quiet for a moment while he listened to her. "You know it, sweetie. See you in a bit." He hung up and slipped the phone into his pocket.

Rick watched the prison disappear behind them. A part of him was relieved to be on the road and back to what loosely resembled a normal life. Another part lingered with Toni and grieved over what might have been. He turned his attention to the road ahead.

"Anything you want to share?" Tom asked.

Rick shook his head. "Not much. I think Alex is right, though. I don't think Toni is up to plotting against me or anyone else. She's angry, but she's also out of it."

Tom nodded.

"Where are we going first?" Rick asked.

"We should get you some clothes for tonight. I also want to check on a lab rat of ours, Edgar Mitchell. Know him?"

"Is that the skinny kid with the ironed jeans?" Rick asked.

"That's the one."

"I've seen him around."

"He was supposed to give me some forensic reports on the BDSM murders Friday, but he never showed up for work. One of the lab techs said he took a personal day. I'll swing by his place and see if he can get the reports for me."

"How's that case going?" Rick glanced out the window.

"Well, let's see. BDSM outfits, but the corsets are cheap, or so says Candy. She told Hodge that the corsets were more like for a costume play or something like that. I was going to check with the store where they were sold, but somehow I lost track of that detail. Maybe I can do that today. Too many damn things to remember. Allyson was definitely stalking Candy. We found his stash of photos, video and audio recordings, and a collection of items he stole from her apartment – trinkets, miscellaneous things. We also found a kidnap kit, complete with duct tape and gloves, but nothing that links him to the BDSM murders."

"Holy shit! You kidding? Damn. Anything in those photos that might tell you who else is following her?"

"Hodge thinks maybe. We need to go through them all, you and me. There's hundreds, mostly digital. It just seems every time I start something, something else comes up."

"What else you got?" Rick wasn't paying as much attention to the murder cases as he should have been, he realized.

"It seems the Pearsons and Lawrence Blackwell were cozy with Paul and Cheryl Burns, but I think I told you that. And then there's the roses."

"Yeah, the ones that came to the house," Rick said.

Tom sighed. "Candy told me about that, and I almost forgot. Damn. I need to sit down and write this shit all up. I think that's the basics. What do you have?"

"For openers, there's what we know about Alex and Jax Saynte and Ant," Rick said. "The only thing keeping me away from the house right now is knowing I'll kill Alex when I see him." Rick's fists tightened. "Piece of shit. I shoulda known he was up to something."

"Might not be a good idea to say that to a cop," Tom told him.

"There's a lot going on with that Max-Mil shit. Fran's father was in over his head in a number of criminal activities, and Jax was his partner in crime. We just don't know everything they were up to yet. Fran seems to think she'll learn something at tonight's party."

They turned into the driveway of Edgar's townhouse. A brick façade boasted three floors of arched windows. Slate steps worked their way up to a small, covered stoop. The door was made of real wood and had two vertical windows of beveled glass.

"Nice place for a lab rat," Rick said.

"I heard it's his dad's house. I think his father is in a nursing home or something. I'll be right back."

Rick checked his cell phone for messages while Tom went up the stairs. When Tom didn't emerge a few minutes later, Rick wondered what happened. He climbed out of the car and hobbled up the steps on his crutches. He hadn't yet made it to the top when Tom walked out.

Tom was pale and shaking. He grabbed the iron railing and sat down.

"You okay? What happened?" Rick asked.

Tom pulled out his cell phone. "Detective Saddler," he said into the phone. "I have a 419 at the Edgar Mitchell residence. Actually, it looks like a 420. I need a forensics team and back up out here ASAP, and let Hodge know." He listened a minute to the response and then hung up.

Rick straightened up and looked at the door.

"Don't," Tom told him. "It's not pretty."

"If I don't look now, I won't be able to later. I won't touch anything."

Tom should have stopped Rick, but he didn't have the energy. Seeing Edgar knocked the wind out of him. His stomach wrenched.

Rick stepped into the shaded hallway and saw the body on the floor. Blood soaked the woven runner. Edgar was still partially disrobed, and the paper towel dowel was still firmly implanted in him. Perched on the body were three sweetbriar roses. Rick groaned. He stepped back onto the stoop and sat next to Tom. "Well, that blows a few theories all to hell. I'd offer you a joint, but –"

"Yeah. Not a great idea. Besides, I'm more of a beer man."

Rick nodded. "Beer it is. I'm buying."

"I've been thinking," Tom said. "I've seen one too many dead bodies lately."

Rick waited.

"I'm due for a career change," Tom continued.

"What would you do?"

"There's a couple of teaching jobs open at the academy. I have a Master's in Law Enforcement and 15 years on the force. I could get in. At least it's worth a shot."

"That's not in Vegas," Rick noted.

"No. I'm looking at Reno."

"And Candy?"

Tom shook his head. "Now, there's a question."

***

Saturday Early Evening

It was nearly 5:30 p.m. when Rick arrived at Fran's house to find Charlie's truck parked at the curb. Tom carried Rick's new suit into the house for him and laid it over the back of a large chair. Rick, still on crutches and swearing at them, came up the stairs as fast as he could. He stepped into the living room behind Tom just as Charlie, still zipping his fly, came out of the bathroom.

"Wash your hands, heathen," Rick barked.

Charlie grunted and returned to the bathroom for a few minutes. When he came back out, he held them up for Rick. "There? Wanna sniff 'em?"

"I'll see you guys later," Tom said as he hurried out the door.

"What took you so long?" Charlie asked.

"We had to deal with a dead guy. Alex here?"

"Not yet. But I got a surprise for you." He grinned and several of his teeth flashed gold.

"Surprise me."

Charlie motioned for Rick to follow him as they went out the kitchen door and into the garage. There, parked in the spot usually taken by Alex's Corvette, was a 1957 Willys Jeep CJ-5, shiny red, with black leather seats.

Rick whistled and hobbled up to it. He ran his hands down the surface and over the seats. Then he popped the hood. "I don't believe it. This thing's all been restored?"

Charlie beamed as he took a bite of beef jerky. "Yup. Labor of love. Like it? I got a lot of sweet equality in that thing."

"Sweat equity," Rick corrected him. "Where'd you get it?" He lowered the hood.

"Well, there's a long story to that, but it's all legit, I swear. I got the papers and everything." Charlie tossed Rick the keys. Rick grabbed for them and nearly lost one of his crutches.

"I know you can't drive it like that —" Charlie started to say.

"To hell I can't," Rick grinned. "How long can I borrow her for?"

"Depends," Charlie said. "How much you wanna pay me for her?"

Rick circled the Jeep and stroked the hood and doors as if petting a cat. "She's a beauty."

"Look, I did some swapping to get it, so I did good. You want it or not? I mean, I can find someone else to take her off my hands for real money."

Rick nodded. "Hell, yeah, I want her. Ten grand?"

"I'll take that."

"Good. I was wondering how I was going to get to that fucking party tonight." Rick pocketed the keys and started toward the kitchen door.

"Hey, don't you wanna take her for a spin?"

"I gotta suit up first. I gotta look good for the princess." Rick winked.

Chapter 20

Fran stepped out of the sun and into the luxurious grand foyer of Rupert Hawksworth's mansion. Her ivory heels fell soft on the gold and brown Persian runner that covered the marble floor. She wore a bronze, sleeveless cocktail dress with a straight skirt and a plunging back. A single-strand diamond choker adorned her throat, and her red hair fell soft and full over her bare shoulders.

Jax Saynte was waiting for her. He rushed up to greet her and quickly took her hand, lifting it to his lips for a kiss. "Fran! How wonderful to see you!"

He was dressed in an elegant, tailor-made, charcoal gray suit, and he wore a large ring with a deep green emerald encircled by diamonds.

Fran just as quickly retrieved her hand. It took a bit of effort for her to not wipe the kiss off.

"Mr. Saynte," she said coolly. She glanced around and spotted the host.

In a room filled with glamor and glitz, Rupert Hawksworth stood out. Even in his eighties, he carried himself with self-confidence and dignity, old school and old money in a room full of wannabes. He was dressed in a simple black suit. He casually dismissed a server trying to give him a drink. "Miss Simone." He smiled as he approached her. "Welcome."

Fran gave him a warm kiss on the cheek. "It's wonderful to see you again, sir."

"Please, call me Hawk. All my friends do. Something left over from my navy days." He ignored Jax and ushered Fran into the party. "Besides, 'sir' is for old men."

Fran glanced around the main room with its vaulted ceilings, tall arched windows, and a smattering of art nouveau-styled furnishings. It wasn't a living room. That phrase implied cozy sofas and intimate conversations. This was more like a grand palace hall. Fran never asked how Rupert Hawksworth came into his money, but he wasn't afraid to spend it.

In the center of the room, a man in a white tux played a grand piano, accompanied by a lady in a regal blue gown playing a violin. The music was just soft enough to allow conversation and just loud enough to waft over everyone, settling a sophisticated dampener on what might otherwise have been a typical, Las Vegas party crowd.

"Did you enjoy yesterday's meeting?" Jax asked.

"Very much," Fran said with a sidelong glance and a grin.

Jax spoke up. "I hope you didn't feel uncomfortable, being there with a group of strangers and –" He never got to finish.

Fran turned around to face him, causing Hawksworth to stop for a moment. She spoke quietly, almost in a whisper, as if a great confidence was being shared with Jax. "I watched my ex-husband's brains get blown away in front of me after he shot me in the gut." Her hand went to her stomach. "I doubt a little thing like a board meeting is going to rattle me."

She pulled back from him and returned to Hawksworth's side.

Jax stared after her a moment before he shook off his stunned reaction and rejoined them.

Several hundred people attended the gathering, and most clustered into small groups throughout the room and onto the adjacent veranda or down the stone stairs to the pool. Waiters in sharp white shirts, bow ties, and black slacks made the rounds, offering up drinks and hors d'oeuvres. Fran even spotted some of the other Max-Mil board members, who glanced in her direction but didn't stop their conversations to greet her.

She wasn't surprised. She was the intruder into their little world. They looked at her as if she was fish bait – a messy but necessary part of their attempts to seize more – more money, more power, more of whatever it was they wanted.

Fran felt Hawksworth's hand squeeze her arm. She looked at him and smiled.

"Give them some rope and they'll do one of two things," he said.

"What's that?"

"Either swing to the next tree or hang themselves." Hawksworth lowered his voice and bent to her ear to finish his thought. "Most of these people are hanging themselves and don't even know it."

Fran nodded. "Perhaps I am too."

Hawksworth shook his head. "I've been watching you, Fran. You haven't done a damn thing with your father's wealth since you inherited it. You're careful, and I know why."

"Why?" Fran was curious about how much Hawksworth knew about her.

"You left home at thirteen. You were on the streets by fifteen. You had to fend for yourself every day until you got into law school." He smiled and nodded as she looked surprised. "I know you received a small trust when you turned eighteen, but everything you did after that – college, law school, building up the firm, surviving your partner's – What shall I call them? Misjudgments? Even fighting for your daughter's life. You did all that on your own. You know the value of a dollar and the sweat and blood that goes into keeping it all together."

"You flatter me," Fran said, although she believed he was right. She did fight her way to success, or at least to survival, and she had the scars to prove it.

"And now you are reassessing. What will you do with your future, Miss Simone?"

Fran chuckled.

"Your partner couldn't make it?" Hawksworth asked.

Jax leaned in closer to listen.

"If you mean Alex, no. He has work to do. My significant other is coming though. Unfortunately, he's running a bit late," she explained as she walked between the two men.

"You have a significant other?" Jax asked, keeping astride of her. "That would be Detective Saddler?"

Fran stopped. "Mr. Saynte, I know you're not that misinformed."

If the partygoers heard her – and they probably did – they ignored the comment. Jax, despite his best efforts, was not the center of their attention. Hawksworth was, and the old man smirked.

"My apologies, Miss Simone. You're right, of course. I took the liberty of making inquiries –"

"Into my personal life. I'm sure you did." Fran turned back to Hawksworth. "I think you'll like Rick. He's a former Marine." She paused. "I find that hard to explain. I'm told there's no such thing as an ex-Marine. Once a Marine, always a Marine, and all that. But he hasn't actively served in the Corps for a very long time, and saying he's a Marine implies he's still active duty. Am I right or wrong?"

"Did I mention I'm a Navy guy?" Hawksworth asked. "I have a feeling that whatever you call him will be fine with him. You are perfect in his eyes."

Fran laughed. "I wish!"

Jax waved a server over and picked up two flutes of champagne. He offered one to Fran. He expected her to simply take it, and when she didn't, he nearly dropped the glass. "Oh, excuse me, Fran. I forgot, your drink is scotch, isn't it?"

"Are you deliberately trying to bait me? My drink is water, or ginger ale, or maybe seltzer."

"It's just champagne, Fran. It won't kill you. It's not like I'm trying to get you drunk and take advantage of you," Jax said with a wink.

"You're damn right," she countered. She leaned close to Jax and whispered in his ear. "I may have come from the streets, but I'm no fucking whore."

Jax rattled her, but she couldn't let him or anyone else at the party know it. Instead, she turned her back on him and left him standing with two drinks in his hands and a shocked look on his face. As Jax looked for a server to take the drinks, Hawksworth took Fran aside and pulled her into another room. He shut the door behind them.

Fran found herself in a small library filled with well-worn, leather-bound books. A heavy rug covered a mahogany floor. The centerpiece was a large desk with its back against a velvet-curtained window. A small fireplace, now cold but filled with ashes and fragments of recently burned wood, stood proudly against one wall. In front of it were two large, wing-backed, burgundy leather chairs. Hawksworth motioned for her to take one.

"We had a break-in last night," he told her as he dropped into his seat. The smile was gone from his face. He looked exhausted.

"Are you alright? Was anyone hurt?" Fran leaned forward and touched the old man's hand.

Hawksworth smiled. "I'm fine. We're all fine. We discovered the theft this morning."

"If you don't mind my asking, what was taken?"

"Your portfolio and a dozen other legal documents."

"Damn. You did say you had another one, right?"

"And that, my dear, is the good news." Hawksworth reached into his pocket and pulled out a key and a piece of paper. "I own a condo downtown. This is the address. Once inside, you'll find a large painting over the sofa. Behind it is a wall safe. The combination is YOUR birthday. Got it?"

"Does Jax know about this place?" Fran asked.

"No. No one does. I've only been there once or twice over the last year." He leaned forward and whispered. "After my wife died, I felt the need for – well – companionship. I may be old Miss Simone, but I still appreciate a beautiful woman by my side. I couldn't bring anyone here, not with all the publicity, and I rather like having a retreat where even Jax can't find me." He pressed the key and paper into her hand. "You'll find the second portfolio there. But I'm begging you, tell no one. No one at all."

Fran bit her lip, looked down at the key and then back up at Hawksworth. "I need to tell Rick."

"Do you trust him with your life?"

"Ten times over."

"Then no one else." Hawksworth pushed himself out of his chair as Fran slipped the key and note into her purse. Then he offered her his hand and escorted her back into the party.

"Ah, there you are," Jax grinned as he approached them. "I was just about to show Fran around the house." He slipped a hand possessively under her arm.

Fran turned and angrily jerked her arm away. "Mr. Saynte, if you don't mind, I can walk perfectly fine by myself."

Jax's eyes clouded over with anger as he stared at her. "I'm sure you realize –" Whatever he was about to say was cut off by a heated discussion at the door.

The three of them – Jax, Fran, and Hawksworth – turned to see what was going on. Jax frowned. Fran smiled. Hawksworth leaned back and watched.

Jax marched up to the door where two men were in a tense conversation.

"I'm sorry, sir," said the doorman. "I don't have your name on our invitation list."

Rick Brandt spoke to the man in a low enough voice so no one else could hear. His eyes flashed and his fist white-knuckled on a new cane, shiny black with a decorative, faux ivory crown. He appeared in an expensive black suit, complete with white shirt and tie and a US Marine Corps tie clasp. He kept his injured arm in a sling, so the suit jacket rested on that shoulder. He'd found sharp dress shoes large enough to accommodate his swollen foot, and he'd managed to shave. He even had a new eyepatch, black.

Fran stared at him. She knew he would dress to fit in, but she didn't know just how damn good he would look, even with the eye patch, which, somehow, in this setting, made him look even more distinguished.

"May I help you?" Jax asked as he walked boldly up to Rick.

Rick looked at Jax critically, assessed him, and then simply said, "No."

Jax tried to reach for Rick's arm, but Rick tensed and glared at him, and Jax froze.

"I think you must be lost," Jax said with a forced smile.

Fran covered her lips to keep from laughing. "Oh, he's not lost." She walked past Jax and up to Rick, nestled herself against his body, and slipped a hand around his waist. "He knows exactly where he is." Fran felt the gun at Rick's back. She touched his cheek with her fingers as she smiled at him. He looked into her eyes and responded by kissing her firmly and slowly. Fran was flushed when she turned her attention back to Hawksworth. "May I present Rick Brandt. Rick, this is Rupert Hawksworth, our host."

She didn't introduce Jax Saynte. She didn't have to, of course. It was clear from the outset that Rick knew exactly who Jax was.

Rick leaned over and whispered in her ear. "We need to find a place to talk – soon."

She glanced up at his worried look and nodded. "Mr. Saynte was just about to show us around the house."

A woman Fran hadn't met yet approached Rick and smiled. "Mr. Brandt? Rick Brandt? The detective?"

"Private investigator, ma'am." Rick glanced at Fran with a quizzical look.

Fran shrugged.

The woman wanted to shake Rick's hand, but he had one hand on his cane and the other in a sling.

"I saw you on the news. The hospital hostage situation? I understand you shot that man – the one who was holding the child at gunpoint. That was so brave of you to go in like that. I couldn't stop watching."

Fran looked away. The last thing she wanted was for anyone to realize that she was the ex-wife of the man Rick had killed. Her grip on Rick tightened.

Rick cleared his throat. "It was a very difficult situation for all involved."

"Oh, I'm sure it was," the woman responded with a blush. A few other people, on overhearing the woman, gathered in the small group and eyed Rick.

"We would have all been happier if it hadn't happened," Rick added.

Fran looked at him and smiled. "Yes, that's true. I'm just glad you were there."

"You're a hero, Mr. Brandt," the woman said.

"My hero." Fran winked at Rick. She leaned closer and whispered in his ear. "Let's get the hell out of here. I want you – alone – now."

Rick pressed his forehead to hers and, in a voice barely loud enough to be heard, said, "You are a wicked little devil, woman."

Fran grinned proudly. For a moment, everyone else in the room disappeared. She wanted to kiss him again and would have but for Hawksworth.

"The tour can wait, right Jax?" Hawksworth continued. "I understand you're a leatherneck, Mr. Brandt."

Rick nodded. "Once a Marine, always a Marine."

"I was in the U.S. Navy myself. Of course, it was well before your time. Where were you stationed?"

"Here and there. Panama, Iraq, a few other places."

"I have a wonderful bottle of bourbon in my study. Perhaps we can swap a few war stories." Hawksworth led Fran and Rick away from the crowd as Jax Saynte straggled behind.

For the second time in as many days, Saynte felt ambushed. He couldn't disguise the angry scowl behind his forced smile.

Hawksworth and Rick sat face to face in the winged-back chairs in the library. Fran pulled a small, embroidered ottoman next to Rick's legs and sat there. She leaned against the arm of his chair. His hand went instinctively to her hair, and he stroked it.

"I was in Korea, myself," Hawksworth said as he sat down. "I was part of Operation Chromite."

"That was quite the operation," Rick noted with some admiration.

"Then Vietnam for a short bit," Hawksworth continued.

"Drink?" Jax asked. He wasn't invited to join them, but that didn't stop him.

Rick looked up at Jax. "Bourbon, neat," he said as if ordering from a waiter. "And seltzer water for the lady."

Fran beamed. She felt as if she was showing him off. She knew Jax was still trying to find some footing around Rick, and she didn't doubt that there would be a confrontation between them somewhere down the road, but not here, and not now, and not in front of Hawksworth in his own home.

Jax poured the drinks from a small bar and carried them back to the others. He offered Rick the bourbon, but Rick reached past it, took the seltzer first, and gave it to Fran.

"Thank you," she told Rick. Her eyes danced.

"You're welcome, beautiful." Rick tried not to laugh. He knew Fran loved the game. It was the lawyer in her, looking for the edge, exploiting the moment, making the connection.

Rick took his drink. "Thanks," he told Jax.

Jax leaned against the large desk as Hawksworth and Rick exchanged war stories until they were interrupted by a soft knock on the door. A beautiful young woman with short auburn hair entered. She was dressed in a simple slip of a dress that showed off her figure, and she seemed to glide across the floor. Fran pegged the woman as being in her early twenties and, from her stance and mannerisms, highly educated. Probably a private prep school, Fran thought. What was intriguing was the woman's air of innocence. Unlike most young women at the event, this one was not a party girl. She had a softness and vulnerability to her that was unexpected and that men noticed.

"Mr. Brandt, Miss Simone, may I introduce my granddaughter, Melody," Hawksworth said proudly.

The young woman smiled warmly at Rick and Fran and took a position behind her grandfather's chair. She leaned over his shoulder and spoke softly. "Everyone's looking for you, Grandpa. They expect a speech, you know."

Hawksworth laughed and took Melody's hand. "I would be lost without her," he said to Rick. Then he turned to his granddaughter. "This is Rick Brandt. I think I mentioned him to you once. And this lovely lady is Attorney Fran Simone."

"Nice to meet you all." Melody glanced at Jax and blushed. "Nice to see you again, sir."

Rick's hand tightened slightly in Fran's hair. Rick's eyes went from Melody to Jax and back again. "The pleasure is ours, Miss Melody," Rick said.

"Yes, a pleasure." Fran rested a hand on Rick's arm and felt how tense he was. "We don't mean to keep you from your party, Mr. Hawksworth."

"If you don't start calling me Hawk, I'm going to take it as a personal insult," the old man said.

"Very well, Hawk."

"Does it hurt much?" Melody asked unexpectedly.

Everyone turned to her and realized she was looking at Rick's eye patch.

Rick glanced uneasily at Fran for a moment, and then looked back up at the girl. "Now and then."

"A fight?" Melody had an unabashed honesty about her that took Rick by surprise.

"Car accident." He waited for the next question that he knew would come.

"Will you be able to see out of it again soon?"

Rick offered his answer to Fran. "No," he said softly as if apologizing. "I was looking for a good time to tell you." He lifted Fran's hand and kissed it.

Fran bit her lower lip. Her hand tightened on his arm. Hot tears stung the back of her eyes. She wanted to reach out and hold him and comfort him, but she didn't move. She was keenly aware that Jax was watching them. She sensed that Jax could never be allowed to see Rick as vulnerable. It would be too dangerous.

"I apologize for my granddaughter." Hawksworth frowned.

"She did nothing wrong." Rick looked at the girl. "Out of the mouths of babes." He raised his glass to Melody and took a drink before turning his attention back to Hawksworth. "The truth is often a bitch," Rick said.

"Melody, tell our guests I'll be out in ten minutes." Hawksworth let go of his granddaughter's hand. "And Jax, go with her."

"She's fine on her own," Jax argued.

Hawksworth turned and looked at him. "Get out."

Jax marched out the door and slammed it behind him.

When they were left alone, Hawksworth turned to Rick. "You know his type. The girl is infatuated with him and he's –" Hawksworth stopped, looking for the right word.

"A snake." Rick put his drink down and rested his cool hand on Fran's warm one. "I'm sorry. I should have told you about the eye sooner."

Fran wiped a tear away with the back of her hand. "When did you find out?"

"This morning. Doc said I would be able to see light and shadows, some movement, but not clearly. They're exploring options, but I know what that means." He tilted her chin up and kissed her. "I'm okay, Fran."

Her hand tightened on his arm. "I love you."

Rick spoke to Hawksworth. "Do you know a New Zealander called Ant?"

Hawksworth leaned back in his chair as if someone shoved him. "I know who you mean. Why?"

"We believe Jax works for him."

"We?" Hawksworth asked.

By now, Fran was sitting straighter and listening carefully.

"Me and certain members of local law enforcement," Rick explained. "We suspect Ant is behind the criminal activity on the Max-Mil properties, but we're looking for proof."

"That's going to be hard to find." Hawksworth finished off his drink and set it aside. "Is he behind the bombing at your office?" Hawksworth asked Fran.

Startled, Fran asked, "How did you know about that?"

"It was on the news. I was wondering –"

"No. We know who did that," Rick said.

"We do?" Fran stared at Rick.

"That's the other thing I wanted to talk to you about. One of the other things. Tom came by the hospital. They got the report back from the lab. The bomb didn't have a timer on it. Someone set it off – someone close by – someone who knew you'd already thrown it over the railing. Someone who didn't want to see you hurt."

Fran gasped, stood up, and turned to the fireplace. She gripped the mantle to keep from falling down. Her legs weakened, and she could barely stand. The shock of his words bolted through her.

Rick pushed himself up, stood behind her, and circled her waist with his strong arm. He pulled her tight against him and whispered into her ear. "I'm sorry, Fran." He kissed her shoulder. "I'm so sorry."

"But why?" Fran turned to face him, tears streaming down her cheeks.

"I don't think he wanted to kill me. I think he chickened out, or he would have let it explode in the office. I think – hell, I'm just guessing here – but Tom and I talked about it, and we think Jax got to him somehow. We think maybe Jax is threatening to hurt Candy. That would explain the vase of roses at the house." Rick sighed and looked down a moment before continuing. "I saw Toni in prison today. She asked if I was gonna testify against her. Alex was right; she's in no condition to be behind this." Rick pulled Fran closer. "If Alex wanted me dead, I'd be dead by now. He had plenty of chances. He didn't use them."

"He should know better than that. I will never forgive him if he hurts you." She paused. "You said, 'One of the other things.'"

"Remember Edgar Mitchell? The forensics guy who's been working with Tom on the Knight murders?" he asked.

"Yeah. Skinny little guy. Used to –" Fran's eyes widened, and she swallowed hard. "Oh, no. Don't tell me."

"Tom and I found the body today. Looks like he was killed a couple of days ago at his apartment." Rick stroked Fran's hand.

"How?"

"Strangled. Dog collar. Roses. You know what this means, don't you?"

"The killer broke his MO."

"Yes. He could be going after anyone who knows Candy," said Rick.

"I could be next. Is there anything else you need to tell me?" She cringed as if expecting another hard blow.

Rick kissed her gently. "Yes, there is. Just one more thing. I love you too."

Fran wrapped her warm arms around Rick's neck and held him close.

Hawksworth frowned. "I was going to ask you for help with my granddaughter, but it sounds like you got your hands full already," he told Rick.

Rick turned slightly to look at Hawksworth. "If it means taking out Jax Saynte, I'm your man."

"I was hoping you'd say that."

Chapter 21

Candy widened her stance and rotated her shoulders a little as she stood in the firing range behind Charlie's store. Pete, Charlie's assistant, stood next to her. He was an older man, thin, wiry, worn around the edges. He smelled heavily of tobacco and wore a broad-brimmed straw hat to protect his bald head from the hot sun.

"A little more to the left," he told her as he adjusted her position. "There, now focus on the target, not the gun. Breathe slowly."

Candy nodded and heard the tinkle of the store bell just before she fired. The .38 went off with a blast and the jolt forced her back a bit. She licked her lips and tried again.

"I'll be right back," Pete said as he went to take care of the customer.

Candy relaxed. Her cell phone rang, and she pulled it out of her pants pocket.

"How's it going?" Charlie asked. He was seated in a dark blue sedan just down the street from Fran's house. He peered at the garage through binoculars to make sure Alex was still there.

"It's going. I could use your steady hand, though," Candy laughed. She heard voices inside the store, but when she turned to look, the shelves blocked her view. "Pete's trying, but he hasn't got your touch." She set the gun down on the railing.

"Well, nothing's going on here. I'm getting hungry. Once I get the go-ahead from Tom, I'm gonna head back and get some supper. Maybe take you up to the farmhouse, show you around the place."

"Why, Charlie, are you trying to seduce me?"

"Don't tempt me, sugar." Charlie grinned through his thick beard and hung up the phone.

Candy smiled, pocketed her phone, and picked up the gun again. She heard footsteps behind her. "Any problems, Pete?"

"Assholes," he muttered as he stood next to her. "I hate people."

Candy glanced at him. "Then why work here?"

"Charlie's the people person," Pete explained. "I just stock shelves and keep the place clean."

The store bells tinkled again, and Pete swore. "Be right back."

Candy picked up the gun and focused on the target. She adjusted her stance. She aimed. The gun exploded in her hand, and she backed up into someone. As she spun around, a cloth covered her face, and her arms were pinned to her side. A few minutes later, the world went black.

Pete woke up with a raging headache. He swore and pushed himself to his feet. He checked the store, he checked the range, he checked Charlie's apartment upstairs, and he checked the parking lot before he called Charlie. "Candy's gone."

"Gone? What do you mean, gone? Did she go somewhere? Is her car there?" Charlie sat up straight in his vehicle and took one last look through the binoculars.

"Her car's here but she's gone. Some guy showed up – tall, mask, hoodie. He maced me, and the next thing I knew I was out like a light. I got one wicked headache."

"Pete, you look again. And then you look again. Everywhere. She could be hiding. I'm on my way." Charlie hung up and immediately dialed Tom Saddler. "I gotta abandon my post. Candy disappeared. I'm headed to the store now."

Tom gripped the phone and felt his chest constrict. "Damn! I'll meet you there." He called Rick.

***

Saturday Night

The evening was pleasant enough. Jax sulked away to some unknown corner of the universe. The Max-Mil board members seemed intent on ignoring Fran and Rick, which suited Rick fine. More than a few people remembered Rick from the news coverage of the hospital shooting. They approached him like they would approach an alligator – with caution and a morbid sense of curiosity. He kept them entertained with a dry wit that bordered on insult.

As the stars twinkled in the darkening sky, Rick stood on the veranda that overlooked the pool and smiled down at Fran. She was with Hawksworth, who was introducing her to some people. Rick considered joining her, but the leg was throbbing, and he wasn't inclined to walk down the long stone steps to the area below.

"She's a beautiful woman." Jax ambled up to Rick and followed his gaze. "A foul-mouthed little bitch, but a beautiful woman."

"Yup." Rick took a drink of his bourbon and leaned against the railing. One hand still gripped his cane.

"I wonder what she sees in you." If Jax was baiting Rick for a reaction, he didn't get it.

Rick just smiled. "I wondered where you went. It seems a shame to miss such a great party."

"You missed me?" Jax took a swig of his own drink. "I had some business to attend to. You know how it is."

"No rest for the wicked."

"You should know." Jax frowned. "She really should take the deal we offered."

Rick turned to look at him. Jax was larger than Rick, taller and wider, and Rick wondered if Jax had been a boxer or wrestler in his youth. Jax also had an edge to him. Despite the fine clothes and expensive ring, he smelled like the streets. It was a scent Rick recognized.

"I think you forget your place," Rick said quietly. "She's the one who owns the company, not you."

Jax raised his eyebrows in surprise. "I didn't take you for business savvy."

"We all have our history, don't we?"

Jax scowled and turned his attention back to Fran and Hawksworth. "Sometimes it's not about the money."

Rick leaned a bit toward Jax as if sharing a confidence. "I think, in this case, it's very much about the money."

Jax backed up a little then leaned on the stone wall that edged the veranda. "Max Simone left one hell of a legacy, and not in a good way. The company is in bed with all sorts of people. But I suspect you already know that. Fran is a sweet girl, intelligent. But she has no idea what she inherited or what that property is really worth, not in dollars but in blood. I'd hate for her to have to find out the hard way."

Much of what Jax said was true, but essential things were left out.

"So, that's your line? A sweet girl? I think you misjudged your target. She's a strong, stubborn, kickass bitch. As for you, you aren't just CEO, you were Max's accomplice," Rick said, "and now you're Ant's lackey."

Jax blinked.

Rick kept going. "Your hands are as dirty as theirs if not more so. And yet here you are, threatening mine as if that won't come back to bite you in the ass." Rick leaned heavily on his cane. "It's this simple, Jax. If you want that property bad enough, she'll probably sell it to you, eventually, but not under your terms and not for your price. Fran isn't cheap. You can take that message straight to Ant, and you can tell him Rick Brandt said so."

"You run in interesting circles, Mr. Brandt." Jax looked at Fran. "But how much do you really love her?"

Rick took a swig of his drink, set it on the stone wall, and glared at Jax. "It's too late. We know about De la Rosa. Consider yourself warned."

Rick's phone went off and he answered it. "Brandt." He listened closely for a few minutes. "When?" he asked, and then, "Where?" He was quiet again. "What do you need me to do?"

Rick caught Fran's eye. He motioned for her to join him. Fran quickly made her apologies and hurried to his side. She arrived just as Rick hung up.

"What is it?" Fran asked, nearly out of breath. She gave a cursory nod to Jax and turned her attention to Rick.

"The party just got cut short, sweetheart." Rick turned and glared at Jax. "Candy's gone."

Fran stared at Rick. "Gone?"

"Someone snatched her from Charlie's store. We need to go." Rick gripped his cane and stepped up to Jax. "If I were you, boy, I'd run like hell."

Rick escorted Fran back through the hall. "We'll take my Jeep and come back for your car later," he said.

"Jeep? What Jeep?"

"I'll explain on the way."

At least a dozen pairs of eyes followed them out the door.

***

When they arrived at the sportsman's shop, Fran and Rick found Pete sitting in a chair with an ice pack over his head, Tom making notes, and Charlie pacing the floor. Charlie ran up to Rick and immediately began apologizing.

"I should have been here. I never thought they'd come to the store." Charlie handed Candy's gun to Rick. "I found this out back by the railing. She must have been shooting when –" Charlie's voice froze up and he just stared at Rick.

"It's my fault," Rick said. "I got sloppy. I should have seen this coming. I figured she was safe here too. I should have realized she ain't safe anywhere. What have we got?" he asked Tom.

"We've got security video of a dark car with no plates in the parking lot," Tom said. "Two men – one came in and one stayed with the car. They came twice. Probably casing the place the first time. Both wore hoodies and ski masks. She was knocked out and tied up. Her head was covered with a black bag, and she was dragged to the car and thrown in the trunk. They didn't make any attempt to hide what they were doing, but they were well disguised."

"Tom, I'm so –" Fran started to say.

"Don't. Just – don't," Tom snapped.

Anger burned up Fran's neck, but she stayed quiet.

Rick shook his head as a warning to say nothing. "What can we do?" he asked.

"I've put out a BOLO on the car. We were able to gather some trace evidence from Pete. It seems Pete put up a bit of a fight before he went down. With any luck, we'll get a hit." Tom turned away and checked his phone for messages, then pocketed it again.

"They had a license plate stashed somewhere," Rick said.

"Probably in the car," Tom agreed. He looked around the room. "Do what you can. I know you will. But until I hear something from forensics, or we get a hit on the car, I don't know where to begin."

"I'm convinced Jax is behind this," Rick said. "I just had an interesting conversation with him. The more I know that man, the more pissed off I get. Candy is his ticket to controlling Alex, and Alex – well, we know what Alex has been up to. Now, all we need is evidence."

"What about the paint?" Pete asked.

"What paint?" Rick looked at Pete.

"The guy who hit me had some kinda red paint on his sleeve."

"I'm not sure that's much help," Tom said. "We already know that Candy's apartment was vandalized with red paint, and it was dry so none of it rubbed off onto anyone." Tom thought a minute, then looked back at Pete. "It was red paint, right? Not blue or yellow or –"

"It was red – a dark red. Like the kind they use to paint houses," Pete said.

"I have an idea I want to check out," said Tom.

"Jax?" Rick asked.

"No. Blackwell. What do you want to do about Alex?"

"I'll handle Alex," said Rick.

Tom stiffened. "Just what do you mean by 'handle'?

"Don't worry. I won't kill him. I'm tempted, but I won't – unless he gives me no choice."

Tom scowled. "If you do, I can't cover for you."

"You won't have to." Rick turned to Fran. "Stay here."

"Like hell! Alex is my friend. I'm coming with you. I've got to be there."

Rick sighed. "Okay, but you're staying in the Jeep, got it? None of your shenanigans, woman!" He limped out the door with Fran close on his heels.

Tom got back on the phone. "Sheriff? I need some help. Candy Knight's been kidnapped from Charlie Cook's store. I'm bringing in some trace evidence and a security video. I need it processed immediately."

He nodded as he listened to Hodge.

"I have a lead I want to follow up on. Could be nothing. Could be everything. I'll drop off what I have and check on that." He looked at Charlie and continued to listen to Hodge. "Simmons got that?" he asked, surprised. "When?" He was quiet for a minute. "She should have told me. That fits with what I'm thinking." He hung up. "I have to go. I'll fill you in later," he told Charlie and Pete.

Before Charlie could object, Tom ran out the door.

***

Rick insisted on driving despite the pain he was in. He didn't want anyone else behind the wheel of the Jeep until he broke her in. When he arrived at Fran's house, he parked the vehicle and marched into the dimly lit, open garage. He winced as the pain sliced through his leg with every step. "De la Rosa!" Rick yelled.

Alex sprang out of his chair and his pen fell to the floor. He wiped his palms on his slacks and backed up. A night breeze swooped into the garage and sent some papers flying off the long table. Alex grabbed at them and put them back. "What's going on?" Alex asked.

"Please! Don't!" Fran yelled as she ran after Rick. She had abandoned her heels in the Jeep, and her stockings tore on the concrete driveway.

Rick raised his hand to stop her. "I told you to stay in the Jeep! Don't interfere!" His eyes were on Alex. "You know damn well what's going on. How long did you think it would take for me to figure it out? You're trying to kill me!"

"No – I – that's not – I didn't want to. It wasn't my idea." Alex backed up. "I tried NOT to kill you. I swear."

"You hate me, don't you?" Rick asked. "Admit it, you little bastard! You hate me for what happened to your sister. You think I betrayed her. You think everything that happened is my fault!"

Alex swallowed hard. "Yes, I hate you," he admitted. He took another step back and waited as Rick came closer. "You had one job, to keep her safe, and instead you turned on her! You went to the cops!" Alex's mouth felt dry as he read the rage on Rick's face.

"Toni is a crazy, murdering bitch who would have killed Fran, but that doesn't matter to you. All you care about is getting back at me. Right?" Rick asked.

"That's not what this is about! Fuck, I have to protect her. I have to!" One more step and Alex found himself pressed against the table.

"Protect who? Toni or Candy? Did Jax Saynte pay you? Bribe you? Threaten you? Threaten Candy? Or did he just appeal to your sense of revenge?" Rick grabbed Alex by the collar.

"This isn't – It wasn't – I can't –" Alex paled and nearly fell over. "It's not what you think!"

Fran screamed, "Rick! Stop!"

Rick let go of Alex, pulled the .45 from the holster at his back, flipped it in his hand, and offered it to Alex. "Either kill me and get it over with or get the fuck outta my face! And don't you ever put Fran or anyone else I love in danger again. Got it?"

Fran screamed again. "What the fuck!"

Rick ignored her. "Take it. I dare you! You want me dead? Do it like a man, straight out and in cold blood. No more bombs. No more stupid stunts. No more threats. No more sneaking around. Do it!"

Alex took the gun and held it in his shaking hand.

"No!" Fran gripped the garage door frame and held on. "No, Alex! Please! Don't! I love him!"

Rick turned once to face her, but he didn't speak. Then he looked back at Alex. "Well, what are you waiting for? You want me dead? Then kill me."

Alex paled and felt like he was about to vomit. He looked down at the gun. It weighed a ton in his hands. He shook his head and closed his eyes for a few seconds. Looking up at Rick, Alex said, "You know I can't do that."

Fran gasped and watched.

Rick, calmer, eyed Alex. He took the gun from Alex's hand and holstered it. "Why? Why can't you kill me?"

Alex looked at Fran with a deep sadness in his eyes. "You know why."

"Get out," Rick ordered.

Alex grabbed his jacket and cell phone and hurried to his car. His tires screeched on the pavement as he roared out of the garage and into the night, leaving Rick standing under the bare bulb, his shadow spread across the concrete floor. Rick turned and looked at Fran.

"You knew he wouldn't kill you," she said softly.

Rick limped up to her and pulled her to him as the adrenaline rushed through his system. "I knew he couldn't. Alex isn't a killer. He never was. He's not like us."

"I don't understand. He tried –"

Rick shook his head. "He tried to scare me off. He hasn't got it in him to kill me. Besides, as much as he hates me, he cares about you more. He knows what killing me would do to you."

Fran rested her head on Rick's shoulder and held him. She was shaking. "You scared the shit out of me, you bastard."

"I know." Rick pulled back a bit and looked into her eyes. "The next time I tell you to stay in the Jeep, you'll listen. Right?"

"There damn well better not be a next time."

Rick kissed her. He reached behind her and flipped the garage door switch. The door closed with a groan and a rattle. Rick took Fran by the arm and led her into the house. "We gotta talk," he said.

***

Candy was trapped in an avalanche. The cutting, freezing ice tumbled around and over her, dragging her down into the blackness. All sensation ceased except the cold that sliced into every inch of her body. She felt it crawling over her skin and sinking into her pores. She felt it moving up her thighs as tendrils of ice seeped into every orifice. She couldn't breathe. Panicked, she forced her eyes open and saw nothing. She clawed at the ice above her and around her until her fingernails bled and scratches formed on her skin.

She tried to scream, but the sound was muffled by a mouthful of oily-tasting cloth. Her tongue wouldn't work. She screamed again, from deep in her lungs as she beat at the black ice that enveloped, encased, and consumed her. Her heart was pounding so hard she thought it would burst through her throat.

"Shut the bitch up," a man said.

Candy stopped moving. She swallowed, savoring what little air she still felt passing through her lungs.

"It's the drugs," someone else said. "She's trying to come out of it."

"Fuck, I don't need that. Put her back under. We'll deal with her later," the first voice instructed.

Candy tried to scream again. So cold, so very cold. The surface under her was hard and gritty. Her eyes hurt. Her body strained against heavy ropes. She realized she was naked and exposed. She heard shuffling and felt the vibration of the ground around her as someone approached. Strong hands grabbed her arms and legs. Something sharp pierced her thigh. The tiny bit of air she'd been clinging to escaped her lips, and the cold blackness swallowed her up again.

Behind the veil of her fear, she saw the morgue. She was standing next to a long, stainless-steel table. The still and pale body of Pamela Mayhew stretched out before her. The only thing that moved was the flow of blood from the puncture wounds around Pamela's throat. Candy wanted to touch her friend, to hold her, and to comfort her, but everything in that room was dead. Hot, salty tears pushed painfully through Candy's eyes. Her breath steamed up like a ghost in front of her blue lips. She was standing as naked as the corpse in front of her, too frozen to even shiver.

"I'm sorry," Candy kept saying in her mind. "I'm sorry. I'm sorry. I'm sorry."

Visions flashed in front of her eyes: the red paint thrown about her apartment, the word REPENT painted across her coffee table, Allyson Stone attacking her at Fran's house, the feel of his hand around her throat.

She shivered and heard the voices again, and the morgue morphed into a coffin of ice. Only this time she didn't move, and she didn't scream. The ice under her turned into rough, filthy, oily concrete. The smell of it wafted up to her nostrils. She was blindfolded.

A hot ache grew inside her icy body. Her mind started clicking through scenarios. Were these the same people who murdered her friends? She tried to organize her thoughts. If she could focus, she told herself, she could deceive them. They would think she was unconscious. She could memorize facts – a voice, a sound, a movement, anything to help her later.

She thought about Tom. Her gut tightened. She wondered, if she tried hard enough, concentrated long enough, could she contact him with her thoughts? It was a silly idea, she knew, but she was desperate. She would try anything.

The ground shifted. Her bed of concrete was moving. She held her breath and waited.

"Got her?" someone asked.

Another man grunted.

Large, calloused hands grasped Candy's bound wrists above her head while another pair of hands grabbed her bound ankles. Her head fell back painfully as she was lifted, swung, and dumped onto a corrugated, metal surface.

"We got her," said one of the voices.

"Why her? She's pretty enough but not as young as the others. I thought he wanted fresh meat."

"Hey, I just follow orders. I deliver; I don't ask questions," came the reply.

Candy swallowed a groan and remained motionless. She'd never been so cold and stiff and sore. She wanted to curl up into a ball and conserve heat, but she was afraid they'd know she was awake. She wondered if she was alone. She listened for some noise – any noise – breathing, crying, moving. She heard nothing.

Steel doors creaked, groaned, and slammed shut. A steel chain rattled into place. Locks clicked closed. The earth rumbled, and the truck moved.

Candy drew her arms lower until her hands reached the blindfold. She peeled it down and peered around the box. She was alone, just her and a few old tires and some tattered tarps. A twin-sized, soiled mattress was pushed into one corner. Slits of light appeared through small rivet holes in the metal box.

She reached for the gag but couldn't move it. It had been strapped, secured, and locked to her head.

A disembodied voice spoke to her. "You can use the mattress, slut. The gag stays on. The cuffs stay on."

Candy curled up, trying to hide her nakedness from unseen eyes. The voice laughed and went silent.

Chapter 22

"I'm going to pick up Jim Pearson, warrant or not," Tom told Hodge over the phone. "The deeper I get into this case, the more he shows up."

"You started to tell me something earlier. You had some idea about the kidnapping?" Hodge asked.

"Yeah, red paint. Candy's living room was splattered with red paint, and the clerk at Cook's store said the guy who took Candy had red paint on the sleeve of his hoodie. He said it looked like house paint."

"Okay, so how does that help us?" Hodge asked.

"When I went to see that preacher guy –" Tom started to say.

"Blackwell?"

"Yes, Blackwell. When I went to see him, I noticed that the handyman, Jim Pearson, was painting the shutters on the church office – rectory? Vestry? Whatever."

"Red?"

"Red. Plus, Pearson shows up a lot in those photos we confiscated from Stone's storage unit. Maybe it's a long shot. Hell, it is a long shot, but I want to bring Pearson in for questioning just in case."

"If Blackwell is behind this, and he gets word of what you're doing –" Hodge began.

"Don't you think I know? Every minute, every second she's out there, she's that much closer to being dead. This isn't a kidnapping for ransom. There's no light at the end of this tunnel. We find her fast or it's all over."

The silence was heavy on the other side of the phone.

"We'll find her," Hodge said finally.

Tom heard, but he didn't believe it.

***

"I didn't kill nobody! I didn't kidnap nobody! I didn't do shit!" Jim Pearson yelled as Tom pushed the man into a chair in the interrogation room at the police department.

Tom seized Pearson's arm and turned it over, revealing splattered drops of red paint on the man's plaid work shirt.

"I know you broke into Candy Knight's apartment. I know you painted the windows and walls in her living room and wrote REPENT on her coffee table with the same red paint you used on preacher Blackwell's shutters. I know you've been stalking her." Panic grew inside Tom. Every possible, horrific scenario played itself out in his head. "You've got one chance to tell me everything you know, or I'm going to pin four murder raps and a kidnapping on you, and I don't give a rat's ass what I have to do to do it."

"I want a lawyer," Pearson screamed, his round face red with fury. He tried to stand, but Tom shoved him back into the chair. Tom sat on the small metal table in front of Pearson and held Pearson down by the shoulders.

"Dr. Candace Knight, kidnapped. Pamela Mayhew, raped and strangled. Andrea Ortiz, raped and strangled. Meghan King, raped and strangled. Edgar Mitchell, sodomized and strangled. Was that one yours, Jim? What did you have against Edgar? He wasn't one of Candy's boys. He wasn't into BDSM. He was just a nice kid who worked here. What happened? The man get in your way once too often? Or do you just get off on strangling people?"

"No! Damn it! I want a lawyer!" Pearson screamed again.

"I don't give a fuck what you want." In truth, Tom didn't care. Nothing mattered except getting Candy back alive.

"I didn't kill nobody!" Pearson's hands trembled.

"Then you damn well better tell me what happened before I have to beat it out of you!" Tom countered.

Sgt. Angela Simmons stood next to Sheriff Hodge on the other side of the soundproof, one-way glass. "He's blowing the case," she complained. "It's a forced confession. We'll never get it into court."

"Yup," Hodge said calmly as he watched Tom work.

"That doesn't bother you?"

Hodge glanced at Simmons. "Dead women bother me. The only thing that matters here is getting Knight back. We can clean up the rest of the mess later."

Inside the interrogation room, Pearson was shaking, sweating, and staring at Tom. "I swear. I didn't kill nobody! All I did was paint that bitch's apartment. I swear. That's all I did!"

Tom took a deep breath and leaned back. "Talk to me," he said in an icy voice. "I want to know everything you did and everyone you saw in detail."

"Look, we checked the place out –" Pearson began.

"We?"

"Me and my wife. We drove around and made sure no one was there. Then I broke in."

"How did you get in?" Tom asked.

"I climbed through the bedroom window."

"That's three floors up!"

"I know," Pearson said. "I told the neighbor lady that we were hired to fix the window. I had my truck. I backed up to the building and put the ladder in the truck bed – leaned it against the outside window frame. Then Melissa held the ladder steady while I climbed up."

"I don't remember the window being broken," Tom said.

"It wasn't. The latch was loose, and I just kept jiggling it until it slipped off. I pushed the window open, put it on the floor, and crawled in."

"And all this time your wife stood in the truck bed and held the ladder."

"Yeah, well, at first, until that guy showed up."

Tom flipped open his file and pulled out a large photo of Allyson Stone. "Is that the man you saw?"

Pearson stared at the photo for a few minutes. "That ain't him."

"That's Allyson Stone. Remember him? He's the guy who promised to re-open your son's murder case. Now, I want you to take a very good look and be absolutely sure that you didn't see this man at Candy's apartment."

"No, sir! That ain't him. That ain't the guy I saw."

Tom slipped the photo back into the file. "Tell me about this guy you saw. What did he look like? Did you talk to him? What did he say?"

Pearson took a deep breath. "I just finished painting the living room when this guy walks in bold as day like he owned the place, you know? Scared the shit outta me. I thought he was gonna have me arrested."

"What do you mean, 'like he owned the place'? He just walked in? He didn't knock or anything?"

"He had a key."

"Then what happened?"

"He says, 'What the hell you doing here?' Or something like that."

"What did you tell him?"

"I didn't tell him nothing. I just high-tailed it outta there."

"Did he chase you? Yell at you? Say anything at all?"

"I don't know. I mean, I didn't wait around. I just ran to the truck, got in and we took off." Pearson wiped sweat off his forehead with his sleeve.

"What about the ladder?"

"It fell off the truck. I left it there. Too bad, too. It was a damn expensive ladder."

Tom sat down across the table from Pearson. "Describe this man to me."

"Well, he wasn't white, for one thing."

Tom raised an eyebrow. "What was he?"

"Kinda Black but not really Black, like maybe a mix or something, like he had a really dark tan, only not. And he was youngish – thirties or forties, maybe. Hard to tell. And tall, real tall. And he was built kinda like you, kinda muscled, you know?"

Tom nodded. "Go on."

"He didn't look like you though."

"What about his hair? His eyes?' Tom asked. "Did he have any tattoos? Did he walk with a limp? Any scars?"

"No, no. That would be the other guy. You know, that investigator guy. It wasn't him."

"Rick Brandt? Is that the investigator you're talking about?"

"Yeah, the guy who killed Paul Burns."

Tom looked confused. "How do you know what Brandt looks like?"

"That Brandt fella killed Paul. It was all over the news," Pearson said.

"Okay, so it wasn't Brandt. Do you remember what the guy in the apartment was wearing?"

"Oh, yeah. Jeans and some kind of sweatshirt like the kids wear."

"A hoodie?"

"Yeah, one of those. Black – or maybe dark blue. I'm not sure about that."

Tom tried not to get his hopes up. Maybe this was just another false lead. Maybe this guy had nothing to do with

Candy's disappearance. But there were too many coincidences to ignore.

"I'm going to get a sketch artist in here, Mr. Pearson. I want every little detail you can remember about this guy. Got it?"

"What about the paint?" Pearson asked nervously.

"You help us find this guy, and we won't charge you with the vandalism. Deal?"

"Deal." Pearson leaned back and sighed. His shoulders dropped.

Hodge was waiting for Tom outside the interrogation room. "Good job," Hodge said.

"I just hope it's worth it. We have to find out who owns Candy's apartment building and track them down. It might be a dead end, but –"

"I'm one step ahead of you." Hodge handed a printout to Tom. "The minute he suggested it might be the landlord, I made some calls. The apartment building is owned by Maxi-Mil Enterprises. Ever heard of them?"

"Max-Mil." Tom shook his head in disbelief. "As a matter of fact, I have. And you will never guess who owns Max-Mil Enterprises."

"Who?"

"Francesca Simone."

"This case just got seriously twisted," Hodge said.

***

With blinding lights shining in her eyes to block her view, Candy's head was covered with a latex mask that was secured to a collar locked around her throat. Memories of the last time she was attacked – when Toni de la Rosa tried to strangle Candy with an electrical cord – ran through Candy's mind. Her throat tightened up. She felt as if she was suffocating. She'd been crying and she was too stuffed up to breathe through her nose. A ball gag kept her from speaking but allowed her some air.

She was dragged over the rusted metal floor of the truck bed and dumped on the concrete floor. Two men grabbed her arms, lifted her, and dragged her a few more feet. Someone else was laughing.

"What we got here?" a man asked.

Large, rough hands squeezed her naked breasts, and invading fingers pressed between her legs and into her. She tried to scream. She tried to twist away. In the blackness of the mask, hot tears gathered against her skin and rained down her cheeks.

"That's enough for now, boys." The voice was deep, powerful, authoritative, and cold. A man's voice. "She's bait. When we're done, then you can play with her."

"Promise?" one man asked.

Several others chuckled.

"What do you want us to do with her?"

"Keep her in the truck," the voice said.

Two sets of hands picked Candy up and carried her. She heard a steel door creek open. She was thrown like a sack of potatoes onto a soggy, smelly mattress. The steel door slammed, but not before Candy heard yelling.

"What the hell do you think you're doing?" It was a new voice – deeper, older, with a British-type accent.

"She's bait," said the voice from earlier. "I couldn't get to Simone, so I settled for Knight. She'll do."

"Bait? For whom? Do you have any clue what the hell you've done! Idiot!"

Candy heard the hard slap of a man's hand against someone's face.

"Brandt will come for her. Just watch. He can't help himself. And once we have Brandt, we have Simone. She'll do whatever I tell her to do," the voice said.

"Rick Brandt? Rick Brandt the investigator? What the fuck does he have to do with any of this?"

"He's sleeping with Fran Simone."

There was a long pause before the second man yelled, "Son-of-a-bitch! What the hell did you just do? Why didn't you tell me he's mixed up in this! That motherfucker won't rest until we're all dead! I had a perfectly good operation going on here, quiet, under the radar, no frills and no hassles. And you, you fucking idiot, you had to drag Rick Brandt into it!"

"Brandt was in it anyway. Simone doesn't make a move without him. They're joined at the hip."

"Does he know I'm involved?"

"He suspects so. He told me to give you a message, something about— "

"I can just guess. Who's going to take him down? You?"

"What the hell is the matter with you people?" said the first voice. "You, De la Rosa, Hawksworth. You all talk about him like he's some kind of superman! He's over the hill, he's blind in one eye, and he can barely walk!"

"And he's still twice the man you are," the second voice interrupted.

"You said to find Simone's weakness and use it against her. You said to do anything I had to do to secure that property. Well, I'm doing it. Brandt is her greatest weakness. Wherever she is, he is, like some damn barnacle on the side of a whale. Immovable."

"You were supposed to woo her, Jax! Pressure her. Influence her. Something. Anything. This fucking scheme of yours won't do that. You have twelve hours to clean up this mess. Twelve fucking hours – and I want them all dead, and their bodies gone."

Heels clicked on the hard concrete floor as the second man walked away. The yelling stopped. The stench of urine, feces, and vomit filled the space where Candy was bound and gagged.

Candy's thoughts turned to Tom. It took some coaxing on her part, but he finally lowered his defenses and surrendered to her. She thought about his warm, strong arms that she would never feel again. She wondered if he would adopt her cat. She wondered how she could be so cold and still be alive. She heard her death sentence, but she thought about Tom and clung to hope.

***

"Tell me you got something," Tom Saddler said as he walked into the police conference room where Rick was pouring over photos taken from Allyson Stone's storage unit.

Fran sat at his side. She was sipping coffee and reviewing everything that Rick pulled up.

"I know Jax is behind this. I was looking straight at him when you called. I could see it in his eyes. Are there more photos?"

"Hundreds, all digital." Tom set down a large laptop, turned it on, and pushed it toward Rick.

"What did Pearson have to say for himself?" Rick flipped through the digital photos and slid some onto a file on the desktop for more careful scrutiny. He stopped a moment to pull another chair closer to him and lift his bad leg onto it with a groan.

"Let me get your painkillers." Fran started to stand up.

Rick grabbed her hand and gently pulled her back down. "Not now. Not yet. They'll screw with my thinking."

"He described a man he saw at Candy's apartment," said Tom as he paced the floor. "He's with a sketch artist now."

"General description?" Rick looked at Tom.

"Tall, athletic, dark skin, and walked around like he owned the place – Pearson's words." Tom looked at Fran. "By the way, Max-Mil owns Candy's apartment building."

Fran's mouth opened.

Rick stopped what he was doing. "You said Pearson's still here, right?"

"Yes. Why?" asked Tom.

Rick grabbed a handful of photos and passed them to Tom. "Have him look at these right now and tell you what he sees."

Tom took the photos and left.

"What is it?" Fran asked.

"Not what, but who, boss. If I'm right, Pearson saw Jax Saynte."

"Jax is in those photos?"

"Some of them. I didn't want Tom to know who I was looking for. I don't want to mess up the photo ID," Rick explained.

"Just because Jax was at Candy's place doesn't mean he kidnapped her or killed anyone."

"No, but –" Rick was cut short when Tom walked back in and slapped three of the photos onto the table in front of Rick.

"Who is this guy?" Tom pointed to one of the men in the photo.

"Jax Saynte, CEO of Max-Mil Enterprises and, I think, a lieutenant for the New Zealand mob boss known as Ant."

"Look, we've got this Jax Saynte guy in Candy's apartment wearing a black hoodie in the middle of a bunch of wet, red paint," Tom explained. "Then we got a guy in a mask and black hoodie with red paint on his sleeve grabbing Candy at Clark's store. How do we find him?"

"We just left him. He was at the Hawksworth party. If he grabbed Candy, he has something in mind. He's rubbing my nose in it. He wants my attention. He'll find me." Rick threw some more photos down on the table. "What we need is to find his boss. Ant won't put up with this shit. He won't protect Jax."

"If we could find that asshole, we would have by now," Tom said. "The man is practically a myth. We don't even know his real name."

"What about the portfolio?" Fran looked at Tom. "Rupert Hawksworth has this portfolio with all the Max-Mil properties in it. It's at his condo downtown."

"We need a search warrant," Tom said as he turned to leave.

"No, we don't." Fran reached into her purse and pulled out a piece of paper and a key. "Hawksworth told me where it was and how to get it. He gave me the address, the key, and the combination to the safe in the condo."

"Let's go," Tom said.

"You two go," Rick said. "I can barely walk, and I want to finish looking at these photos. I may find something to tell us where Candy is."

Fran kissed Rick before following Tom out the door.

A few minutes later, seated in Tom's cruiser as he pulled into traffic, Tom and Fran spoke at the same time.

"I didn't mean for –" Tom began.

"I know how hard this must be –" Fran started.

They both stopped.

"I just wanted you to know –" Tom tried again.

"Candy told me about you and –" Fran stopped.

An awkward silence hung between them for a few minutes. They exchanged nervous glances.

"She told you? About us? I mean, about her and me?" Tom asked.

"Sleeping together. Yes. She wanted my blessing, or at least for me not to be pissed at her."

"Why should you be pissed at her? You have no right –"

"I know! That's what I told her!" Fran snapped. "I know," she said again, quieter this time. "I said I was happy for you – for both of you."

"It wasn't like it happened overnight," Tom said defensively. "It's been coming for a while."

Fran nodded. "I want you to know that I love you. I love both of you. I want you both to be happy, together."

Tom's shoulders dropped and his fists tightened on the steering wheel. "I can't lose her. Not like this. I just can't."

Fran squeezed his arm.

**

Despite the late hour, a tall, gray-haired man in a burgundy uniform stood at attention before the swinging glass door of the luxurious apartment building.

"I'll get this," Tom said, pulling out his ID and badge.

But before Tom and Fran could get up the stairs, the uniformed man graciously opened the door for them. "Nice to see you, Miss Simone. I've been expecting you." Then he nodded at Tom. "Good evening, sir."

Fran stopped and smiled. "What's your name?"

"Earl, ma'am. Do you have your key?"

"Key?" She thought a minute. "Oh, the key. Yes." Fran dug it out of her purse and handed it over.

If you need anything, just buzz me." Earl used the key to unlock the elevator box, then punched a code into the pad. "This will take you right up." The doors opened, and Earl gave the key back to Fran.

"Thank you, Earl."

Tom silently followed her into the elevator. "That was strange," he said as the doors swished closed on them.

"Not really. Not for Hawk."

"Hawk?"

"Rupert Hawksworth," Fran explained.

"You're suddenly buddy-buddies with this billionaire?"

"Something like that. He wants Rick and me to take down Jax Saynte."

"Why?"

"He suspects Jax has been using the Max-Mil properties for a number of illegal activities. Since I now own a majority interest in the company –"

"Of course. It looks like he got what he wanted."

"I have a feeling Hawk usually gets what he wants," Fran said.

The condo was not what Fran expected. Instead of the classic elegance of the Hawksworth mansion, the condo felt like a decadent boudoir. The walls were covered in red damask wallpaper. Layers of rugs were topped with piles of oversized pillows. The furniture was gilded. The lights shone dimly through heavily embossed lampshades trimmed in glass beads. There was even a hookah in one corner of the main room.

"Damn." Tom eyed the place. "Who IS this guy?"

Fran spotted the painting hanging over a long, low, velvet sofa. "There. Give me a hand." She kicked off her shoes and climbed onto the sofa.

The painting was of a reclining Rubenesque woman and was framed in bronze.

"I gotta hand it to you, Fran. You sure make interesting friends."

Fran almost said she wished Rick was there to see the condo, but she decided to keep that thought to herself. She peered around the edge of the painting. "I think we can just lift this off."

Tom removed his shoes and joined her on the sofa. Together, they lifted the heavy painting from its hooks and set it on the floor. A long wall safe, measuring about four feet in width and two feet high, was revealed. Fran immediately started playing with the dials. It took three tries, but finally the heavy door swung downward.

"Custom job," Tom said, admiring the safe.

Fran nodded and started pulling out binders and handing them to Tom. "That looks like it," she said with excitement.

Tom stepped off the sofa, plopped the binders onto a small table, and leafed through them. "Yes this is good, but there are so many properties."

"Sixty-one. Or was it sixty-three? I can't remember now."

"Where do we begin?" Tom asked as he looked at her.

"Let's get these back to the department."

Fran felt almost giddy. Candy had to be at one of the properties, Fran thought. It was a clue, something tangible that Fran could sink her claws into.

Tom had a different reaction. The number of properties worried him. Every minute that went by brought Candy closer to her death. For all he knew, she could be lying somewhere and bleeding out at that minute.

They gathered up the binders, locked the condo, and headed down the elevator. When the elevator reached the ground floor and the doors opened, Fran froze.

"What?" Tom asked.

"Earl is gone." She poked her head out.

They heard a repetitive thudding noise as they stepped cautiously out of the elevator and into the lobby. They saw the doorman sprawled out on the floor; one leg caught in the doors of the second elevator. Each time the doors tried to shut, they ran up against his thigh and re-opened.

"Shit!" Fran dropped the binders, grabbed Earl by the arm, and started dragging him away from the elevator.

Tom joined her. He then radioed for backup and an ambulance as Earl groaned.

"It's okay. Take it easy," Fran told Earl.

"The stairs," Earl said. "They took the stairs."

Tom drew his gun, went to the stairwell, and tried the door. It was locked.

"They took my keys," Earl added.

"Any other way in or out of the building?" Tom asked.

Earl tried to nod. "There's a service entrance out back, but that should be locked up. And there's an underground garage." He reached into the pocket of his jacket and handed Tom a small notebook. "The elevator key codes," said Earl. His eyes closed and his head went back into Fran's lap.

Fran checked Earl's pulse. "He's out." She heard the sirens approaching as she spoke. "Are you going after them?"

"I don't have time. Not if we're going to find Candy." Tom snatched the notebook from Fran's hand, went to the front door, and opened it for the police and medics.

"There's a burglary in progress in the Hawksworth penthouse," Tom told the first officers to walk through the door. "More than one person. They assaulted the doorman. You need these to get upstairs. It has the elevator code." He turned to Fran. "The key?"

She reluctantly handed it over.

Tom handed the book and key to the police and told them what he knew. He didn't mention the safe or its contents. Then he gathered up the binders as the medics took Earl away on a gurney.

Chapter 23

Rick sat in the conference room and stared at the photos in front of him. He was about to open a Pandora's Box of trouble, and he was missing a key piece to the combination lock.

His phone made a soft sound and he answered it without looking. It was Fran. She texted him and said that she and Tom had the portfolio and were headed back to the police station. He texted her "ok" and put the phone down. Leaning forward, Rick went through the photos again. His cell phone rang a second time, and again he picked it up without looking. "Is there a problem?" Rick asked.

"You tell me," said an altered male voice.

Rick sat up straight and checked the number. When he didn't recognize it, he slowly exhaled. "What the fuck do you want?"

"I want $250,000 in non-sequential bills delivered to the Max-Mil parking garage. You know the place. No cops. No one comes but you. You don't show, Candace Knight dies."

Rick was quiet a minute, thinking.

"Did you hear me?" the voice asked.

Rick pressed the phone to his ear and said nothing.

"Did you hear me, Brandt?" the voice shouted.

"You're full of shit. Let me tell you what I heard," Rick said. "You don't give a damn about the money. If you did, you'd ask for a lot more and know I could get it. No, you don't want the money. What you want is me. You could have called anyone, but you called me. Why?"

"Deliver the money or she dies!"

"Tell Jax he's full of shit. He's gonna kill Candy anyway. If I show up, we both die. My question is: Why do you want to kill me?"

The phone went dead.

Rick was glad Tom and Fran weren't there to hear the call. He leaned back, crossed his arms, and waited for the phone to ring again. When it did, Candy was on the line.

She had been yanked to her feet and she stood, still naked and blindfolded, shivering in the cold. The ball gag was removed, and the barrel of a gun was pressed to her temple. A man held the phone up to her ear.

"Speak," someone ordered.

"Hello?" Candy spoke tentatively into the darkness.

"Candy! Are you alright?" Rick's throat went dry. They were keeping her alive, at least until he surrendered himself.

"I'm bait! It's a trap! They want –" was all she said.

Someone batted her across the face with the butt of a gun. Her head jerked back, and she fell to the floor. The phone went dead.

"Fuck!" Rick slammed the phone down. He waited. He knew now that it was a "they" and that they weren't done with him. There was nothing else he could do, and the helplessness ate at him. He was raging when the phone rang again.

"You want her or not?" asked the voice.

"I want her."

"You know what to do." The phone went silent again.

Rick picked up the phone, pocketed it, and limped out the door. He was squealing out of the parking lot as Fran and Tom pulled in.

"What the hell! Where's he going?" Fran asked.

Tom immediately turned his car around to give chase. A minute later, Tom's cell phone rang. He put it on speaker.

"Get off my tail, or they'll kill her," Rick said.

"What the fuck are you doing?" Fran shouted.

"They don't want her. They want me. They're just using her as bait."

"Someone called?" Tom asked.

"Yeah."

"Did he recognize the voice?" Fran asked Tom.

"Did you –" Tom started to ask.

"I heard that. Shit. He altered his voice. He knew I'd recognize it. He knows me. I know him. That fucking son-of-a-bitch!" Rick slammed his steering wheel hard with both hands.

"Who?" Tom asked.

"Jax Saynte. That's the guy in the photos. That's the guy at the party. That's the guy on the phone. I'm sure of it. Fuck!"

"Why the hell does he want Candy?" Fran asked.

"To get to me, babe," said Rick. "To get to you."

"But why would –" Fran froze.

Tom struggled to breathe. "Look, buddy. You're both going to end up dead. You know that, right?"

"I got no choice," said Rick.

Tom immediately stepped on the brakes and pulled the car to a screeching stop.

"What are you doing?" Fran yelled. "Go after him!"

"I can't. Not this way." Tom watched the taillights of Rick's Jeep disappear down the road. "Rick's right. I can't just barge into this. We won't have a chance. Not against these guys. We need help, big time help, and we have to find Candy fast."

"I'm meeting them at the Max-Mil garage," Rick said, still on the phone. "I spoke with Candy. She's alive. Check those properties. See which one is nearest the garage and could be used for hiding her. That's where she'll be."

"Got it." Tom turned the cruiser around.

"But won't she be at the garage?" Fran asked.

"She won't be there," Rick said.

"He's right," Tom agreed.

"Keep Fran safe," Rick told Tom. "Listen, boss, I love you. Do what Tom says. I'll see you on the other end of this thing." He hung up the phone.

Fran swore.

"Who else knows about these properties?" Tom asked as they sped back to the police station.

"Alex. He's been researching them for me."

Tom picked up his radio. "Alex de la Rosa is a person of interest in a possible kidnapping," Tom told the dispatcher. "I need him found and delivered to the police station ASAP."

"Oh, god, Rick. Don't die," Fran prayed as she sunk into her seat. Her voice shook with desperation.

"That's probably what these guys are counting on." Tom reached over and squeezed her hand. "Hang on, Fran. Hang on."

***

Rick swore at himself as he drove toward the rendezvous point. He didn't have a plan, and he hated not having a plan.

This wasn't about the Pearsons trying to get justice for their dead son. Rick could reason with people like that. It wasn't about some desperate amateurs in need of an instant payday. Rick had dealt with that kind before. And it wasn't about some lovesick stalker. Allyson was behind bars, and this had nothing to do with BDSM or sweetbriar roses. This was different. These guys were professionals. They had no empathy, no conscience, and no moral code. There was no way to appeal to them. They would kill without flinching and probably already had. They were completely indifferent to the value of human life.

There would be at least three of them and maybe as many as five or six. They would come at him from all sides. If they didn't kill him right away, they would frisk him thoroughly, which meant he might as well leave his gun in the car. If he had to shoot them – and he was sure he would – he would have to disarm one of them first and take the chance that he could hit them with his right hand. The left one was still in a sling. The odds were not in his favor. He didn't bother with the ransom money, which gave him a little more time. He knew it was a ruse. He wondered if Candy was still alive.

Several blocks from the garage, he pulled the Jeep over and called Charlie. "You still got those M40s we borrowed from Iraq?" Rick asked.

"Borrowed? Hell, that's a nice way of putting it. Yeah, I got three or four of 'em in the kitty. Why? What the fuck did you get yourself into this time?"

"I got twenty minutes before I get my ass blown off. They called me about Candy. These guys are pros. They want me for her."

"Shit. They're gonna kill both of you," Charlie said.

"Yup."

"Why?"

"It's complicated. I got a lot of theories and no solid answers."

"Where they keeping her?" Charlie asked.

"Tom's working on that."

"Where you meeting 'em?"

"The Max-Mil parking garage. You know the place?"

"Yeah. Twenty minutes, huh? Guess I'd better hurry." The phone went quiet.

Rick shut off the ringer to his phone and turned on the GPS unit. He then shoved the phone between the seat cushions. At the very least, the cops might be able to find his body, he reasoned. He locked his .45 in his glove compartment. His heart pounded, his leg throbbed, and the only weapon he had was his cane. He knew he could do a lot with the cane, but not enough against a handful of gunmen intent on killing him.

Night had fallen and the parking garage was dark and abandoned. Rick drove the Jeep past the automated ticket booth and through the wooden gate, smashing it to pieces. He would apologize to Fran later if he lived long enough.

Without wanting to, he triggered her memory. She was probably furious with him. She was probably scared. It was also possible that, if he made it out alive, Fran would walk out of his life rather than go through this again. That possibility gave him a deep, aching sadness.

Rick revved the engine as he drove the Jeep up the steep ramps to the third level of the garage. He parked in the travel lane and left the Jeep running with the headlights on. Stepping out of the vehicle, he grabbed his cane, limped to the front of the vehicle, and stood there, waiting. The garage was warm from soaking up the heat of the day. It smelled of oil and exhaust.

Rick heard the familiar click of a gun – one, two, three. The first gunman was to Rick's rear left. The second was to his direct right, and the third was to his front right. Only three, Rick thought. That meant one sharpshooter was hiding in the garage.

"Down on your knees! Hands on your head!" the frontman ordered.

"You want me to fall over?" Rick asked.

"You heard me!" the man yelled.

Rick dropped the cane, and it clattered to the floor at his feet. He slowly lowered himself to his knees and put his right hand on his head.

"Where's the money?" the frontman asked.

"Don't be an idiot. Why would I bring cash to my own execution? Or doesn't Jax pay you enough?"

There was a moment of silence. Footsteps drew closer. Rick saw the gunman's shadow on the floor. The pistol moved close to his head. Rick closed his eye. He thought of Fran's smooth skin, her soft blue eyes, and the way she moaned when he made love to her.

A rifle shot exploded nearby, and Rick hit the ground. He grabbed the cane and swept the first guy off his feet. They struggled, and Rick grabbed the man's gun and shot. Two dead; two to go. He rolled and shot, again. Bullets hit the concrete next to him. He felt a sharp sting as one grazed his shoulder. He yelped as he took shelter behind his Jeep. Another rifle shot echoed in the garage.

Three men lay dead, one downed by Rick and two by Charlie. The fourth shooter, the sniper, was exchanging gunfire with Charlie, who was well hidden.

Rick lay on his back for a few seconds while he gathered his strength. Gritting his teeth, he circled the Jeep on his hands and knees until he spotted the fourth gunman. The man had left his post and was now trying to get into a vehicle. Charlie stopped shooting as Rick pushed himself to his feet and slammed his gun into the back of the gunman's head. The man went down with a heavy thud. Rick sank to his knees, lost consciousness, and fell over.

Rick awoke for a few minutes to find himself inside an ambulance and strapped to a gurney. He stared up at the faces of strangers in dark blue uniforms before he passed out again.

Charlie called Fran. The first words out of his mouth were, "He's okay."

"You were there! Thank God! Thank you, Charlie! I owe you! What happened?"

Fran put the phone on speaker so Tom could hear.

"Three dead. One in custody with a nasty headache thanks to your boyfriend," Charlie said. "No sign of that Jax fella."

"Maybe we can get that one guy to talk," Fran suggested to Tom.

"Not likely," Tom and Charlie both said at the same time.

"Thanks, again, Charlie." Fran hung up the phone. She turned to Tom. "Why not? We could make him a deal."

"Because you don't cross the Ant and live."

***

Early Sunday Morning

It was midnight when Alex was roused from his sleep and escorted to the police station. He was dressed in jeans and a sweatshirt, his hair was mussed, and he felt as if he was walking in a bad dream.

"What's up? Do I need a lawyer?" he asked with a yawn as he entered the conference room. He glanced from Tom to Fran and back. He expected Tom to say yes.

"Not this time," Tom said with a bite to his voice. "We need your help to find Candy and get her back."

Alex stared at Tom. "Back from where? Something happened to Candy? When? Why didn't anyone tell me?"

"Back from wherever Jax Saynte is stashing her," Tom snarled.

"He took her?" Alex stumbled into a nearby chair and sat down. "That fucking son-of-a-bitch! He swore he wouldn't touch her!"

"We believe Jax works for a New Zealand mob boss known as Ant," Tom explained. "The guy is practically a myth. We don't even have a real name for him. He seems to have his fingers in everything, but we don't know who he is."

Alex looked stunned. "But why would Jax take her? He's got everything he wanted. All he can get. I don't get it."

"I think it has something to do with Rick, but we're not sure."

"No. Rick is just Jax's ticket to Fran. Where is Rick anyway?" Alex asked.

"He got a call from the kidnappers. He went to meet them. There was a gunfight. We have one of them in custody but no Candy."

"Is he alright?" Alex asked.

Fran nodded. "Yes."

"What can I do, Fran?"

"You studied the Max-Mil properties. Rick met the kidnappers at the Max-Mil parking garage. If you were going to hold someone near there, where would it be?"

"Is that the property portfolio?" Alex indicated the binders on the table.

"Yes." Tom pushed them toward Alex.

"Jax would kill to get his hands on these," Alex muttered as he started flipping through them. "Maybe he already has. This is probably what they want, but they need to get it from you," he told Fran.

"They have a portfolio," Fran argued.

"Yes, but they don't want anyone else to have one." Alex looked up at Fran. "There's a lot of information in this thing, enough to expose their entire operation."

"And you knew this?" Tom asked.

"I was just beginning to get a handle on it when, well –" Alex looked at Fran. "What Jax wants is you. He wants to control you, to manipulate you, to get you to sign your holdings over to him. He thinks if Rick is out of the picture, you'll break and he'll get the portfolios and the property, and maybe you, as well. Like I said, Fran. You're a commodity. Bright, beautiful, and an heiress. And thanks to your dad, you probably have investments in every dirty scheme in Vegas. Controlling you means controlling a lot of assets."

"Ambushing Rick and kidnapping Candy would get to Fran." Tom pushed himself out of his chair and paced the room.

Hodge poked his head in. "Any luck?"

"Not yet," Tom said as he nodded toward Alex. "He's looking."

"Our guys are at the parking garage now," Hodge told Fran. "Looks like your boy made it out alive."

"That's what Charlie said." Fran willed tears away. Rick was safe – this time. He scared the shit out of her again, but he was safe.

Tom read the worry on Fran's face. He put his hands comfortingly on her shoulders. Hodge looked at them a moment, grunted, and headed out the door.

"This one," Alex said as he opened the book on the table.

Tom looked at the document. "That's a motel."

"An old motor lodge. Yes. It's abandoned, closed down. No one's using it. And it's only ten minutes from the garage."

"Are you sure?" Tom asked.

"I've been there. I'm as sure as I can be."

Tom nodded.

"I'm going with you." Fran stood up.

"No! Not you! Definitely not you!" Tom told her. "We're going to have a SWAT team and bullets will be flying. And I, for one, don't want to be explaining to Rick how you ended up in the crossfire."

"But Tom!"

"I swear, Fran, I'll have you arrested and thrown into protective custody if you so much as move an inch!" Tom turned to Alex. "I suppose you want to come, too."

"Candy's the reason I came back to Vegas. She's also the reason I stayed. I only helped the police arrest my sister because Toni tried to kill Candy. I owe her. I'm going."

"Okay. Just stay out of the line of fire, preferably in the cruiser. Got it?"

"Got it. I don't want to get shot tonight."

Fran watched the two men charge out of the building and into the parking lot where the SWAT team was assembling.

Frustrated, Fran tried calling Rick but got no answer. She glared out the window and then called Charlie. "Are you home yet?"

"Not yet, darling." Charlie looked at Rick who was stretched out on an examining table and beginning to feel the effects of a strong sedative. "We're still at the hospital."

Fran frowned. "I thought you said Rick was okay."

"Oh, he's fine. They're just checking him out 'cause of the leg, is all. The whole thing kinda got him wiped out, you know?"

"Bullshit," Fran barked. "Let me talk to him."

"Ah, well, that's not possible right now, sweetheart. They gave him some meds and he's kinda outta it."

"Don't sweetheart me! What the hell is going on?"

"Now, now. No need for the language."

"Charlie, are you going to put Rick on the phone, or do I have to come down there?"

Charlie sighed. "You might as well come down here."

Fran's heart skipped. "He's alright, though, right? Tell me, Charlie. Tell me he's alright." Fran felt the panic in her bones.

"On my word, Fran, he's alright. He's just doped up."

"Ok, I'm on my – Oh, shit. I don't have my car. It's at Hawk's place," said Fran.

"Hawk?" Charlie asked.

"Never mind. I'll get a cab. I'll be right there!"

***

"Thanks," Rick's voice was slurred.

"No problem," Charlie said. "You know she's gonna come here and find out what's really going on, right? You're in so much shit with her."

Rick tried to grin through the haze that threatened to swallow him whole. "They're gonna get tired of seeing me here."

"You're damn right," Dr. Sam Kaul said as he walked into the examining room. "Can you excuse us, please?" he asked Charlie and a nurse who had just walked in.

Once they were gone, the doctor turned his attention to Rick. "Are you trying to kill yourself?" He leaned forward and stared at his patient. "Or do you just have some kind of pathological hero complex? I can arrange for a nice, comfy room in the mental ward if you want."

"I didn't have a choice. All I did was –" Rick began. He could barely keep his eyes open.

"Run headfirst unarmed into what you knew was an ambush, on a leg you had no business walking on, on the chance – the chance! – you might buy enough time for the police to rescue a kidnap victim. Did I get all of that right?"

Rick felt himself fading away.

The doctor continued. "Those cops out there – the ones who brought you in – and your friend Charlie, they all think you're some kind of hero. But you know what I see? I see a middle-aged man with a need to prove himself and who doesn't care if he lives or dies."

"Listen, Sam," Rick started to object. He was getting angry, but the drugs sapped the punch out of him.

"I'm not done," Kaul said. "You lost a hell of a lot of blood this week. You had three transfusions just a few days ago and you were bleeding internally when you got here. I don't know what kind of lies you're telling that girlfriend of yours, but she's not stupid. One of these days either you're going to be dead or she's going to be gone. Either way, it's not a happy ending."

Kaul, beet red with anger, turned and marched out of the room. A few minutes later, Charlie popped back in.

"Did he say you could go?" Charlie asked.

"Charlie, what's a hero complex?" Rick asked with a yawn.

"It's when some jackass can't stop himself from saving the world, even if it means doing something stupid that'll get him killed. Why?"

"Sam said –" Rick stopped a second. "Do you think I got a hero complex?"

"Nah, just a big ego – and you're hooked on the rush." Charlie laughed.

"That's better?" Rick asked skeptically. His head was buzzing. He couldn't open his eyes.

"Well, you're done being a hero today. We'll get you tanked up on this stuff..." Charlie indicated the IV, "...and maybe we can go drinking tomorrow."

"Any word on Candy?"

"Not a peep."

***

Fran's heart pounded all the way to the hospital. Her mind skipped from Tom and Candy to Rick. Charlie said that Rick was alright, but between Rick and Charlie, who the hell knew what that meant? She wondered if Charlie would lie to her. Of course, he would, if Rick told him to. But that would require Rick being alright.

Fran forced her heart to slow down. Her chest hurt. She knew it was the tension. The emotional rollercoaster ride with Rick was getting to her. She loved him deeply. She didn't want to lose him, but right now she wanted to kill him.

Charlie was waiting outside Rick's hospital room door when Fran arrived. She was out of breath and marching as if going to war. Charlie was leaning against the wall, and he came to attention when she accosted him.

"Ma'am," he said with a mock salute.

"Report," Fran ordered. She wasn't smiling.

"It's the bum leg, Fran," Charlie said, getting serious. "He passed out. They gave him more blood, patched him up, and drugged him up so he can't go anywhere."

"Thank God for that," Fran turned to walk into Rick's room, but Charlie latched onto her arm and stopped her. "Any word on Candy?"

"Not yet. Tom and Alex think they know where she is. They went after her with a SWAT team."

"I should be there," Charlie said.

"Tom would disagree. He's already got Alex to deal with."

"Yeah, but Alex can't shoot worth shit."

Fran crossed her arms and eyed him curiously. "And exactly how would you know that?"

"Ah, well now, that's a long story for another day." Charlie stepped away from the door to let her pass. "Okay, sweetheart, he's all yours. Just don't kill him."

"Thanks." Fran gave Charlie a hug. "And thanks for keeping him alive." Her throat choked on the words.

"Happy to do it." Charlie hugged her back and walked away.

When Fran entered Rick's hospital room, her feeling of panic was replaced by anger. She was sick and tired of seeing Rick in the hospital with tubes running out of his arms and monitor wires taped to his skin. She was furious with him for running headlong into a no-win situation and scaring her to death. When she realized how close she came to losing him time and again, it made her sick.

Fran pulled a chair up to the side of the bed and brushed her fingers through his hair. He was pale and unconscious. He murmured slightly when she touched him as if trying to wake up but then sleep claimed him again.

Fran didn't notice she was crying until Dr. Kaul stepped in and handed her a box of tissues. She wiped the tears from her cheeks.

"You're a gutsy lady," the doctor said.

"Is that what I am? And here I thought I was either a masochist or an idiot."

"Look, I'll be honest with you," Kaul said. "If he doesn't stay off that leg for at least six weeks, he's going to get gangrene, and he's going to lose it. For a man like him, as active as he is, that's going to be tough."

Fran nodded. "I know. I just don't know how to keep him off his feet."

The doctor chuckled. "I suppose you'll figure something out. In the meantime, it's bed rest and crutches or a wheelchair. No cane. No walking. And no saving the world."

"Did you tell him that?" Fran asked.

"I did."

"And you're still standing?"

"He was too doped up to argue with me," Kaul told her with a grin. The smile soon disappeared. "He takes too many risks. You know that, don't you?"

Fran squeezed Rick's hand. "You don't know the half of it." She remembered how Rick handed Alex a loaded gun and told Alex to kill him "like a man."

"I've treated guys like him before. I think Vegas attracts them. They think they're invincible, and then one day their luck runs out."

"You're lecturing to the choir."

The doctor checked Rick over and left Fran to her thoughts.

"Why the hell do you do this to me?" Fran didn't want to wake Rick, and she didn't expect an answer. She rested her head on the edge of the bed.

Chapter 24

The police ran silent and without lamps as they approached what remained of the Pearly Bass Motor Lodge. The building appeared abandoned. Windows were boarded up with graffiti-covered plywood. The main office featured a dark, gaping hole where a door once hung. All that was left of the sign were two naked aluminum poles reaching into the night sky. The parking lot was littered with trash. Someone had attempted to secure the property with a chain link fence, but most of the fence had either fallen down or been torn down.

The surrounding properties weren't in much better shape. Most were brick and heavily covered with graffiti. The few that looked secure were dark, their windows barricaded behind black iron gates. Cars didn't park on the dark street. There was one large box truck in the rear of the motor lodge. Whatever lettering had once been on its cab doors had long since peeled away.

The police were circling the building on foot, weapons drawn, when two cars pulled into the yard. In moments, gunfire erupted. A spray of bullets drove police to the ground. As the gunfire continued, several men in dark clothes and ski masks emerged from two of the motor lodge rooms.

Tom crawled, rolled, and fired in the direction of the unknown assailants. "Don't shoot the building!"

He saw Angela Simmons take a hit, grab her leg, and go down. "Angela!"

"I'm okay," she yelled back as she dragged herself into the shadows and kept firing.

A bullet zinged past Tom's head.

Three of the gunmen jumped into one of the vehicles and sped away. Another dropped to his knees, lowered his weapon, and surrendered.

Tom took a quick look around. Other than Angela, none of the police appeared hurt, and someone was already helping her.

The police then surrounded the doors and demanded anyone inside to surrender. When no one appeared, they cautiously entered.

Each room held a young girl, usually naked but sometimes in cheap lingerie. Several were shackled to the massive beds. Most had welts or bruises. The girls were terrified and shaking. One screamed.

Tom went from room to room as he searched for Candy. When he didn't find her, he stepped out into the parking lot, bent over with his hands on his knees, and took several deep breaths. She had to be there, he told himself. If she wasn't, she was already dead.

"We got the truck open!" someone yelled.

Gripping a thread of hope, Tom rushed to the box truck where police were unloading some boxes and checking the contents.

Tom heard her before he saw her. She was deep in the truck. Someone had removed her gag and she was sobbing Tom's name. He couldn't get to her fast enough. He climbed into the box and found his way through the darkness to where she huddled in the corner. One policeman was taking photos while another removed her shackles and tossed them aside.

"I'm here, Candy. I'm here." Tom knelt down, stripped off his nylon jacket, and pulled it over her shivering body. Then he wrapped his arms around her and rubbed her back. "I'm here. I'm here." He heard the police talking outside. The patrol car's flashing lights danced around the truck.

Tom cupped Candy's cheek and raised her head so he could look into her eyes. "You knew I'd find you, right?"

She nodded as she stared at him.

"I'm going to hang onto you, Candy. You hear me? No matter what, I'm going to hang onto you. You're safe now."

Candy clung to him, pale and shaking. Her skin felt like ice. He got her to her feet and led her to the edge of the truck bed, then he jumped down and caught her as she collapsed into his arms. He carried her to his cruiser, bundled her up in a blanket, and turned the heat on in the vehicle as the ambulances arrived.

That's when Tom noticed that Alex was gone. Tom didn't know where Alex went or when, and he didn't care. He pulled Candy close to his body and rubbed her to make her warm.

"I knew you'd come," she whispered, her voice shaky.

"I'm here."

"I'm glad you're still a cop."

"Yeah, me too."

***

"Hey."

Fran woke up to the sound of Rick's voice and the feel of his hand in her hair. She yawned and looked around. For a moment, she forgot they were in the hospital. For a moment, things were normal again.

"How are you feeling?" she asked as she sat up and brushed back her tangled hair.

Rick had propped up the head of the bed and finally had some color in his face. The IVs were gone, and the monitor wires had been removed and were draped over the machine.

"Better."

Fran knew by now that a better from Rick didn't mean good, it meant a little better than a day or two ago.

"What time is it?"

"A little after two a.m. We got company."

Fran rubbed her eyes and looked up to see Tom standing at the side of the bed and looking exhausted. Fear clenched at her heart. "Did you –" she started to ask.

"We got her." Relief showed in his eyes. "I got her," he corrected himself.

"Is she okay?"

"No, but she's alive. She's in shock, and she has hypothermia. She also got bruised and banged up, but she's alive."

Fran offered a weak smile.

"Rick," Tom said, "this isn't the first time, and it probably won't be the last, but thank you. What you did was ballsy and stupid, but it bought us enough time to find her. It worked, and I owe you, man."

"How about we call it even and you won't have to beat me up?" Rick asked with a grin.

"You got a deal," said Tom.

"What was that all about?" Fran asked after Tom left.

"About you, boss. Why don't you go home and get some sleep.?"

"Because you're not there." Fran squeezed his hand. "I'm furious at you, you know."

"I kinda figured." Rick's leg throbbed again. He wondered if that pretty young nurse would be back with something to numb it.

"Then I don't have to tell you why." Still sleepy, Fran rested her head on her arm on the side of the bed. "If I wasn't so damn tired, I'd strangle you."

Rick stroked her head as she nodded off. "You can always strangle me tomorrow, boss."

***

Alex watched from the shadows as Tom carried Candy to his cruiser and wrapped her in a blanket. Alex wanted to go to her, to hold her, to make sure she was safe, but he knew she was in good hands with Tom.

Alex understood shady business deals. He understood narcotics, loansharking, prostitution, and money laundering. He suspected Jax was mixed up in most if not all of that in the Vegas scene. But he never saw girls treated like cattle before; he never saw cattle treated so poorly. The whole thing made him sick to his stomach. When he thought about what Jax did to Candy, Alex couldn't contain his rage.

He waited until everyone was distracted at the motor lodge before he snuck up to the remaining car that had been abandoned by Jax's men. The car door was riddled with bullet holes, but the keys were in the ignition. Several of Jax's men rushed past the car. One was shot and fell against the hood. Ducking bullets, Alex grabbed the man and pulled him to the ground. The man's pistol fell at Alex's feet. He looked at it for a minute and remembered the .45 that Rick had put in his hand. Despite his fear, Alex picked up the gun, got into the car, and drove off. A few minutes later, he called Jax.

"The cops just raided the motor lodge," Alex said.

"Shit! What about Brandt?"

"He's alive. I heard he took down three of your men."

"Damn fucker. And Knight?"

"Detective Saddler has her." Alex steered the car with one hand and gripped the phone tightly to his ear. "Where are you?"

"Don't worry. I'm safe," Jax said.

"We need to meet."

"Why?"

"I have the second portfolio," Alex lied. "If you don't want it –"

"I want it," Jax said.

"Well, it's been a long night." Alex tried to sound casual. "I suppose it can wait 'til tomorrow."

"No. Tonight. Meet me at the office building," Jax said.

"Which one?"

"The one you so neatly blew up."

"I don't know why you wanted me to do that."

"To put Rick Brandt out of commission. You couldn't even do that right."

"It wasn't necessary," Alex argued.

"If you killed him when you had the chance, the Knight woman wouldn't have been taken and none of this would have happened. Now I have to clean up your mess and hope my boss doesn't hunt down both of us."

"No one was supposed to die."

"Don't be stupid," Jax said. "We don't play with pop guns."

"Rick knows I set that bomb. He thought Toni put me up to it. He didn't know –"

"And he never will," Jax finished.

Alex spotted a patrol car, and he parked his vehicle in a dark alley until the police passed.

"I have orders to clean up this mess, and that means Rick Brandt, Fran Simone, and Candace Knight. Brandt won't live long enough to hurt us."

Alex didn't respond.

"You wouldn't be stupid enough to warn him, would you?" Jax asked.

"I don't have to. I'm sure he knows you're coming for him by now. But you promised me – You promised me you wouldn't hurt Candy."

Jax grunted. "Show up with the portfolio and we'll talk." He hung up.

Alex called Charlie. "She's alive. Candy's alive and safe. Tom has her. Jax plans to kill Rick, and Fran, and Candy."

"You gotta plan?"

"I'm meeting Jax in a few minutes at Fran's old office building. I'm going to try and stop him."

"You got a gun?" Charlie asked.

"Yes."

"The last time I saw you with one, you couldn't shoot your own foot."

"I've never killed someone," Alex admitted. "After tonight, I won't be a virgin."

"Or you'll be dead."

The streets were quiet. A soft rain fell, making the pavement black and shiny. As Alex approached the office building, his headlights flashed against the black windows. A portion of the lower level was boarded up, and bright yellow police tape encircled the structure. Alex parked on the side of the building nearest the fire escape stairs.

As he stepped out of the car, he looked at the windows where Fran's – and his – office had been. He remembered them huddled over the library table and pouring over legal cases. He remembered teasing her and flirting with her and arguing with her, and even the time he kissed her. He remembered the cat figurine that Toni gave him, which stared down at them disapprovingly from the top of a file cabinet.

Headlights turned the corner and spread Alex's shadow against the stucco wall. He raised his hand to shield his eyes. The car crept closer until the headlights were almost at Alex's knees. He didn't move.

Jax left his car running and stepped out of it. He was as calm and unruffled as ever, a sharp contrast to Alex. Jax glanced at Alex's car. "That looks like one of mine," he said, noting the bullet holes.

Alex looked at the car and then back at Jax. "Yes. I had to improvise."

Jax nodded. "You got the binders?"

"In the trunk." Alex stepped behind the car. His hands shook, and he had trouble getting the key into the lock. "You should have never taken Candy."

Jax glanced into the trunk and realized it was empty. "What the fuck?"

In that same second, Alex pulled the gun from his pocket, but Jax was prepared. He seized the gun with one hand and Alex's wrist with the other, and the two men wrestled. Jax was the stronger man and soon had Alex pinned against the car, his back painfully arched. Alex was able to trip Jax, but Jax only fell forward, on top of Alex.

The gun exploded between them. Alex gasped. He dug his fingernails into Jax's neck, ripping at the skin as a searing heat penetrated Alex's body. He panicked when he couldn't get enough air. His chest was pinned tight against Jax's, and both were soaked in blood. Jax stepped back. Alex grew cold, slid off the trunk of the car, and hit the wet pavement. It was the last thing he ever felt.

***

Sunday Morning

Fran awoke to a warm sun on her face, Rick's arm tightly around her, and the sound of the news on the television set.

"Hey," she said as she smiled at him.

Rick didn't look at her. He was staring at the TV.

"What is it?" Fran asked.

"The police found a body by your old office building," Rick said slowly. "Apparent homicide. No identification released yet." His jaw tightened.

Fran's gut twisted sickeningly. She sat up in bed, grabbed the remote, and turned up the sound. "No. No, it can't be. No. Oh my God, no."

She was pale and shaking her head when Tom stepped through the door. The look on his face told her everything.

"No!" Fran couldn't breathe.

"I'm sorry, Fran," Tom said. "They found Alex about an hour ago. I just got the word."

Fran ran to the bathroom, fell hard to her knees, and threw up in the toilet.

Rick sat up on the edge of the bed. "How?"

"It appears Alex and Jax fought over a gun. Alex lost."

Rick looked at Fran, who was curled up on the bathroom floor and sobbing.

"Alex called Charlie last night to warn us that Jax was coming for us. Alex said he was going to try and stop him." Rick grabbed his crutches and started to get up, but Fran yelled at him.

"Don't you dare stand on that leg!" Still shaking, she pushed herself up from the floor, flushed the toilet, and washed her face. Then she rinsed out her mouth, found her purse, and grabbed a few mints. "How's Candy? Does she know?"

"Not yet," Tom said. "I'm going there next."

"You need some rest." Fran wiped fresh tears from her face. "You look like shit."

Tom rested a hand on Fran's shoulder.

She shrugged it off. "I don't want to be touched right now."

"Okay." Tom walked away, his shoulders drooping, his head bent in exhaustion, pain and anger written on his face.

"Fran," Rick said.

She put up her hand to silence him. "Not now." She grabbed her shoes and purse and started toward the door.

"Where are you going?"

"I need some air." She slipped out of the room and walked down the sterile hallway.

Fran had been angry at Alex for a long time, for the way he betrayed her, the way he abandoned her, and the way he defended his sister when Toni wanted to kill Fran. Despite all of that, the last thing he did was try to save their lives. Fran wondered if Toni knew about her brother's death yet and how she would take it. For a minute, Fran considered going to the prison to see Toni, but it would only make things worse. Toni always blamed Fran for everything that happened to Alex. This would only cement that delusion.

As Fran stepped into the sunny parking lot, she came face to face with Margo, who was crying.

"I just heard," Margo said.

Fran gathered the young woman into her arms to comfort her. "Go see Rick. I need to do something. Can I borrow your car?"

Margo gave Fran the keys and continued into the hospital.

Fran drove around for nearly an hour before she found herself at the medical examiner's office.

Hodge met her in the foyer. "You don't need to do this."

"Yes, I do. I have to see him. I have to know he's really gone."

Hodge took her arm and led her into the examining room.

"You were expecting me," Fran noted.

"Rick called. He thought you might come here."

Hodge followed Fran to the steel table where a white sheet covered a man's body. Hodge gave a signal to the medical examiner who lifted back the sheet.

Fran knew what to expect, and still she was shaken. Her knees weakened. Hodge steadied her.

Alex de la Rosa lay expressionless on the table, his eyes closed peacefully, and his thick dark hair curled around his ears. He had a bit of stubble on his chin.

The body had been cleaned and three bullet holes were evident. They had entered from below the sternum and had been fired directly into Alex's heart.

"He went fast," the medical examiner said. "He didn't suffer."

Fran choked back tears as she ran her fingers one last time through Alex's hair. "He suffered his whole life. He just never talked about it." She bent over and kissed Alex gently on the lips. "Goodbye, my friend. Thank you."

Fran let Hodge guide her out of the room and back into the warm hallway.

"Let me take you home," Hodge said.

Fran shook her head no.

"Then where do you want to go?"

They stepped through the doors and into the parking lot. A hot sun had dried up the early morning rain. People were coming into work, some carrying cups of coffee and bags of muffins. The world was going about its business as if nothing happened.

Fran looked down at the pavement and felt like she was walking on nothing – on the belief that something was holding her up even though she couldn't see it at her feet. She panicked. She seized the sheriff's arm.

"You okay?" Hodge asked.

She shook her head no and took a step.

"Fran?"

"You can buy me a drink. Then follow me to the hospital. I have Margo's car."

"I'll drive. I'll have someone bring Margo's car. Where do you want it?"

"She's at the hospital."

Hodge took the keys and stepped inside the building for a minute. When he returned, he helped her into his vehicle. Several hours later, Fran, with scotch on her breath and an intense look in her eyes, walked into Rick's hospital room. "I've been drinking," she announced.

"I figured as much." Rick sat on the edge of the bed, and he motioned her to come to him. "Not driving, I hope."

"No, I took care of that. I'd better get going," Hodge said.

"Not yet. I need you to stay a couple of minutes."

Hodge raised an eyebrow and waited.

When Fran got to Rick, he took her by the shoulders and studied her. "How do you feel?"

"Like shit," she admitted.

"You know I love you, don't you?"

She nodded and lowered her eyes.

"I want you to turn around, look directly at Joe, and tell him why this was a really bad idea," Rick told her.

Her eyes widened. "But –"

"No buts." Rick pressed a finger gently to her lips. "No buts, no excuses. You need to own this. Now, turn around." He pressed on her shoulders until she had her back to Rick and was facing Hodge. Her lip trembled and tears swelled in her eyes. "Tell him," Rick said softly in her ear.

Fran lowered her head. Rick put his hand under her chin and lifted it up.

"Look him in the eyes and tell him." Rick's voice was low and demanding.

Fran closed her eyes a second and nodded. She looked at Joe and stammered, "I'm an alcoholic."

Fran felt her legs cave in under her. She didn't need this. She had all she could handle already. She wanted to dig a hole and disappear. She wanted to hate Rick for putting her through this, even though she knew he loved her. Even though she knew he was trying to help her.

Rick caught her and pulled her back against him. "Good girl," he whispered in her ear.

Hodge stared at them. "I'm sorry, Rick. If I'd known –"

Rick nodded. "Well, now you know." He turned Fran around to look at him. "I understand why you did this. I know how much you're hurting. But everything has a consequence. We pay somehow, somewhere, for every stupid thing we do."

"Don't leave me," Fran whispered.

Rick kissed her. "I'm not going anywhere, but I need you to be strong. Be strong for me, Francesca."

She nodded and wrapped her arms around his neck, as Hodge slipped quietly out the door.

"Still pissed at me?" Rick asked her.

"Yes." Fran wiped away her tears and sat on the bed. "I wouldn't be so mad if I didn't love you so much."

"I know." Rick took her hand and kissed it. "Same here."

"I want us to live together," Fran said.

"Lauren –" Rick started to object.

"It's going to be tough. I know. Lauren will have to adjust. I know it'll be hard on both of you, but you're still her Uncle Rick. She still cares about you."

"I killed her father." Rick tried again.

"It was self-defense. You saved a lot of lives that day, including mine. Besides, I need you. I don't want to spend another night without you in my bed. I don't want to wake up another morning and not see your face next to mine. I want to see you in the shower. I want to find your clothes on the bedroom floor. I want the smell of you in the house."

He tried to interrupt, but she stopped him by pressing her fingers to his lips. "You're the kind of guy who runs headlong into flying bullets. I know that. I know you're not going to change. But the day that bullet finds your heart, the day it takes you away from me, I don't want to look back and have regrets. I want to know that you and I made the most out of our time together, that we shared every second that we could. I need to know that."

Rick smirked. "You know, I could end up an 84-year-old man who chases young women."

"I'm going to hold you to that," Fran said.

Rick held her and kissed her until Fran felt the earth touch her feet again.

Chapter 25

Candy knew before anyone told her that Alex was dead. She felt it in her bones. She heard the nurses whisper near her hospital bed. They were talking about her and about Alex. She didn't know what they knew or how they knew it, but there was a tenor to their voices that disturbed her thoughts, that pulled her out of the cocoon of her sleep. Alex, she thought. Something was wrong with Alex.

"Tom?" Candy's voice was weak and searching. She didn't know if he was there. She just needed to feel safe again. She didn't want to close her eyes. The cold wouldn't leave her body. It burrowed deep into her bones. Her muscles ached. Her head reeled, and the sensation made her nauseous.

"Tom? Are you there?"

Then she heard his voice as he ushered the nurses out the door and told them to leave her alone. He was there. She was safe now. She closed her eyes and drifted back into unconsciousness.

When she woke, Tom was sitting next to her bed. He was holding her hand and he looked drained and pale. He didn't smile. She squeezed his fingers. The fear crept into her chest and tightened. For a few seconds, she was afraid to breathe. "Alex," she said softly. Her eyes filled with tears.

Tom nodded. "You know?"

"I overheard the nurses talking. Something about a shooting. He was trying to rescue me?"

"Something like that. The man who kidnapped you was Jax Saynte. Alex went after him and confronted him. Jax –" Tom stopped and looked down. "Jax –" He had to stop again, choking on what he had to say next. "He killed Alex."

Candy turned her face into the pillow and sobbed, her hand gripping Tom's. She'd felt Alex's presence seep out of her life. She had believed, for so long, that no matter what happened, the two of them would survive it. Now he was gone. "Damn. I want that fucking son-of-a-bitch. I want Saynte strung up, gutted, and beat until he bleeds out."

"We have to catch him first." Tom understood her rage and pain. More importantly, he understood her grief. Alex was an integral part of their lives for years. His death left a hole no one could fill.

"You look like death warmed over," Candy said.

"Now, there's a phrase I haven't heard in a long, long time."

"You need sleep," she told him.

"We all do."

"How is everyone else?"

"Rick messed up that leg of his pretty bad, but they have him patched up. The rest of us, we're as okay as we can be right now."

"What did Rick have to do with this?" Candy asked.

"A lot. He bought us the time we needed to find you. We'll talk about it when you're feeling better."

"Has anyone told Toni yet?"

Tom shook his head no. "That's on my list of things to do today."

"I don't envy you."

***

Sunday was one of the worst days of Tom Saddler's life. He thought breaking up with Fran was the worst. Seeing her with Rick and returning the house key cut Tom deeply. He was angry and trying desperately to let it all go. He wanted her back, but he could tell from the look in her eyes that what he wanted wouldn't happen. She belonged to Rick now, and Tom had no choice but to accept it.

Then Candy was kidnapped, and that became the worst day. After nearly a year of working on him, she finally coaxed him into her bed. He was resistant. She was beautiful and smart and sexy as hell, but she was also brilliant, intimidating, and a dominatrix. The combination scared the shit out of him. She wasn't at all what he was looking for – a nice, normal woman who would keep his life on a steady keel.

But neither was Fran.

Now Candy was safe and recovering in the hospital. Tom allowed himself to breathe until he got the news that Alex de la Rosa was dead.

Tom was surprised at how hard the news hit him. Toni had been his partner on the police force until she went on a murderous rampage. Tom had worked with Alex for years. Tom was, in a manner of speaking, part of Alex's entourage, along with Fran, Candy, Rick, Margo, and, of course, Toni.

Alex was dead, and Tom found himself at the women's prison in Las Vegas with the self-appointed task of breaking the news to Toni.

Tom stepped out of the hot sun and through the doors of the prison. The receptionist checked his credentials and had him surrender his gun. Tom then moved past the first set of security doors and through the metal detector. The guard scanned him and let him pass. Tom went through the second set of security doors, each step painful, deliberate and forced. He was digging his way into her world.

He was admitted into a small room with a large glass window that looked into the hallway, where a guard could keep an eye on them. Tom glanced at the heavy metal table that was bolted to the floor. He didn't sit down right away. The tension in his chest felt like an iron band. He took a deep breath and waited.

Toni appeared in a navy jumpsuit with her wrists and ankles shackled together. Both were then chained to a leather belt around her waist. She was emaciated, and Tom knew she wasn't eating. She was on suicide watch, her fragile mind still reeling from Alex betraying her and leaving her in prison. Her dark hair had grown out a little and now curled under her ears, much like Alex's had. There were dark circles under her eyes. She looked like a stray puppy that was starved and beaten nearly to death.

It took a few minutes for Toni to recognize Tom. She leaned back in her chair, her eyes foggy, and stared at him. A wry smile worked its way across her lips. "Damn. Never thought I'd see you again."

"How have you been?" Tom sat leaning forward, elbows on the table, hands clasped. He wanted to avoid her eyes but couldn't.

She shrugged. "They keep me on happy pills. You?"

He scratched the back of his neck. "I've been okay. I've been busy."

Toni frowned. "You didn't come here to shoot the shit or see how I was, did you?" Even with the drugs in her system, the mind was still working. "What the hell happened, Tom?"

"There was an incident." Even as Tom said those words, he recognized what a complete understatement that was. "Candace Knight was kidnapped."

Toni frowned. "Did you save her sorry ass?"

"Yeah, yeah. We did." Tom cleared his throat. This was proving to be harder than he anticipated.

"So, why should I give a shit?"

"Because Alex helped us." Tom's eyes froze on hers.

"Alex." Her lips formed her brother's name, but no sound came out. "Alex," she said again, louder this time. She gripped her hands together and stared at Tom. "What happened?"

"A man named Jax Saynte shot him."

Toni inhaled deeply as if the wind was knocked out of her. "He's alive though, right? He's not--"

"I'm sorry, Toni. Alex is dead." Tom wanted to reach out and touch her hand, but he knew that wasn't allowed. He wanted to hug her and tell her how sorry he was, and he truly was, but he knew it wouldn't help. All he could do was sit there helplessly as Toni crumpled in front of him.

She didn't cry. She barely breathed. "This Jack guy."

"Jax. Jax Saynte."

"You're gonna make him pay, right?" Toni asked.

"You bet your sweet ass."

"I knew this would happen. I knew if I wasn't there to protect him, he'd do something stupid, he'd get himself killed. And because of Candy Knight, huh? Yeah. Of course, it would be over a woman. He had a weakness for women – especially her type." Toni pushed herself up from the table and the guard walked in. "Goodbye, Tom," she said.

He didn't answer. He watched her being led away. He had the gut-twisting sense that he would never see her again.

***

"It goes against my better judgment," Dr. Kaul said as he signed Rick's release papers.

Rick was already half dressed. He pulled on his sweatpants and dug through the plastic bag Fran brought to find a shirt. "No undershirts," he muttered as he balanced on his good leg and leaned against the bed for support.

There was a soft knock at the door and a woman cleared her throat.

Rick looked up in surprise. "Cheryl? What are you doing here?" He quickly slipped on his shirt and buttoned it up.

Dr. Kaul nodded at the woman and stepped out of the room.

"I didn't realize you had so much…" Cheryl Burns hesitated a moment.

"What?" Rick asked.

"…ink."

"Oh." Rick chuckled a bit. "I had a wild youth."

"You have a wild present, as well," Cheryl said stiffly.

Rick looked at her again and frowned. It was uncanny how much she resembled Fran, but then, that's why Paul had married her. The man had been obsessed with Fran. The obsession had killed him.

"Did you need something?" Rick asked.

"I was looking for Fran."

"Margo took Fran to pick up her car. Have you tried calling her?" Rick sat on the edge of the bed and reached for his socks. He grimaced as he pulled them on. Then he tried the shoes.

"No. I was hoping to catch the two of you here together. We need to talk."

Fran had brought Rick a pair of beaten sneakers that she found at his apartment. His good foot slipped in fine, but the bad one required removing the laces. With a grunt, he pushed it on and looked down. "I'm sick and tired of this shit." He looked back up at Cheryl. "Sorry. Talk about what?"

"Lauren. May I sit down?"

Rick straightened up and frowned. "What's this all about?"

Cheryl sat on a nearby chair and gripped her purse with both hands. "About my adopting Lauren."

"Adopting? What are you talking about? I thought all you wanted to do was keep Lauren away from me."

"I talked to child services. They are going to file to terminate Fran's parental rights and arrange for me to adopt Lauren," Cheryl explained.

Rick stared at her a moment. "Terminate? As in she'll never see Lauren again?"

"Well, at least until she's eighteen. Then Lauren will be free to do what she wants."

Rick curled his hands around the edge of the bed to control his temper. "You can't do this to Fran. It's one thing to limit visits; it's another to cut her off from her child. That's just wrong. And mean. And – Why would you do that?"

Cheryl looked down a minute. Rick scared her just by being Rick. She forced herself to look back at him. "Lauren needs permanency."

"What the hell does that mean?"

"She needs to have security. She needs to know where she lives and what she's doing. She needs –" Cheryl tried to continue.

"Her mother," Rick snapped.

Cheryl scowled angrily. "Not as long as you're in Fran's life."

Rick leaned back as if he'd been slapped. "I know Lauren is upset with me. I'm doing my best to stay out of her way. I'm not trying to cause her any grief."

"You and Fran aren't good for her, and you know it," Cheryl said. "If you're not shooting someone, then you're getting shot at, and Fran can't keep her hands off a scotch bottle."

"She's been sober for four months." Rick lied.

"Until when? How long will it be until you're in crisis again or she's drunk again? Can you promise Lauren it won't happen?" Cheryl stood up. "Fran needs to make up her mind what she wants most – her daughter or you." She turned to walk out the door.

"I love her," Rick said. "I love both of them. I won't let this happen."

Cheryl glanced back over her shoulder. "You don't have a choice."

"Yes, I do," he muttered under his breath after she was gone.

He didn't say anything to Fran when she picked him up. She seemed so fragile. Losing Alex was enough pain for the day.

When they got home, they found a note on the kitchen table from Candy. She was spending the night at Tom's. "He's in bad shape," Candy wrote. "I need to cheer him up."

"It's probably mutual," Fran said.

Rick approached Fran from behind, slipped his arm around her, and held her tight. He buried his face in her hair and inhaled the scent of her shampoo. "You're a strong woman, Fran. Don't ever forget that."

She turned and saw the sad look on his face. Her fingers went up to the patch over his eye. "Let me see it."

"You don't need to do that."

"No, I don't. But I want to." She pulled the patch off and revealed the damaged eye and the scar that ran above and below it. She touched the scar with her fingertips. "You said there were options. What kind of options?"

Rick took her hand and lowered it, then put the patch back on. "They thought – They thought –" He stopped. "Damn." He turned away from her and walked into the living room, limping on his bad leg, and ignoring his cane.

"Rick?"

He shook his head, keeping his back to her. Finally, he sighed and turned around. "Dr. Kaul was exploring some options, but nothing seems likely at this point. I could always get a prosthetic eye, and some cosmetic surgery would help. At least it would look somewhat normal. But the longer it takes to repair the damage, the harder it will be. I don't want to talk about this."

Fran nodded. "Fine, then we'll talk about something else, but first, sit down and get off that leg."

Rick lowered himself into the large armchair, and Fran scooted an ottoman under his leg. As she did so, he took her hand and pulled her into his lap. He brushed back her hair from her face and ran his fingers down her throat. "You know I love you, don't you?"

"You mentioned that."

"Even when I don't say so?"

"You tell me all the time, just by how you take care of me." She frowned a little in concern. "Why, Rick? What happened?"

"Cheryl came to the hospital today."

Fran tensed in his arms. "What did she say?"

"She wants to adopt Lauren."

Fran sat up and turned to face him. "That little bitch is NOT getting my daughter! She's mine. She can't take her away from me."

"She said child services is trying to terminate your right." Rick watched as Fran teared up. He pressed his hand to her cheek.

"I'm a good mother! I took care of her fine for twelve years. That's got to count for something!"

"It's my fault," said Rick. "Remember when I told you that we all pay the consequences for our actions sooner or later? Well, the bill is due. Lauren doesn't want to be here so long as you and I are together. Either she's in your life or I am. That's the ultimatum."

"No, no, oh no." Fran grew angrier by the moment. "That's not fair. That's just not right. I can't lose you. Hell, I can't lose her! Oh my god, Rick, what the hell are we supposed to do?" She wrapped her arms around his neck and held onto him.

"I'm working on that," he whispered in her ear. "It's not gonna be easy, I know, but I need you to be strong, Francesca. Promise me you'll be strong through this."

"I'll do whatever you want," she told him.

"I'm going to do whatever it takes to get her back to you. I promise."

She nodded.

***

Sunday Night

Fran couldn't sleep. She kept rolling Cheryl's words around in her head: termination of parental rights, adoption of Lauren, Rick was no good for the child, every girl deserved a safe home. Fran never felt so safe as she did with Rick, but she also knew that Rick killed Lauren's father. The shooting was justified, she reminded herself. That was a word that wouldn't let her sleep, either. Making sure she didn't disturb Rick, she crawled out of bed, slipped on a robe, and padded barefoot down the carpeted hallway to Lauren's unused bedroom.

As Fran looked around the room, she realized it could use some redecorating. Lauren was thirteen now, and most of what was in here was geared toward a younger child. Fran hugged herself in the dark.

"Fran?" Rick asked quietly from the doorway.

She only half heard him, as if in a dream. She didn't look up.

"Fran?" he said again, a little louder.

She jumped and turned around.

He stood in the dark, still naked, his hand resting on the door frame as he studied her. "Are you alright?"

She almost laughed. Instead, she rolled her eyes as she tried to sound nonchalant. "I can't sleep."

He walked quietly into the room and rested his hand on her arm. "It's going to work out. You'll see. One way or another, Lauren will come home."

"But Cheryl said –" Fran began.

"I know what she said. I know how upset you are. That's why I took the other apartment, so I won't have to be here when Lauren is here." He smoothed her hair back as he spoke to her. "I'm never going to come between you and your daughter. Believe me."

"I don't want to lose you."

"Come back to bed," he said.

She leaned on his shoulder and wrapped her arms around his neck. It was late. The week had been insane. All she wanted was a good night's sleep.

Rick led her back to the bedroom, slipped the robe off her cool shoulders, and laid her on the bed. He covered her up and lay next to her. He couldn't sleep, either.

Chapter 26
Monday Morning

Rick woke in his own bed, or in what he had come to think of as his own bed, at Fran's house. He was up most of the night trying to work some sense into the custody situation. The few times when he was able to doze off, Fran woke him with recurring nightmares. As Rick rolled over in bed to hold her, he found her gone and her spot cool.

Frowning, Rick listened for the shower but didn't hear it. Instead, he heard some sounds coming from the kitchen, and he smelled the aroma of fresh coffee. Rick sat up, slipped on his sweatpants, grabbed his crutches, and hobbled out to see what was going on.

Candy was busy making breakfast. She was dressed professionally in navy slacks and a white blouse and heels, and she wore a single strand of pearls around her throat.

"Morning, sleepyhead," she said with a smile as she eyed him up and down. "Damn, you look good this morning."

"Liar. When did you get here?" Rick asked, startled to see her.

"About an hour ago. I had to get a change of clothes." She poured him a cup of coffee and set it on the table.

He eyed her carefully. He was surprised the hospital released her the night before, but he was more surprised that she seemed unaffected by all that happened to her. "Are you okay?" he asked as he sat down.

Candy stopped a moment and glanced at him. There was a flash of fear on her face and then it subsided. "I am as long as no one talks about it." She sat opposite him.

He nodded. "Going somewhere?"

"I'm being considered for a full-time position at the university. I have to meet the department head in about an hour." She glanced at the kitchen clock.

"Shitty timing," Rick noted. "Where's Fran?"

"Running errands. I think she's going to the funeral parlor to put a deposit down on everything." Candy's face paled. She took a drink of coffee.

Rick reached out to take her hand, but she pulled it away and stood up. Rick started to speak when the doorbell rang. "I'll get it," he said.

He wielded his way to the hall and opened the door. Two middle-aged women in pantsuits were standing on the front porch. Rick groaned. In that second, Rick thought he should have put on a shirt and shoes, but it was too late now.

"I'm sorry. We don't accept solicitations," he said as he started to close the door.

"Mr. Brandt?"

Rick stopped and looked at the speaker.

"I'm Ruth Miller and this is Jill Moreland. We're from child services. We have an appointment with Mrs. Simone."

"Miss Simone," Rick corrected. "She's not in this morning, and I don't think she was expecting you." He turned a bit and called out to Candy. "Did Fran say anything about a meeting with some social workers this morning?"

"Nope," Candy responded. She grabbed her coffee cup and joined him at the front door.

Rick turned back to the women on the porch. "Well, she's not here." He felt a little woozy and leaned against the doorframe.

"I left a message with the nice young man who answered the phone Friday," Miller said. "Alex something?"

Candy stepped back a bit. Her grip tightened on her mug.

"Alex is dead," Rick said bluntly. "Fran is out making funeral arrangements. I suggest you call her later."

The two women exchanged concerned glances.

"May we come in?" Miller asked as she stepped forward.

"Not on my watch." Rick straightened up and blocked the door. He struggled to keep his balance on the crutches.

"And you are?" Miller asked Candy.

"Late for work," Rick interrupted.

"Oh my god! The eggs!" Candy hurried back to the kitchen.

"I take it you live here?" Miller asked Rick as she eyed his shirtless chest.

"I have my own place."

"Then you just sleep here. You certainly aren't dressed like someone who just stopped in for a visit."

Rick considered lying to her, but he sensed it would come back to bite him in the ass. Instead, he chose to ignore the accusation. "Like I said, you can call Fran later."

"Mr. Brandt, I'm sure you realize how important it is for us to assess the condition and safety of Mrs. Simone's home before we can permit her daughter to return," Moreland interjected.

Rick stiffened. "Don't give me that bullshit. You just want an excuse to search the house so that bitch Cheryl Burns can steal MISS Simone's daughter!" The second the words left his mouth, he regretted saying them.

"I've gotta run!" Candy said as she grabbed her purse and keys. She gave Rick a kiss on the cheek and scooted past the women on the porch.

"Have a good day, sweetheart," Rick said with a smirk.

"Mr. Brandt!" Miller said. "The only person standing between MISS Simone and her daughter is YOU. You're the one who killed Lauren's father. You're the one with a history of violence. You're the one Lauren is afraid of, and you're the one who is shacking up with Lauren's mother. Do you see the problem here?"

Rick wanted to say that he was also the person who kept Fran alive and sober, but he realized that would only make Fran look bad. "We're done here," Rick said as he slammed the door on them. He staggered back to the living room and collapsed into a chair.

When his head cleared and he had showered and dressed, Rick called Candy. "I blew it."

"Yeah. I was there."

"Any suggestions?"

"Look sweetie, these people mean well," Candy told him. "They're overworked and underpaid, and they do have the kid's welfare at heart. As long as you see them as the bad guys, you're not going to get anywhere."

Rick groaned. "They see me as the bad guy."

"You know the old saying, you can't beat city hall? No matter what you do, these guys have bigger guns." When he didn't respond, she added, "Go down there. Make nice. Get them on your side."

"It's not going to work. I know the type. They take one look at me and run the other way, usually screaming."

"It can't hurt to try," Candy said.

Rick rubbed his tense neck and nodded. "Okay, I'll give it a try, but I'll have you to blame if it blows up in my face."

"I'm tough. I can handle it. Gotta go!"

An hour later, Rick huddled on a small chair in the child services waiting room. Across from him, a little boy played in a toy box, making zooming noises and driving a wooden truck around. Every so often he looked up at Rick and stared at him, then Rick looked away and the boy went back to playing. A few women came and went, one with a baby on her hip. She was wearing beach sandals, stretch shorts that were several sizes too small and rode up her ass, and a low plunging, striped tank top. She held a cell phone to her ear and talked as she checked in. When she caught Rick looking at her and the baby, she gave him the finger.

Rick picked up a magazine and flipped through it. He was relieved when they finally called him in. He was escorted to a small conference room and told to wait. Rick leaned his crutches against the table and lowered himself into a chair with a grunt. He wanted to take his meds that morning, but he was worried about being alert during this meeting. This might be the only chance he had to salvage his relationship with Fran and Lauren. He had to be sharp.

A man entered and smiled at Rick. He sat down across from him and put a thick file on the table. "Hi. I'm Andy Doyle. You're Rick Brandt?"

Rick nodded and sized up the man. He was fortyish, with light brown hair that harbored a few gray strands. His eyes were blue and keen behind glasses. He was clean-shaven and wore a button-down shirt and khakis. Rick had the feeling he was looking at a relative of Tom's.

"So, you're here to talk about Lauren Burns," Doyle said.

Rick shifted in his chair and leaned forward, his hands on the table. "I had a run-in with two of your workers this morning, Miller and – I can't remember the other one."

"Moreland. Yes, they told me. In detail." Doyle smiled.

Rick rubbed his eyes. "Look, I just got outta the hospital. I gotta bum leg, and they got me doped up on meds. I was rude to them. I'm sorry. They shouldn't hold that against Fran. She's a good woman. She deserves to have Lauren back."

Doyle tapped the folder in front of him and studied Rick a moment. "You're not the kind of man who apologizes much, are you?"

Rick looked down at his hands. "Fran –" he started to say.

"This isn't about Miss Simone," Doyle interrupted. "This is about Lauren Burns, about her needs, and about how she feels."

"I understand how she feels. I don't blame her. I've made a point to keep my own place and stay away when she's around. I don't want to cause that little girl any grief."

Doyle sighed and leaned back. "I read the police report. I know you didn't have a choice. Any man in your shoes would have done the same thing. Nonetheless, you shot and killed Paul Burns. Right or wrong, that's traumatic for a thirteen-year-old girl."

Rick nodded.

"If it stopped there, maybe we'd be more lenient, but –" Doyle hesitated.

"But what?" Rick glanced at the thick file and back at Doyle. Rick felt the tension go up in the room. He was about to be hit with both barrels and he knew it. Somehow, kneeling on the ground in front of three men trying to assassinate him seemed easy in comparison.

"It's your history we're worried about," Doyle said as he opened the file and pulled out some notes. "You've been involved in numerous shootings. You are reported to have a gambling addiction. You expose yourself to high-risk situations. You've been in jail –"

"Juvie," Rick protested. "Hell, that was a lifetime ago!"

"Juvie, then." Doyle made a note. "You aided a murder suspect in escaping the country."

"That charge was dropped."

"And you already surrendered one child to the state," Doyle finished. He looked back up at Rick.

Rick's hands clenched together. "I didn't surrender nothing. I was sixteen. We eloped. Her parents annulled the marriage and took my son. They signed him away, not me. I didn't have any say in the matter."

"Still, you –" Doyle began again.

"Twenty-seven minutes." Rick's fists clenched. "Twenty-seven minutes: that's how long I got to hold my son. You know how I remember? Because they told me I had thirty minutes to say goodbye, and I was holding him and watching the clock, and they took him away three minutes early. I was sixteen and that was probably the most important day of my life."

"Regardless," said Doyle, "that's not the kind of history we look for when we want to place a child in a home."

"I'm not asking for Lauren to live with me," Rick argued. "I'm asking for Fran. She loves that girl. She'd do anything for her."

"And you love Miss Simone?"

Rick nodded. "Yeah, I do."

"How much?" Doyle closed the file and waited.

How much do you love her? Why was that question haunting him? Jax asked it. Doyle asked it. What did he have to do to prove how much? "I'm here, ain't I?"

"Look, here's the deal," Doyle said. "You're not good for Lauren. Heck, I'm not sure Fran is good for Lauren, but at least she's her mother. Bottom line, if you're in Fran's life, you're in Lauren's life, and we don't want you in Lauren's life. So, it comes down to this, just how much do you love Fran Simone? What are you willing to do to help her get her daughter back?"

Rick was steaming. His mind battled over all the things he wanted to say and yet knew better than to say. Instead, he picked up his crutches and pushed himself up. Without another word, he turned and hobbled out.

***

Monday Afternoon

Tom knew Rick was home. Rick's Jeep was parked in the driveway in front of the open garage door. A large duffle bag was on the front seat. No one answered the front door, but jazz played loudly throughout the house, and Tom was sure the bell wasn't being heard. He circled around to the garage and entered.

The long tables that Alex used as a workspace were still there. The piles of papers and folders hadn't been touched. Tom turned away from them and tried the kitchen door. It was open. He walked into Fran's home, made his way to the living room, and turned off the music. In seconds, Rick appeared, a small silver gun case in his hand.

"Hey. You startled me. I thought that was Fran." Rick was using his cane and tentatively walking on his bad leg against medical orders.

"Why would Fran coming home startle you?"

Rick didn't answer. He limped into the kitchen, put the case on the counter, and started preparing a thermos.

Tom followed. "Where are you going?"

"Home." Rick gripped the edge of the counter as if he was going to break it in half. He took a deep breath and focused on the coffee again.

"To your apartment?"

"For now."

Tom walked up to Rick and roughly put a hand on his shoulder to turn Rick around. Rick shrugged Tom off at first but eventually faced him. Rick had dark circles under a swollen and bloodshot eye, and he was exhausted. He smelled of pot.

"What's going on?" Tom asked.

"None of your damn business."

"Bullshit." Tom's gut tightened. "You're leaving her, aren't you?"

"What are you talking about?" Rick limped over to the table and sat down. The leg was throbbing again, and he swore under his breath. He set the cup down and stretched out the leg to relieve the pressure.

"I saw the duffle bag in the Jeep. You look like shit. There's only one thing I know of that would upset you like this – Fran. You're leaving her."

Rick groaned and leaned against the table. His head and shoulders drooped.

"I don't get it. What the hell's going on, Rick?"

"Child services won't let Lauren come home unless I'm completely outta the picture." Rick looked up at Tom.

"That's not right." Tom sat down opposite Rick. "I have some pull at child services. I can talk to someone for you."

"It's not that simple." Rick looked at his thermos, unscrewed the lid, and took a drink, then put the lid back on. "I fucked up, and not just once. My whole life is one big fuck up." He looked back at Tom. "I had a visit from some social workers this morning. I said some things."

"Things you regret."

"Yup. Something like that. Well, things I shouldn't have said, anyway."

"How are you going to fix it?"

"Candy suggested I go talk to child services downtown, so I did." Rick scoffed. "Like that did me any good. That son-of-a-bitch sat right there and told me my life's story, all the bad parts. They even dug up my juvie record. Damn."

"I know you have a history. We all know it. But you're a good man and you love her. This isn't right." Tom leaned against the table. "Hey, I WANT you to go! I wish you'd never come back. But I'm not an idiot. I know how much she loves you. This'll kill her! Let me see what I can do. Let me talk to these people."

"I've got to get outta here before Fran comes home. I'm going to my apartment for a bit and figure things out."

"You mean you're going to break her heart," Tom snapped.

"What choice do I have?" Rick wanted to smash something. "If I stay, she doesn't get her daughter back. I can't be responsible for that. I can't stop that from happening."

"Have you talked to Cheryl?" Tom asked quietly, hoping to calm Rick down.

"Yes. She came to the hospital. She warned me. Child services will terminate Fran's parental rights and –"

"Terminate? I thought you were just talking about visitation or not letting Lauren live here, but terminate her rights? That's serious shit."

"They read me the riot act. If I'm not gone, Fran loses Lauren for good." Rick shook his head. "Fran shouldn't have to choose. Hell, she can't choose. She can't give up Lauren.

I know that." He took a deep breath. "If I stay – I can't do that to her."

"Stay. Tell her. Talk it out with her," Tom urged.

"I'm doing the right thing," Rick argued.

"Damn it, man! Sometimes you can do the right thing the wrong way."

"I've played that recording over in my head a hundred times," said Rick. "It never ends well."

"There's got to be a better way."

"You find it, you let me know. You got my number."

Tom stood up. "Just wait a few days, Rick. Give me some time to think about it. Let me see what I can do."

"Did you want something?" Rick asked. "You never said why you were here."

"You weren't picking up your phone. Fran asked me to look in on you. She's worried about you."

Rick closed his eye and slumped back in the chair. "Fuck."

"We still have our hands full, you know. Jax Saynte is on the loose, and I've yet to figure out who's killing Candy's friends. You want to be helpful? I could use a hand."

"I won't be far. You got my number." Rick picked up his cane, the thermos, and the gun case and limped out to his Jeep.

"At least leave her a note!" Tom yelled after him.

Chapter 27
Monday Evening

Fran called Rick repeatedly that afternoon. She went to the funeral home that morning, grabbed a quick lunch with Margo, and then ran to court to file some papers. When Rick didn't answer, she frantically called Tom to check on Rick. When Tom didn't get back to her either, she had a sinking feeling in her gut that she tried to ignore. Rick was recovering. He was exhausted. He was probably asleep or in the shower or had his phone turned off. If something was wrong, Tom would have called her. Right? She bit her nail and then chided herself. Rick was fine, she was sure, but things had been in such a crisis for so long that she was having a hard time adjusting to a normal day.

Fran wanted to look at some property with Rick, to move her office out of her garage and into more pleasant surroundings – surroundings that didn't remind her of Alex. She needed help with Alex's funeral arrangements. She wasn't sure she was emotionally ready to pick out a casket or gravestone or memorial cards. She was weepy. Rick could help her with that. He always helped her with everything. He was the rock that held her together.

She tried calling him again. Her call went directly to voicemail.

When Fran got home, her heart sank when she saw that Rick's new Jeep was gone. She parked in the driveway and opened the garage door, which brought her face-to-face with Alex's ghost in the form of long, folding tables covered with files, folders, boxes, and papers. Several folding metal chairs edged a table at an angle, facing each other. She'd brought him food – leftovers from something Margo had made.

Fran walked up to Alex's chair and rested her hands on the back of it. The grief of his loss overwhelmed her. Her knees weakened, and she sank into the chair next to his, rested her head on her arms, and fought back her tears. Her thoughts were crowded with memories, good and bad, starting with the day they first met at his law office, the very office that would eventually become hers, and including the day Rick confronted Alex and forced him out.

Then there was the last time Fran saw Alex alive, at the police station when Alex left with Tom to rescue Candy. It never occurred to Fran that she wouldn't see him again. She didn't kiss him or hug him or even tell him to be careful. She never imagined that he wouldn't come back.

Fran picked up her head and wiped away the tears. There were things to do and plans to make.

Fran called Rick's name when she walked into the kitchen, even though she knew his Jeep wasn't there. It was a habit. She came home and she called out for him. She went to his room in case he was napping, but there was no sign of him. It wasn't until she returned to the kitchen to make coffee that she saw the note, folded in half and pitched like a tent next to the coffee maker.

Fran frowned and picked it up. She immediately recognized Rick's handwriting.

"I went to child services today. They told me you gotta choose – me or Lauren. If I stay, they'll take her away for good. I got too much history and they don't like it. They don't like me. I can't do that to you, babe. You shouldn't have to choose. This sucks. Love you. Be strong. Rick."

Fran crumpled up the note and threw it on the floor. She couldn't breathe. She stumbled backward until she fell into a chair. Her chest ached with a stabbing pain that doubled her over. She gasped for air and slipped to the floor. Curled up in a ball, she fought the hyperventilation that threatened to knock her unconscious. At last, her sobs broke free, followed by an angry, shrieking cry that flooded the house.

Fran didn't know how long she was on the kitchen floor. It didn't matter. She was cold and stiff, her head pounded, and her entire body ached. She crawled to the kitchen sink, opened the cupboard, and started plowing through various cleaning products until she got to her secret stash, the $400 bottle of scotch. A gift, Alex said. He didn't know from whom, but Fran could guess. She was sure Jax sent it, the bastard. She had no intention of drinking it until now.

She didn't know what she was going to do, only that she couldn't bear the thought of losing Rick. She stood up, opened the bottle in her hand, took a couple of swigs, and dragged herself into the living room where Rick had smashed her last bottle of scotch against the wall. It was the booze or him, he said. Only now he was gone, and what did she have to lose? It was going to be a long, lonely night. She might as well spend it drunk.

She spotted the fireplace poker and picked it up. It was black and sooty and heavy in her small hand. At first, she just wanted to hit something – anything – to make the pain go away. She started with the glass doors to the secretary desk that had housed her bar. She could still see Rick's reflection in the beveled glass when he stood behind her the first night they made love. The glass shattered into crystal splinters around her feet.

Then she started on the lamps, then the pictures on the shelves, and then the television set. Somehow, she lost track of what she was smashing or why; she couldn't stop.

When she was forced to quit, she stumbled into the kitchen and gripped her throbbing head. She dropped the poker. She closed her eyes against the pain that sliced through them. When she opened them again, bright lights danced around her. Her stomach clenched, and she bent over the sink and threw up. Fran rinsed her mouth with water and pulled out the painkillers from the kitchen cabinet. She took a couple for the headache, stared at the bottle for a few minutes, and took four more. She was going to need them to get through the pain. She wanted to be numb.

Then she picked up the bottle of scotch and headed for the bedroom, her head spinning. She was swearing at Rick all the way. She took four more swigs of scotch as she sat on the edge of the bed. The room began to swim. She grabbed the nightstand, but it seemed to slide out of her hand. She went down hard on the floor as the scotch soaked the rug.

***

"Did you get the job?" Tom asked Candy. They met in the parking lot outside the police station as the sun was beginning to set.

She leaned against the car, arms crossed, and smiled. "What do you think?"

Tom grinned and hugged her. "I'm proud of you."

"I have a favor to ask." Candy looked tired and pale.

Tom wondered if she should have been released from the hospital so soon. "Anything. What do you need?"

"Can you take me home?"

"You mean Fran's place?" Tom glanced around but couldn't find Candy's car.

She nodded yes and showed him her trembling hands. "I think I pushed myself a bit too hard today. I'm exhausted. I don't trust myself to drive."

"How did you get here?"

"Uber."

Tom was about to ask why she didn't have the driver take her directly home, but he decided to keep that idea to himself. "Of course." Tom led her over to his car and helped her in, then he leaned over her and hooked her seatbelt.

"I'm not going to break," she said quietly in his ear.

He smiled a little and kissed her. "I know."

Despite her reassurance, Tom felt how emotionally fragile Candy was at that moment. "Are you sure you want to go back to Fran's place?" he asked, hoping she would suggest his place instead.

"Where else am I going to go?"

Tom sighed, shut her door, and got into the driver's seat. He glanced sideways at her.

Candy rested her hand on his arm. "Thanks."

The drive back to Fran's was quiet. Candy put her head back, closed her eyes, and nodded off. Tom didn't bother with the radio. They would have enough to deal with at the house without listening to news reports of the police raid on a human trafficking ring or anything about Alex's death.

When they arrived at Fran's, her car was in the driveway. Tom stroked Candy's cheek with his fingers to wake her up. She yawned and dug her house key out of her purse as Tom opened her car door.

"Service with a smile," he told her with a wink. He held her hand as they walked up the front steps; then he waited as she unlocked the door.

The air conditioning was on full blast and the house was chilly. Tom went to turn it down. He stepped into the living room and froze. Anything and everything breakable was smashed as if someone had taken a baseball bat to the room. Pictures, books, and figurines were dumped off the shelves and destroyed. The lampshades were in tatters and the lamps smashed. The television set was on the floor and broken.

He remembered his conversation with Rick and knew immediately what happened. Tom swore under his breath. Nevertheless, to be cautious, he pulled his gun and moved through the house room by room. Everywhere he went, furniture was tipped over and items were either smashed or damaged. The only room that was untouched was Lauren's.

Tom opened the door to Fran's bedroom. The bed was unmade, and clothes were scattered on the floor, but that wasn't unusual for Fran. He didn't see her right away, but as he went to check the bathroom, he saw her leg on the floor beside the bed. His heart jumped and he holstered his gun. "Damn you, Fran," he muttered.

"Oh God!" Candy yelled behind Tom.

Tom knelt at Fran's side and checked her pulse. "She's alive." He pulled out his phone and called 911 as the scotch-logged carpet soaked his pant legs.

Candy stepped around Tom. "What the hell?"

Tom lifted Fran onto the bed. He slapped her gently to rouse her, but she didn't respond. He checked her pulse again. It was slow and weak.

"Bastard," Tom muttered. "That son-of-a-bitch fucking bastard!"

Candy stared at Tom. "Who?"

"Rick Brandt, who else? That shithead left her!"

"No. I don't believe it. He wouldn't do that. He's crazy about her. Why would he?"

"He told me he was leaving," Tom admitted. "It's about the custody battle. Fran can't have –" Tom stopped when he heard the sirens. "Get the door. Let the medics in." Tom gripped Fran's wrist and couldn't let go.

Candy ran to the front door as an ambulance pulled up to the house. The medics rushed in, and Candy pointed down the hall. "Last room on the left," she told them. "Watch out for broken glass."

Candy backed into the kitchen to get out of their way. As she turned, she stepped on the crumpled note. Curious, she bent over, picked it up, and read it. "You stupid idiot," Candy said as she pocketed the note. "Tom?" she called out.

The medics retrieved Fran and were reeling the gurney to the ambulance when Tom emerged from the bedroom, pale and angry, the knees of his pants soaked, and the bottle of scotch, with less than a cupful still in it, gripped tightly in his hand.

"She must have taken more than just scotch," he said. "Most of the bottle is in the rug."

Candy held up the note. "Find Rick. He can't be far. Put a BOLO out. Do whatever you have to do to find that man but get him back. She won't make it without him."

"I need to go to the hospital."

"I'll do that. I'll take Fran's car. You go get him and bring him back here!" Furious, Candy dumped Fran's purse on the kitchen table, found the car keys, and headed out the door.

"No!" Tom grabbed Candy by the arm. "You're not up for this. We go together." He escorted her out the door, locked the house, and steered her into his car.

By the time they reached the hospital, Candy had called Cheryl Burns. She told Cheryl that Fran had an accident and to bring Lauren to the hospital. Then Candy hung up and called Charlie. "Where is that bastard?"

"Which bastard, darling?" Charlie asked in surprise.

"Rick! Who else?"

"Hon, I ain't my brother's keeper. Why? What's he done now?"

"He took off! He left Fran! Something about Lauren, about not making Fran choose."

"Oh, yeah, he told me about that. He was pretty upset about it," Charlie said. "He talked to some social worker and –"

"That bastard doesn't know the meaning of the word upset," Candy yelled. "You call him. You text him. Hell, you hunt his ass down, Charlie!"

"He's just trying to –" Charlie started to say.

"Fran overdosed! The ambulance just took her to the hospital. She might not make it! Find him!"

"Yes, ma'am," Charlie said before hanging up.

***

After Fran's fourth attempt to reach him, Rick turned off his phone. He leaned on his cane as he drank his beer on the front porch of Charlie's "camp" – a rambling, two-story farmhouse built with a mix of brick and white clapboard and facing a western vista northwest of Vegas. The sun was beginning to set, and the horizon was on fire. Fran would have liked this place, he thought.

But by now, Fran would have found the note. By now, she probably wanted to kill him. It was for the best. The deep ache he felt would go away someday. Fran would go to bed angry, but tomorrow she would see Lauren. The girl was thirteen. In a few years, most of the pain of her father's death would be gone. In a few years, maybe Rick could come back. Maybe. If Fran let him. He winced.

Rick finished his second beer when he saw Charlie's brown truck kicking up dust on the dirt road to the camp. Rick frowned. He planned on staying there a day or two until he figured out where to go next. He thought about going home to Philadelphia. He still had contacts there. Maybe L.A. He hadn't been there in a long time. With any luck, certain people would have forgotten about him. And then there was always Mexico.

He watched as Charlie drove up to the porch and jumped out of the truck.

"Overdose," Charlie said as soon as he was within earshot.

"What?"

"Your little redhead. She overdosed. She's in the hospital."

Rick stood there, stunned.

"Move it! Now!" Charlie yelled.

Rick grabbed his cane, tossed the beer can aside, and climbed into Charlie's truck. He slammed the door as Charlie got in and put the vehicle in gear. "Fuck!" Rick yelled. Of all the scenarios Rick played out in his head, he never saw this one coming. He should have, he realized. Fran was still struggling. She wasn't strong enough. He should have – He sighed. His life was full of should-haves. Rick closed his eyes and groaned. "Fool woman."

"You shoulda figured that out by now," said Charlie. "She fell for you, didn't she?"

Rick scowled. "How'd you find out?"

"Candy called looking for you. She knew I'd find you. You really don't understand women, do you?"

They didn't speak for the rest of the trip.

***

Candy stood by Fran's bed and held her limp hand. The beeps of the monitors weren't reassuring.

Tom walked into the room, stood next to Candy, and put his warm arm over her shoulders. "Nothing yet."

"If anyone can find Rick, Charlie can," Candy said. At least, that was her hope.

"Not if he doesn't want to be found."

"I want to kill him."

"Get in line," Tom said.

"Cheryl and Lauren are on their way."

"I know. You think that's a good idea?"

"Yes. Lauren needs to be here."

Dr. Kaul stepped into the room and nodded at them. "Detective, Dr. Knight," he said by way of a greeting. "Where's Rick?"

"We haven't located him yet," Tom said. "How's she doing?"

"It's a good thing you got there when you did," the doctor said. "All things considered, she's doing well. We have an IV going, trying to counteract the dehydration and wash the alcohol and oxycodone out of her system." He looked at his notes. "I'm calling it an accidental overdose. I don't think she intended to kill herself. She probably took the pills first and –"

"Pills?" Candy asked. "I didn't see any pills."

"You didn't find a pill bottle there?" Kaul asked.

"No," Candy said, shaking her head.

"What was the BAC?" Tom asked.

"Blood alcohol content was point two three. That's almost three times the legal limit, although it shouldn't have done this much damage." Dr. Kaul looked back at Candy. "No painkillers?"

Candy whistled. "That's a lot of scotch."

"Yeah, and half of it spilled on the rug," said Tom. "Maybe the pill bottle fell under the bed. I didn't look. Or maybe— " His thought drifted.

"We're using oxygen therapy and hydration to treat her, and she's responding well, but we're going to monitor her carefully for a while. Did you happen to bring the liquor bottle with you?" Kaul asked Tom.

Tom nodded. "Yes. Why?"

"Just a hunch. Where is it?"

"In my car."

"Get it for me, please. I want to run some tests on it," Kaul said.

A nurse poked her head in. "There are some people here to see you, Dr. Knight."

"That will be Lauren," Candy told Tom. "Stay with Fran."

"And miss this? Like hell. I'm coming with you."

They found Cheryl, Lauren, and Lawrence Blackwell in a small waiting room across the hall. Lauren was curled on the sofa, and Cheryl was pacing the rug.

"What the hell is he doing here?" Tom asked without thinking.

"He's our minister," Cheryl said. "I asked him to come."

"Good evening detective, Miss Knight," Blackwell leaned on his cane and strained to be courteous.

"He's got no business here," Tom told Cheryl.

"What the hell is going on, Tom?" Cheryl demanded to know. "We get called here for some kind of accident just to find out Fran is drunk again. Is this really an emergency? What happened to her?"

Tom glanced past her and saw Lauren sitting on a small sofa and looking frightened. He pushed past Cheryl, walked up to the girl, and kneeled in front of her. She threw her arms around his neck and hugged him. She may have been thirteen, but she felt so small and fragile in his arms. He wanted to hold her until all her fears went away.

"She's going to be okay, sweetie," Tom told her softly as he held her tight. "It was an accident. She's going to be just fine. Trust me."

Lauren nodded her head and held him tighter.

"What happened?" Cheryl asked again.

"You are what happened!" Candy faced Cheryl.

"Stay out of this, you whore," Blackwell snapped, stepping between Candy and Cheryl. He was still in his gardening clothes, and his pant legs were muddy. He gripped the top of his cane and stared down at her.

Candy stepped back and stared at him in shock. She would have hit him, but Tom let go of Lauren, stood up, and stepped in front of Blackwell.

Tom looked past Blackwell to Cheryl. "You're taking Lauren away from Fran? That was your grand plan? Why? Why not just let the girl live with you and still see her mother? Why terminate Fran's rights? What the hell is wrong with you?"

Cheryl glanced at Blackwell and back at Tom. "It's for Lauren's own good. The child needs a stable home – someplace where people aren't shooting at each other, for god's sake."

"I realize Lauren is upset over what happened with her father. I get it. I do," Tom argued. "But you can't do this to Fran. You just can't."

"Yes, she can," a cool woman's voice said.

Tom spun around to find a middle-aged woman in a lavender pantsuit standing in the doorway.

"Who are you?" Candy asked with irritation.

"Ruth Miller from child services. We met this morning at Mrs. Simone's house. I understand there's a problem."

"I called her," said Cheryl. "They have a right to know what happened here."

"My best friend could have died because YOU made her choose between her daughter and Rick!" Candy screamed at Cheryl. "That's what's wrong with Fran!"

"That shouldn't be a choice!" Cheryl yelled back. "Of course, Lauren comes first. If Lauren doesn't come first with Fran, then Fran shouldn't have her. It's that simple."

"Stop it! Stop fighting!" Lauren screamed.

"First, yes," Candy agreed. "But Fran needs Rick in her life. He keeps her stable. He keeps her sober. She's a stronger person because of him."

"So strong that she tried to kill herself," Cheryl charged.

"Stop! Stop! Stop!" Lauren screamed again.

"That's not what the doctor said," Tom chimed in. He wanted to go to Lauren, but he didn't dare leave Blackwell and Candy with free access to each other.

"Then what did he say?" Cheryl asked. "Fran just accidentally fell off the wagon and nearly drowned in her own self-pity?"

Candy stepped towards Cheryl, but Tom grabbed Candy by the arm and pulled her back.

"That won't help," he told her.

"Damn it, Tom! I need to hit somebody!" Candy yelled.

Lauren burst into tears and ran to Tom. She threw her arms around his waist and hung on as she sobbed. "I want to see Mommy. I want to see Mommy right now. Please, Tommy? Please let me see her."

Tom held the girl and rocked her. "Of course. I'll take you to see her."

"You don't get to make that decision," Cheryl said stiffly. "I'm her guardian, and I decide what she does."

"Fran is still her mother." Tom's face flushed with anger.

"We don't believe –" Miller started to say.

"Shut up!" Candy yelled at the social worker.

"I knew we shouldn't have come." Cheryl looked to Blackwell to back her up. "Lauren's a child. She doesn't need to be exposed to this. And she especially doesn't need to be around Rick Brandt."

Tom looked down at the child. "Lauren, sweetie, are you really that afraid of Rick?"

"Leave her alone!" Cheryl yelled.

Lauren frowned. "No, of course not. I'm never afraid of Uncle Rick."

It was Tom's turn to frown. "Then you're mad at him because of your dad getting shot."

"I said leave her alone!" Cheryl repeated.

Lauren lowered her eyes. "It's all my fault." She buried her face in Tom's chest.

"That's enough!" Cheryl interrupted.

"I agree. You have no business questioning that child," Miller said.

"Well, it's not like YOU'RE doing your job," Candy barked.

"What do you mean, Lauren?" Tom ignored the women.

"Daddy wanted me to go with him, and I didn't. If I went with him, Uncle Rick wouldn't have shot him. It's all my fault."

Tom held her tightly. "No, honey. It's not. It's not your fault at all. Don't you see? If you went with your dad, he would have killed you, too. He was all mixed up that day. That's why he had a gun. That's why he shot your mom. It wasn't your fault at all."

"That's enough!" Cheryl said. "Lauren, we're going home!"

"No! I want to see Mommy!" Lauren clung to Tom.

Tom looked at Cheryl, Miller, and Blackwell a moment before talking to Lauren again. "Look, Rick isn't here, but he could show up. If you're with your mom and Rick walks in, will you be okay?"

"Will you be there?" Lauren asked.

"Yes, of course, I will."

"And he won't be mad at me?"

Tom was stunned. "Mad at you? Why in the world would Rick be mad at you?"

"Because I made him shoot daddy."

Tom was trying to wrap his brain around the concept when Lauren continued.

"Tommy, why didn't you marry Mommy, like you were supposed to?" Lauren asked. "I wanted you to be my dad, not Uncle Rick. You were supposed to marry Mommy, and we were supposed to live together, and none of this would have happened."

Tom closed his eyes as he held her. When he opened them, he looked at Candy before speaking to Lauren. "Hon, for two people to get married, they have to love each other the same way and the same amount at the same time. Your mom and I love each other, but not the same way and not the same amount."

"But you were sleeping together," Lauren said.

Tom shook his head. "I know. We shouldn't have done that. Is that why you don't want Rick around? Because you want your mom to marry me?"

Lauren shrugged. "Maybe. A little. I know…" she stammered, "…I know Daddy did a terrible thing. I know he shot Mommy, but it was my fault." She tightened her grip on Tom. "I don't want Uncle Rick to be mad at me anymore."

"He never was mad at you," Tom said. "Your mom loves you. You know that. But she also needs Rick. She shouldn't lose you because she cares about him."

"But Cheryl said Mommy had to choose. I want her to choose me."

"Why would you tell her that?" Tom glared at Cheryl.

"Rick Brandt is dangerous," Cheryl snapped. "He killed my husband, for god's sake! Am I the only one who gives a damn about that?"

"So, this is about revenge?" Tom asked. "I don't get it. Paul held your son at gunpoint. Rick rescued him. What is it you want? To get back at Rick by hurting Fran? Or to get back at Fran because Paul never got over her? What's your game?"

"It's not about getting back at anyone! He's dangerous. He's not good for Lauren. Anyone with two eyes can see that."

"I have to agree," Miller said, nodding.

"I concur," said Rev. Blackwell.

"You don't count," Candy snapped at Blackwell.

"I'm taking Lauren in to see her mother," Tom announced. He took the girl's hand and led her into the hallway.

Chapter 28
Monday Night

Rick leaned heavily on his cane and winced as he limped into the hospital with Charlie running to keep up. Rick felt gutted and exposed. He knew whatever he was walking into wasn't going to be good. Fran overdosed, and he didn't know if she was alive. The thought seized in his throat. His chest hurt from fear. He stopped when he ran into the others in the hallway in front of Fran's room. His attention immediately went to Lauren, who was holding Tom's hand and hiding behind him, her eyes red and her face covered in tears. If Lauren was there, it couldn't be good. Rick prepared himself for the worst. "How is she?" he asked Tom.

Time stopped.

"Now can I hit somebody?" Candy asked as she faced Rick.

Tom said, "Have at it." He turned and pulled Lauren into Fran's room.

Candy let her fist fly, catching Rick in the jaw.

"Damn!" Charlie exclaimed.

Rick winced and stepped back but didn't try to block her. Instead, he leaned on his cane and quietly stared her down. "You need to do that again?"

"You bastard!" Candy screamed. "How dare you!"

"The whore can hit," Blackwell muttered.

Rick turned on his heel and used his cane to slam Blackwell against the wall and pin him by the throat. Blackwell squawked and stared at Rick. Everyone went silent. A few centimeters more and Blackwell would be dead, and they all knew it. Rick, as if coming out of a daze, took a deep breath and stepped back. Blackwell gasped for air. As Rick turned, he saw the shocked look on Miller's face. He scowled at her, and she retreated as Dr. Kaul walked out of Fran's room.

Kaul sighed in relief when he saw Rick. "Thank god you're here."

"How is she, Sam?" Rick asked.

Behind him, Blackwell stood up and picked up his own cane to ram it into Rick's side, but Rick turned, blocked the blow, and plowed the top of his cane into Blackwell's jaw. Blackwell stumbled backward and fell to the floor, his hand grabbing his face.

"Get down and stay down!" Rick yelled.

"Jesus!" Cheryl screamed.

Kaul grabbed Rick by the arm. "She's alive but in rough shape. It was touch and go for a bit." The doctor pulled Rick towards Fran's room. "We don't have time for this. We need to talk. Now."

Rick looked at Cheryl, Miller, and Blackwell. "Get out of here," he said in a low, threatening tone. "All of you, out of here."

"You can't do that!" Cheryl yelled. "I'm Lauren's guardian and I'm not leaving without her."

"You're not going in Fran's room. If you're gonna stay, you're gonna stay in there." Rick pointed to the waiting room.

"You have no right –" Rev. Blackwell interjected as he pushed himself up from the floor.

Rick took a half-step toward Blackwell and started to raise his arm to strike. Blackwell shrank back.

"Sergeant! Stand down!" Kaul barked.

Rick stepped back.

"He has every right," Dr. Kaul explained. "Miss Simone gave Mr. Brandt the power to make all medical decisions for her in the event she can't do so herself. So, if Mr. Brandt says you can't go in, you can't go in." He crossed his arms and stood in front of the door as if daring them to defy him. No one moved. "We need to talk, Rick," he said again. "Now." Kaul stepped into Fran's room.

Candy angrily grabbed Rick's arm as he limped past her.

Rick stopped and folded his hand over hers. He slowly peeled her fingers from his arm and looked her in the eyes. "You want to hate me? Hate me. You want to tell me I fucked up? Fine. I fucked up. You can yell at me later. This is not a good time to push my buttons, sweetheart."

Candy took a deep breath and backed off. "She's my best friend. This shouldn't have happened."

Rick nodded. "You're right. It shouldn't have. So go be with her. Be her friend."

Charlie tapped Rick on the arm. "I'm headed out. I'll be back for you later."

Candy hurried into the hospital room. Rick followed Kaul through the door as Cheryl yelled at them. Miller was on the phone.

Once in Fran's room, Kaul pulled Rick to the side and spoke quietly. "It's not just the booze. I believe she took some painkillers – oxycodone – with a scotch chaser, but not enough to do this. I had the lab run some tests. She was poisoned. Someone dumped a ton of oxy into that bottle of booze. She's damn lucky Saddler found her in time."

"Poisoned? What the fuck." Rick fought to contain his rage. "Has she woken up?"

"Not yet. But there were other complications."

"What kind of complications?" Rick stared at Fran from across the room.

"She lost the baby," the doctor said quietly so no one else would hear. "I'm sorry."

Rick felt dizzy. He took a deep breath and leaned against the wall to keep from falling. "She never said –" He looked at the doctor. "Did she even know she was pregnant? She wouldn't drink if she knew. There's no way."

The doctor shook his head. "I don't know. I just assumed you both knew. She might have suspected but, honestly, I can't tell you. As far as I can tell from her medical records, she hasn't had any tests done or seen a doctor for that."

"She was using birth control," Rick whispered.

"An IUD. We had to remove it when she hemorrhaged. She'll need to see an OBGYN once she's up and around again."

Rick looked at Lauren who was sitting on the bed and holding her mother's hand. Tom stood next to the girl with his arm over her shoulder. The perfect family, Rick thought. If only he hadn't come back from Mexico, Tom and Fran would have been married by now. They might have even had a child on the way. Everything would have been fine. He closed his eye for a second to chase away those thoughts. If he hadn't come back from Mexico, Toni would have killed Fran by now. There wouldn't have been a happy family. It was an illusion. A dream. Not even his dream. He had ripped someone else's dream into shreds and now he was paying for it.

Someone tried to kill Fran. Someone killed *their* unborn child.

Lauren looked up at Rick.

"I'm sorry," he said. He felt drained.

Lauren nodded at him as if giving him permission to approach. "Me, too."

Rick circled the bed and stood on the other side by Fran. He brushed her hair back and ran his fingers down her still cheek. She seemed so peaceful, but he knew there was a storm brewing underneath. He raised her hand to his lips and kissed it. There was so much he wanted to say and nothing that he could say, not like this, not with everyone here. He bent over and whispered in her ear, "Come back to me, boss."

"You're supposed to be on crutches," Dr. Kaul said as he slid a stool over to Rick.

"I was in a hurry." Rick sat next to Fran. His cane clattered to the tile floor.

"You can't go around playing god," Candy snapped at Rick. Tom tried to hush her but failed. "You had no right to do that to her."

"I knew she'd be mad, but at least she'd have Lauren back. I never thought —"

"You never think," Candy spat. "You rush in with bullets flying because you know everything, because you're always right, because you have to be the damn hero."

"Candy, that's enough," Tom said, reeling her in.

"I wasn't trying to be a fuckin' hero," Rick interjected.

"Shut up," Candy ordered. "Fran had a choice to make. No matter how much it hurt her, it was still her choice. You don't get to take that away from her."

"She didn't have a choice," Rick said without looking at them. "She could never lose Lauren. That wouldn't happen."

"You're right, she couldn't give up Lauren. But that didn't mean she had to let you go. Damn, why are men such idiots?"

Rick was in a mood to give Candy an argument, but a warning look from Kaul made him stop. This was not the time and not the place.

"Sam, talk to Tom. Tell him what you found out." Rick squeezed Fran's hand tighter. "About the scotch. About what was in it."

Dr. Kaul motioned for Tom and Candy to follow him into the hallway.

***

Tuesday Morning

Fran awoke with a raging headache, cramps, an upset stomach, and no idea where she was. She stared at a white tiled ceiling that threatened to disappear at any moment. Her eyes hurt. She moaned and closed them for a while. When she opened them again, Rick was standing over her.

"Where am I? What happened?"

"You're at the hospital, boss." He was holding the bedrail so tightly that his knuckles were white.

She stared up at him for a minute and then she frowned. "Don't you dare look at me that way!" Her words were immediately followed by a loud and painful groan as she reached for her splitting head.

"You scared the shit outta me, Fran. Outta me and everyone else, including your daughter. You almost died."

"You left me!" The pain in her head worsened. "What the fuck do you care!"

"You don't understand. Someone poisoned the scotch. Someone tried to kill you. Someone counted on you getting drunk." He took a deep breath. "I expected you to yell. I expected you to throw a fit or scream or smash something. I never expected you to go for the scotch. I didn't. I should have, but I didn't."

"I did smash something. I smashed every damn thing in the house!" Sobbing, she rolled onto her side, buried her head in her arms, and whimpered, "You bastard, you left me."

"You promised me you'd be strong. You promised me you wouldn't drink." Rick sat on the edge of the bed, gathered her up in his good arm, and rocked her. "I'm sorry. I'm so sorry, baby."

"I can work it out. I can find a way. Damn it, Rick. You don't get to leave me. You just don't. You understand?"

"Francesca, you're not listening to me," Rick said, forcing her to look directly at him. "Someone poisoned the scotch. Someone nearly killed you!" He buried his face in her hair and held her tighter. "You nearly died. It could cost you Lauren. It could cost you everything. Don't you get that?"

"I just want the pain to go away."

"Me, too," Rick said softly in her ear.

Fran pushed herself out of his arms and looked up at him. For the first time in the ten years she'd known him, there were tears on his face. He looked away and wiped his face with his sleeve.

"Poisoned?" she asked, stunned, the information finally taking hold in her brain. "What the hell. How did that happen? I didn't —"

"Fran, where did the scotch come from?" Rick asked.

"I assumed it was from Jax," she said, trembling. "It arrived, no note, the good stuff. You know, $400 a bottle kind of good stuff. It was there, on the table. Alex said," she hesitated. "Alex said – someone –dropped it – off." She looked up at Rick. "Alex knew it was from Jax. He must have. He just didn't – He must not have realized what was in it. He wouldn't do that to me. Oh shit." She kissed Rick. "Don't leave me. Please, don't leave me."

"You need to talk to Lauren. I'm going to tell her that you're awake." She felt so warm and alive in his arm. He didn't want to let her go.

"She's here?" Fran asked with surprise.

"Of course, she's here. Everyone's here. We're all worried about you. Don't you understand? What you do affects all of us." Rick kissed her cheek, stood, and walked out of the room.

Lauren and Tom were asleep on separate sofas in the waiting room. Candy was with them, awake, stretched out on a recliner with Tom's jacket on and watching television on mute. Blackwell, Cheryl Burns, and Miller had disappeared.

"She's awake," Rick said as he stood in the doorway. It was nearly five a.m., and the room was still dark except for a small lamp in one corner and the flickering of the television set.

"I hope she gave you a piece of her mind," Candy said sharply.

"Where's Godzilla and her keeper?" Rick asked, referring to Cheryl.

"They left. They'll be back."

Rick sank into a chair and held his head. He didn't have the energy to deal with Candy's anger. "Fran wants to see Lauren."

Candy got up from her chair and roused the girl. "Your mom's awake and asking for you."

Lauren immediately sat up and looked at Rick. "Is Mommy okay?"

He nodded.

When Lauren headed to the door, Rick reached out and grasped her hand. She stopped and looked at him.

"Lauren," Rick said, his voice shaky, "I want you to know that I will do anything I have to do to fix this. No matter what, I want you to be with your mom and for both of you to be safe."

Lauren nodded, slipped her small hand out of Rick's rough one, and left the room.

Candy turned toward Rick as if to speak.

"Shut up," Rick said.

"Excuse me?"

"I said shut the fuck up." Rick pushed himself to his feet. "I'm going for coffee. I'll be back."

"There's coffee here," Candy told him.

"Then I'm going to get away from you."

"Listen to me, Buster," Candy began.

"No, you listen to me," Rick confronted her. "If Fran loses her daughter, it will be my fault. I'm the one who pulled the trigger. I'm the one who put Fran in danger. I'm the one who got her so upset she fell off the wagon. I'm the one child services wants out the door. No matter how I play this, I'm screwed. I can stay and save her life, or I can leave and hope Lauren goes home with her. You got any bright ideas?"

"You selfish bastard." Candy slapped him hard.

By now, Tom was awake and listening.

"Hell, yeah, I'm selfish." Rick rubbed his stinging cheek. "I need that woman in my life. I don't want to give her up. But if I have to, if that's what it takes for her to keep Lauren, then that's exactly what I'll do, no matter what you think."

She swung again, but this time Rick caught her arm in his strong hand and stopped her. "Enough, woman!" Rick released her arm, turned, and limped out of the room.

Rick made his way to the cafeteria. Breakfast was just getting started. People were wandering into work, some half-asleep, some in hospital uniforms, a few in suits. Rick was on his second cup of coffee when Charlie showed up, still in the ripe clothes he wore the day before.

"I thought you went home," Rick said.

"I was too tired. I fell asleep in the truck until some cop rapped on my window and told me to move it or lose it." Charlie yawned. He sat opposite Rick. "How's she doing?" He unwrapped a piece of beef jerky and took a bite.

"This is the place where it all started going downhill."

"The place?" Charlie asked.

"Where I killed Paul Burns." Rick pointed to a cement pillar in the middle of the room. He shaped his hand into the form of a gun and pretended to fire. "Right there. Bam. Blew the bastard's brains out."

Charlie glanced at the pillar and nodded. "Not your first kill."

"No, but it was the one that changed my life." Rick put his hand down and took another drink of coffee. "I thought I was doing the right thing."

"Yeah. We always get fucked up when we think that."

Rick closed his eye. He remembered the night he first made love to Fran. She asked him, "What do you want?" and he told her "Everything." That's what she gave him, everything. He opened his eye. "I was wrong to leave. I should have trusted her to work it out."

"Whatcha gonna do?"

Rick shrugged. "Wait for the ax to fall, I guess. She really doesn't have a choice, not if she wants Lauren back. And I know she wants Lauren back."

Charlie nodded. "Then what?"

"Then, we'll see."

Tom approached the table, nodded to Charlie, and sat down. Rick looked at him and said nothing.

"I've been thinking," Tom began.

"Oh?" Rick asked.

"You shouldn't have left her. I still believe that. And I warned you, but she didn't have to dive into a bottle of scotch, either, poisoned or not. That's on her, not you."

"Poison?" Charlie asked.

"Yes. The scotch was loaded with oxy. Someone tried to kill her," Tom explained.

Rick looked down. He was grateful for Tom's comment, but it didn't change anything.

"Fran told me how you made her choose – the scotch or you," Tom said.

Rick nodded.

"Now what? Now that she screwed up, is it over between you two? Are you going to walk away?"

Rick shook his head no. "It's her choice. It's always been her choice. After all of this, she may not want me back."

"What the hell do you want, Rick?" Tom asked as he leaned forward. "Do you love her or don't you? Do you want her or don't you? Are you going to see this through or walk away and let her drown?"

"I walked away once and look what happened," Rick said bitterly.

"Are you ready to fight for her?"

Rick frowned and eyed Tom. "What have you got in mind?"

Tom cleared his throat. "I spent some time talking to Lauren and Cheryl yesterday when all this happened. I think this whole choice thing is Cheryl's doing. I'm not sure why. She may be mad at Fran for some reason or simply using it to get to you, but I do know this: Lauren isn't mad at you, and she isn't afraid of you. She is scared, though. She's convinced the shooting was all her fault. She knows you killed Burns, at least in part, to save her. Seeing you reminds her of that. It's like holding a mirror up to her and telling her she's the bad guy. That's why she gets so upset when you're around. That's why she doesn't want you to marry Fran."

"Her fault? She's just a kid. She didn't – Hell, Tom, that shooting was my doing. I made that choice. It was Burns or Fran. This whole mess is on Cheryl?"

"Which I probably would have found out if you'd only given me a couple of days," Tom said.

Rick rubbed his tired eye. "Fuck. Now what?"

"Now it's up to you. Are you willing to fight for them?"

Rick thought about how much Tom loved Fran and how all of this could have been avoided if only Rick hadn't kissed her. He then thought about losing Fran – about what that would do to her and what it was doing to him. "I'm in."

Tom nodded and stood up to leave the table.

"Tom. There's one more thing you need to know – you and Candy."

"What's that?"

Rick took a deep breath. "The doc told me – Sam said – Fran was pregnant. This – mess – made her lose the baby. She miscarried."

Tom's eyes widened.

"I just want you to know. I want Candy to know 'cause Fran doesn't know yet. And when she finds out, it's gonna be hard on her. She's gonna need to talk to someone, to talk to Candy."

"She didn't know she was pregnant?" Tom asked.

"I don't think so," said Rick. "If she knew, she wouldn't have done this. She wouldn't have mixed booze and pills. I don't believe that."

Tom nodded. "Okay." Then he left.

Charlie turned to Rick. "You remember that big fight we had about, oh, eight, ten years ago?"

Rick frowned. "You mean when I was drunk out of my mind and still gambling, and you locked me in a shed?" Rick shook his head. "Hell, yeah, I remember. It was a damn stupid thing for you to do, but it worked."

"No, I don't think so," said Charlie. "I think you're still gambling, only you don't use money anymore. You gamble with your life." Charlie pushed himself up from the table. "Need a ride somewhere?"

Rick felt anger burn at his neck. He shook his head. "I'm gonna try and clean up my mess here, first. I'll manage. Thanks."

As Charlie walked away, Rick stared down at his empty coffee cup and swore.

***

Tuesday Afternoon

"Did you ever talk to that store owner?" Hodge asked Tom over the phone.

The question woke Tom from his drowsy state. He was stretched out on the sofa in his apartment and listening to Candy making lunch in the kitchen. He was beyond exhausted, but that seemed to be his normal state these days. He groaned. "Damn. No, I didn't."

"Well, Simmons did," Hodge told him. "I had her take some photos from Allyson Stone's stash over to the store. The clerk picked out two possible suspects. One was Jim Pearson."

Tom sat up. He remembered the old man with his work hands, his soiled clothes, and his poor teeth. "What the hell would he be doing with six cheap corsets?"

The question drew Candy's attention. She stopped what she was doing, stepped into the living room, and sat next to Tom. He took her hand as he put Hodge on speaker so she could hear.

"That's the interesting part," Hodge said. "The order was called in and the guy gave a fake name. He had Pearson pick up the corsets and pay in cash. But get this: According to the clerk, the corsets were to be securely boxed and taped and the clerk was under orders not to tell Pearson what was in the box. In the clerk's words, 'It was supposed to be a surprise.' So, apparently, Pearson didn't know what he was getting."

"Blackwell," Tom said.

"It looks like it, but we need more than someone who looks like Pearson who picked up those corsets. Remember, the clerk picked out two suspects from the photo lineup. For all we know, Pearson set the whole thing up so he'd look innocent."

"We need to get close to Blackwell, talk to people he knows, see what we can find out about him," Tom said.

"You know anyone like that?" Hodge asked.

"Maybe. Let me see what I can do."

"We're running out of time on this case," Hodge said. "We're still short one victim, or two if you count your new girlfriend." His tone was sarcastic, and Candy winced, but she didn't say anything.

"I'll get back to you." Tom hung up the phone.

"What are you thinking?" Candy asked.

"We know Blackwell has some kind of fixation on you, but we don't know why. It's one thing for him to be upset over the handling of the Bryce Pearson case, it's another to stalk you and torment you by killing your friends. There's got to be a motive out there that we're missing," Tom began.

"Maybe he's just your garden variety psychopath."

"We really don't know enough about him, other than Pearson works for him, he's cozy with Cheryl Burns, and he's got a hot temper and a big mouth."

"What do we need to know? What evidence are we looking for?" She was getting excited. Not only did this mean she was closer to being safe, but she was reliving her days at the crime lab. She felt useful instead of helpless. She liked the change.

"We can start by showing he has some connection to sweetbriar roses," Tom said.

"Didn't you say he gardened?"

"Yes. He and Mrs. Pearson mentioned that, and he showed up at our meeting covered in dirt, and again at the hospital with mud on his pants and shoes. Of course, for all we know, he was rummaging in a cabbage patch."

Despite the seriousness of the matter, Candy had to stifle a giggle.

"Okay, so we need proof he grows or has easy access to the roses. What else?" she asked.

"Means. We need to show he had access to the dog collars," Tom said.

"That's going to be harder than pinning the corsets on him. Almost every store sells dog collars. He could buy one here and one there. Hell, does he even own a dog?"

"And he could use cash, but we could look at credit card receipts, anyway, just in case."

"Assuming we have enough evidence for a search warrant," Candy agreed.

"What else? Oh, opportunity. We have to make sure he has no alibi."

"That's going to be hard. You know the Pearsons will lie for him."

"Will they? Jim Pearson has a lot on the line, and I've already had him on the hot seat once. I'm sure the minister will provide an alibi, but I'm not so sure Pearson will back it up."

"Okay. Anything else?" Candy asked.

"The paint. Pearson admitted to vandalizing your apartment. That meant he had your address. He doesn't strike me as particularly sophisticated. I bet Blackwell told him where you lived."

"And we have the photos from Allyson Stone," Candy added. "Was Blackwell in them?"

"Yes," Tom said with a smile. "A number of times."

"I think we have enough for a warrant."

"Let me check the ME's report on Edgar and see if there's anything there. His murder came out of the blue. It didn't fit the pattern, other than he knew you and was choked to death and his throat sliced with the dog collar." He glanced up at her and saw her go pale. "Sorry. I didn't need to say that."

Candy stood up and walked over to the window. She hugged herself. Her fingers went to her throat. Every time she thought about what happened to her girls and to Edgar, she remembered Toni's assault on her. She shuddered. "I keep asking myself why. If someone wanted to kill me, why not just kill me? Why put me through this?"

"We need a profiler," Tom suggested.

"You haven't talked to one, yet?" Candy asked in surprise.

"I haven't been able to keep on top of everything," Tom admitted. He leaned forward, elbows on his knees, and shook his head. "I'm telling you, honey, I'm burned out. I've been putting in –" He suddenly stopped. "You know, this isn't about me. I don't need a pity party. Let's check with Hodge and the ME and see what we can find out."

Simmons was waiting for them at the police department. She eyed Candy with a critical look, but Candy ignored her. They pulled their chairs around the table in the conference room. Photos and reports were strewn between them.

"What have you got and what do you need?" Hodge asked as he sat down, one hand gripping a cup of coffee and the other balancing the thickening file.

"We have a lot," Candy said.

Simmons scowled at her, and Candy bristled. "Look, I may not work here anymore, but this case IS about me, and I damn sure know what I'm doing."

Tom put a hand on her arm to calm her down. "What we need is a warrant to search Lawrence Blackwell's house, car, computer, emails, phone records, and credit card receipts."

Hodge nodded. "I thought as much." He turned to Simmons. "Angela, fill him in on the latest."

Simmons pulled out the report from the medical examiner. "Edgar had a number of wounds, but what was particularly interesting was that he apparently attacked his killer by scratching him."

"DNA?" Candy asked.

"The killer scraped the cells out with some kind of sharp object, but he must have been in a hurry because some of the skin cells fell on Edgar's clothing and on the rug. So, yes, we got DNA, but no match in CODIS or the NDIS."

"Blackwell would have no reason to be in Mitchell's home – at least none that I'm aware of. If we get his DNA, that could close this case," Tom said.

"You mentioned someone being close to Blackwell," Candy said.

"Yes," Tom responded. "But I don't think the Pearsons or Cheryl Burns are going to give me anything."

"What about Lauren Burns?" Candy asked.

Hodge looked up. "Lauren Burns?"

"Fran's daughter. She's thirteen and lives with Cheryl, and from what we saw at the hospital, Cheryl and Blackwell were more than a little friendly."

"Lovers?" Hodge asked.

"Maybe not lovers," Tom admitted. "Definitely co-conspirators, at least with regards to getting custody of Lauren away from Fran."

"That doesn't make them criminals," Simmons pointed out.

"No, but Lauren may know about the roses if she's been around Blackwell enough," said Candy.

"Okay," said Hodge. "I'm going to take what we got and try for a warrant. No promises, but I think we might get it. In the meantime, Tom, you interview Lauren. I take it you know her well?"

"Very well," Tom said.

"Maybe she'd feel better talking to a woman," Simmons suggested.

"She's good with me," Tom insisted. "I've known her a long time."

Hodge nodded. "Angela, we need more background information on this Blackwell guy. Who are his friends? Where does he hang out? Does he have an Internet presence? What's his history? How did he get to Vegas and from where?"

"You got it, sir," she said as she stood up.

"Good luck."

Once Simmons was gone, Hodge turned to Tom. "She's good, you know. She's still green and needs a little prompting now and then, but she'll do a good job. And as for you two, I don't want to fuck this case up because you two got a thing going on. Every scrap of evidence needs to be independently verified. Got that? The prosecutor may not be able to put you on the stand, Tom. Just keep that in mind. Dismissed."

Tom was annoyed but didn't say anything.

Candy took him by the arm and dragged him out of the conference room. "Where to now?"

"Let's check on the lab results on that bottle found at Fran's place," he said.

"You're suddenly switching gears on me?"

"It just seems odd that Jax would try to poison Fran. He had other plans. I'm wondering if it's related to your case." Tom stretched his back. "What happened to lunch?"

"I put it back in the fridge," Candy admitted. "Look, going back to Fran's won't help us. For one thing, whatever you find there won't be admissible simply because YOU found it. You heard Hodge. If Fran was poisoned by someone targeting me, then we need forensics at the house to look around."

"Jeanette. We need Jeanette." Without explanation, Tom turned and headed toward the lab.

Chapter 29
Late Tuesday Afternoon

"Lauren's missing?" Tom stood in the cramped, littered office of social worker Ruth Miller and stared at her. "When did this happen? I have to talk to her."

"Why?" Miller asked as she frowned at him over the top of her glasses. She'd shed a lime green jacket and rolled up the sleeves of her shirt. She was surrounded by stacks of files, and her normally neat hair was escaping the twist at the back of her neck.

"She's a witness in a murder case. Why didn't you tell me she was gone?"

"We can't report it to the police for twenty-four hours," Miller said. "Besides, she's thirteen, and her mother just overdosed. She's bound to overreact. I'm sure we'll find her sooner or later." She picked up another file, made a notation in it, and tossed it onto the growing pile on the floor.

"I need to find her. I need to talk to her."

"So? Find her, then."

"And for the record, Fran didn't overdose. Someone tried to kill her."

Miller took off her glasses and leaned forward, her hands folded. "That's supposed to be better? I don't think you understand my job, detective. My job is to make sure Lauren Burns has a safe home to live in. The fact that her mother, a known alcoholic, reached for a bottle of scotch because of a fight with her boyfriend, or that someone tried to murder her, is NOT comforting. If anything, it goes against the notion that we would ever place Lauren at Fran's house."

"But you placed her with Cheryl Burns," Tom countered, his temper flaring. "That woman –" He stopped and got control of himself. "Once I find Lauren, I take it you have no objection to my questioning her about the murders."

Miller frowned. "Murders? Plural? I thought you were talking about the attempted murder of her mother. What murders?"

"We have a serial killer who murdered four people so far and, according to our information, is after at least two more. Lauren may hold information that's key to solving this case."

"I doubt that very much." Miller leaned back. "Look, I've seen you with Lauren. I know she considers you a friend. I trust you to protect her. So I'm going to allow this. But if I hear one peep that you abused this privilege, that you in any way upset that child –"

"I know." Tom fled the office as if being chased by flying wasps. Everything about being there made him uncomfortable, but he had to concede that Miller was right. She was only doing her job, even if that job meant taking Lauren away from Fran.

Candy waited in the parking lot. She leaned against the unmarked cruiser, her dark hair pushed back behind her ears, her large sunglasses obscuring most of her features.

Her arms were crossed as she watched the main door for signs of Tom.

"What'd she say?" Candy asked the minute he appeared.

"Lauren ran away. I've got to find her before Blackwell does."

Candy's heart skipped. "Where do you think she is?"

"Possibly the hospital, but if she was there, they would have found her by now. Maybe Fran's house?"

"More likely."

Fran's house was locked tight when Tom and Candy arrived. Candy had keys. They entered through the kitchen door. The house had been empty since Monday and the air was stale. Two entryways went to the main part of the house from the kitchen, one into the living room and one into the long hallway. Candy and Tom entered through the hallway to avoid the broken glass and debris in the living room. They went from room to room, first checking Candy's room, then Rick's across the hall, then Fran's – last on the left – and Lauren's across from that. They found Lauren fast asleep in the bed her mom had bought for her. She was covered with a soft quilt and hugging an old doll.

Candy teared up and stepped back into the hallway. "Let's leave her for a bit. She probably hasn't had a moment's rest since this whole thing with her mom started."

Tom nodded and followed Candy back into the kitchen. "I'm going to have to wake her sooner or later. The crime lab guys will be here, and I don't want them to find her. If she goes back to Cheryl and Blackwell before I talk to her, we're screwed." Tom started making coffee.

Candy poked her head into the fridge. "This thing needs to be cleaned out before they get home." She pulled out some leftovers and dumped them in the trash.

"Once the lab boys are done, we should clean up that glass before someone cuts themself," Tom added.

"Themselves," Candy corrected.

Tom, surprised, glanced up at her. "Since when did you become a grammar witch?"

Candy pulled some bagels out of the fridge and cut a couple open, then placed them in the toaster oven and found some cream cheese. "Behave, boy," she said, slapping his ass as she walked by.

Tom turned, grabbed her, and pushed her up against the counter. Candy yelped.

"I'm not your boy, and I never will be." He bent down and kissed her firmly on the lips.

Candy moaned, wrapped her arms around his neck, and kissed him back. "That's better. I missed that this morning."

Tom smiled. "Just so we're clear." He let her go and went back to the coffee.

"Really, guys, you should get a room," Lauren said from the doorway. She was yawning and clinging to her doll.

Tom and Candy spun around.

"Hey, there, sleepyhead," Candy said with a smile. "Want a bagel? There's not much else to eat in the house."

Lauren nodded. She plopped down in a chair and looked up at Tom. "Are you going to arrest me?"

Tom shook his head. "I didn't come here to arrest you. I was worried about you."

Candy glanced at him sideways. Lauren noticed.

"I also need to talk to you," Tom admitted, caught between the two.

"About what?" Lauren asked.

Candy set a bagel and a glass of juice in front of Lauren. Tom poured his coffee, added some milk, and sat across from the girl.

"About Lawrence Blackwell," he said.

Lauren crinkled up her nose. "I'll make you a deal."

"Wow," Candy responded. "You can tell HER mama's a lawyer." She laughed as she put the rest of the bagels on the table, grabbed some coffee, and joined them.

"What kind of a deal?" Tom asked.

"Are you guys dating?" Lauren asked, putting them both on the spot.

"I'm not sure you'd call it dating, exactly," Candy admitted. She looked at Tom. "You know, you have yet to ask me on a date."

Tom groaned. "First things first."

Lauren grinned.

"What kind of deal?" Tom asked again.

"I'll answer all your questions if you agree to take me to see mom. I tried to get Cheryl to do that this morning, but she said no."

"So that's why you ran away? To see your mom?" Tom asked.

Lauren nodded as she bit into her bagel.

"Why not just go straight to the hospital?"

"Cause Larry's there," Lauren said with a grimace. "He was hanging out in the parking lot, and I didn't want him to see me, so I thought I'd come here for a while."

"How'd you get there?" Candy asked.

"The bus," said Lauren.

Tom looked at Candy. "Why the hell would Blackwell be there?"

"Any number of reasons. That doesn't mean –"

"He's going to talk to mom, to make sure she lets me live with Cheryl." Lauren sniffled. "I don't want to live with Cheryl. I want to come home."

Tom nodded. "Okay, we have a deal. I'll take you to see your mom, but you have to tell me about Larry."

Lauren nodded eagerly.

Candy got up and refilled their coffee mugs as they talked.

"For openers, what can you tell me about Larry's flowers?" Tom asked.

Lauren frowned. "That matters?"

"Yes."

"Okay. Well, he's got tons of them, a bunch in the garden at the church, and a bunch on the farm, plus the greenhouse."

"What farm?" Tom asked.

"What greenhouse?" Candy asked.

"Jim's farm. I can't remember how we got there, but it was a long drive."

"Jim and Melissa Pearson?" Tom asked, to be sure.

Lauren nodded. "They got a farm. Got some vegetables, lots of flowers, a couple of goats, and a couple – no, three – pigs. What else? Oh, yeah, the pony. Larry let me ride the pony."

"Did Cheryl go with you?" Tom asked.

Lauren shook her head no. "I don't think she's ever been there. She had to do something – some kind of meeting or appointment or something – so she let me go with him."

"How did he treat you?" Candy, worried, asked Lauren. She was listening intently, her foot pressed up against Tom's under the table.

Lauren shrugged. "He was okay, I guess. I mean, he wasn't mean to me or anything. He kinda ignored me. He was busy with something."

"Tell me more about the flowers," Tom said. "Do you know what kind they are?"

Lauren shook her head. "All kinds: pink, blue, yellow, red. Some just had leaves. I don't know what was in the greenhouse, though. He told me I couldn't go in there. Something about bees."

"Any place else you couldn't go?" Candy asked.

"Yeah, upstairs in the barn. There's a ladder and a trap door. I tried to peek, but he keeps it locked."

"Is he dating Cheryl?" Tom asked.

Lauren laughed. "I don't think so. He's gay."

"Gay?" Tom looked at Candy and back at Lauren. "Are you sure? He didn't seem gay to me."

"You couldn't tell?" It was Lauren's turn to be surprised. "Yeah, I think that's why he's always talking about it, you know, about how terrible it is and how people go to hell for it and stuff. He's got this idea that people who are gay can get over it, and I think he keeps trying, but –" She shrugged again. "Believe me, he's gay."

"Anything else I should know about him?" Tom asked.

Lauren frowned. "No, I don't think – Oh, yeah, there is one thing. It probably doesn't matter, though. Well, two things, actually."

Tom could tell the child's mind was sorting things out. "Just tell me."

"Once I helped Melissa with the laundry, and she had some shirts, and I think they were Larry's. Anyway, they had blood stains on them, all over the back, like stripes."

"Go on," Tom said.

"I asked what the stains were, and she said, 'Never you mind,' and that was that."

"You said there was something else," Tom said.

Lauren frowned. "There was. I forgot. I'll have to think about it."

Tom nodded and pulled out his cell phone. When Lauren looked worried, he patted her arm. "It's not about you," he whispered.

She relaxed.

"Give me the sheriff," he said into the phone. He waited a minute, then spoke again. "You know that warrant? We need one for the Jim and Melissa Pearson farm, too. I'll find an address." He Paused. "Yes, well, we got him admitting to the vandalism and picking up the corsets, plus evidence of a large flower greenhouse on the property. That should be enough for probable cause." He listened a bit, then hung up.

"Now, about that hospital visit," he said with a smile.

***

Tom and Candy drove quietly to the hospital. Lauren, sitting in the back seat, stared out the window. She was lost in her thoughts. Tom glanced in the mirror once in a while to make sure the child was okay, then he looked at Candy, who shrugged. No one wanted to break the silence.

When they arrived, Tom parked as close to the entrance as he could, locked his gun in the trunk of his car, and followed the women into the main lobby. Lauren looked around as if expecting trouble. She hung close to Tom. No one bothered them on their way to Fran's room.

When they got there, Dr. Kaul was standing in the hallway and looking over his chart. He glanced up at Tom. "Glad you're here. I had to chase that damn preacher off twice this afternoon, already."

"Did he say what he wanted?" Tom asked.

"Other than insisting that he talk to Fran, no. You got the toxicology, right?"

Tom nodded. He gave a furtive glance in Lauren's direction as a warning not to say anything in front of her. "How's Fran doing?"

Kaul frowned. "Better. Exhausted, but better." He glanced at Candy. "You know about the other thing, right?"

She nodded. She assumed he meant the baby, but he wasn't going to say so out loud, especially in front of Lauren.

"I haven't spoken to her about that yet," Kaul said, "so it might be a good idea not to bring it up until I do."

"Of course," Candy said.

"About what?" Lauren asked, curious.

"About seeing another doctor when she gets out," Candy said. It was a half-lie. Fran did have to see a gynecologist. The why part was left out. "We just want to make sure she's okay."

Lauren nodded.

"They're sleeping," Kaul told Tom.

"They?" Tom asked.

"They," Kaul repeated.

Tom opened the door to the room and found Rick stretched out on the recliner and snoring softly. Fran was asleep in his lap, her head on his chest and his arm around her as if he was holding a child. Tom felt like he was spying on them. Lauren didn't hesitate to go to her mom, put her hand on her arm and wake her up.

"Hey there, sweetie," Fran yawned. She slipped off of Rick's lap, sat down on the hospital bed, and pulled her daughter into her arms.

Rick continued sleeping.

"We won't stay long." Tom checked the hall. "Lauren ran away this morning and child protective services is looking for her."

"You ran away?" Fran held her daughter by the shoulders and looked at her. "What's going on?"

"I missed you." Lauren wrapped her arms around her mother's neck and clung to her.

Rick snorted in his sleep, turned sideways a bit, and continued to snore.

"Why don't we talk in the waiting room," Candy suggested. She picked up a soft white blanket and carefully laid it over Rick.

Tom watched her with mild surprise. Yesterday, she was ready to flatten Rick with whatever she could put her hands on. Today, she treated him like her child. He shook his head in bewilderment and led the group into the waiting room.

Once they were settled, Tom cleared his throat and looked at Fran.

"We think – that is, Candy and I, and the sheriff think that either Blackwell or Jim Pearson may be behind the sweetbriar rose murders," Tom said.

"Whose Jim Pearson?" Fran asked.

"Blackwell's handyman," Candy explained.

"Oh. I forgot about him. I'm afraid I'm not thinking clearly yet." Fran looked at Lauren, frowned, and looked back at Tom. "But isn't –" She stopped, suddenly not sure what to say. She glanced back at Lauren and hugged the girl. "What are you going to do?" she asked Tom.

"Well, for one, we're doing a forensic sweep of your house," Tom said.

"My house? Why my house?" Fran asked.

"The scotch was poisoned," Tom explained. "We don't think –" He sighed and rephrased his statement. "I don't think Jax was behind that. He had a different agenda. He needed you alive. So, either someone else sent that scotch, or someone tampered with it after you got it."

"Why would someone try and poison me?"

Candy bit her lip and looked from Tom to Fran and back again. "You know about Edgar, right?"

Fran nodded. "Yes, but –" Her hold on Lauren tightened. "You think I'm the new number five?"

"It's just speculation at this point," said Tom. "We'll see what forensics has to say. In the meantime–"

"In the meantime, what?" Rick asked from the doorway. He leaned on his cane. His clothes were disheveled. He wasn't happy. Charlie Cook stood behind him.

Lauren smiled at him but clung to her mother.

"In the meantime, she shouldn't be alone." Tom didn't intend for the statement to be anything more than a suggestion. He wasn't trying to be critical or hurtful, and yet he could see the pain on Rick's face. Tom thought he could say something to explain, to fix that awkward moment, but Candy put her hand on his arm and quieted him.

"We think Blackwell is behind the killings, but we need more information," Candy said. "Lauren gave us some, and we have a warrant coming for the Jim Pearson farm. We'll know more soon."

"Why the Pearson farm?" Rick asked.

"They have a big garden and a greenhouse with a lot of flowers," Lauren stated. She looked at the others. "What? You think I can't hear? You think the killer got his flowers from there, right?"

"In the meantime?" Rick asked again.

"We need to make sure Lauren and Fran are safe and Blackwell doesn't get his hands on them," Tom said.

Rick nodded. "I know a place." He turned to Charlie. "I don't have my Jeep. We'll need a ride."

"No problem," Charlie said.

"Where is it?" Tom asked.

"Charlie has a camp, a farmhouse really, outside of town. That's where I was when you…" He nodded at Candy, "…called. I can take them there for now. But you know what this means, don't you? We could all be in deep shit."

Candy looked confused. "What does it mean?"

"Custodial interference," Tom said. "We would essentially be kidnapping Lauren."

"But as a police officer –" Candy said.

"Right. I talked to child protective services. They gave me permission to find her and talk to her. They didn't say anything about hiding her, but they didn't say anything about WHERE I could talk to her, either," he explained. "It's dicey, but we can give it a try."

"I'm worried they're going to show up here, again," Candy said.

"Child services?" Fran asked.

"No, Blackwell and Cheryl. The last thing we need is another fight in the hospital." She glanced at Rick. "I know, I know. I started the last one."

"You started a fight? How long was I out for, anyway?" Fran asked.

Rick leaned down a bit and put a hand on Fran's shoulder. "It's not important. What matters is getting you and Lauren away from here and someplace safe."

Tom nodded. "I'll keep Lauren with me for now so I can record a statement. You guys can pick her up at the police department."

"Oh, that reminds me." Candy dug into her purse and pulled out Fran's keys. "The house is still a disaster, and forensics hadn't arrived yet so be careful, stay away from the glass, and don't touch anything."

Fran sighed and looked like she was going to cry. "Look, guys, I owe you all an apology." She looked up at Rick. "Especially you. I should have –"

Rick shook his head. "This one's on me. Besides, I'm sure I can make you pay for it later." He winked at her to cheer her up.

Fran smiled.

"We better get going," Tom said.

Fran gave Lauren a hug. Charlie, Rick, and Fran were standing side by side as the others headed down the hallway.

***

Tom knew that some days it didn't pay to fight. This wasn't one of those days.

Tom Saddler and Lawrence Blackwell faced off in the hospital parking lot. Cheryl stepped back and looked from one man to the other. Candy, unsure what she should do, glanced at Tom. Lauren turned on her heel and ran back into the hospital.

"Go home, minister. You've caused enough trouble here already," Tom said.

"You're telling me what to do now?" Blackwell's hand tightened on his cane.

Tom had seen what that cane could do. He'd also seen Blackwell's short temper. Tom stepped back a bit to defuse the situation. "I'm taking Lauren to the station with me to answer some questions."

Blackwell's eyes widened. He glanced nervously at Cheryl and then back at Tom. "What kind of questions?"

"You can't do that!" Cheryl shouted. "I have custody and —"

"Not yet, you don't," Tom reminded her. "The state has custody. You just get to babysit. And her social worker said that if I could find her, I could question her." He glanced over his shoulder at the hospital and saw Lauren staring at them through the window. He didn't want to let her down, not when they were so close. He turned back to Cheryl and Blackwell. "It seems all roads lead to you, minister."

"All roads? What are you talking about?" Blackwell tensed.

"The red paint that was used to vandalize Candy's apartment matches the paint used on your shutters," Tom began. "Jim Pearson admitted the vandalism."

"I doubt he implicated me," Blackwell said.

"As a matter of fact, he didn't. He took credit for that all by himself."

Blackwell relaxed a bit.

"He did admit to picking up a box for you at the Whip, though," Tom said.

"The Whip?" Blackwell frowned.

"Yes, the costume store. Something about six black and pink corsets? I don't suppose you wear those kinds of things at a church play, now, do you?"

"I don't know what you're talking about," Blackwell said coolly.

"Funny, because the store clerk picked out Jim Pearson from a photo lineup, and Jim admitted picking up the box for you." Tom was stretching the truth. Pearson never admitted to picking up a box from anyone, and the store clerk was vague about Pearson's description. When shown a photo lineup, the clerk had identified two possible suspects, one of which was Pearson.

But Blackwell didn't need to know that. Tom realized he should be having this discussion at the police station with witnesses and recording equipment and backup – especially backup. He looked at Candy to make sure she was alright.

"You can't protect that little bitch forever," Blackwell hissed.

Tom grew warm with anger. "I know about the roses, too," Tom bluffed. Tom was ninety percent sure Blackwell ordered the corsets used on the dead women. If that was the case, he had to have access to sweetbriar roses.

Tom glanced downward at the muddy stains on Blackwell's slacks and shoes. "It's convenient to have a green thumb." The tension in Tom's neck and shoulders stung. Was Blackwell going to simply deny everything and walk away? Or was he going to bolt and run? Or stand and fight?

Blackwell chuckled. "Roses? Seriously? You're going to pin three murders on me based on some common roses?" he asked.

"Four murders. That's where you screwed up. You broke the pattern with Edgar Mitchell. He was an innocent in all this, and you raped him." Tom shook his head. "There's a special kind of place in hell for men like you."

"I never touched him."

"No, not skin to skin, but he sure as hell touched you." Tom looked at Blackwell's arm where a long sleeve covered his wrist. "He ripped the skin right off of your body."

"If you have DNA on me, arrest me," Blackwell growled.

"You were in a hurry. You were careless. You –" Tom suddenly froze as a dozen scenarios rushed through his mind.

Cheryl started to step around the men and head toward the hospital, but Tom caught her eye. "I wouldn't move, if I were you," he told her. "Right now, I can charge you with obstruction. You try to interfere with Lauren, and I'll call it accessory to commit murder. Got it?"

Cheryl frowned. "You know damn well I don't know anything about murder, and you're crazy if you think Larry does. It's that bitch of yours that's behind this, isn't it? Her and her so-called lifestyle. Does she have a collar around your neck, Tom? Is she leading you around with a leash?"

Tom bristled and signaled for Candy to step back. The last thing he needed was a fight between the women.

"I'm taking Lauren to the station to make a statement. I expect you to get out of my way. If you don't, I'm arresting you," Tom told Blackwell. He looked at Cheryl. "Both of you."

Blackwell frowned and stepped forward. Tom's fists tightened. Tom wasn't sure of Blackwell's guilt before, but the confrontation in the parking lot confirmed his hunch. He regretted leaving his pistol in the police car.

"You sick bastard," Candy sputtered. "You killed my girls? Why? They never did anything to you. They never did anything to anyone."

Blackwell looked at her strangely, like a mouse eyeing a lump of cheese that he knew was in a trap. There was disdain, and there was pity, and there was something else – a kind of morbid fascination. Tom didn't like the look in Blackwell's eyes, but he never could have predicted what happened next.

Blackwell gave up all pretense of needing his cane and tossed it aside. It struck a car door and clattered to the pavement. The two men circled each other. Tom was surprised at how light Blackwell was on his feet, how he crouched like a cat about to pounce. Tom kept his distance at first and assessed his opponent. When Blackwell finally charged, Tom easily side-stepped out of his way and Blackwell landed, hands first, against a car. He spun quickly. Tom lowered his body and kept his stance wide. Blackwell swung and missed as Tom ducked. Blackwell swung again and grazed Tom's jaw. Tom spun on his heel and landed a kick to Blackwell's kidney. The preacher fell back against the car but regained his footing. The two men circled again – Blackwell angry and on the attack, Tom cautious and looking for his opportunity.

Blackwell stepped twice toward Tom as Tom stepped back, braced himself against a car, and kicked with both feet, landing a blow to Blackwell's chest that sent him crashing to the ground. Tom pounced, but Blackwell rolled and eluded him. Tom scrambled to his feet as Blackwell hit him from behind and landed a blow to the base of Tom's back that sent him sprawling. Blackwell lunged. Tom rolled out of the way and came back to his feet. His eyes flared with fire. He bent his head down like a bull about to charge. Blackwell looked at the detective with derision.

Tom lunged, pulled back, lunged again, each time watching where Blackwell stepped, each time learning the man's moves. The third time, Tom landed a right cross into Blackwell's jaw, and the man's head went back hard. He flailed as he stumbled into a car. Shaking his head to clear it, Blackwell could taste the blood in his mouth.

"You're going to kill him!" Cheryl screamed as she rushed toward Tom.

Candy caught the woman by the arm and yanked her back, pushed her to the ground, and sat on her. "Now, who's the bitch, bitch?" Candy yelled.

Blackwell and Tom circled again. Blackwell dodged and slid into Tom. His elbow went into Tom's gut and Tom doubled over. Blackwell seized Tom from behind and body slammed him onto the hood of a car. Tom kicked wildly and broke loose, then slid hard to the pavement. As Blackwell circled, Tom scrambled away and regained his footing. He was hurting. His shirt was torn. He kept the car between them for a few minutes to catch his breath.

Blackwell suddenly jumped over the hood of the car and landed on top of Tom, knocking him to the ground again. Blackwell swung at Tom's head – once, twice, three times. Tom blocked each blow but couldn't get out from under the big man. Blackwell then spotted his cane and leaned sideways to snatch it. The move threw him off balance, and Tom was able to tip Blackwell over and fall hard on his chest, straddling him. The two men wrestled over the cane.

Blackwell finally twisted the cane out of Tom's grip and slugged Tom in the face with the heavy head of it. Tom roared, stood, and backed up, his hand going to his face. He turned to avoid another blow and twisted his knee sharply as the cane struck and dented the hood of the car behind Tom. The car's alarm went off. Blackwell struck again, and this time Tom was able to grab the cane and use it as leverage to slam Blackwell back into the ground.

Behind him, Tom heard Candy screaming for Rick and Charlie. With no time to think about it, Tom tried to straddle his opponent, but Blackwell twisted free and jumped up. Tom, grasping the cane, raised it to strike. He stepped forward and his knee suddenly gave out under him. Tom landed hard on the pavement with a yelp as Blackwell fled the parking lot on foot, bleeding and beaten, but still free.

Charlie was the first to reach Tom, who was now prone on the ground and gripping his leg. Charlie turned Tom over and poked him a little. "Hey, you okay?"

Rick hobbled up on his cane and stared down at Tom.

Tom wanted to laugh, but he hurt all over. "No, I'm not okay. Damn motherfucker got away!"

Rick and Charlie bent over and helped Tom to his feet, but Tom couldn't put any weight on his bad knee.

Tom turned to Cheryl, who was still pinned under Candy and screaming like crazy. "One down," Tom muttered. "You're under arrest."

Cheryl tried to claw at Candy, but Charlie grabbed both of Cheryl's hands and held her still. "Now what?" Charlie asked.

"Call 911?" Tom suggested. "We could use a cop."

Some days, it didn't pay to fight, Tom thought. This wasn't one of those days. He picked up the cane and smiled. "You know what we call this, Charlie?"

"A cane?"

"We call it a weapon, and in this case, we also call it evidence." Tom looked at Cheryl. "Your ass is on the line, sweetie. Got anything you want to say to me now?"

Chapter 30
Wednesday Afternoon

Tuesday night, Tom called the office and said he was taking Wednesday off. The police secured the Pearson farm and were waiting on the warrant to search the property. Blackwell was on the run. Jax disappeared to god-knows-where, and Tom could barely walk. It was a torn ligament, Sam Kaul said, as if that would get rid of the pain.

Tom and Candy went back to his apartment, fell into bed, and slept. It was all either of them could do. They were beyond exhaustion. The sleepless nights only added to the emotional stress. It was nearly four a.m. when they finally crawled between the covers, and nearly noon when Tom was forced awake by the phone.

Tom sat up, dropped his feet to the floor, and yawned. He was still in his clothes and needed a shower. He picked up the phone. "Saddler," he said.

"It's Hodge."

"I'm taking the day off," Tom said sleepily.

"I'm not calling you in."

"Then what?"

"It's Toni de la Rosa. Suicide. She was found around five this morning. I just got word. I thought you'd like to know."

Tom groaned. His stomach plunged. Her face flashed in front of his eyes. She was eating a hamburger; the ketchup was dripping on the plate; she was kicking him under the table at the diner and teasing him; she had him pinned to the mat in the police department gym. She had been a handful, a livewire. "Yeah, thanks. Let the coroner know I'll take care of arrangements."

"You got it," Hodge said.

"I thought she was on suicide watch. What happened?"

"Sure you want to know?"

"Not really."

"They moved her into the infirmary. She was eating so little, they were going to try to force-feed her. While she was there, she said she had to use the bathroom. Idiot medic left her alone on the toilet." He was quiet for a moment. "She started swallowing the toilet paper until she choked to death."

"Fuck." Tom closed his eyes. Bile rose in his mouth.

"I'm sorry," Hodge said. "There'll be an investigation. It shouldn't have happened."

"Well, there was no stopping her. Sooner or later, she would have pulled it off. Thanks for calling." Tom hung up the phone and slumped back into his pillow.

"What is it? Who died?" Candy rolled over on the bed and rested her hand on Tom's warm back.

"Toni," he said without looking at Candy. "She killed herself."

"How?" Candy propped herself up on her elbow. "I thought she was on suicide watch."

"She was in the infirmary. A medic got careless." Tom tried to wipe the fatigue from his eyes. "I don't want to talk about it."

Candy quietly rubbed his back. "Hold me. I can't stop being cold."

Tom stretched out next to her and pulled her close to him. "You will."

"You said you'll take care of Toni's funeral?"

"Somebody has to. Fran's clearly not up to it, and Alex is dead."

"I know Fran said she'd pay for Alex's. I can pay for Toni's," Candy offered.

"Why?" Tom brushed back her hair and looked into her eyes. "The woman tried to kill you. Why would you do that?"

"She was Alex's sister. I'm doing it for him."

Tom closed his eyes. "Damn. I've got to tell Rick." He kissed Candy firmly on the lips as if doing so could delay the inevitable.

"He's probably still at the hospital with Fran."

Tom nodded.

"How about a hot shower?" Candy asked.

"I was just thinking that. I really hate to get up and leave you here, though."

"Who said you have to leave me here? I've seen your shower. It'll be a little crowded, but we can manage."

"You need fresh clothes."

"I'll just borrow one of your shirts until we can stop at Fran's."

"Ah, shit!" Tom leaned back on his pillow and covered his head with his arm.

"What now?" Candy asked.

"We still have that mess to clean up at Fran's. Forensics should have been in and out of there by now and the place is –" He growled.

"Like hell," Candy snapped. "I'm sick and tired of cleaning up after those two. They can damn well take care of it themselves. You've got more than enough to deal with."

Tom looked at her and smiled at the fire in her eyes. He reached up, caressed her cheek, and pulled her into a kiss. "You were saying something about a shower?"

Candy straddled him and started removing her clothes. Still sore from the fight, Tom winced a bit. He admired her firm body and soft skin. He reached up to fondle her breasts, but she grabbed his wrists and pushed them back into his pillow, one on each side of his head. Candy bent down and kissed him slowly and lovingly.

She whispered in his ear, "Last one in the shower is a rotten egg!" Laughing, she scooted off the bed and made a dash for the bathroom.

Tom groaned and snatched at her but missed. He tried to stand up and nearly fell over when the pain hit. Swearing, Tom shed his clothes and hopped on one foot to the bathroom. By the time he got there, Candy had turned on the water. She squealed when he grabbed her by the waist, hoisted her into the shower, and pinned her face first to the shower wall. He pressed his chest into her back, gripped her hands over her head, and began kissing her neck and shoulders.

"Oh, god, that feels good," Candy moaned.

"I'm not done yet," Tom whispered in her ear.

Balancing on his good leg, he held her tightly as he kissed and fondled her until she was a bundle of nerves. Then he took a soapy sponge and bathed her. Finally, he washed her hair, his hands massaging her scalp. When he was done bathing her, he knelt on one knee, pressed his lips to her, and played with her body until she shrieked and nearly fell over. Tom stood up, held her tightly in his arms, and said, "Your turn."

It was the longest shower he ever had.

***

Tom and Candy ran into Rick and Margo in the hospital lobby. "Going somewhere?" Tom asked. He was adjusting to a pair of crutches and having little luck.

"We're heading to the house. Fran said she left the place in a bit of a mess." Margo was in bright pink that day, right down to the streaks in her black hair. "I thought we'd go pick it up."

Tom had so many responses to that but fortunately Candy cut him off.

"We were just there. Forensics left, so it's all yours." Candy eyed Rick. "I'd get a dumpster, if I were you."

Margo raised an eyebrow.

"Tornadoes do less damage," Tom said.

"I know a few cleaning crews in town," Candy said. "I'm sure we can get some help."

"We?" Tom asked.

"It's okay. I got it," Margo said with a smile. "I know people."

"I just bet you do," Tom grinned.

"Checking on Fran?" Rick asked.

"I was looking for you," said Tom. "I got a call from the sheriff about Toni." Tom hesitated, unsure how to continue. Toni had been Tom's partner, but she had been Rick's lover.

The silence hurt Rick's ears. He turned and started to walk toward the exit.

"Rick!" Candy called out.

Rick stopped and looked at them. "This one I did see coming." Then he headed out the door.

"She's gone?" Margo asked.

Tom nodded. "Suicide."

"Damn. That's so sad." Margo ran after Rick. She found him leaning against her car and shaking. "I'm so sorry," she said as she opened the door for him. Hot air escaped from inside the vehicle.

"It's okay, kid." Rick slid into the car and put the window down. "Toni died a long time ago. It just took a while for her body to catch up."

As Rick and Margo drove away, Candy turned to Tom. "What now? Fran?"

He nodded.

They found Fran fully dressed and sitting up.

"Going home?" Tom asked.

"I was supposed to, but the doctor insisted on a psych eval this afternoon – as if there's anything I don't know about myself."

"They're just being thorough," Candy said.

"He also wants me to see a gynecologist. Something about –" Fran caught her breath and tears welled in her eyes. "Something about my IUD failing. They had to remove it, and I need a new one."

Candy walked up to Fran's chair, knelt in front of her, and hugged her. "I'm so sorry. Did you know?"

Fran shook her head no. "I had no idea. I can't believe it. Of all the – Fuck. I was about six weeks along. What am I going to tell Rick?"

"We just saw Rick," Tom said. "I'm afraid I'm the bearer of more bad news."

"What now?" Fran clasped her hands together and waited.

"Toni took her own life early this morning. We just gave Rick the news."

Fran bowed her head a moment as if in prayer. "Rick's going to blame himself. How did he take it?"

"Calmly," said Candy.

"Like he was expecting it," Tom added.

"Well, I guess there's nothing left to do except bury the dead." Fran wiped tears from her eyes and composed herself.

"Yes, we need to talk about that," said Tom. "And a few other things."

"What kinds of other things?" Fran asked.

Tom cleared his throat. "Well, let's start with Lauren. I take it Rick filled you in on what happened with Blackwell and the murder cases?"

"Yes."

"Blackwell's on the run. Cheryl spent the night in jail. Lauren spent the night at Paul's parents' house, but they don't want to keep her. I'm thinking, with everything that's going on, my mom and I could take care of her for a while, at least until things get settled."

Candy's eyes widened. "You never told me –"

Fran sighed. "Child services isn't going to send her home to me, are they?" Some little part of her still held out hope.

"Not likely, and certainly not anytime soon. That's why I thought it would be better to have her with me than with strangers." Tom looked apologetic.

"You have a pretty dangerous job, yourself," Fran noted. It was a half-hearted argument. In truth, she was relieved Tom would take Lauren.

"For now. I'm quitting. I gave my notice."

"Okay, wait a minute!" Candy stood up and faced Tom. "I just spent the last – what? 48 hours? – with you, and you never mentioned a damn thing to me. When did this all come up?"

"I told you I wanted a career change." Tom scowled. "You didn't think I was waiting for your permission, did you?"

Candy was silent for a stunned minute before responding softly. "No, no. You're right, Tom. You don't need my permission. You don't even need to tell me. You don't need to do a damn thing." She turned on her heel and walked out of the room.

"Damn," Tom muttered.

"Go after her," Fran said.

"I'm not her 'boy,' Fran."

"I know, but she's not used to –" Fran stopped. She sensed she was jumping in where she didn't belong.

"Think about my offer," Tom said. "The sooner you agree, the sooner I can talk to child protective services, the sooner we can get her back."

"I think it's a good idea. She likes you. It's the next best thing to her being home."

Tom walked up to Fran, took her face in his hands, and gently kissed her lips. "I know this has been hard on you. It's been hard on me too. We're all adjusting. When I look at Rick and you, I get it. I can see how much he loves you, and how much you need him. I can't say it doesn't hurt, but – I guess I'm trying to say that I've accepted it, that I've moved on. That everything is going to be okay. Understand?"

"I love you, too, sweetie." Fran kissed him one more time. "Now, go fix things with your girl. She's not used to waiting."

"She's not used to a lot of things. We both have a lot to learn." He smiled and left Fran to her thoughts.

Tom found Candy pacing the floor in the waiting room and wiping tears from her cheeks. He walked up to her, took her in his arms, and said, "Tell me what just happened here."

She shook her head and started to cry again.

Tom cupped her cheek in his hand and brushed away the tears with his thumb. "I'm not one of your boys, Candy. I told you that, and you said that's what you want. And yet now you're upset that I don't clear everything with you first. Well, it's not going to happen. I make my own decisions about my life. That doesn't stop me from loving you, but if you're going to make this work with me, you have to accept who and what I am. Otherwise, this isn't going anywhere."

Candy wrapped her arms around his neck. "Okay, you need to make your own decisions," she said with a sigh. "Could you at least give me a warning, first? Maybe a heads up before you announce it to the world?"

Tom grinned. "I'll do my best."

***

Late Wednesday Afternoon

"Remember when I said I wasn't calling you in?" Hodge asked.

Tom took a minute to scowl at the cell phone before putting it back to his ear. "I'm on crutches. I tore a ligament in that scuffle with Blackwell."

"From what I heard, that was more than a scuffle. I need you to come out to the Pearson farm and bring Candy. Things are pretty interesting out here, to say the least. I just want your input."

"Candy?" Tom asked.

"Yeah. I tried calling her earlier, but she didn't answer," said Hodge.

"Oh, yeah. We were – er – busy." Tom immediately regretted saying those words to his boss.

"Too much information, detective. Just get your asses out here ASAP."

Tom nodded and looked across the kitchen table at Candy as she waited for him to fill her in.

"Okay. We'll head right out." Tom hung up.

"The sheriff?" Candy took a bite of her salad and pushed Tom's plate toward him.

He looked down at the meal and frowned. He didn't like salad, but he picked up a fork and poked at it in a lame attempt to be polite.

"Yes. He wants us at the Pearson farm. Seems they found a few interesting things."

"Us?"

"Us." Tom swallowed his resistance and ate.

"I wonder how Joe defines 'interesting,'" Candy mused.

For once, the weather was nice, warm but with a soft, cool breeze. A few clouds managed to shade the earth from the autumn sun. The ride into the country was pleasant. Tom put his window down and enjoyed the fresh air. If they weren't still looking for a serial killer, it would have been the perfect day.

Candy was driving her car. She had one arm out the window and the wind tossed her dark hair around her oversized sunglasses. Tom smiled at her. She had such passion, such determination, a clear-headedness about her that he admired. He drew a finger down her cheek, and she leaned slightly into his touch and grinned.

When they arrived at the farm, a police officer directed them to the smaller of two barns, a rectangular building about eighteen by twenty-four feet, with a second level and a Dutch roof, and painted in farmhouse yellow with forest green trim. Candy, who had chosen capris, a tank top, and white sandals for the occasion, helped Tom out of her car and handed him his crutches.

"I'm beginning to understand Rick's frustration," Tom noted as he struggled to get his balance.

"You did great driving the cruiser earlier," Candy noted.

"Driving isn't my problem. Walking is." Tom looked around and saw Hodge waving to them from the hayloft opening. The sheriff had an odd look on his face, something between satisfaction and confusion. Tom shook a crutch at Hodge, but the sheriff ignored him.

The barn itself was more like a workshop – clean and tidy, with rakes and shovels aligned on wall hooks, a four-wheeler parked in the corner, shelves that held jars of screws and assorted items, and a carpenter's worktable framed by neatly sorted tools.

A thick, steeply tilted ladder led to the upstairs. Tom took one look at Candy, and she poked him.

"Just take it easy," she said. "I'll be right behind you."

"I'm beginning to hate this job," Tom muttered. He left the crutches on the first floor and slowly worked his way up the ladder, using his upper body strength to pull himself up most of the way.

Upstairs, Hodge gave Tom a hand and pulled him to his feet. "You're gonna love this." Hodge frowned. "I think."

The room was plain, unpainted, and, for the most part, unfurnished. A large canvas tarp was suspended from the ceiling and painted with a primitive, large red cross. In front of it was an old church kneeler, built of solid, rustic wood and untrimmed. Dark spots covered the kneeler and the floor around it, and Tom knew he was looking at blood. He shuddered.

"Son-of-a-bitch," Candy said behind him.

"Over here." One of the forensics guys opened a large wooden chest. The lid creaked until it hit the wall and stopped. Wearing latex gloves, he pulled items out of the box: heavy chains, floggers, paddles, cuffs. He straightened his back and looked up as Hodge and Tom studied the contents.

Jeanette climbed spryly up the ladder with one of Tom's crutches in her grasp. She glanced at the men. "What do you think? Quite the cache, isn't it?" She handed the crutch to Tom.

"What's behind curtain number one?" Tom indicated the tarp.

"Oh, you're gonna love this." Jeanette acted as if she'd found the mother lode. She snapped her gloves into place, grabbed a cane-like instrument, and drew back the tarp.

Candy felt dizzy. She reached out and grabbed Tom's arm.

A large, rustic, wooden altar stood against the wall. A white linen tablecloth was thrown over the top and several whips were stretched over it, the blood from the whips staining the cloth. A large crucifix rose over the altar. More startling were the photographs, each one that of a young man in his twenties, each one carefully framed, each one with a votive candle in front of it. The photos included one of Edgar Mitchell. None of them were Candy's girls.

"Did you ever see such shit? Seriously? Ever?" Hodge turned to Jeanette. "I need one of them shrink guys in here. I want every inch of this photographed. I want to know exactly how many men he tortured up here."

"He only tortured one up here," Candy said softly as she approached the altar. She knew better than to touch anything. Her eyes teared up as she focused on Edgar's photo.

"One?" Hodge asked.

Candy nodded. "Yes. Himself." She turned to face Tom and Hodge. "This is where Lawrence Blackwell beat himself up, where he did penance for his sins; and I'm pretty sure these young men…" Candy indicated the photos on the altar. "…are the reason why. They're his victims. He used self-flagellation to either try and control his compulsion or to pay for what he did to them."

"Why aren't the women up here, then?" Tom asked. "Pamela, Andrea, Meghan?"

"Because they weren't his victims." Candy looked back at the photos. "I wonder which one is Bryce Pearson."

"Victims? Or sacrifices?" Jeanette asked. "After all, it IS an altar."

Candy shuddered.

"Bryce Pearson's killer went to jail." Hodge backed up toward the large loft opening to get some fresh air.

"Maybe. Maybe not," Candy said. "Maybe Blackwell killed him. Or maybe Blackwell contributed to his death somehow. We won't know for sure until we examine each of these victims. That will tell us what's going on inside Blackwell's head." Candy slipped into saying 'us' as if she was still part of the crime lab.

Hodge groaned. "So, we started out trying to solve four murders and ended up having to solve, how many?"

Tom counted the photos on the altar. "Twelve. Fifteen, if you include the three women."

"Maybe sixteen. I don't think any of these guys is Bryce. The twelve men are like the twelve apostles," Candy noted. "Could be a coincidence."

"I wonder if Bryce was the Judas, the thirteenth apostle, the one not saved," said Tom.

"What else did our people find?" Candy asked.

The 'our' was a slip of the tongue. Hodge ignored it. "Your sweetbriar roses in the greenhouse."

"I just came from there," Jeanette said. "It gets worse. The flowers were planted on a bed of fresh soil, and the soil —"

"Is a gravesite." Candy finished the thought.

Jeanette nodded. "Yes. We're digging up bodies as we speak. Anyone care to come see?"

Candy shook her head. "I'm going to pass on that one."

Jeanette turned to Tom. "By the way, you'll be happy to hear we got a hit on Fran's place."

"A hit?" Tom and Hodge both asked at once.

Jeanette nodded almost gleefully. "The liquor bottle from Fran's had a partial print that matches Blackwell's print from his cane, and the dirt found in Fran's bathroom matched that on the cane and is a possible match for what's in the greenhouse."

"What dirt in the bathroom? Damn." Tom caught his breath. "That son-of-a-bitch was in the bathroom when we found Fran!"

"It was the only place we didn't look," Candy said. "She was in the bedroom and –"

Tom nodded. "He was right there. The whole time. And we didn't know it. He could have killed her. Hell, he could have killed you!"

"I don't get it," Hodge admitted. "If he was into killing young men and then beating himself up over it, why did he suddenly focus on you and your girls? What broke the pattern?"

"Bryce, apparently," Tom said. "Something about his death sparked this. We just don't know why, yet." He leaned a bit on Candy as he limped back to the ladder and sat down on the floor. "Let's get outta here."

"You gonna let Rick know about Blackwell, or should I?" Hodge asked.

"This one's all yours. I'm off today, remember?"

***

Wednesday Evening

Rick nodded as he listened over the phone to Hodge's report. He hung up without saying goodbye and glanced at Fran. Her eyes were closed, and she hadn't spoken since they got into Rick's Jeep.

Rick and Margo had boxed up the law office files and put away the tables. When Rick arrived at the house, he drove his Jeep into the garage and closed the garage door behind them. Then he got out, went around to Fran's side of the vehicle, and helped her out of it.

"I can manage," she said, although she was surprised at how weak she still felt.

"I know." He didn't let that stop him from helping her. He put an arm around her waist and steered her into the house. He was still limping, but he left the cane behind. "Where do you want to go? Sofa? Bed?"

Fran turned toward him and curled her arms around his waist. "My room. I want you to sleep with me there. Do you mind?"

They had never made love in her room. It was the room she'd shared with Tom and was somehow off limits to Rick. He kissed her forehead. "Sure, boss." He led her into the bedroom where he helped her undress. Then he crawled into bed with her.

Fran lay next to him, her fingers running gently over his powerful chest, tracing the lines of his tattoos. "Tell me about the ink."

"What do you want to know?"

Fran propped herself up a bit and studied his chest as she talked. "Well, let's start with this one, the bulldog. What's that for?"

"Ah, that's my Marine buddy," he explained. "The bulldog is the Marine Corps mascot." He pointed to another tattoo. "The eagle, globe, and anchors are also Marine Corps, as is this, the Marine Corps motto, Semper Fidelis."

"What does it mean?" she asked.

"Always Faithful," he told her.

"Do you miss it? Being in the Marines?"

Rick shrugged. "I'm still a Marine. I do miss the corps. I was a kid. It was one hell of a way to grow up fast."

"What's this one for?" She looked at his chest and read the date inked on it, "July 6, 1985."

"That's the day my son was born."

"Your son? What son? You never told me you had a son."

"I don't." Rick's eyes met hers. "I was sixteen. The state took him, put him up for adoption. I never saw him again."

Fran bit her lip. "Sam told me – He said – Damn. I talked to the gynecologist. He told me –"

"Shhh." Rick stroked her cheek. "It's okay. I already know."

"Fuck," Fran moaned as she buried her head in his chest. "I'm so sorry, Rick. I'm so sorry."

"It's okay, baby. I got no business being a dad. Maybe it's for the best." He stroked her hair. "Now, this one," he said, pointing to a small black rosebud with wings for thorns, "was for an old sweetheart of mine who died in a car crash. I was in Panama at the time. She was back in Philly. She'd been out partying with some friends."

"What was her name?" Fran asked.

"Angela," he said.

"Like Detective Simmons," Fran noted.

Rick laughed. "Believe me, VERY different personality."

"You must have loved her very much."

"Enough to marry her."

"What?" Fran looked up in surprise.

"I was sixteen. We were kids. She was pregnant. Her folks found out, arranged an annulment. Then they took the baby and signed it away. I never saw either of them again."

"Damn. That sucks. What's with the barbed wire around your throat?"

"It's supposed to be a crown of thorns," Rick explained. "Never took me for the religious type, did you?"

"Are you religious?" Fran asked.

"I don't sit still and listen to any preaching if that's what you mean, but when you face death a lot, you gotta believe in something." He pulled himself up a bit as he spoke. "After Iraq, I was pretty depressed. I went back to Philly, but I couldn't seem to adjust to being a civilian. Went through a rough spell. Ended up on the streets for a while with a bunch of other vets that weren't making it. One night …" He hesitated a few moments, reluctant to go on. "One night it got pretty cold. It was snowing. Three or four of us ate at a soup kitchen and were looking for a place to sleep. We curled up behind some dumpsters with cardboard boxes for blankets." He sighed. "Anyway, one of my buddies – Aces we called him, I never knew his real name – anyway, he died in his sleep that night. Aces always told me that when he died the angels were gonna take him someplace nice and warm, and I should keep an eye out 'cause I'd see them, and then I'd get converted." Rick chuckled. "I didn't believe him, of course, but that night," he looked up at Fran, "I swear to God, Fran, that night, I saw them take him." He looked down again. "Now, I ain't saying what I saw was real. I could have been hallucinating. I was drinking pretty heavy at the time. It could have been a dream. Hell, I don't know. But I saw something, and the next day I went out and got the tat."

"There are so many things I don't know about you," Fran said.

Rick pulled her up and kissed her. "Don't worry. You got plenty of time to find out."

She smiled. "How about I get a tattoo?" she suggested.

Rick laughed. "Where? On that sweet little ass of yours?" He gave her a light spank.

Fran flushed red. "Well, that's one place. Or on my neck, or shoulder, or shoulder blade, or, right here, over my breast." She drew an invisible line with her finger.

"Just what kind of tattoo did you have in mind?"

"Hmm, let's see. Something pretty. Something delicate. Something just for you."

Rick frowned as he thought about it. "You come up with an idea and I'll let you know if it's okay." He kissed her again. "If you're really into wearing my mark, I gotta admit, I find that hot, but I think you need to think about this."

"Sure thing, boss," Fran said with a grin.

***

Early Thursday Morning

"I just want you to keep an eye on the house. Make sure she's safe while she sleeps, and make sure she's okay if she wakes up." Rick told Charlie.

They stood in the darkness in front of Fran's house as her living room clock struck midnight. Rick was dressed in black with a .38 holstered to his back. He had abandoned the cane and the sling. He downed a handful of pills to dull the pain in his leg.

"Sure thing." Charlie was munching on a bag of candy and popped a nonpareil into his mouth. "What should I tell her if she asks where you are?"

"Tell her I had to run to the camp. You don't know why. Something like that."

"Lie to her, you mean," Charlie raised an eyebrow. "You're not gonna tell me where you're going, are you?"

"You don't want to know." Rick looked back over his shoulder at the house. "I won't be long. An hour, maybe two. Three tops. And I won't mess up your truck." Rick smirked.

Charlie handed over his keys. "You'd better not. I just got her painted – three years ago." He laughed. He was standing on the sidewalk and eating his candy as Rick pulled away from the curb.

About a mile out of Vegas, Rick stopped at a junkyard, parked the truck, and slipped on a pair of leather driving gloves. He wore a black hoodie that hid most of his eyes and a mask over his mouth. A single bulb dangled from a wire inside the small office. Rick knocked once.

"It's open," someone yelled.

Rick stepped in and nodded to the short, bald man behind the desk. "We all set?"

The man picked up some keys and tossed them to Rick. "It's out back. The black one. The plates are on magnets."

"Thanks." Rick laid five hundred in cash on the desk and walked out. He removed the plates long before he got to the Pearson farm.

Rick saw the glimmer of a flashlight in the greenhouse. The place was cordoned off, but no police were around. The Pearsons were both in jail. Shovels and dirt, left from digging up the bodies, were stacked by the building. A lone flood lamp streamed light over the front yard of the farmhouse, but the greenhouse was in the shadows.

Rick approached with no headlights and parked the car away from the building. He stepped out, pulled the .38 from his back holster, and kept low as he skirted the building. He had no doubt Blackwell would find his way back to the farm as soon as the police cleared the scene. Rick expected to wait for Blackwell, but the man had returned earlier than expected.

The night was hot and dry. Rick moved slowly and kept to the shadows. When he finally entered the greenhouse, he found Blackwell sitting in the dirt, legs crossed, head bent as if in prayer, the flashlight shedding a glow on the ground around him. He was shirtless and held a flogger in his hand. His shoulders and back were covered in blood.

"Are you my executioner?" Blackwell asked as he looked up. His face was pale gray in the dim light.

"Yes."

"Why? I did my penance. Why not just arrest me? Call the police? What do you want with me?"

"There are good men in this world, and there are evil men," said Rick. "I've been both, and now I stand between the two. You came after those I protect. You attacked the weak, tortured and murdered those stupid enough to trust you, and now you want the law to protect you. You invaded my world, and in my world, I am the law.

"Your woman lived," Blackwell argued. Still on his knees, he straightened up.

Rick tightened his grip on the gun. "Mine was pregnant. Did you do your penance for *my* dead child?"

Blackwell's eyes widened in shock. "God will forgive me."

"God doesn't even know your name." Rick approached, his gun leveled at Blackwell's head.

Blackwell opened his mouth to speak. Rick fired.

A half-hour later, Rick brushed the rest of the dirt from his slacks. He returned to the car, stripped, and put the clothing, gloves, and boots in a garbage bag. He put on fresh clothes, returned to the junkyard, and threw the garbage bag into a burning pile of trash. He wiped down the car and keys, left the keys behind the visor, and drove the truck to Charlie's camp where he showered and changed clothes again.

Fran was still sleeping when Rick returned to the house. He entered quietly and nodded at Charlie, who was sitting at the kitchen table and drinking some coffee. Rick handed him the truck keys and the .38.

"We good?" Rick asked.

Charlie gulped down the last of the coffee and left.

The front door closed just as Fran walked into the kitchen. "Who was that?" she asked with a yawn.

"Charlie. Just checking on us." That part, at least, was the truth. Rick pulled her into his lap and kissed her. "Sleep well?"

"Like a rock, but where did you go? I woke up and you weren't there," Fran complained.

"My leg was acting up. I was up and down all night. Don't worry, boss, I'm still here." He kissed her again, this time much harder. "Now, about that tattoo –"

Chapter 31

Thursday Morning

"I need to see your gun," Joe Hodge said as he stood in the doorway of Fran's house around 9 a.m. Thursday morning.

Rick shrugged. "Sure. Why?"

"You got a problem with that?" Hodge asked.

"I gotta problem anytime someone wants my gun. If you were anyone else, I'd say get a warrant." Rick, gripping his cane, stepped out of the way. "It's in the Jeep. I'll get it."

"No. I'll get it." Hodge followed Rick into the kitchen and through the door to the garage where the vehicle was parked. It was the first time Hodge had seen the 1957 Willys Jeep CJ-5. "She's a beauty. Restored?"

"Yup. Bought her off of Charlie. The gun's in the glove compartment."

Hodge nodded, opened the glove compartment, and lifted out a back holster and the .45. "This the one?"

Rick nodded again. He leaned against the doorway to the kitchen and watched.

"Ever use a .38?" Hodge asked.

"Hell, Joe. I've used every gun ever made. Why?"

"Forensics guys went back to the Pearson farm this morning. They took cadaver dogs to look for other bodies." Hodge turned to face Rick. "They found Blackwell."

"He's in custody?

Joe raised an eyebrow. "He's dead. They found his body."

Rick grunted and frowned. "Well, good for them." He turned slowly and deliberately, limped back into the kitchen, and poured himself a cup of coffee.

Hodge put the gun back in the Jeep and followed Rick into the house. "You wouldn't know anything about that, would you?"

Rick sat down with a groan. He put the cane on the table. "Spit it out. Let's get this over with."

"Did you murder Lawrence Blackwell?"

"No. Any other questions?"

"Yeah, just one. Would you tell me if you had?"

Rick chuckled. "Good point. No, I probably wouldn't. Want some coffee?"

Hodge relaxed a little and shook his head no. "Does Fran know?"

"About what?"

"About Blackwell," said Hodge.

"She suspects he tried to kill her if that's what you mean. I didn't tell her about the forensic report. She's got enough to deal with."

Hodge nodded. "Where is she, anyway?"

"She ran to the store. We're low on everything."

"I take it you guys will be here all day?" Hodge asked.

"In case you want to question me some more?"

"Something like that."

"We're going to Charlie's camp. You can reach us up there if you need us."

Hodge studied Rick for a moment before walking out the door. Rick, using the cane, stood up and followed Hodge onto the front porch. Once Hodge was gone, Rick leaned against the railing and took a deep breath.

***

Thursday Evening

"If I knew we were going to be a foursome, I would have brought more food." Candy hopped out of her car and ran up to the wide porch that encircled the white clapboard farmhouse Charlie fondly called 'the camp.' She was carrying two bottles of wine, one in each hand. She sat them down on the top step.

Rick and Fran were seated side by side on a mismatched pair of Adirondack chairs. They were sharing a footrest, drinking iced tea, and looking at the vista as the sun sank into a pool of deep orange on the horizon.

"It's a five-some, and Charlie's getting the food," Rick said with a grin. He motioned to the side of the building where a large fire pit was set up and the flames were just getting started.

"I hope he brings something I can eat." Candy turned her nose up.

"Speaking of which, where's your other half?" Fran asked.

"He's on his way," Candy said happily.

"So, I take it you kissed and made up?"

Rick gave Fran a sideways glance. "None of your business, sweetheart."

Fran rolled her eyes.

Candy laughed it off. She walked onto the porch wearing jeans and cowboy boots, her heels clicking on the wooden floor; then she sat down on the railing in front of Rick and Fran. "I guess I have to change how I handle things a bit. I just didn't expect –" She shrugged.

"Expect what?" Rick asked as he took another drink.

"I thought you said it was none of our business," Fran smirked.

"No, woman, I said it was none of YOUR business. Now, if Candy here wants to tell me a story, who am I to stop her?" Rick stretched out and grinned at the two women.

"First things first, then," Candy said. "Tom wants to quit the force and do something less dangerous. He mentioned the idea to me once, but I didn't realize he was actually set on resigning. So when he told Fran he was quitting his job, I was a bit, well, surprised."

"You don't like surprises?" Rick teased.

"Not from the men I'm sleeping with, no," Candy admitted. "And then when he talked about having Lauren live with him –"

Rick almost choked on his iced tea. He turned to look at Fran. "You didn't say anything to me about that."

"See? That's what I'm talking about," Candy exclaimed. "That was my reaction, exactly."

Fran nodded. "With Blackwell on the run and Cheryl in prison –"

"Blackwell's not on the run. He's dead," said Rick.

"What?" both women asked at once.

"Hodge came by this morning and told me. Forensics found his body at the Pearson farm this morning."

"Suicide?" Fran asked.

"You'll have to ask Hodge, but I don't think so."

"Men!" Candy sputtered.

Fran rolled her eyes.

"You were talking about Lauren?" Rick asked.

Fran explained. "She ended up at her grandparents' house, but she can't stay there. Tom seems to think child services will let her stay with him, and he's willing to take her for now. At least he won't be pushing for custody. We can get visitation back on track and –" She looked up at Rick. "It'll give us time, Rick. Time to work something out. Time to fix this."

"By this, you mean me," Rick said quietly. He slipped the empty bottle of iced tea to the floor, reached into a small cooler for a second one, and unscrewed the cap.

Candy stretched her leg up and kicked Rick in the foot. "Nah. No one can fix you." She winked at him.

Rick leaned back and frowned. "Don't play with me, woman," he growled.

Candy stopped kicking, not sure if he meant it or not.

Rick turned back to Fran. "It's not a bad idea. I'll talk to Tom and see how this will play out. I told you, whatever I can do to get her back for you, I'm gonna do it."

"Don't go there, Rick. Not tonight," Fran said. "I'm not going to make the same mistake twice. I don't want you to, either."

Candy felt the tension in the air and cleared her throat. She glanced up as Tom's unmarked cruiser came up the driveway, the car kicking up dust as it approached. Tom barely had the vehicle in park before Lauren jumped out of the passenger seat and ran up the porch and into her mother's arms. Fran squealed happily and hugged her daughter.

Rick pushed himself out of his seat to greet Tom. He gave up using the cane, but his leg was still dicey. He leaned on the railing. "The ladies were just filling me in on your plan with Lauren."

Tom nodded from the bottom of the stairs. "There's a lot to talk about, I know, but it's a start." He glanced at Lauren and Fran. "Besides, I kinda like having the kid around, although Candy's going to have to start keeping her clothes on when she's at my place."

"What?" Fran asked, startled.

The others laughed at her reaction.

"Well, one down and one to go." Tom kept his eyes on Rick as he spoke, but the message was for everyone.

Rick just nodded. "Hodge told me."

"He suspects you," Tom said.

"Yup, he told me that too," said Rick.

"Suspects him of what?" Fran asked as she cuddled her daughter on her lap.

"You didn't tell her?" Tom asked.

Rick shrugged. "I told her he was dead."

Tom turned to Fran. "Blackwell's dead. Forensics found his body at the Pearson farm this morning. One bullet to the head."

"Oh my god." Fran took a deep breath and shuddered. "Suicide?"

"Nope," was all Tom said.

Fran's mouth opened in shock. "Hodge thinks –" She stopped and looked from Tom to Rick. "Fuck. Of course, he does!"

"Mommy!" Lauren complained.

"Sorry, darling. I used a bad word. I'll be more careful."

Tom smiled. "This should be an interesting evening." He looked back at Rick. "Be careful with Hodge. He's a bulldog. Once he gets his teeth into something, that's it."

"He doesn't want to test me," Rick said.

Tom bristled slightly and glanced at Candy, who shrugged and tilted her head as if to say, 'What did you expect?' Tom turned back to Rick. "Just be careful." He then looked at Fran. "Both of you."

"Who's that?" Lauren asked as Charlie's truck approached.

"Santa Claus," Rick said with a grin. "And he's bringing lots of food!"

"Yeah!" Candy yelled.

Lauren, Tom, and Candy went to meet the truck.

Rick leaned down, one hand on either of Fran's armrests, and gave her a deep kiss.

She pulled him close and whispered in his ear, "I won't ask, and you won't have to lie to me."

Rick looked into her eyes and kissed her again before joining the others. Fran leaned back and smiled, watching her friends as the sun dipped over the horizon.

***

"Is this a party, or what?" Charlie yelled from the fire pit. The sun was slipping behind the horizon and the air had chilled.

"More like an old-fashioned Irish wake," Candy noted as she grabbed a beer for herself. "Where's the rest of the food?"

They just about had dinner cooked when Sheriff Hodge showed up in the cruiser. By now, Fran had joined the others, and she and Rick sat side by side near the fire, holding hands. As Hodge approached, her grip on Rick tightened. She smiled at Hodge.

"Anything new?" Tom asked as everyone turned to listen.

"Yeah." Hodge looked around. "You got one of those beers for me?"

Charlie smiled, opened a longneck, and handed it to Hodge.

"So, don't keep us guessing," Candy said as she sat down next to Tom and leaned against him.

Hodge pulled up a camp chair and sat down. "We collected most of Blackwell's papers. I thought you might like to know what we learned."

"I'm not sure I do," Candy admitted.

Tom took her hand and held it.

Hodge cleared his throat. "Well, it seems Blackwell was gay and had what he called a 'sinful compulsion' to enjoy the company of younger men. Now, as far as we can tell, the relationships were consensual. Where they got weird was when the boyfriends would want to break up. Blackwell got this idea that they were all going to hell for the sin of sodomy, so he, being a good preacher that he was, had to save their souls for all eternity."

"I'm sorry," Candy said. "This is just too sick for young ears. Excuse us." She got up, grabbed Lauren by the hand, and dragged the girl into the house.

"Continue," said Tom as his eyes followed Candy.

"Blackwell would meet them, force them at knifepoint to confess their heinous sins, absolve them, and then kill them. That way they go straight to heaven and escape damnation," Hodge explained.

Fran kept looking over her shoulder at the house, but Rick held tightly onto her.

"Okay, so far, but what does any of this have to do with Candy?" Tom asked.

"It seems Blackwell couldn't get Bryce Pearson to confess fast enough. Bryce found another lover and moved out. Blackwell couldn't control him. When Bryce died, he went straight to hell, as far as Blackwell was concerned, which made Blackwell guilty of a mortal sin. He got some weird idea in his head that if Bryce had been murdered, that would somehow mitigate the sin. Not sure how, but anyway –"

Tom nodded.

"Candy didn't find evidence of murder, though. That meant she was personally responsible for Bryce going to hell. Blackwell's solution was to 'rescue' Candy's followers – her apostles – from her by luring them away, forcing confessions out of them, and killing them while they were still in a state of grace."

"Fuck." It was Rick's only comment so far.

"And Edgar?" Tom asked.

"You were able to save two of Fran's girls, so Blackwell had to cast his net in other waters."

"Can we forget the Bible metaphors?" Fran shuddered.

"Sorry." Hodge continued. "Blackwell met Edgar at the diner when we were investigating the Ortiz murder. He made a connection with Candy and simply added him to the list to make up for the one that got away."

"And Fran?" Rick asked.

"Same thing. She was a substitute sacrifice on the altar of –"

"Shut up, already!" Fran snapped. She stood up and stomped into the house in search of Candy.

Hodge glanced around at the guys who were all staring him down. "You could at least offer me some supper," he said.

***

Friday Morning

"It should be raining. Isn't it supposed to rain at funerals?" Fran stood barefoot in front of her closet and tried to find something to wear. She was in her panties, a bra, and a slip, and she still felt warm. Outside, a hot sun beat down on the house and pried its way through her closed bedroom shades.

She heard the door open and close behind her. She didn't turn around. Rick walked up to her, rested his hand on her shoulder, and kissed her neck. His warm bare chest pressed against her back. She closed her eyes.

"I don't have anything black," she said.

"What about your navy suit?"

"I hate that suit."

"Well, how about the peach one, then? It always makes you feel good." He pulled her hair back and ran his fingers through it.

"I lost the jacket in the explosion."

He turned her around to face him. "You could always go naked."

"Not funny," Fran countered, although the comment made her smile a little.

"Look, funerals are for the living, not the dead." Rick pressed his forehead to hers. "They're a ritual we use to let us grieve. Until we grieve, we can't let go."

"I don't want to let go!" Fran admitted.

"I know." Rick pulled her closer and held her. "Wear whatever makes you feel good. Forget about black."

Fran sighed. "I can't believe we're doing this. I keep thinking it's a bad dream, and I'm going to wake up. I keep expecting Alex to walk through the front door. I'm still mad at him, damn it! I never made peace with him."

Rick reached into the closet and pulled out a soft, pastel green dress with a cropped, three-quarter sleeve jacket. "This one," he said as he laid it on the bed.

"You don't think— " Fran started to ask.

"This one." He kissed her forehead and then her lips. "I'm going to change. I'll meet you in the kitchen."

"You're wearing your new suit?"

"Of course."

She let him slip away, and then she picked up the dress.

***

Alex and Toni de la Rosa had been raised Roman Catholic, but neither attended Mass since they were teenagers, although Toni continued to wear a small gold crucifix around her neck. When planning the funeral, Fran had opted to skip the viewing and church service, and instead settled on having a minister at the cemetery.

The mourners arrived in separate cars: Rick with Fran, Tom with Candy, Margo with her current girlfriend, Charlie, and Hodge. A few others were there – people Fran didn't recognize, although she was told that two were cousins of the De la Rosa family. They didn't approach her, and she didn't talk to them.

The matching caskets were set side by side, each on pedestals, each a simple dark wood with a gold trim. The graves were dug and were covered with a green carpet-like material to hide them. The caskets wouldn't be lowered until the mourners left. A slight breeze wove around the gravestones and kicked up a little dust.

Candy arranged for a basket of single stemmed roses – red for Alex and white for Toni. No one was surprised when Rick approached Toni's casket with a red rose. He put his hand on the soft wood and leaned gently against it. His eye closed as he said goodbye. Rick turned away from the casket and sought out Fran's eyes. She approached him and held him as the rest of the mourners went from casket to casket with their roses and prayers.

"Let's go home," Fran said softly into Rick's ear.

Leaving the others behind, they walked arm in arm toward Rick's Jeep. He opened the door for Fran just as a large, dark car drove up and stopped behind them. Rupert Hawksworth stepped out, escorted by his willowy granddaughter.

"Now what?" Rick whispered to Fran. He turned to face Hawksworth.

"I can't help but feel responsible for this," Hawksworth said as he glanced at the mourners near the gravesite. "I knew Jax was dangerous, but I didn't know, I didn't realize –" Hawksworth looked at Fran. "Rumor has it you might not reopen the law practice."

"I'm thinking of opening a law clinic to help the victims of people like Jax and my father." Fran clung to Rick's arm.

"And you? What will you do?" Hawksworth asked Rick.

"Before or after I kill Jax Saynte?"

Hawksworth's granddaughter paled and shirked back.

Hawksworth nodded. "There's a job for you, if you want it, as head of my security team. It's a bigger job than you might imagine. I have multiple holdings."

Rick noticed the mourners breaking up. "Tom Saddler's looking for a new job. He's a good man. You might want to make that offer to him."

Hawksworth offered Rick his hand. "Good luck, Sergeant."

Rick shook it. "Same to you, Hawk."

Fran and Rick got into the car, and he started the engine. He reached over and squeezed Fran's hand before taking the wheel and driving away.

It wasn't until everyone was back at Fran's house that Tom took Rick aside. They stood on the front porch, each gripping a beer and looking uncomfortable. Rick had given up the sling but still leaned heavily on his cane. Tom was managing to handle one crutch.

"I wanted you to be the first to know that we have a line on Jax Saynte," Tom said. "He fled to South Africa. I guess he can't get far enough away from you."

"Shit. And here I was looking forward to personally breaking his fucking neck. No extradition, I take it."

"None. Do you want to tell Fran or should I?"

"I'd love to give you that job," Rick said.

"But you won't," Tom concluded.

"You're right. I won't. Well, at least we won't see him for a while. Any luck with Ant?"

"Nothing yet. He seems to have disappeared."

"I doubt that," said Rick. "Jax will be back. They both will. Men like that always come back."

"What will you and Fran do now?"

"She's talking about reworking the law practice, doing something different with it. She's a lawyer, you know. It's in her blood. She wants to help the victims."

"She could do anything," Tom said.

"She could," Rick agreed.

"Do you think you two –?" Tom left the question hanging.

Rick shrugged. "We'll see. A lot depends on Lauren."

"Fran's hard to pin down," Tom noted.

Rick smirked. Pinning Fran down was suddenly foremost on his mind. He was sure he could do it quite easily once they were alone.

Fran stepped onto the porch. Tom smiled at her and went back into the house to leave them alone.

"Conspiring against me?" Fran asked as Rick put his arm around her.

"Something like that. Did you have a good time at Charlie's camp yesterday? I thought we could spend a long weekend up there. You, me, maybe Candy." He winked.

Fran laughed. "That's exactly what you want. A threesome!"

"Well, it's a thought." He took a drink of beer. "I suppose, if I have to, I could let Tom come, just to keep Candy occupied, you understand."

Fran leaned into him. "We should get away for a while. It would be nice to relax for a bit and not wait for the next shoe to fall."

As they were talking, a dark blue Lincoln pulled up to the curb and parked. Fran, curious, looked at the car. Rick tensed next to her. The next shoe fell.

A beautiful woman stepped out from behind the wheel. She was dressed in a chauffeur's uniform. She opened the back door.

"Go in the house," Rick whispered. "Tell Tom to stand down. Got it? Stand DOWN."

Fran felt the panic growing. She stared up at Rick. "What is it? Who is it?"

"Don't argue." Rick pushed her toward the door. He set his beer on the porch railing and walked down the steps to the sidewalk. Fran hovered just inside the front door.

A man emerged from the car. His grayish-blond hair protruded from a Panama straw hat. Keen gray eyes crinkled at the edges. Khaki pants ended in boat shoes. He wore a loose-fitting polo shirt and a tense smile. He met Rick face-to-face on the sidewalk: the same height, the same stance, the same tilt of the head.

"Come to pay your respects?" Rick asked curtly. He held his cane in front of him, both hands on the top, using it for balance and at the same time prepared to use it as a weapon.

"I came to apologize," Ant said in his New Zealand accent. "Jax Saynte is an idiot and an ass. I told him to stay away from you and yours. He didn't listen, and now we both have messes to clean up."

"What do you want with me, Anthony?"

Ant chuckled. "Damn, Ricky, no one's called me that in ages." He glanced at the house where Tom and Fran were poised in the front door, out of earshot but watching. "I want to make you a deal. I won't play in your backyard if you won't play in mine."

Rick lowered his head a bit, absorbing the words. He scowled and tapped his cane on the sidewalk a few times. "I'm going to find Saynte and kill him. Will that be in your backyard?"

Ant nodded. "Yeah, but I'll make an exception for that as long as it doesn't interrupt any other part of my operation."

"And how will I be sure of that?"

Ant pursed his lips together in thought, pushed his hat back a little, and eyed Rick carefully. "I guess I'll just have to let you know when the time comes."

"You could just deliver Saynte to me, with or without his head attached. I won't complain."

"I could, but what fun would that be?"

"It would save us both a lot of grief," said Rick.

"Ah, hell, Ricky. Guys like you and me, we thrive on grief." Ant smiled and nodded. "I don't have a beef with you or your friends. I told Jax not to mess with you and not to drag Knight into this, but he wouldn't listen. Damn big ego of his got in the way of common sense."

Rick grinned. "Sounds familiar."

"I heard about that stunt you pulled at the garage. You always were a crazy son-of-a-bitch."

"Yeah, well, my options were limited."

Ant looked at Fran and tipped his hat to her. "Boys like Jax and Alex with their dime store egos, they're tin gods in little worlds. A few girls, some cocaine, a bribe here and there. They think it's all about that shit. But you and I see the big picture." He looked back at Rick. "You know the kind of resources I have. You've been on the inside."

"I remember. I got out," Rick reminded him. "If this is your idea of a recruitment drive, save your breath. You almost killed me once. Once was enough."

Ant shook his head. "Now, I know better. You changed. You're not the kid I used to know. I've seen what you can do. These people…" He nodded toward the house. "…have no clue. They only see what you let them, and with a little sleight of hand, they'll never know just how cold-blooded you can be."

"Fran's holdings –" Rick began.

"Are going to be a problem, I know. I got the portfolios now. All of them. Even the one from the police station. I still want the properties. I'm not going to kill your girl to get them, but you can bet I'll do anything short of that."

"What's your offer?" Rick asked.

"Seven million and I take the liabilities," Ant said.

"I'll get back to you," said Rick.

"I'm giving Ricky your email address," Ant told his driver as he pulled out his cell phone and messaged the address to Rick without asking his number.

She nodded.

Rick's phone buzzed in his pocket; he didn't bother to look at it.

Ant extended his hand and Rick shook it. Then Ant got into his car, his driver shut the door, and the vehicle pulled away. As Rick leaned back and watched the car leave, Tom and Fran walked out of the house and down the stairs.

"Was that Ant?" Tom grabbed Rick by the arm. "You let him walk away?"

Rick frowned and faced Tom. "What were you gonna do? Have a shootout right here? At our home? Now? With Lauren here and a house full of drunk mourners?"

"I could have called for backup."

"He would've been gone before you hung up the phone. Besides, he's got the portfolio from the police station. He's got people on the inside."

"You could have helped."

"I don't know about you, but I've had enough killing for a while. Besides, if he came for a fight, we wouldn't be standing here."

"What does he want?" Fran asked.

"He said Jax didn't act on his orders. He wants me to know that he isn't coming after you. If I want – if WE want – to go after Jax, he won't stand in our way."

"Mighty nice of him," Tom said sarcastically.

It was, Rick thought without saying so.

"Let's go inside." Fran shivered.

Rick nodded, took her hand, and returned to the house.

***

Endings

Candy stood next to her car and watched the mourners at the gravesite of Pamela Mayhew. The investigation was done. The body had finally been released. People could bury their dead. Candy came alone. She remembered standing inches from Pamela's body in the chilled room at the coroner's office. Pamela had an iconic beauty that, even in death, was forever printed in Candy's mind.

Candy didn't approach the others. Other than Pamela's husband, her family didn't know about the little BDSM group. They didn't want to know.

Trembling, Candy slipped into her Mini Cooper, covered her face, and cried. The nightmare was finally over. Seventeen families were grieving, eighteen if you included Cheryl Burns. Whatever her relationship with Lawrence Blackwell, she would be mourning today as well.

Candy finally started the car and drove away.

***

Tom sat at the table in his mother's kitchen. Maryanne was her usual smiling self. She was neatly dressed in slacks and a light sweater, and she wore a simple set of pearls. She had just come from church and "a woman never leaves without her pearls," she said. She primped her hair and looked across the table at Lauren.

The thirteen-year-old was a bit uncomfortable. She didn't know what to expect, but she knew and trusted Tom. They held hands around the table: Lauren and Tom and Candy and Maryanne. Tom bowed his head and said grace. It was

Sunday afternoon at the Saddler home. For a little while, the world felt normal.

When they had finished praying, Maryanne passed the meatloaf and asked, "So, are you going to take the job?"

"What job?" Candy asked, surprised. "Tom? What job?"

"Rupert Hawksworth called. He wants me to run his security for him. I'm thinking about it."

"What's to think about?" Candy asked.

"I had planned to teach," said Tom.

"Which meant moving to Reno," said Maryanne. She looked miffed. "I want you and Candy and Lauren right here where I can keep an eye on you."

Candy smiled. "I like the way your mother thinks."

"You do, huh?" Tom laughed. He glanced from one woman to the next, and then his eyes went to Lauren. "And what do you think?"

"I don't want to live in Reno," she told him. "It's too far from Mom."

Tom sighed. "Then it looks like I've been ambushed. I'll call Hawk in the morning."

Maryanne got up to get some coffee. She stopped by Tom's chair, gave him a kiss on the cheek, and said, "That's my boy."

Candy laughed.

***

Charlie carefully packed a shipment of small guns for the Reno gun show. Each weapon was carefully cleaned and tested. The paperwork was all in order. There was a larger than usual demand for the .38s, but Charlie didn't mind. He had plenty. He pulled out a small box, opened it, and unwrapped the pistol from the soft cloth. Lifting it, he made sure it was empty. He even took time to wipe down each bullet that had been inside before slipping them into an ammo box. Charlie grunted, repackaged the gun, and put it with the others.

***

Fran sat on the kitchen counter at Charlie's camp. Rick stood between her legs, his arm around her waist and her arms around his neck. He was kissing her, gently at first, but the kisses quickly increased in intensity.

"I want to buy this place," Fran said. "I love it up here."

Rick laughed. "You'd miss the city. Besides, I'm pretty sure Charlie doesn't want to sell."

"I could make him an offer he can't refuse."

Rick brushed her hair back and kissed her again. "Give any more thought to what you want to do next?"

"Other than make wild, passionate love to you all day?" she asked with a grin.

"Yeah, other than that."

"God, I can't believe –" Fran started to say.

"What?"

"All these years, Rick. Ten years. You were right there, right in front of me. Holding me, propping me up, rescuing me from all kinds of shit. And you never once made a pass at me. I never knew, I never even imagined." She shook her head in disbelief.

"Oh, I made a pass or two," he said with a wink. "Your mind was somewhere else, boss."

"I wish you'd kissed me sooner.

"Me, too," he agreed as he kissed her again. "So, what now?"

Fran laughed. Her fingers reached up to caress the edge of his eyepatch. She remembered how panicked she was when Margo told her about the accident. "Why? Antsy?"

"Hell, yeah. I want to know what I'm doing tomorrow."

"Well, after we sort through all the Max-Mil shit and the law cases, Margo and I will revamp the law office, turn it into a clinic to help victims. I'm going to ask Charlie if we can at least rent this place for now – live here, work here. We could represent those who can't afford an attorney. We could fundraise for advocacy groups and shelters. We could lobby for legislation to battle human trafficking. We could –"

"Whoa!" Rick laughed. "I get the idea!"

Fran smiled. "Approve?"

"Sweetheart, you don't need me to approve anything you do with your career. You know that." He bent his head down a moment in thought before looking back up at her. "Now, if you're talking tattoos, that's another matter." He kissed her harder.

"Mmmmm. I was thinking of something small and sexy."

"I get it. Something impersonal, so if you break up with me –"

Fran pounded his arm and laughed. "If you think, after all of this, that I'm going to walk away from you, you're out of your mind!"

She felt his shoulders relax a little. Surprised, she realized he was worried about her leaving him. She caressed the back of his neck. "You tell me what you'd like to see. What kind of tattoo. What would you like?"

"Anything that says you're mine." He went back to kissing her.

Made in the USA
Columbia, SC
19 August 2023